The 1978
Annual World's Best
SF

THE 1978 ANNUAL WORLD'S BEST SF

EDITED BY

DONALD A. WOLLHEIM
with Arthur W. Saha

DAW BOOKS, INC.

DONALD A. WOLLHEIM, Publisher
1301 Avenue of the Americas
New York, N.Y.   10019

Contents

The 1978
Annual World's Best
SF

Introduction

At a conference of the men and women who sell and distribute the paperback books I publish, I was asked how do I distinguish between what is science fiction and what is fantasy. For a moment I was hard put to give an answer that would not get too involved with semantic hair-splitting or ridiculously complex definitions. What I said was that the line between the two categories had become very smudged and shadowy in recent years and that what might have been labeled fantasy in the past can now find acceptance from confirmed science fiction addicts without much questioning.

This seems to be generally the case and a book line devoted to science fiction novels may present a work of fantasy without anyone being the wiser. What's the reason for this? Why has the distinction become so unclear?

One answer possibly may be that the readers of imaginative fiction have become more liberal in their interpretations. They read for pleasure and entertainment, and they have come to accept many premises which could hardly withstand the scrutiny of a hard-core scientific analyst.

Some part of this breakdown between what was once regarded as two classes of literature can be ascribed to the widespread influence of Tolkien's *Lord of the Rings*—a fantasy work surely, whose depth of background and ring of verisimilitude carries the depiction of a world that simply makes no claim to real existence here or anywhere else. Add the influence of the Witch World books of Andre Norton—which started off on the slim science fiction premise that her world of witchery is an actual planet, simply so remote from our part of the universe that the very laws of science are different. This supplies the sort of logical transition that brings an sf-devotee across into a world identical with the creations of sword-and-sorcery writers.

It is always possible to devise pseudo-scientific arguments to justify the plausibility of the farthest-out fantasy. The adventures of Conan twenty thousand years ago might have taken place because we are not absolutely certain of what human societies existed then and we are not able to disprove that various "magics" and "monsters" did not exist then which we cannot explain away now simply because of lack of laboratory data.

The theory of alternate worlds and alternate universes, and even of alternate or changed scientific laws, has now penetrated the halls of academic science. Hypotheses are advanced in scientific journals which can be used as jump-off points for just about anything one wishes to dream up. The margin between science and speculation has therefore become smudged, too. And the readership of speculative fiction now finds that its horizons have enlarged to encompass just about everything.

Still . . . one can pick out extreme examples. To take two from my own last year's list of novels, consider Tanith Lee's *Volkhavaar* and C.J. Cherryh's *Hunter of Worlds*. The first is surely as "fantasy" as can be found—virtually a grown-up fairy tale utilizing many of the premises of the fairy tale. The second is just as certainly a work of science fiction involving space ships, star flights, psychological manipulation, linguistics, evolution of societies and species, etc. So there is a distinction after all, if you seek extremes.

Yet the Tanith Lee novel was read by regular science fiction readers without complaint and with evident enjoyment. Acceptance is on the order of the day.

And now we enter the years of *Star Wars*. This film, which burst on the world in 1977, will, we think, harvest its crop during the present year, too. *Star Wars* is presented as science fiction and utilizes the standard clichés of the action-sf of the early days of the sf pulps, not to mention the elements that made Buck Rogers and Flash Gordon popular comic strips for millions for a couple of decades. Like many popular science fiction works, *Star Wars* would not stand up under the severe scrutiny of a humorless science and literary analyst. But the key word is entertainment and the lesson given was that science fiction is fun. The millions who saw it and will be seeing it will agree to this last. For them this will be a pleasing introduction to "science fiction."

We expect that this year will possibly see the expansion of science fiction (fantasy) reading as never before. We hope that the millions who found *Star Wars, Close Encounters of the Third Kind,* and the many films that are sure to follow on their heels will want to feed this new-found appetite in their reading. We understand that every publisher is interested in adding science fiction (fantasy) to his immediate list, and sales and the display of sf in shops were never greater.

Some part of this readership will drop away eventually—their new-found tastes easily sated. We hope that some part will remain. But how much and what percentage remains to be seen. There is a boom in science fiction this year. There will be a letdown sometime after . . . but meanwhile let's enjoy it.

Donald A. Wollheim

IN THE HALL OF
THE MARTIAN KINGS

by John Varley

Writing a story about Martians has become exceedingly difficult now that we know too much about the actualities of that not quite so glamorous ball of dust. But in this novelette there has been combined both solid space technology, an acceptance of the hard Mars facts, and that extra bit of imagination that even engineers really relish.

It took perseverance, alertness, and a willingness to break the rules to watch the sunrise in Tharsis Canyon. Matthew Crawford shivered in the dark, his suit heater turned to emergency setting, his eyes trained toward the east. He knew he had to be watchful. Yesterday he had missed it entirely, snatched away from him in the middle of a long, unavoidable yawn. His jaw muscles stretched, but he controlled it and kept his eyes firmly open.

And there it was. Like the lights in a theater after the show is over: just a quick brightening, a splash of localized bluish-purple over the canyon rim, and he was surrounded by footlights. Day had come, the truncated Martian day that would never touch the blackness over his head.

This day, like the nine before it, illuminated a Tharsis radically changed from what it had been over the last sleepy ten thousand years. Wind erosion of rocks can create an infinity of shapes, but it never gets around to carving out a straight line or a perfect arc. The human encampment below him broke up the jagged lines of the rocks with regular angles and curves.

The camp was anything but orderly. No one would get the impression that any care had been taken in the haphazard arrangement of dome, lander, crawlers, crawler tracks, and scattered equipment. It had grown, as all human base camps seem to grow, without pattern. He was reminded of the footprints around Tranquillity Base, though on a much larger scale.

Tharsis Base sat on a wide ledge about halfway up from the uneven bottom of the Tharsis arm of the Great Rift Valley. The site had been chosen because it was a smooth area, allowing easy access up a gentle slope to the flat plains of the Tharsis Plateau, while at the same time only a kilometer from the valley floor. No one could agree which area was most worthy of study: plains or canyon. So this site had been chosen as a compromise. What it meant was that the exploring parties had to either climb up or go down, because there wasn't a damn thing worth seeing near the camp. Even the exposed layering and its archaeological records could not be seen without a half-kilometer crawler ride up to the point where Crawford had climbed to watch the sunrise.

He examined the dome as he walked back to camp. There was a figure hazily visible through the plastic. At this distance he would have been unable to tell who it was if it weren't for the black face. He saw her step up to the dome wall and wipe a clear circle to look through. She spotted his bright red suit and pointed at him. She was suited except for her helmet, which contained her radio. He knew he was in trouble. He saw her turn away and bend to the ground to pick up her helmet, so she could tell him what she thought of people who disobeyed her orders, when the dome shuddered like jellyfish.

An alarm started in his helmet, flat and strangely soothing coming from the tiny speaker. He stood there for a moment as a perfect smoke ring of dust billowed up around the rim of the dome. Then he was running.

He watched the disaster unfold before his eyes, silent except for the rhythmic beat of the alarm bell in his ears. The dome was dancing and straining, trying to fly. The floor heaved up in the center, throwing the black woman to her knees. In another second the interior was a whirling snowstorm. He skidded on the sand and fell forward, got up in time to see the fiberglass ropes on the side nearest him snap free from the steel spikes anchoring the dome to the rock.

The dome now looked like some fantastic Christmas ornament, filled with snowflakes and the flashing red and blue lights of the emergency alarms. The top of the dome heaved over away from him, and the floor raised itself high in the air, held down by the unbroken anchors on the side farthest from him. There was a gush of snow and dust; then the floor settled slowly back to the ground. There was no motion now but the leisurely folding of the depressurized dome roof as it settled over the structures inside.

The crawler skidded to a stop, nearly rolling over, beside the deflated dome. Two pressure-suited figures got out. They started for the dome, hesitantly, in fits and starts. One grabbed the other's arm and pointed to the lander. The two of them changed course and scrambled up the rope ladder hanging over the side.

Crawford was the only one to look up when the lock started cycling. The two people almost tumbled over each other coming out of the lock. They wanted to *do* something and quickly, but didn't know what. In the end, they just stood there silently twisting their hands and looking at the floor. One of them took off her helmet. She was a large woman, in her thirties, with red hair shorn off close to the scalp.

"Matt, we got here as . . ." She stopped, realizing how obvious it was. "How's Lou?"

"Lou's not going to make it." He gestured to the bunk where a heavyset man lay breathing raggedly into a clear plastic mask. He was on pure oxygen. There was blood seeping from his ears and nose.

"Brain damage?"

Crawford nodded. He looked around at the other occupants of the room. There was the Surface Mission Commander, Mary

Lang, the black woman he had seen inside the dome just before the blowout. She was sitting on the edge of Lou Prager's cot, her head cradled in her hands. In a way, she was a more shocking sight than Lou. No one who knew her would have thought she could be brought to this limp state of apathy. She had not moved for the last hour.

Sitting on the floor huddled in a blanket was Martin Ralston, the chemist. His shirt was bloody, and there was dried blood all over his face and hands from the nosebleed he'd only recently gotten under control, but his eyes were alert. He shivered, looking from Lang, his titular leader, to Crawford, the only one who seemed calm enough to deal with anything. He was a follower, reliable but unimaginative.

Crawford looked back to the newest arrivals. They were Lucy Stone McKillian, the red-headed ecologist, and Song Sue Lee, the exobiologist. They still stood numbly by the airlock, unable as yet to come to grips with the fact of fifteen dead men and women beneath the dome outside.

"What do they say on the *Burroughs?*" McKillian asked, tossing her helmet on the floor and squatting tiredly against the wall. The lander was not the most comfortable place to hold a meeting; all the couches were mounted horizontally since their purpose was cushioning the acceleration of landing and takeoff. With the ship sitting on its tail, this made ninety percent of the space in the lander useless. They were all gathered on the circular bulkhead at the rear of the life-system, just forward of the fuel tank.

"We're waiting for a reply," Crawford said. "But I can sum up what they're going to say: not good. Unless one of you two has some experience in Mars-lander handling that you've been concealing from us."

Neither of them bothered to answer that. The radio in the nose sputtered, then clanged for their attention. Crawford looked over at Lang, who made no move to go answer it. He stood up and swarmed up the ladder to sit in the copilot's chair. He switched on the receiver.

"Commander Lang?"

"No, this is Crawford again. Commander Lang is . . . indisposed. She's busy with Lou, trying to do something."

"That's no use. The doctor says it's a miracle he's still breathing. If he wakes up at all, he won't be anything like you knew him. The telemetry shows nothing like the normal brain wave. Now I've got to talk to Commander Lang. Have her come up." The voice of Mission Commander Weinstein was accustomed to command, and about as emotional as a weather report.

"Sir, I'll ask her, but I don't think she'll come. This is still her operation, you know." He didn't give Weinstein time to reply to that. Weinstein had been trapped by his own seniority into commanding the *Edgar Rice Burroughs,* the orbital ship that got them to Mars and had been intended to get them back. Command of the *Podkayne,* the disposable lander that would make the lion's share of the headlines, had gone to Lang. There was little friendship between the two, especially when Weinstein fell to brooding about the very real financial benefits Lang stood to reap by being the first woman on Mars, rather than the lowly mission commander. He saw himself as another Michael Collins.

Crawford called down to Lang, who raised her head enough to mumble something.

"What'd she say?"

"She said take a message." McKillian had been crawling up the ladder as she said this. Now she reached him and said in a lower voice, "Matt, she's pretty broken up. You'd better take over for now."

"Right, I know." He turned back to the radio, and McKillian listened over his shoulder as Weinstein briefed them on the situation as he saw it. It pretty much jibed with Crawford's estimation, except at one crucial point. He signed off and they joined the other survivors.

He looked around at the faces of the others and decided it wasn't the time to speak of rescue possibilities. He didn't relish being a leader. He was hoping Lang would recover soon and take the burden from him. In the meantime he had to get them started on something. He touched McKillian gently on the shoulder and motioned her to the lock.

"Let's go get them buried," he said. She squeezed her eyes shut tight, forcing out tears, then nodded.

It wasn't a pretty job. Halfway through it, Song came down the ladder with the body of Lou Prager.

"Let's go over what we've learned. First, now that Lou's dead there's very little chance of ever lifting off. That is, unless Mary thinks she can absorb everything she needs to know about piloting the *Podkayne* from those printouts Weinstein sent down. How about it, Mary?"

Mary Lang was lying sideways across the improvised cot that had recently held the *Podkayne* pilot, Lou Prager. Her head was nodding listlessly against the aluminum hull plate behind her, her chin was on her chest. Her eyes were half-open.

Song had given her a sedative from the dead doctor's supplies on the advice of the medic aboard the *E.R.B.* It had enabled her to stop fighting so hard against the screaming panic she wanted to unleash. It hadn't improved her disposition. She had quit, she wasn't going to do anything for anybody.

When the blowout started, Lang had snapped on her helmet quickly. Then she had struggled against the blizzard and the undulating dome bottom, heading for the roofless framework where the other members of the expedition were sleeping. The blowout was over in ten seconds, and she then had the problem of coping with the collapsing roof, which promptly buried her in folds of clear plastic. It was far too much like one of those nightmares of running knee-deep in quicksand. She had to fight for every meter, but she made it.

She made it in time to see her shipmates of the last six months gasping soundlessly and spouting blood from all over their faces as they fought to get into their pressure suits. It was a hopeless task to choose which two or three to save in the time she had. She might have done better but for the freakish nature of her struggle to reach them; she was in shock and half believed it was only a nightmare. So she grabbed the nearest, who happened to be Doctor Ralston. He had nearly finished donning his suit; so she slapped his helmet on him and moved to the next one. It was Luther Nakamura, and he was not moving. Worse, he was only half suited. Pragmatically she should have left him and moved on to save the ones who still had a chance. She knew it now, but didn't like it any better than she had liked it then.

While she was stuffing Nakamura into his suit, Crawford arrived. He had walked over the folds of plastic until he reached the dormitory, then sliced through it with his laser normally used to vaporize rock samples.

And he had had time to think about the problem of whom to save. He went straight to Lou Prager and finished suiting him up. But it was already too late. He didn't know if it would have made any difference if Mary Lang had tried to save him first.

Now she lay on the bunk, her feet sprawled carelessly in front of her. She slowly shook her head back and forth.

"You sure?" Crawford prodded her, hoping to get a rise, a show of temper, *anything*.

"I'm sure," she mumbled. "You people know how long they trained Lou to fly this thing? And he almost cracked it up as it was. I . . . ah, nuts. It isn't possible."

"I refuse to accept that as a final answer," he said. "But in the meantime we should explore the possibilities if what Mary says is true."

Ralston laughed. It wasn't a bitter laugh; he sounded genuinely amused. Crawford plowed on.

"Here's what we know for sure. The *E.R.B.* is useless to us. Oh, they'll help us out with plenty of advice, maybe more than we want, but any rescue is out of the question."

"We know that," McKillian said. She was tired and sick from the sight of the faces of her dead friends. "What's the use of all this talk?"

"Wait a moment," Song broke in. "Why can't they . . . I mean they have plenty of time, don't they? They have to leave in six months, as I understand it, because of the orbital elements, but in that time. . . ."

"Don't you know anything about spaceships?" McKillian shouted. Song went on, unperturbed.

"I do know enough to know the *Edgar* is not equipped for an atmosphere entry. My idea was, not to bring down the whole ship but only what's aboard the ship that we need. Which is a pilot. Might that be possible?"

Crawford ran his hands through his hair, wondering what to say. That possibility had been discussed, and was being studied. But it had to be classed as extremely remote.

"You're right," he said. "What we need is a pilot, and that pilot is Commander Weinstein. Which presents problems legally, if nothing else. He's the captain of a ship and should not leave it. That's what kept him on the *Edgar* in the first place. But he did have a lot of training on the lander simulator back when he was so sure he'd be picked for the ground team. You know Winey, always the instinct to be the one-man show. So if he thought he could do it, he'd be down here in a minute to bail us out and grab the publicity. I understand they're trying to work out a heat-shield parachute system from one of the drop capsules that were supposed to ferry down supplies to us during the stay here. But it's very risky. You don't modify an aerodynamic design lightly, not one that's supposed to hit the atmosphere at ten thousand-plus kilometers. So I think we can rule that out. They'll keep working on it, but when it's done, Winey won't step into the damn thing. He wants to be a hero, but he wants to live to enjoy it, too."

There had been a brief lifting of spirits among Song, Ralston, and McKillian at the thought of a possible rescue. The more they thought about it, the less happy they looked. They all seemed to agree with Crawford's assessment.

"So we'll put that one in the Fairy Godmother file and forget about it. If it happens, fine. But we'd better plan on the assumption that it won't. As you may know, the *E.R.B.-Podkayne* are the only ships in existence that can reach Mars and land on it. One other pair is in the congressional funding stage. Winey talked to Earth and thinks there'll be a speedup in the preliminary paperwork and the thing'll start building in a year. The launch was scheduled for five years from now, but it might get as much as a year boost. It's a rescue mission now, easier to sell. But the design will need modification, if only to include five more seats to bring us all back. You can bet on there being more modifications when we send in our report on the blowout. So we'd better add another six months to the schedule."

McKillian had had enough. "Matt, what the hell are you talking about? Rescue misson? Damn it, you know as well as I that if they find us here, we'll be long dead. We'll probably be dead in another year."

"That's where you're wrong. We'll survive."

"How?"

"I don't have the faintest idea." He looked her straight in the eye as he said this. She almost didn't bother to answer, but curiosity got the best of her.

"Is this just a morale session? Thanks, but I don't need it. I'd rather face the situation as it is. Or do you really have something?"

"Both. I don't have anything concrete except to say that we'll survive the same way humans have always survived: by staying warm, by eating, by drinking. To that list we have to add 'by breathing.' That's a hard one, but other than that we're no different than any other group of survivors in a tough spot. I don't know what we'll have to do, specifically, but I know we'll find the answers."

"Or die trying," Song said.

"Or die trying." He grinned at her. She at least had grasped the essence of the situation. Whether survival was possible or not, it was necessary to maintain the illusion that it was. Otherwise, you might as well cut your throat. You might as well not even be born, because life is an inevitably fatal struggle to survive.

"What about air?" McKillian asked, still unconvinced.

"I don't know," he told her cheerfully. "It's a tough problem, isn't it?"

"What about water?"

"Well, down in that valley there's a layer of permafrost about twenty meters down."

She laughed. "Wonderful. So that's what you want us to do? Dig down there and warm the ice with our pink little hands? It won't work, I tell you."

Crawford waited until she had run through a long list of reasons why they were doomed. Most of them made a great deal of sense. When she was through, he spoke softly.

"Lucy, listen to yourself."

"I'm just—"

"You're arguing on the side of death. Do you want to die? Are you so determined that you won't listen to someone who says you can live?"

She was quiet for a long time, then shuffled her feet awkwardly. She glanced at him, then at Song and Ralston. They were waiting, and she had to blush and smile slowly at them.

"You're right. What do we do first?"

"Just what we were doing. Taking stock of our situation. We need to make a list of what's available to us. We'll write it down on paper, but I can give you a general rundown." He counted off the points on his fingers.

"One, we have food for twenty people for three months. That comes to about a year for the five of us. With rationing, maybe a year and a half. That's assuming all the supply capsules reach us all right. In addition, the *Edgar* is going to clean the pantry to the bone and give us everything they can possibly spare and send it to us in the three space capsules. That might come to two years or even three.

"Two, we have enough water to last us forever if the recyclers keep going. That'll be a problem, because our reactor will run out of power in two years. We'll need another power source, and maybe another water source.

"The oxygen problem is about the same. Two years at the outside. We'll have to find a way to conserve it a lot more than we're doing. Offhand, I don't know how. Song, do you have any ideas?"

She looked thoughtful, which produced two vertical punctuation marks between her slanted eyes.

"Possibly a culture of plants from the *Edgar*. If we could rig some way to grow plants in Martian sunlight and not have them killed by the ultraviolet. . . ."

McKillian looked horrified, as any good ecologist would.

"What about contamination?" she asked. "What do you think that sterilization was for before we landed. Do you want to louse up the entire ecological balance of Mars? No one would ever be sure if samples in the future were real Martian plants or mutated Earth stock."

"What ecological balance?" Song shot back. "You know as well as I do that this trip has been nearly a zero. A few anaerobic bacteria, a patch of lichen, both barely distinguishable from Earth forms—"

"That's just what I mean. You import Earth forms now, and we'll never tell the difference."

"But it could be done, right? With the proper shielding so the plants won't be wiped out before they ever sprout, we could have a hydroponics plant functioning—"

"Oh, yes, it could be done. I can see three or four dodges right now. But you're not addressing the main question, which is—"

"Hold it," Crawford said. "I just wanted to know if you had any ideas." He was secretly pleased at the argument; it got them both thinking along the right lines, moved them from the deadly apathy they must guard against.

"I think this discussion has served its purpose, which was to convince everyone here that survival is possible." He glanced uneasily at Lang, still nodding, her eyes glassy as she saw her teammates die before her eyes.

"I just want to point out that instead of an expedition, we are now a colony. Not in the usual sense of planning to stay here forever, but all our planning will have to be geared to that fiction. What we're faced with is not a simple matter of stretching supplies until rescue comes. Stopgap measures are not likely to do us much good. The answers that will save us are the long-term ones, the sort of answers a colony would be looking for. About two years from now we're going to have to be in a position to survive with some sort of lifestyle that could support us forever. We'll have to fit into this environment where we can and adapt it to us where we can. For that, we're better off than most of the colonists of the past, at least for the short term. We have a large supply of everything a colony needs: food, water, tools, raw materials, energy, brains, and women. Without these things, no colony has much of a chance. All we lack is a regular resupply from the home country, but a really good group of colonists can get along without that. What do you say? Are you all with me?"

Something had caused Mary Lang's eyes to look up. It was a reflex by now, a survival reflex conditioned by a lifetime of fighting her way to the top. It took root in her again and pulled her erect on the bed, then to her feet. She fought off the effects of the drug and stood there, eyes bleary but aware.

"What makes you think that women are a natural resource, Crawford?" she said, slowly and deliberately.

"Why, what I meant was that without the morale uplift provided by members of the opposite sex, a colony will lack the push needed to make it."

"That's what you meant, all right. And you meant women, available to the *real* colonists as a reason to live. I've heard it before. That's a male-oriented way to look at it, Crawford." She was regaining her stature as they watched, seeming to grow until she dominated the group with the intangible power that marks a leader. She took a deep breath and came fully awake for the first time that day.

"We'll stop that sort of thinking right now. I'm the mission commander. I appreciate you taking over while I was . . . how did you say it? Indisposed. But you should pay more attention to the social aspects of our situation. If anyone is a commodity here, it's you and Ralston, by virtue of your scarcity. There will be some thorny questions to resolve there, but for the meantime we will function as a unit, under my command. We'll do all we can to minimize social competition among the women for the men. That's the way it must be. Clear?"

She was answered by quiet assent and nods of the head. She did not acknowledge it but plowed right on.

"I wondered from the start why you were along, Crawford." She was pacing slowly back and forth in the crowded space. The others got out of her way almost without thinking, except for Ralston who still huddled under his blanket. "A historian? Sure, it's a fine idea, but pretty impractical. I have to admit that I've been thinking of you as a luxury, and about as useful as the nipples on a man's chest. But I was wrong. All the NASA people were wrong. The Astronaut Corps fought like crazy to keep you off this trip. Time enough for that on later flights. We were blinded by our loyalty to the test-pilot philosophy of space flight. We wanted as few scientists as possible and as many astronauts as we could manage. We don't like to think of ourselves as ferry-boat pilots. I think we demonstrated during Apollo that we could handle science jobs as

well as anyone. We saw you as a kind of insult, a slap in the face
by the scientists in Houston to show us how low our stock has
fallen."

"If I might be able to—"

"Shut up. But we were wrong. I read in your resume that you
were quite a student of survival. What's your honest assessment of
our chances?"

Crawford shrugged, uneasy at the question. He didn't know if it
was the right time to even postulate that they might fail.

"Tell me the truth."

"Pretty slim. Mostly the air problem. The people I've read
about never sank so low that they had to worry about where their
next breath was coming from."

"Have you ever heard of Apollo 13?"

He smiled at her. "Special circumstances. Short-term problems."

"You're right, of course. And in the only two other real space
emergencies since that time, all hands were lost." She turned and
scowled at each of them in turn.

"But we're *not* going to lose." She dared any of them to disa-
gree, and no one was about to. She relaxed and resumed her stroll
around the room. She turned to Crawford again.

"I can see I'll be drawing on your knowledge a lot in the years
to come. What do you see as the next order of business?"

Crawford relaxed. The awful burden of responsibility, which he
had never wanted, was gone. He was content to follow her lead.

"To tell you the truth, I was wondering what to say next. We
have to make a thorough inventory. I guess we should start on
that."

"That's fine, but there is an even more important order of business. We have to go out to the dome and find out what the hell
caused the blowout. The damn thing should *not* have blown; it's
the first of its type to do so. And from the *bottom*. But it did blow,
and we should know why, or we're ignoring a fact about Mars that
might still kill us. Let's do that first. Ralston, can you walk?"

When he nodded, she sealed her helmet and started into the
lock. She turned and looked speculatively at Crawford.

"I swear, man, if you had touched me with a cattle prod you

couldn't have got a bigger rise out of me than you did with what you said a few minutes ago. Do I dare ask?"

Crawford was not about to answer. He said, with a perfectly straight face, "Me? Maybe you should just assume I'm a chauvinist."

"We'll see, won't we?"

"What is that stuff?"

Song Sue Lee was on her knees, examining one of the hundreds of short, stiff spikes extruding from the ground. She tried to scratch her head but was frustrated by her helmet.

"It looks like plastic. But I have a strong feeling it's the higher life-form Lucy and I were looking for yesterday."

"And you're telling me those little spikes are what poked holes in the dome bottom? I'm not buying that."

Song straightened up, moving stiffly. They had all worked hard to empty out the collapsed dome and peel back the whole, bulky mess to reveal the ground it had covered. She was tired and stepped out of character for a moment to snap at Mary Lang.

"I didn't tell you that. We pulled the dome back and found spikes. It was your inference that they poked holes in the bottom."

"I'm sorry," Lang said, quietly. "Go on with what you were saying."

"Well," Song admitted, "it wasn't a bad inference, at that. But the holes I saw were not punched through. They were eaten away." She waited for Lang to protest that the dome bottom was about as chemically inert as any plastic yet devised. But Lang had learned her lesson. And she had a talent for facing facts.

"So. We have a thing here that eats plastic. And seems to be made of plastic, into the bargain. Any ideas why it picked this particular spot to grow, and no other?"

"I have an idea on that," McKillian said. "I've had it in mind to do some studies around the dome to see if the altered moisture content we've been creating here had any effect on the spores in the soil. See, we've been here nine days, spouting out water vapor, carbon dioxide, and quite a bit of oxygen into the atmosphere. Not much, but maybe more than it seems, considering the low concentrations that are naturally available. We've altered the biome.

Does anyone know where the exhaust air from the dome was expelled?"

Lang raised her eyebrows. "Yes, it was under the dome. The air we exhausted was warm, you see, and it was thought it could be put to use one last time before we let it go, to warm the floor of the dome and decrease heat loss."

"And the water vapor collected on the underside of the dome when it hit the cold air. Right. Do you get the picture?"

"I think so," Lang said. "It was so little water, though. You know we didn't want to waste it; we condensed it out until the air we exhausted was dry as a bone."

"For Earth, maybe. Here it was a torrential rainfall. It reached seeds or spores in the ground and triggered them to start growing. We're going to have to watch it when we use anything containing plastic. What does that include?"

Lang groaned. "All the air-lock seals, for one thing." There were grimaces from all of them at the thought of that. "For another, a good part of our suits. Song, watch it, don't step on that thing. We don't know how powerful it is or if it will eat the plastic in your boots, but we'd better play it safe. How about it, Ralston? Think you can find out how bad it is?"

"You mean identify the solvent these things use? Probably, if we can get some sort of work space and I can get to my equipment."

"Mary," McKillian said, "it occurs to me that I'd better start looking for airborne spores. If there are some, it could mean that the airlock on the *Podkayne* is vulnerable. Even thirty meters off the ground."

"Right. Get on that. Since we're sleeping in it until we can find out what we can do on the ground, we'd best be sure it's safe. Meantime, we'll all sleep in our suits." There were helpless groans at this, but no protests. McKillian and Ralston headed for the pile of salvaged equipment, hoping to rescue enough to get started on their analyses. Song knelt again and started digging around one of the ten-centimeter spikes.

Crawford followed Lang back toward the *Podkayne*.

"Mary, I wanted . . . is it all right if I call you Mary?"

"I guess so. I don't think 'Commander Lang' would wear well over five years. But you'd better still *think* commander."

He considered it. "All right, Commander Mary." She punched him playfully. She had barely known him before the disaster. He had been a name on the roster and a sore spot in the estimation of the Astronaut Corps. But she had borne him no personal malice, and now found herself beginning to like him.

"What's on your mind?"

"Ah, several things. But maybe it isn't my place to bring them up now. First, I want to say that if you're . . . ah, concerned, or doubtful of my support or loyalty because I took over command for a while . . . earlier today, well. . . ."

"Well?"

"I just wanted to tell you that I have no ambitions in that direction," he finished lamely.

She patted him on the back. "Sure, I know. You forget, I read your dossier. It mentioned several interesting episodes that I'd like you to tell me about someday, from your 'soldier-of-fortune' days—"

"Hell, those were grossly overblown. I just happened to get into some scrapes and managed to get out of them."

"Still, it got you picked for this mission out of hundreds of applicants. The thinking was that you'd be a wild card, a man of action with proven survivability. Maybe it worked out. But the other thing I remember on your card was that you're not a leader. No, that you're a loner who'll cooperate with a group and be no discipline problem, but you work better alone. Want to strike out on your own?"

He smiled at her. "No, thanks. But what you said is right. I have no hankering to take charge of anything. But I do have some knowledge that might prove useful."

"And we'll use it. You just speak up, I'll be listening." She started to say something, then thought of something else. "Say, what are your ideas on a woman bossing this project? I've had to fight that all the way from my Air Force days. So if you have any objections you might as well tell me up front."

He was genuinely surprised. "You didn't take that crack seriously, did you? I might as well admit it. It was intentional, like that cattle prod you mentioned. You looked like you needed a kick in the ass."

"And thank you—But you didn't answer my question."

"Those who lead, lead," he said, simply. "I'll follow you as long as you keep leading."

"As long as it's in the direction you want?" She laughed, and poked him in the ribs. "I see you as my Grand Vizier, the man who holds the arcane knowledge and advises the regent. I think I'll have to watch out for you. I know a little history, myself."

Crawford couldn't tell how serious she was. He shrugged it off.

"What I really wanted to talk to you about is this: You said you couldn't fly this ship. But you were not yourself, you were depressed and feeling hopeless. Does that still stand?"

"It stands. Come on up and I'll show you why."

In the pilot's cabin, Crawford was ready to believe her. Like all flying machines since the days of the windsock and open cockpit, this one was a mad confusion of dials, switches, and lights designed to awe anyone who knew nothing about it. He sat in the copilot's chair and listened to her.

"We had a back-up pilot, of course. You may be surprised to learn that it wasn't me. It was Dorothy Cantrell, and she's dead. Now I know what everything does on this board, and I can cope with most of it easily. What I don't know, I could learn. Some of the systems are computer-driven; give it the right program and it'll fly itself, in space." She looked longingly at the controls, and Crawford realized that, like Weinstein, she didn't relish giving up the fun of flying to boss a gang of explorers. She was a former test pilot, and above all things she loved flying. She patted an array of hand controls on her right side. There were more like them on the left.

"This is what would kill us, Crawford. What's your first name? Matt. Matt, this baby is a flyer for the first forty thousand meters. It doesn't have the juice to orbit on the jets alone. The wings are folded up now. You probably didn't see them on the way in, but you saw the models. They're very light, super critical, and designed for this atmosphere. Lou said it was like flying a bathtub, but it flew. And it's a *skill,* almost an art. Lou practiced for three years on the best simulators we could build and still had to rely on things you can't learn in a simulator. And he barely got us down in one piece. We didn't noise it around, but it was a *damn* close thing. Lou was young; so was Cantrell. They were both fresh from flying. They flew every day, they had the *feel* for it. They were tops." She slumped back into her chair. "I haven't flown anything but trainers for eight years."

Crawford didn't know if he should let it drop.

"But you were one of the best, everyone knows that. You still don't think you could do it?"

She threw up her hands. "How can I make you understand? This is nothing like anything I've ever flown. You might as well. . . ." She groped for a comparison, trying to coax it out with gestures in the air. "Listen. Does the fact that someone can fly a biplane, maybe even be the best goddamn biplane pilot that ever was, does that mean they're qualified to fly a helicopter?"

"I don't know."

"It doesn't. Believe me."

"All right. But the fact remains that you're the closest thing on Mars to a pilot for the *Podkayne*. I think you should consider that when you're deciding what we should do." He shut up, afraid to sound like he was pushing her.

She narrowed her eyes and gazed at nothing.

"I have thought about it." She waited for a long time. "I think the chances are about a thousand to one against us if I try to fly it. But I'll do it, if we come to that. And that's *your* job. Showing me some better odds. If you can't, let me know."

Three weeks later, the Tharsis Canyon had been transformed into a child's garden of toys. Crawford had thought of no better way to describe it. Each of the plastic spikes had blossomed into a fanciful windmill, no two of them just alike. There were tiny ones, with the vanes parallel to the ground and no more than ten centimeters tall. There were derricks of spidery plastic struts that would not have looked too out of place on a Kansas farm. Some of them were five meters high. They came in all colors and many configurations, but all had vanes covered with a transparent film like cellophane, and all were spinning into colorful blurs in the stiff Martian breeze. Crawford thought of an industrial park built by gnomes. He could almost see them trudging through the spinning wheels.

Song had taken one apart as well as she could. She was still shaking her head in disbelief. She had not been able to excavate the long insulated taproot, but she could infer how deep it went. It extended all the way down to the layer of permafrost, twenty meters down.

The ground between the windmills was coated in shimmering plastic. This was the second part of the plants' ingenious solution to survival on Mars. The windmills utilized the energy in the wind, and the plastic coating on the ground was in reality two thin sheets of plastic with a space between for water to circulate. The water was heated by the sun then pumped down to the permafrost, melting a little more of it each time.

"There's still something missing from our picture," Song had told them the night before when she delivered her summary of what she had learned. "Marty hasn't been able to find a mechanism that would permit these things to grow by ingesting sand and rock and turning it into plasticlike materials. So we assume there is a reservoir of something, like crude oil down there, maybe frozen in with the water."

"Where would that have come from?" Lang had asked.

"You've heard of the long-period Martian seasonal theories? Well, part of it is more than a theory. The combination of the Martian polar inclination, the precessional cycle, and the eccentricity of the orbit produces seasons that are about twelve thousand years long. We're in the middle of winter, though we landed in the nominal 'summer.' It's been theorized that if there were any Martian life it would have adapted to these longer cycles. It hibernates in spores during the cold cycle, when the water and carbon dioxide freeze out at the poles, then comes out when enough ice melts to permit biological processes. We seem to have fooled these plants; they thought summer was here when the water vapor content went up around the camp."

"So what about the crude?" Ralston asked. He didn't completely believe that part of the model they had evolved. He was a laboratory chemist, specializing in inorganic compounds. The way these plants produced plastics without high heat, through purely catalytic interactions, had him confused and defensive. He wished the crazy windmills would go away.

"I think I can answer that," McKillian said. "These organisms barely scrape by in the best of times. The ones that have made it waste nothing. It stands to reason that any really ancient deposits of crude oil would have been exhausted in only a few of these cycles. So it must be that what we're thinking of as crude oil must be something a little different. It has to be the remains of the last generation."

"But how did the remains get so far below ground?" Ralston asked. "You'd expect them to be high up. The winds couldn't bury them that deep in only twelve thousand years."

"You're right," said McKillian. "I don't really know. But I have a theory. Since these plants waste nothing, why not conserve their bodies when they die? They sprouted from the ground; isn't it possible they could withdraw when things start to get tough again? They'd leave spores behind them as they retreated, distributing them all through the soil. That way, if the upper ones blew away or were sterilized by the ultraviolet, the ones just below them would still thrive when the right conditions returned. When they reached the permafrost, they'd decompose into this organic slush we've postulated, and . . . well, it does get a little involved, doesn't it?"

"Sounds all right to me," Lang assured her. "It'll do for a working theory. Now what about airborne spores?"

It turned out that they were safe from that imagined danger. There were spores in the air now, but they were not dangerous to the colonists. The plants attacked only certain kinds of plastics, and then only in certain stages of their lives. Since they were still changing, it bore watching, but the airlocks and suits were secure. The crew was enjoying the luxury of sleeping without their suits.

And there was much work to do. Most of the physical sort devolved on Crawford and, to some extent, on Lang. It threw them together a lot. The other three had to be free to pursue their researches, as it had been decided that only in knowing their environment would they stand a chance.

The two of them had managed to salvage most of the dome. Working with patching kits and lasers to cut the tough material, they had constructed a much smaller dome. They erected it on an outcropping of bare rock; rearranged the exhaust to prevent more condensation on the underside, and added more safety features. They now slept in a pressurized building inside the dome, and one of them stayed awake on watch at all times. In drills, they had come from a deep sleep to full pressure-integrity in thirty seconds. They were not going to get caught again.

Crawford looked away from the madly whirling rotors of the windmill farm. He was with the rest of the crew, sitting in the dome with his helmet off. That was as far as Lang would permit anyone to go except in the cramped sleeping quarters. Song Sue Lee was at the radio giving her report to the *Edgar Rice Burroughs*. In her hand was one of the pump modules she had dissected out of one of the plants. It consisted of a half-meter set of eight blades that turned freely on Teflon bearings. Below it were various tiny gears and the pump itself. She twirled it idly as she spoke.

"I don't really get it," Crawford admitted, talking quietly to Lucy McKillian. "What's so revolutionary about little windmills?"

"It's just a whole new area," McKillian whispered back. "Think about it. Back on Earth, nature never got around to inventing the wheel. I've sometimes wondered why not. There are limitations, of course, but it's such a good idea. Just look what *we've* done with it. But all motion in nature is confined to up and down, back and forth, in and out, or squeeze and relax. Nothing on Earth goes round and round, unless we built it. Think about it."

Crawford did, and began to see the novelty of it. He tried in vain to think of some mechanism in an animal or plant of Earthly origin that turned and kept on turning forever. He could not.

Song finished her report and handed the mike to Lang. Before she could start, Weinstein came on the line.

"We've had a change in plan up here," he said, with no preface. "I hope this doesn't come as a shock. If you think about it, you'll see the logic in it. We're going back to Earth in seven days."

It didn't surprise them too much. The *Burroughs* had given them just about everything it could in the form of data and supplies. There was one more capsule load due; after that, its presence would only be a frustration to both groups. There was a great deal of irony in having two such powerful ships so close to each other and being so helpless to do anything concrete. It was telling on the crew of the *Burroughs*.

"We've recalculated everything based on the lower mass without the twenty of you and the six tons of samples we were allowing for. By using the fuel we would have ferried down to you for takeoff, we can make a faster orbit down toward Venus. The departure date for that orbit is seven days away. We'll rendezvous with a drone capsule full of supplies we hadn't counted on." And besides, Lang thought to herself, it's much more dramatic. *Plunging sunward on the chancy cometary orbit, their pantries stripped bare, heading for the fateful rendezvous. . . .*

"I'd like your comments," he went on. "This isn't absolutely final as yet."

They all looked at Lang. They were reassured to find her calm and unshaken.

"I think it's the best idea. One thing; you've given up on any thoughts of me flying the *Podkayne?*"

"No insult intended, Mary," Weinstein said, gently. "But, yes, we have. It's the opinion of the people Earthside that you couldn't do it. They've tried some experiments, coaching some very good pilots and putting them into the simulators. They can't do it, and we don't think you could, either."

"No need to sugar-coat it. I know it as well as anyone. But even a billion to one shot is better than nothing. I take it they think Crawford is right, that survival is at least theoretically possible?"

There was a long hesitation. "I guess that's correct. Mary, I'll be frank. I don't think it's possible. I hope I'm wrong, but I don't expect. . . ."

"Thank you, Winey, for the encouraging words. You always did know what it takes to buck a person up. By the way, that other mission, the one where you were going to ride a meteorite down here to save our asses, that's scrubbed, too?"

The assembled crew smiled, and Song gave a high-pitched cheer. Weinstein was not the most popular man on Mars.

"Mary, I told you about that already," he complained. It was a gentle complaint, and, even more significant, he had not objected to the use of his nickname. He was being gentle with the condemned. "We worked on it around the clock. I even managed to get permission to turn over command temporarily. But the mockups they made Earthside didn't survive the re-entry. It was the best we could do. I couldn't risk the entire mission on a configuration the people back on Earth wouldn't certify."

"I know. I'll call you back tomorrow." She switched the set off and sat back on her heels. "I swear, if the Earthside tests on a roll of toilet paper didn't . . . he wouldn't. . . ." She cut the air with her hands. "What am I saying? That's petty. I don't like him, but he's right." She stood up, puffing out her cheeks as she exhaled a pent-up breath.

"Come on, crew, we've got a lot of work."

They named their colony New Amsterdam, because of the windmills. The name of whirligig was the one that stuck on the Martian plants, though Crawford held out for a long time in favor of spinnakers.

They worked all day and tried their best to ignore the *Burroughs* overhead. The messages back and forth were short and to the point. Helpless as the mother ship was to render them more aid, they knew they would miss it when it was gone. So the day of departure was a stiff, determinedly nonchalant affair. They all made a big show of going to bed hours before the scheduled breakaway.

When he was sure the others were asleep, Crawford opened his eyes and looked around the darkened barracks. It wasn't much in the way of a home; they were crowded against each other on rough pads made of insulating material. The toilet facilities were behind a flimsy barrier against one wall, and smelled. But none of them would have wanted to sleep outside in the dome, even if Lang had allowed it.

The only light came from the illuminated dials that the guard was supposed to watch all night. There was no one sitting in front of them. Crawford assumed the guard had gone to sleep. He would have been upset, but there was no time. He had to suit up, and he welcomed the chance to sneak out. He began to furtively don his pressure suit.

As a historian, he felt he could not let such a moment slip by unobserved. Silly, but there it was. He had to be out there, watch it with his own eyes. It didn't matter if he never lived to tell about it, he must record it.

Someone sat up beside him. He froze, but it was too late. She rubbed her eyes and peered into the darkness.

"Matt?" she yawned. "What's . . . what is it? Is something—"

"Shh. I'm going out. Go back to sleep. Song?"

"Um hmmm." She stretched, dug her knuckles fiercely into her eyes, and smoothed her hair back from her face. She was dressed in a loose-fitting bottoms of a ship suit, a gray piece of dirty cloth that badly needed washing, as did all their clothes. For a moment, as he watched her shadow stretch and stand up, he wasn't interested in the *Burroughs*. He forced his mind away from her.

"I'm going with you," she whispered.

"All right. Don't wake the others."

Standing just outside the airlock was Mary Lang. She turned as they came out, and did not seem surprised.

"Were you the one on duty?" Crawford asked her.

"Yeah. I broke my own rule. But so did you two. Consider yourselves on report." She laughed and beckoned them over to her. They linked arms and stood staring up at the sky.

"How much longer?" Song asked, after some time had passed.

"Just a few minutes. Hold tight." Crawford looked over to Lang and thought he saw tears, but he couldn't be sure in the dark.

There was a tiny new star; brighter than all the rest, brighter than Phobos. It hurt to look at it but none of them looked away. It was the fusion drive of the *Edgar Rice Burroughs,* heading sunward, away from the long winter on Mars. It stayed on for long minutes, then sputtered and was lost. Though it was warm in the dome, Crawford was shivering. It was ten minutes before any of them felt like facing the barracks.

They crowded into the airlock, carefully not looking at each other's faces as they waited for the automatic machinery. The inner door opened and Lang pushed forward—and right back into the airlock. Crawford had a glimpse of Ralston and Lucy McKillian; then Mary shut the door.

"Some people have no poetry in their souls," Mary said.

"Or too much," Song giggled.

"You people want to take a walk around the dome with me? Maybe we could discuss ways of giving people a little privacy."

The inner lock door was pulled open, and there was McKillian, squinting into the bare bulb that lighted the lock while she held her shirt in front of her with one hand.

"Come on in," she said, stepping back. "We might as well talk about this." They entered, and McKillian turned on the light and sat down on her mattress. Ralston was blinking, nervously tucked into his pile of blankets. Since the day of the blowout he never seemed to be warm enough.

Having called for a discussion, McKillian proceeded to clam up. Song and Crawford sat on their bunks, and eventually as the silence stretched tighter, they all found themselves looking to Lang.

She started stripping out of her suit. "Well, I guess that takes care of that. So glad to hear all your comments. Lucy, if you were expecting some sort of reprimand, forget it. We'll take steps first thing in the morning to provide some sort of privacy for that, but, no matter what, we'll all be pretty close in the years to come. I think we should all relax. Any objections?" She was half out of her suit when she paused to scan them for comments. There was none. She stripped to her skin and reached for the light.

"In a way it's about time," she said, tossing her clothes in a corner. "The only thing to do with these clothes is burn them. We'll all smell better for it. Song, you take the watch." She flicked out the lights and reclined heavily on her mattress.

There was much rustling and squirming for the next few minutes as they got out of their clothes. Song brushed against Crawford in the dark and they murmured apologies. Then they all bedded down in their own bunks. It was several tense, miserable hours before anyone got to sleep.

The week following the departure of the *Burroughs* was one of hysterical overreaction by the New Amsterdamites. The atmosphere was forced and false; an eat-drink-and-be-merry feeling pervaded everything they did.

They built a separate shelter inside the dome, not really talking aloud about what it was for. But it did not lack for use. Productive work suffered as the five of them frantically ran through all the possible permutations of three women and two men. Animosities developed, flourished for a few hours, and dissolved in tearful reconciliations. Three ganged up on two, two on one, one declared war on all the other four. Ralston and Song announced an engagement, which lasted ten hours. Crawford nearly came to blows with Lang, aided by McKillian. McKillian renounced men forever and had a brief, tempestuous affair with Song. Then Song discovered McKillian with Ralston, and Crawford caught her on the rebound, only to be thrown over for Ralston.

Mary Lang let it work itself out, only interfering when it got violent. She herself was not immune to the frenzy but managed to stay aloof from most of it. She went to the shelter with whoever asked her, trying not to play favorites, and gently tried to prod them back to work. As she told McKillian toward the first of the week, "At least we're getting to know one another."

Things did settle down, as Lang had known they would. They entered their second week alone in virtually the same position they had started: no romantic entanglements firmly established. But they knew each other a lot better, were relaxed in the close company of each other, and were supported by a new framework of interlocking friendships. They were much closer to being a team. Rivalries never died out completely, but they no longer dominated the colony. Lang worked them harder than ever, making up for the lost time.

Crawford missed most of the interesting work, being more suited for the semiskilled manual labor that never seemed to be finished. So he and Lang had to learn about the new discoveries at the nightly briefings in the shelter. He remembered nothing about any animal life being discovered, and so when he saw something crawling through the whirligig garden, he dropped everything and started over to it.

At the edge of the garden he stopped, remembering the order from Lang to stay out unless collecting samples. He watched the thing—bug? turtle?—for a moment, satisfied himself that it wouldn't get too far away at its creeping pace, and hurried off to find Song.

"You've got to name it after me," he said as they hurried back to the garden. "That's my right, isn't it, as the discoverer?"

"Sure," Song said, peering along his pointed finger. "Just show me the damn thing and I'll immortalize you."

The thing was twenty centimeters long, almost round, and dome-shaped. It had a hard shell on top.

"I don't know quite what to do with it," Song admitted. "If it's the only one, I don't dare dissect it, and maybe I shouldn't even touch it."

"Don't worry, there's another over behind you." Now that they were looking for them, they quickly spied four of the creatures. Song took a sample bag from her pouch and held it open in front of the beast. It crawled halfway into the bag, then seemed to think something was wrong. It stopped, but Song nudged it in and picked it up. She peered at the underside and laughed in wonder.

"Wheels," she said. "The thing runs on wheels."

"I don't know where it came from," Song told the group that night. "I don't even quite believe in it. It'd make a nice educational toy for a child, though. I took it apart into twenty or thirty pieces, put it back together, and it still runs. It has a high-impact polystyrene carapace, nontoxic paint on the outside—"

"Not really polystyrene," Ralston interjected.

" . . . and I guess if you kept changing the batteries it would run forever. And it's *nearly* polystyrene, that's what you said."

"Were you serious about the batteries?" Lang asked.

"I'm not sure. Marty thinks there's a chemical metabolism in the upper part of the shell, which I haven't explored yet. But I can't really say if it's alive in the sense we use. I mean, it runs on *wheels!* It has three wheels, suited for sand, and something that's a cross between a rubber-band drive and a mainspring. Energy is stored in a coiled muscle and released slowly. I don't think it could travel more than a hundred meters. Unless it can re-coil the muscle, and I can't tell how that might be done."

"It sounds very specialized," McKillian said thoughtfully. "Maybe we should be looking for the niche it occupies. The way you describe it, it couldn't function without help from a symbiote. Maybe it fertilizes the plants, like bees, and the plants either do-nate or are robbed of the power to wind the spring. Did you look

for some mechanism the bug could use to steal energy from the rotating gears in the whirligigs?"

"That's what I want to do in the morning," Song said. "Unless
Mary will let us take a look tonight?" She said it hopefully, but
without real expectation. Mary Lang shook her head decisively.

"It'll keep. It's *cold* out there, baby."

A new exploration of the whirligig garden the next day revealed
several new species, including one more thing that might be an animal. It was a flying creature, the size of a fruit fly, that managed
to glide from plant to plant when the wind was down by means of
a freely rotating set of blades, like an autogiro.

Crawford and Lang hung around as the scientists looked things
over. They were not anxious to get back to the task that had occupied them for the last two weeks: that of bringing the *Podkayne* to
a horizontal position without wrecking her. The ship had been
rigged with stabilizing cables soon after landing, and provision had
been made in the plans to lay the ship on its side in the event of a
really big windstorm. But the plans had envisioned a work force of
twenty, working all day with a maze of pulleys and gears. It was
slow work and could not be rushed. If the ship were to tumble and
lose pressure, they didn't have a prayer.

So they welcomed an opportunity to tour fairyland. The place
was even more bountiful than the last time Crawford had taken a
look. There were thick vines that Song assured him were running
with water, both hot and cold, and various other fluids. There
were more of the tall variety of derrick, making the place look like
a pastel oilfield.

They had little trouble finding where the matthews came from.
They found dozens of twenty-centimeter lumps on the sides of the
large derricks. They evidently grew from them like tumors and
were released when they were ripe. What they were for was another matter. As well as they could discover, the matthews simply
crawled in a straight line until their power ran out. If they were
wound up again, they would crawl farther. There were dozens of
them lying motionless in the sand within a hundred meter radius
of the garden.

Two weeks of research left them knowing no more. They had to abandon the matthews for the time, as another enigma had cropped up which demanded their attention.

This time Crawford was the last to know. He was called on the radio and found the group all squatted in a circle around a growth in the graveyard.

The graveyard, where they had buried their fifteen dead crewmates on the first day of the disaster, had sprouted with life during the week after the departure of the *Burroughs*. It was separated from the original site of the dome by three hundred meters of blowing sand. So McKillian assumed this second bloom was caused by the water in the bodies of the dead. What they couldn't figure out was why this patch should differ so radically from the first one.

There were whirligigs in the second patch, but they lacked the variety and disorder of the originals. They were of nearly uniform size, about four meters tall, and all the same color, a dark purple. They had pumped water for two weeks, then stopped. When Song examined them, she reported the bearings were frozen, dried out. They seemed to have lost the plasticizer that kept the structures fluid and living. The water in the pipes was frozen. Though she would not commit herself in the matter, she felt they were dead. In their place was a second network of pipes which wound around the derricks and spread transparent sheets of film to the sunlight, heating the water which circulated through them. The water was being pumped, but not by the now-familiar system of windmills. Spaced along each of the pipes were expansion-contraction pumps with valves very like those in a human heart.

The new marvel was a simple affair in the middle of that living petrochemical complex. It was a short plant that sprouted up half a meter, then extruded two stalks parallel to the ground. At the end of each stalk was a perfect globe, one gray, one blue. The blue one was much larger than the gray one.

Crawford looked at it briefly, then squatted down beside the rest, wondering what all the fuss was about. Everyone looked very solemn, almost scared.

"You called me over to see this?"

Lang looked over at him, and something in her face made him nervous.

"Look at it, Matt. Really look at it." So he did, feeling foolish, wondering what the joke was. He noticed a white patch near the top of the largest globe. It was streaked, like a glass marble with swirls of opaque material in it. It looked *very* familiar, he realized, with the hair on the back of his neck starting to stand up.

"It turns," Lang said quietly. "That's why Song noticed it. She came by here one day and it was in a different position than it had been."

"Let me guess," he said, much more calmly than he felt. "The little one goes around the big one, right?"

"Right. And the little one keeps one face turned to the big one. The big one rotates once in twenty-four hours. It has an axial tilt of twenty-three degrees."

"It's a . . . what's the word? Orrery. It's an orrery." Crawford had to stand up and shake his head to clear it.

"It's funny," Lang said, quietly. "I always thought it would be something flashy, or at least obvious. An alien artifact mixed in with cave man bones, or a spaceship entering the system. I guess I was thinking in terms of pottery shards and atom bombs."

"Well, that all sounds pretty ho-hum to me up against *this*," Song said. "Do you . . . do you *realize* . . . what are we talking about here? Evolution, or . . . or engineering? Is it the plants themselves that did this, or were they made to do it by whatever built them? Do you see what I'm talking about? I've felt funny about those wheels for a long time. I just won't believe they'd evolve naturally."

"What do you mean?"

"I mean I think these plants we've been seeing were designed to be the way they are. They're *too* perfectly adapted, *too* ingenious to have just sprung up in response to the environment." Her eyes seemed to wander, and she stood up and gazed into the valley below them. It was as barren as anything that could be imagined: red and yellow and brown rock outcroppings and tumbled boulders. And in the foreground, the twirling colors of the whirligigs.

"But why this thing?" Crawford asked, pointing to the impossible artifact-plant. "Why a model of the Earth and Moon? And why right here, in the graveyard?"

"Because we were expected," Song said, still looking away from them. "They must have watched the Earth, during the last summer season. I don't know; maybe they even went there. If they did, they would have found men and women like us, hunting and living in caves. Building fires, using clubs, chipping arrowheads. You know more about it than I do, Matt."

"Who are *they?*" Ralston asked. "You think we're going to be meeting some Martians? People? I don't see how. I don't believe it."

"I'm afraid I'm skeptical, too," Lang said. "Surely there must be some other way to explain it."

"No! There's no other way. Oh, not people like us, maybe. Maybe we're seeing them right now, spinning like crazy." They all looked uneasily at the whirligigs. "But I think they're not here yet. I think we're going to see, over the next few years, increasing complexity in these plants and animals as they build up a biome here and get ready for the builders. Think about it. When summer comes, the conditions will be very different. The atmosphere will be almost as dense as ours, with about the same partial pressure of oxygen. By then, thousands of years from now, these early forms will have vanished. These things are adapted for low pressure, no oxygen, scarce water. The later ones will be adapted to an environment much like ours. And *that's* when we'll see the makers, when the stage is properly set." She sounded almost religious when she said it.

Lang stood up and shook Song's shoulder. Song came slowly back to them and sat down, still blinded by a private vision. Crawford had a glimpse of it himself, and it scared him. And a glimpse of something else, something that could be important but kept eluding him.

"Don't you see?" she went on, calmer now. "It's too pat, too much of a coincidence. This thing is like a . . . a headstone, a monument. It's growing right here in the graveyard, from the bodies of our friends. Can you believe in that as just a coincidence?"

Evidently no one could. But likewise, Crawford could see no reason why it should have happened the way it did.

It was painful to leave the mystery for later, but there was nothing to be done about it. They could not bring themselves to uproot the thing, even when five more like it sprouted in the graveyard.

There was a new consensus among them to leave the Martian plants and animals alone. Like nervous atheists, most of them didn't believe Song's theories but had an uneasy feeling of trespassing when they went through the gardens. They felt subconsciously that it might be better to leave them alone in case they turned out to be private property.

And for six months, nothing really new cropped up among the whirligigs. Song was not surprised. She said it supported her theory that these plants were there only as caretakers to prepare the way for the less hardy, air-breathing varieties to come. They would warm the soil and bring the water closer to the surface, then disappear when their function was over.

The three scientists allowed their studies to slide as it became more important to provide for the needs of the moment. The dome material was weakening as the temporary patches lost strength, and so a new home was badly needed. They were dealing daily with slow leaks, any of which could become a major blowout.

The *Podkayne* was lowered to the ground, and sadly decommissioned. It was a bad day for Mary Lang, the worst since the day of the blowout. She saw it as a necessary but infamous thing to do to a proud flying machine. She brooded about it for a week, becoming short-tempered and almost unapproachable. Then she asked Crawford to join her in the private shelter. It was the first time she had asked any of the other four. They lay in each other's arms for an hour, and Lang quietly sobbed on his chest. Crawford was proud that she had chosen him for her companion when she could no longer maintain her tough, competent show of strength. In a way, it was a strong thing to do, to expose weakness to the one person among the four who might possibly be her rival for leadership. He did not betray the trust. In the end, she was comforting him.

After that day Lang was ruthless in gutting the old *Podkayne*. She supervised the ripping out of the motors to provide more living space, and only Crawford saw what it was costing her. They drained the fuel tanks and stored the fuel in every available container they could scrounge. It would be useful later for heating, and for recharging batteries. They managed to convert plastic packing crates into fuel containers by lining them with sheets of

the double-walled material the whirligigs used to heat water. They
were nervous at this vandalism, but had no other choice. They
kept looking nervously at the graveyard as they ripped up meter-
square sheets of it.

They ended up with a long cylindrical home, divided into two
small sleeping rooms, a community room, and a laboratory-
storehouse-workshop in the old fuel tank. Crawford and Lang
spent the first night together in the "penthouse," the former cockpit, the only room with windows.

Lying there wide awake on the rough mattress, side by side in
the warm air with Mary Lang, whose black leg was a crooked line
of shadow lying across his body, looking up through the port at
the sharp, unwinking stars—with nothing done yet about the problems of oxygen, food, and water for the years ahead and no assurance he would live out the night on a planet determined to kill him
—Crawford realized he had never been happier in his life.

On a day exactly eight months after the disaster, two discoveries
were made. One was in the whirligig garden and concerned a new
plant that was bearing what might be fruit. They were clusters of
grape-sized white balls, very hard and fairly heavy. The second
discovery was made by Lucy McKillian and concerned the absence
of an event that up to that time had been as regular as the full
moon.

"I'm pregnant," she announced to them that night, causing Song
to delay her examination of the white fruit.

It was not unexpected; Lang had been waiting for it to happen
since the night the *Burroughs* left. But she had not worried about
it. Now she must decide what to do.

"I was afraid that might happen," Crawford said. "What do we
do, Mary?"

"Why don't you tell me what you think? You're the survival expert. Are babies a plus or a minus in our situation?"

"I'm afraid I have to say they're a liability. Lucy will be needing
extra food during her pregnancy, and afterward, and it will be an
extra mouth to feed. We can't afford the strain on our resources."
Lang said nothing, waiting to hear from McKillian.

"Now wait a minute. What about all this line about 'colonists' you've been feeding us ever since we got stranded here? Who ever heard of a colony without babies? If we don't grow, we stagnate, right? We *have* to have children." She looked back and forth from Lang to Crawford, her face expressing formless doubts.

"We're in special circumstances, Lucy," Crawford explained. "Sure, I'd be all for it if we were better off. But we can't be sure we can even provide for ourselves, much less a child. I say we can't afford children until we're established."

"Do you want the child, Lucy?" Lang asked quietly.

McKillian didn't seem to know what she wanted. "No. I . . . but, yes. Yes, I guess I do." She looked at them, pleading for them to understand.

"Look, I've never had one, and never planned to. I'm thirty-four years old and never, never felt the lack. I've always wanted to go places, and you can't with a baby. But I never planned to become a colonist on Mars, either. I . . . things have changed, don't you see? I've been depressed." She looked around, and Song and Ralston were nodding sympathetically. Relieved to see that she was not the only one feeling the oppression, she went on, more strongly. "I think if I go another day like yesterday and the day before—and today—I'll end up screaming. It seems so pointless, collecting all that information, for what?"

"I agree with Lucy," Ralston said, surprisingly. Crawford had thought he would be the only one immune to the inevitable despair of the castaway. Ralston in his laboratory was the picture of care-free detachment, existing only to observe.

"So do I," Lang said, ending the discussion. But she explained her reasons to them.

"Look at it this way, Matt. No matter how we stretch our supplies, they won't take us through the next four years. We either find a way of getting what we need from what's around us, or we all die. And if we find a way to do it, then what does it matter how many of us there are? At the most, this will push our deadline a few weeks or a month closer, the day we have to be self-supporting."

"I hadn't thought of it that way," Crawford admitted.

"But that's not important. The important thing is what you said from the first, and I'm surprised you didn't see it. If we're a colony, we expand. By definition. Historian, what happened to colonies that failed to expand?"

"Don't rub it in."

"They died out. I know that much. People, we're not intrepid space explorers anymore. We're not the career men and women we set out to be. Like it or not, and I suggest we start liking it, we're pioneers trying to live in a hostile environment. The odds are very much against us, and we're not going to be here forever, but like Matt said, we'd better plan as if we were. Comment?"

There was none, until Song spoke up, thoughtfully.

"I think a baby around here would be fun. Two should be twice as much fun. I think I'll start. Come on, Marty."

"Hold on, honey," Lang said, dryly. "If you conceive now, I'll be forced to order you to abort. We have the chemicals for it, you know."

"That's discrimination."

"Maybe so. But just because we're colonists doesn't mean we have to behave like rabbits. A pregnant woman will have to be removed from the work force at the end of her term, and we can only afford one at a time. After Lucy has hers, then come ask me again. But watch Lucy carefully, dear. Have you really thought what it's going to take? Have you tried to visualize her getting into her pressure suit in six or seven months?"

From their expressions, it was plain that neither Song nor McKillian had thought of it.

"Right," Lang went on: "It'll be literal confinement for her, right here in the *Poddy*. Unless we can rig something for her, which I seriously doubt. Still want to go through with it, Lucy?"

"Can I have a while to think it over?"

"Sure. You have about two months. After that, the chemicals aren't safe."

"I'd advise you to do it," Crawford said. "I know my opinion means nothing after shooting my mouth off. I know I'm a fine one to talk; I won't be cooped up in here. But the colony needs it. We've all felt it: the lack of a direction or a drive to keep going. I think we'd get it back if you went through with this."

McKillian tapped her teeth thoughtfully with the tip of a finger.

"You're right," she said. "Your opinion *doesn't* mean anything." She slapped his knee delightedly when she saw him blush. "I think it's yours, by the way. And I think I'll go ahead and have it."

The penthouse seemed to have gone to Lang and Crawford as an unasked-for prerogative. It just became a habit, since they seemed to have developed a bond between them and none of the other three complained. Neither of the other women seemed to be suffering in any way. So Lang left it at that. What went on between the three of them was of no concern to her as long as it stayed happy.

Lang was leaning back in Crawford's arms, trying to decide if she wanted to make love again, when a gunshot rang out in the *Podkayne*.

She had given a lot of thought to the last emergency, which she still saw as partly a result of her lag in responding. This time she was through the door almost before the reverberations had died down, leaving Crawford to nurse the leg she had stepped on in her haste.

She was in time to see McKillian and Ralston hurrying into the lab at the back of the ship. There was a red light flashing, but she quickly saw it was not the worst it could be; the pressure light still glowed green. It was the smoke detector. The smoke was coming from the lab.

She took a deep breath and plunged in, only to collide with Ralston as he came out, dragging Song. Except for a dazed expression and a few cuts, Song seemed to be all right. Crawford and McKillian joined them as they lay her on the bunk.

"It was one of the fruit," she said, gasping for breath and coughing. "I was heating it in a beaker, turned away, and it blew. I guess it sort of stunned me. The next thing I knew, Marty was carrying me out here. Hey, I have to get back in there! There's another one . . . it could be dangerous, and the damage, I have to check on that—" She struggled to get up but Lang held her down.

"You take it easy. What's this about another one?"

"I had it clamped down, and the drill—did I turn it on, or not? I can't remember. I was after a core sample. You'd better take a look. If the drill hits whatever made the other one explode, it might go off."

"I'll get it," McKillian said, turning toward the lab.

"You'll stay right here," Lang barked. "We know there's not enough power in them to hurt the ship, but it could kill you if it hit you right. We stay right here until it goes off. The hell with the damage. And shut that door, quick!"

Before they could shut it they heard a whistling, like a teakettle coming to boil, then a rapid series of clangs. A tiny white ball came through the doorway and bounced off three walls. It moved almost faster than they could follow. It hit Crawford on the arm, then fell to the floor where it gradually skittered to a stop. The hissing died away, and Crawford picked it up. It was lighter than it had been. There was a pinhole drilled in one side. The pinhole was cold when he touched it with his fingers. Startled, thinking he was burned, he stuck his finger in his mouth, then sucked on it absently long after he knew the truth.

"These 'fruit' are full of compressed gas," he told them. "We have to open up another, carefully this time. I'm almost afraid to say what gas I think it is, but I have a hunch that our problems are solved."

By the time the rescue expedition arrived, no one was calling it that. There had been the little matter of a long, brutal war with the Palestinian Empire, and a growing conviction that the survivors of the First Expedition had not had any chance in the first place. There had been no time for luxuries like space travel beyond the moon and no billions of dollars to invest while the world's energy policies were being debated in the Arabian Desert with tactical nuclear weapons.

When the ship finally did show up, it was no longer a NASA ship. It was sponsored by the fledgling International Space Agency. Its crew came from all over Earth. Its drive was new, too, and a lot better than the old one. As usual, war had given research a kick in the pants. Its mission was to take up the Martian exploration where the first expedition had left off and, incidentally, to recover the remains of the twenty Americans for return to Earth.

The ship came down with an impressive show of flame and billowing sand, three kilometers from Tharsis Base.

The captain, an Indian named Singh, got his crew started on erecting the permanent buildings, then climbed into a crawler with three officers for the trip to Tharsis. It was almost exactly twelve Earth-years since the departure of the *Edgar Rice Burroughs*.

The *Podkayne* was barely visible behind a network of multicolored vines. The vines were tough enough to frustrate their efforts to push through and enter the old ship. But both lock doors were open, and sand had drifted in rippled waves through the opening. The stern of the ship was nearly buried.

Singh told his people to stop, and he stood back admiring the complexity of the life in such a barren place. There were whirligigs twenty meters tall scattered around him, with vanes broad as the wings of a cargo aircraft.

"We'll have to get cutting tools from the ship," he told his crew. "They're probably in there. What a place this is! I can see we're going to be busy." He walked along the edge of the dense growth, which now covered several acres. He came to a section where the predominant color was purple. It was strangely different from the rest of the garden. There were tall whirligig derricks but they were frozen, unmoving. And covering all the derricks was a translucent network of ten-centimeter-wide strips of plastic, which was thick enough to make an impenetrable barrier. It was like a cobweb made of flat, thin material instead of fibrous spidersilk. It bulged outward between all the crossbraces of the whirligigs.

"Hello, can you hear me now?"

Singh jumped, then turned around, looked at the three officers. They were looking as surprised as he was.

"Hello, hello, hello? No good on this one, Mary. Want me to try another channel?"

"Wait a moment. I can hear you. Where are you?"

"Hey, he hears me! Uh, that is, this is Song Sue Lee, and I'm right in front of you. If you look real hard into the webbing, you can just make me out. I'll wave my arms. See?"

Singh thought he saw some movement when he pressed his face to the translucent web. The web resisted his hands, pushing back like an inflated balloon.

"I think I see you." The enormity of it was just striking him. He kept his voice under tight control, as his officers rushed up around him, and managed not to stammer. "Are you well? Is there anything we can do?"

There was a pause. "Well, now that you mention it, you might have come on time. But that's water through the pipes, I guess. If you have some toys or something, it might be nice. The stories I've told little Billy of all the nice things you people were going to bring! There's going to be no living with him, let me tell you."

This was getting out of hand for Captain Singh.

"Ms. Song, how can we get in there with you?"

"Sorry. Go to your right about ten meters, where you see the steam coming from the web. There, see it?" They did, and as they looked, a section of the webbing was pulled open and a rush of warm air almost blew them over. Water condensed out of it in their faceplates, and suddenly they couldn't see very well.

"Hurry, hurry, step in! We can't keep it open too long." They groped their way in, scraping frost away with their hands. The web closed behind them, and they were standing in the center of a very complicated network made of single strands of the webbing material. Singh's pressure gauge read 30 millibars.

Another section opened up and they stepped through it. After three more gates were passed, the temperature and pressure were nearly Earth-normal. And they were standing beside a small oriental woman with skin tanned almost black. She had no clothes on, but seemed adequately dressed in a brilliant smile that dimpled her mouth and eyes. Her hair was streaked with gray. She would be—Singh stopped to consider—forty-one years old.

"This way," she said, beckoning them into a tunnel formed from more strips of plastic. They twisted around through a random maze, going through more gates that opened when they neared them, sometimes getting on their knees when the clearance lowered. They heard the sound of children's voices.

They reached what must have been the center of the maze and found the people everyone had given up on. Eighteen of them. The children became very quiet and stared solemnly at the new arrivals, while the other four adults. . . .

The adults were standing separately around the space while tiny helicopters flew around them, wrapping them from head to toe in strips of webbing like human maypoles.

"Of course we don't know if we would have made it without the assist from the Martians," Mary Lang was saying, from her perch on an orange thing that might have been a toadstool. "Once we figured out what was happening here in the graveyard, there was no need to explore alternative ways of getting food, water, and oxygen. The need just never arose. We were provided for."

She raised her feet so a group of three gawking women from the ship could get by. They were letting them come through in groups of five every hour. They didn't dare open the outer egress more often than that, and Lang was wondering if it was too often. The place was crowded, and the kids were nervous. But better to have the crew satisfy their curiosity in here where we can watch them, she reasoned, than have them messing things up outside.

The inner nest was free-form. The New Amsterdamites had allowed it to stay pretty much the way the whirlibirds had built it, only taking down an obstruction here and there to allow humans to move around. It was a maze of gauzy walls and plastic struts, with clear plastic pipes running all over and carrying fluids of pale blue, pink, gold, and wine. Metal spigots from the *Podkayne* had been inserted in some of the pipes. McKillian was kept busy refilling glasses for the visitors who wanted to sample the antifreeze solution that was fifty percent ethanol. It was good stuff, Captain Singh reflected as he drained his third glass, and that was what he still couldn't understand.

He was having trouble framing the questions he wanted to ask, and he realized he'd had too much to drink. The spirit of celebration, the rejoicing at finding these people here past any hope; one could hardly stay aloof from it. But he refused a fourth drink regretfully.

"I can understand the drink," he said, carefully. "Ethanol is a simple compound and could fit into many different chemistries. But it's hard to believe that you've survived eating the food these plants produced for you."

"Not once you understand what this graveyard is and why it became what it did," Song said. She was sitting cross-legged on the floor nursing her youngest, Ethan.

"First you have to understand that all this you see," she waved around at the meters of hanging soft-sculpture, causing Ethan to nearly lose the nipple, "was designed to contain beings who are no more adapted to *this* Mars than we are. They need warmth, oxygen at fairly high pressures, and free water. It isn't here now, but it can be created by properly designed plants. They engineered these plants to be triggered by the first signs of free water and to start building places for them to live while they waited for full summer to come. When it does, this whole planet will bloom. Then we can step outside without wearing suits or carrying airberries."

"Yes, I see," Singh said. "And it's all very wonderful, almost too much to believe." He was distracted for a moment, looking up to the ceiling where the airberries—white spheres about the size of bowling balls—hung in clusters from the pipes that supplied them with high-pressure oxygen.

"I'd like to see that process from the start," he said. "Where you suit up for the outside, I mean."

"We were suiting up when you got here. It takes about half an hour; so we couldn't get out in time to meet you."

"How long are those . . . suits good for?"

"About a day," Crawford said. "You have to destroy them to get out of them. The plastic strips don't cut well, but there's another specialized animal that eats that type of plastic. It's recycled into the system. If you want to suit up, you just grab a whirlibird and hold onto its tail and throw it. It starts spinning as it flies, and wraps the end product around you. It takes some practice, but it works. The stuff sticks to itself, but not to us. So you spin several layers, letting each one dry, then hook up an airberry, and you're inflated and insulated."

"Marvelous," Singh said, truly impressed. He had seen the tiny whirlibirds weaving the suits, and the other ones, like small slugs, eating them away when the colonists saw they wouldn't need them. "But without some sort of exhaust, you wouldn't last long. How is that accomplished?"

"We use the breather valves from our old suits," McKillian said. "Either the plants that grow valves haven't come up yet or we haven't been smart enough to recognize them. And the insulation isn't perfect. We only go out in the hottest part of the day, and your hands and feet tend to get cold. But we manage."

Singh realized he had strayed from his original question.

"But what about the food? Surely it's too much to expect for these Martians to eat the same things we do. Wouldn't you think so?"

"We sure did, and we were lucky to have Marty Ralston along. He kept telling us the fruits in the graveyard were edible by humans. Fats, starches, proteins; all identical to the ones we brought along. The clue was in the orrery, of course."

Lang pointed to the twin globes in the middle of the room, still keeping perfect Earth time.

"It was a beacon. We figured that out when we saw they grew only in the graveyard. But what was it telling us? We felt it meant that we were expected. Song felt that from the start, and we all came to agree with her. But we didn't realize just how much they had prepared for us until Marty started analyzing the fruits and nutrients here.

"Listen, these Martians—and I can see from your look that you still don't really believe in them, but you will if you stay here long enough—they know genetics. They really know it. We have a thousand theories about what they may be like, and I won't bore you with them yet, but this is one thing we do know. They can build anything they need, make a blueprint in DNA, encapsulate it in a spore and bury it, knowing exactly what will come up in forty thousand years. When it starts to get cold here and they know the cycle's drawing to an end, they seed the planet with the spores and . . . do something. Maybe they die, or maybe they have some other way of passing the time. But they know they'll return.

"We can't say how long they've been prepared for a visit from us. Maybe only this cycle; maybe twenty cycles ago. Anyway, at the last cycle they buried the kind of spores that would produce these little gismos." She tapped the blue ball representing the Earth with one foot.

"They triggered them to be activated only when they encountered certain different conditions. Maybe they knew exactly what it would be; maybe they only provided for a likely range of possibilities. Song thinks they've visited us, back in the Stone Age. In some ways it's easier to believe than the alternative. That way they'd know our genetic structure and what kinds of food we'd eat, and could prepare.

" 'Cause if they didn't visit us, they must have prepared other spores. Spores that would analyze new proteins and be able to duplicate them. Further than that, some of the plants might have been able to copy certain genetic material if they encountered any. Take a look at that pipe behind you." Singh turned and saw a pipe about as thick as his arm. It was flexible, and had a swelling in it that continuously pulsed in expansion and contraction.

"Take that bulge apart and you'd be amazed at the resemblance to a human heart. So there's another significant fact; this place started out with whirligigs, but later modified itself to use human heart pumps from the genetic information *taken from the bodies of the men and women we buried.*" She paused to let that sink in, then went on with a slightly bemused smile.

"The same thing for what we eat and drink. That liquor you drank, for instance. It's half alcohol, and that's probably what it would have been without the corpses. But the rest of it is very similar to hemoglobin. It's sort of like fermented blood. Human blood."

Singh was glad he had refused the fourth drink. One of his crew members quietly put his glass down.

"I've never eaten human flesh," Lang went on, "but I think I know what it must taste like. Those vines to your right; we strip off the outer part and eat the meat underneath. It tastes good. I wish we could cook it, but we have nothing to burn and couldn't risk it with the high oxygen count, anyway."

Singh and everyone else was silent for a while. He found he really was beginning to believe in the Martians. The theory seemed to cover a lot of otherwise inexplicable facts.

Mary Lang sighed, slapped her thighs, and stood up. Like all the others, she was nude and seemed totally at home with it. None of them had worn anything but a Martian pressure suit for eight years. She ran her hand lovingly over the gossamer wall, the wall that had provided her and her fellow colonists and their children protection from the cold and the thin air for so long. He was struck by her easy familiarity with what seemed to him outlandish surrounds. She looked at home. He couldn't imagine her anywhere else.

He looked at the children. One wide-eyed little girl of eight years was kneeling at his feet. As his eyes fell on her, she smiled tentatively and took his hand.

"Did you bring any bubblegum?" the girl asked.

He smiled at her. "No, honey, but maybe there's some in the ship." She seemed satisfied. She would wait to experience the wonders of Earthly science.

"We were provided for," Mary Lang said, quietly. "They knew we were coming and they altered their plans to fit us in." She looked back to Singh. "It would have happened even without the blowout and the burials. The same sort of thing was happening around the *Podkayne,* too, triggered by our waste; urine and feces and such. I don't know if it would have tasted quite as good in the food department, but it would have sustained life."

Singh stood up. He was moved, but did not trust himself to show it adequately. So he sounded rather abrupt, though polite.

"I suppose you'll be anxious to go to the ship," he said. "You're going to be a tremendous help. You know so much of what we were sent here to find out. And you'll be quite famous when you get back to Earth. Your back pay should add up to quite a sum."

There was a silence, then it was ripped apart by Lang's huge laugh. She was joined by the others, and the children, who didn't know what they were laughing about but enjoyed the break in the tension.

"Sorry, Captain. That was rude. But we're not going back."

Singh looked at each of the adults and saw no trace of doubt. And he was mildly surprised to find that the statement did not startle him.

"I won't take that as your final decision," he said. "As you know, we'll be here six months. If at the end of that time any of you want to go, you're still citizens of Earth."

"We are? You'll have to brief us on the political situation back there. We were United States citizens when we left. But it doesn't matter. You won't get any takers, though we appreciate the fact that you came. It's nice to know we weren't forgotten." She said it with total assurance, and the others were nodding. Singh was uncomfortably aware that the idea of a rescue mission had died out only a few years after the initial tragedy. He and his ship were here now only to explore.

Lang sat back down and patted the ground around her, ground that was covered in a multiple layer of the Martian pressure-tight web, the kind of web that would have been made only by warm-blooded, oxygen-breathing, water-economy beings who needed protection for their bodies until the full bloom of summer.

"We *like* it here. It's a good place to raise a family, not like Earth the last time I was there. And it couldn't be much better now, right after another war. And we can't leave, even if we wanted to." She flashed him a dazzling smile and patted the ground again.

"The Martians should be showing up any time now. And we aim to thank them."

A TIME TO LIVE

by Joe Haldeman

With The Forever War *and* Mindbridge, *Haldeman established himself among the top ranks of science fiction writers. And it would take a talent such as that to be able to put the infinity of time and space into one short story and make it stick.*

The Man Who Owns the Moon they called him while he was alive, and The Man Who Owned the Moon for some time thereafter. D. Thorne Harrison.

Born 1990 in a mean little Arkansas strip-mining town. Formal education terminated in 2005, with his escape from a state reformatory. Ten years of odd jobs on one side of the law or the other. Escalating ambition and power; by the age of thirty-five, billionaire chairman of a diversified, mostly legitimate, corporation. Luck, he called it.

One planet was not enough. About a week before his fortieth birthday, Harrison fired his board of directors and liquidated an awesome fortune. He sank every penny of it into the development and exploitation of the Adams-Beeson drive. Brought space travel to anyone who could afford it. Bought a chunk of the Moon to give them someplace to go. Pleasure domes, retirement cities, safaris for the jaded rich. Made enough to buy the votes to initiate the terraforming of Mars.

As the first trickle of water crawled down the Great Rift Valley, Harrison lay in his own geriatrics hospital, in Copernicus City, in his hundred and twentieth year. The excitement may have hastened his passing.

"Move it move it *move* it!" Down the long white corridor two orderlies pushed the massive cart, drifting in long skips in the lunar gravity, the cart heavy with machines surrounding a frail wisp of a human body: dead cyborg of D. Thorne Harrison. Oxygenated fluorocarbon coursing through slack veins, making the brain think it still lived.

Through the bay doors of the cryonics facility, cart braked to a bumpy stop by the cold chamber, tubes and wires unhooked and corpse slid without ceremony inside. Chamber locked, pumped, activated: body turned to cold quartz.

"Good job." Not in the futile hope of future revival.

The nuts had a field day.

Harrison had sealed his frozen body into a time/space capsule, subsequently launched toward the center of the Galaxy. Also in the capsule were stacks of ultrafiche crystals (along with a viewer) that described humankind's nature and achievements in exhaustive detail, and various small objects of art.

One class of crackpots felt that Harrison had betrayed humanity, giving conquering hordes of aliens a road map back to Earth. The details of what they would do to us, and why, provided an interesting refraction of the individual crackpot's problems.

A gentler sort assumed *a priori* that a race of aliens able to decipher the message and come visit us must necessarily have evolved away from aggression and other base passions; they would observe; perhaps help.

Both of these groups provided fuel for solemn essays, easy master's theses, and evanescent religions. Other opinions:

"Glad the old geezer got to spend his money the way he wanted to."

"Inexcusable waste of irreplaceable artistic resources."

"He could have used the money to feed people."

"Quixotic gesture; the time scale's too vast. We'll be dead and gone long before anybody reads the damned thing."

"I've got more important things to worry about."

None of the above is true.

Supposedly, the miniature Adams-Beeson converter would accelerate the capsule very slowly for about a century, running out of fuel when the craft had attained a small fraction of the speed of light. It would pass the vicinity of Antares in about five thousand years.

The capsule had a preprogrammed signal generator, powered by starlight. It would accumulate power for ten years at a time, then bleat out a message at the 21-centimeter wavelength. The message lasted ninety minutes and would be repeated three times; any idiot with a huge radio telescope and the proper ontological prejudices could decode it: "I am an artifact of an intelligent race. My course is thus and so. Catch me if you can."

Unfortunately, the craft carried a pretty hefty magnetic field, and ran smack-dab into Maxwell's Equations. Its course carried it through a tenuous but very extensive cloud of plasma, and through the years it kept turning slowly to the right, decelerating. When it came out of the cloud it was pointed back toward the Earth, moving at a very modest pace.

In twenty thousand years it passed the place where Earth had been (the Sun having wandered off in the natural course of things) and continued to crawl, out toward the cold oblivion between the galaxies. It still beeped out its code every decade, but it was a long time before anybody paid any attention.

I woke up in great pain, that didn't last.

"How do you feel?" asked a pretty young nurse in a starched green uniform.

I didn't answer immediately. There was something wrong. With her, with the hospital room, the bed. The edges were wrong. Too sharp, like a bad matte shot at the cubies.

"How do you feel?" asked a plain, middle-aged nurse in a starched green uniform. I hadn't seen the change. "Is this better?"

I said it didn't make much difference. My body, my body was a

hundred years younger. Mind clear, limbs filled with springy muscle. No consciousness of failing organs. I am dead, I asked her,
told her.

"Not really," she said and I caught her changing: shimmer*click*.
Now a white-haired, scholarly-looking doctor, male. "Not any
more. You were dead, a long time. We rebuilt you."

I asked if he/she would settle on one shape and keep it; they
pulled me out of a capsule, frozen solid?

"Yes. Things went more or less as you planned them."

I asked him what he meant by more or less.

"You got turned around, and slowed. It was a long time before
we noticed you."

I sat up on the bed and stared at him. If I didn't blink he might
not change. I asked him how long a time?

"Nearly a million years. 874,896 from the time of launch."

I swung to the floor and my feet touched hot sand.

"Sorry." Cold tile.

I asked him why he didn't show me his true form. I am too old
to be afraid of bogeymen.

He did change into his true form and I asked that he change
back into one of the others. I had to know which end to talk to.

As he became the doctor again, the room dissolved and we were
standing on a vast plain of dark brown sand, in orderly dunes. The
vague shadow in front of me lengthened as I watched; I turned
around in time to see the Milky Way, rather bright, slide to the horizon. There were no stars.

"Yes," the doctor said, "we are at the edge of your galaxy." A
sort of sun rose on the opposite horizon. Dim red and huge, nebu-
lous at its boundaries. An infrared giant, my memory told me.

I told him that I appreciated being rebuilt, and asked whether I
could be of some service. Teach them of the ancient past?

"No, we learned all we could from you, while we were putting
you back together." He smiled. "On the contrary, it is we who owe
you. Can we take you back to Earth? This planet is just right for
us, but I think you will find it dull."

I told him that I would very much like to go back to Earth, but
would like to see some of his world first.

"All of my world is just like this," he said. "I live here for the lack of variety. Others of my kind live in similar places."

I asked if I could meet some of the others.

"I'm afraid that would be impossible. They would refuse to see you, even if I were willing to take you to them." After a pause he added, "It's something like politics. Here." He took my hand and we rose, his star shrinking to a dim speck, disappearing. The Galaxy grew larger and we were suddenly inside it, stars streaming by.

I asked if this were teleportation.

"No, it's just a machine. Like a spaceship, but faster, more efficient. Less efficient in one way."

I started to ask him how we could breathe and talk but his weary look cut me off. He seemed to be flickering, as if he were going to change shape again. But he didn't.

"This should be interesting," he said, as a yellow star grew brighter, then swelled to become the familiar Sun. "I haven't been here myself in ten, twelve thousand years." The blue-and-green ball of Earth was suddenly beneath us, and we paused for a moment. "It's a short trip, but I don't get out often," he said, apologetically.

As we drifted to the surface, it was sunset over Africa. The shape of the western coast seemed not to have changed much.

The Atlantic passed beneath us in a blur and we came to ground somewhere in the northeastern United States. We landed in a cow pasture. Its wire fence, improbably, seemed to be made of the same shiny duramyl I remembered from my childhood.

"Where are we?" I asked.

He said we were just north of Canaan, New York: There was a glideway a few kilometers to the west; I could find a truck stop and catch a ride. He was flickering very fast now, and even when he was visible I could see the pasture through him.

"What're you talking about?" I said. "They wouldn't, don't, have truck stops and glideways a million years in the future."

He regarded me with fading scorn and said we were only five or ten years in my future; after the year of my birth; that is. Twenty at the outside. Didn't I know the slightest thing about relativity? And he was gone.

A farmer was walking toward me, carrying a wicked-looking scythe. There was nothing in the pasture to use it on, but me.

"Good morning," I said to him. Then saw it was afternoon.

He walked to within striking distance of me and stopped, grim scowl. He leaned sideways to look behind me. "Where's the other feller?"

"Who?" I'd almost said I was wondering that myself. "What other fellow?" I looked back over my shoulder.

He rubbed his eyes. "Damn contacts. What're you doin' on my propitty anyhow?"

"I got lost."

"Don't you know what a fence is?"

"Yes, sir, I'm sorry. I was coming to the house to ask directions to Canaan."

"Why you out walkin' with a funny costume on?" I was wearing a duplicate of the conservative business suit Harrison was buried in.

"It's the style, sir. In the city."

He shook his head. "Kids. You just go over that fence yonder," he pointed, "and head straight 'til you get to the road. Mind you don't touch the fence an' watch out for my God damn beans. You get to the road and Canaan's to the left."

"Thank you, sir." He had turned and was stumping back to the farmhouse.

In the truck stop, the calendar read 1995.

It's not easy to be penniless in New York City, not if you have a twenty-year-old body and over a century's worth of experience in separating people from their money.

Within a week, the man who had been Harrison was living in a high-class flat behind the protection of the East Village wall, with enough money stacked away to buy him time to think.

He didn't want to be Harrison again, that he knew for sure. Besides the boredom of living the same life over, he had known (as Harrison) by the time he was fifty that his existence was not a particularly happy one, physically addicted to the accumulation of wealth and power, incapable of trusting or being trusted.

Besides, Harrison was a five-year-old in Arkansas, just beginning the two decades of bad luck that would precede a century of nothing going wrong.

He had this sudden cold feeling.

He went to the library and looked up microfiches of the past few years' *Forbes* and *Bizweek*. And found out who he was, by omission.

For less than a thousand dollars, he gave himself a past. A few documents to match counterfeit inserts in government data banks. Then a few seemingly illogical investments in commodities that made him a millionaire in less than a year. Then he bought a failing electronics firm and renamed it after himself: Lassiter Electronics.

He grew a beard that he knew would be prematurely white.

The firm prospered. He bought a plastics plant and renamed it Lassiter Industries. Then the largest printing outfit in Pennsylvania. A fishery after that.

In 2010 he contrived to be in a waterfront crap game in Galveston, where he lost a large sum to a hard-eyed boy who was fairly good at cold-rolling dice. Lassiter was better, but he rolled himself crapouts. It was two days after Harrison's twentieth birthday, and his first big break.

A small bank, then a large one. An aerospace firm. Textiles. A piece of an orbital factory: micro-bearings and data crystals. Now named Lassiter, Limited.

In 2018, still patiently manufacturing predestination, he hired young D. Thorne Harrison as a time-and-motion analyst, knowing that all of his credentials were false. It would give Harrison access to sensitive information.

By 2021 he was Junior Vice-President in charge of production. By 2022, Vice-President. Youngest member of the board, he knew interesting things about the other board members.

In 2024, Harrison brought to Lassiter's office documents proving that he had voting control of 51% of Lassiter, Limited. He had expected a fight. Instead, Lassiter made a cash settlement, perplexingly small, and dropped out of sight.

With half his life left to live, and money enough for much longer, Lassiter bought comfortable places in Paris, Key West, and

Colorado, and commuted according to the weather and season. He took a few years for a leisurely trip around the world. His considerable mental energies he channeled into the world of art, rather than finance. He became an accomplished harpsichordist, and was well-known among the avant-garde for his neopointillist constructions: sculptures of frozen light, careful laser bursts caught in a cube of photosensitive gel. Beautiful women were fascinated by this man who had done so well in two seemingly antagonistic fields.

He followed Harrison's fortunes closely: the sell-out in 2030, buying out the Adams-Beeson drive (which seemed like a reckless long shot to most observers), sinking a fortune in the Moon and getting it back a hundredfold.

And as the ecologic catalyzers were being seeded on Mars, Harrison an old man running out of years to buy, Lassiter lay dying in Key West.

In the salt breeze on an open veranda, not wanting to clutter up his end with IV tubes and rushing attendants and sterile frigid air, he had sent his lone nurse away on an errand that would take too long, his last spoken words calm and reassuring, belying the spike of pain in his chest. The house downstairs was filled with weeping admirers, friends he had not bought, and as the pale blue sky went dark red, he reckoned himself a happy man, and wondered how he would do it next time, thinking he was the puppeteer, even as the last string was pulled.

THE HOUSE OF COMPASSIONATE SHARERS

by Michael Bishop

One of last year's new science fiction magazines,
Cosmos, *launched its initial issue with this as its
first story. With such an auspicious beginning, it is
a shame to report that* Cosmos *did not survive the
year . . . but we are sure it did not have anything
to do with this unusual and thought-compelling
novelette, which gives an insight into one advanced
kind of psychiatric treatment.*

> *And he was there, and it was not far enough, not
> yet, for the earth hung overhead like a rotten fruit,
> blue with mold, crawling, wrinkling, purulent and
> alive.*
>
> —*Damon Knight, "Masks"*

In the Port Iranani Galenshall I awoke in the room Diderits
liked to call the "Black Pavilion." I was an engine, a system, a

series of myoelectric and neuromechanical components, and The Accident responsible for this clean and enamel-hard enfleshing lay two full D-years in the past. This morning was an anniversary of sorts. I ought by now to have adjusted. And I had. I had reached an absolute accommodation with myself. Narcissistic, one could say. And that was the trouble.

"Dorian? Dorian Lorca?"

The voice belonged to KommGalen Diderits, wet and breathy even though it came from a small metal speaker to which the sable curtains of the dome were attached. I stared up into the ring of curtains.

"Dorian, it's Target Day. Will you answer me, please?"

"I'm here, my galen. Where else would I be?" I stood up, listening to the almost musical ratcheting that I make when I move, a sound like the concatenation of tiny bells or the purring of a stopecar. The sound is conveyed through the tempered porcelain plates, metal vertebrae, and osteoid polymers holding me together, and no one else can hear it.

"Rumer's here, Dorian. Are you ready for her to come in?"

"If I agreed, I suppose I'm ready."

"Dammit, Dorian, don't feel you're bound by *honor* to see her! We've spent the last several brace-weeks preparing you for a resumption of normal human contact." Diderits began to enumerate: "Chameleodrene treatments . . . hologramic substitution . . . stimulus-response therapy. . . . You ought to want Rumer to come in to you, Dorian."

Ought. My brain was—is—my own, but the body Diderits and the other kommgalens had given me had "instincts" and "tropisms" peculiar to itself, ones whose templates had a mechanical rather than a biological origin. What I ought to feel, in human terms, and what I in fact felt, as the inhabitant of a total prosthesis, were as dissimilar as blood and oil.

"Do you *want* her to come in, Dorian?"

"All right. I do." And I did. After all the biochemical and psychiatric preparation, I wanted to see what my reaction would be. Still sluggish from some drug, I had no exact idea how Rumer's presence would affect me.

At a parting of the pavilion's draperies, only two or three meters from my couch, appeared Rumer Montieth, my wife. Her garment of overlapping latex scales, glossy black in color, was a hauberk designed to reveal only her hands, face, and hair. The way Rumer was dressed was one of Diderits's deceits, or "preparations": I was supposed to see my wife as little different from myself, a creature as intricately assembled and synapsed as the engine I had become. But the hands, the face, the hair—nothing could disguise their unaugmented humanity, and revulsion swept over me like a tide.

"Dorian?" And her voice—wet, breath-driven, expelled between parted lips . . .

I turned away from her. "No," I told the speaker overhead. "It hasn't worked, my galen. Every part of me cries out against this."

Diderits said nothing. Was he still out there? Or was he trying to give Rumer and me a privacy I didn't want?

"Disassemble me," I urged him. "Link me to the control systems of a delta-state vessel and let me go out from Diroste for good. You don't want a zombot among you, Diderits—an unhappy anproz. Damn you all, you're torturing me!"

"And you, us," Rumer said quietly. I faced her. "As you're very aware, Dorian, as you're very aware. . . . Take my hand."

"No." I didn't shrink away; I merely refused.

"Here. Take it."

Fighting my own disgust, I seized her hand, twisted it over, showed her its back. "Look."

"I *see* it, Dor." I was hurting her.

"Surfaces, that's all you see. Look at this growth, this wen." I pinched the growth. "Do you see that, Rumer? That's sebum, fatty matter. And the smell, if only you could—"

She drew back, and I tried to quell a mental nausea almost as profound as my regret. . . . To go out from Diroste seemed to be the only answer. Around me I wanted machinery—thrumming, inorganic machinery—and the sterile, actinic emptiness of outer space. I wanted to be the probeship *Dorian Lorca*. It hardly seemed a step down from my position as "prince consort" to the Governor of Diroste.

"Let me out," Rumer commanded the head of the Port Iranani Galenshall, and Diderits released her from the "Black Pavilion."

Then I was alone again in one of the few private chambers of a surgical complex given over to adapting Civi Korps personnel to our leprotic little planet's fume-filled mine shafts. The Galenshall was also devoted to patching up these civkis after their implanted respirators had atrophied, almost beyond saving, the muscles of their chests and lungs.

Including administrative personnel, Kommfleet officials, and the Civi Korps laborers in the mines, in the year I'm writing of there were over a half million people on Diroste. Diderits was responsible for the health of all of them not assigned to the outlying territories. Had I not been the husband of Diroste's first governor, he might well have let me die along with the seventeen "expendables" on tour with me in the Fetneh District when the roof of the Haft Paykar diggings fell in on us. Rumer, however, made Diderits's duty clear to him, and I am as I am because the resources were at hand in Port Iranani and Diderits saw fit to obey his Governor.

Alone in my pavilion, I lifted a hand to my face and heard a caroling of minute, copper bells. . . .

Nearly a month later I observed Rumer, Diderits, and a stranger by closed-circuit television as they sat in one of the Galenshall's wide conference rooms. The stranger was a woman, bald but for a scalplock, who wore gold silk pantaloons that gave her the appearance of a clown, and a corrugated green jacket that somehow reversed this impression. Even on my monitor I could see the thick sunlight pouring into their room.

"This is Wardress Kefa," Rumer informed me.

I greeted her through a microphone and tested the cosmetic work of Diderits's associates by trying to smile for her.

"She's from Earth, Dor, and she's here because KommGalen Diderits and I asked her to come."

"Forty-six lights," I murmured, probably inaudibly. I was touched and angry at the same time. To be constantly the focus of your friends' attentions, especially when they have more urgent matters to see to, can lead to either a corrosive cynicism or a humility just as crippling.

"We want you to go back with her on *Nizami*," Diderits said, "when it leaves Port Iranani tomorrow night."

"Why?"

"Wardress Kefa came all this way," Rumer responded, "because we wanted to talk to her. As a final stage in your therapy she's convinced us that you ought to visit her . . . her establishment there. And if this fails, Dorian, I give you up; if that's what you want, I relinquish you." Today Rumer was wearing a yellow sarong, a tasseled gold shawl, and a nun's hood of yellow and orange stripes. When she spoke she averted her eyes from the conference room's monitor and looked out its high windows instead. At a distance, I could appreciate the spare aesthetics of her profile.

"Establishment? What sort of establishment?" I studied the tiny Wardress, but her appearance volunteered nothing.

"The House of Compassionate Sharers," Diderits began. "It's located in Earth's western hemisphere, on the North American continent, nearly two-hundred kilometers southwest of the gutted Urban Nucleus of Denver. It can be reached from Manitou Port by 'rail."

"Good. I shouldn't have any trouble finding it. But what is it, this mysterious house?"

Wardress Kefa spoke for the first time: "I would prefer that you learn its nature and its purposes from me, Mr. Lorca, when we have arrived safely under its several roofs."

"Is it a brothel?" This question fell among my three interlocutors like a heavy stone.

"No," Rumer said after a careful five-count. "It's a unique sort of clinic for the treatment of unique emotional disorders." She glanced at the Wardress, concerned that she had revealed too much.

"Some would call it a brothel," Wardress Kefa admitted huskily. "Earth has become a haven of misfits and opportunists, a crossroads of Glatik Komm influence and trade. The House, I must confess, wouldn't prosper if it catered only to those who suffer from rare disassociations of feeling. Therefore a few—a very few—of those who come to us are kommthors rich in power and exacting in their tastes. But these people are exceptions, Governor Montieth, KommGalen Diderits; they represent an uneasy compromise we must make in order to carry out the work for which the House was originally envisioned and built."

A moment later Rumer announced, "You're going, Dor. You're going tomorrow night. Diderits and I, well, we'll see you in three E-months." That said, she gathered in her cloak with both hands and rearranged it on her shoulders. Then she left the room.

"Good-bye, Dorian," Diderits said, standing.

Wardress Kefa fixed upon the camera conveying her picture to me a keen glance made more disconcerting by her small, naked face. "Tomorrow, then."

"Tomorrow," I agreed. I watched my monitor as the galen and the curious-looking Wardress exited the conference room together. In the room's high windows Diroste's sun sang a Capella in the lemon sky.

They gave me a private berth on *Nizami*. I used my "nights," since sleep no longer meant anything to me, to prowl through those nacelles of shipboard machinery not forbidden to passengers. Although I wasn't permitted in the forward command module, I did have access to the computer-ringed observation turret and two or three corridors of auxiliary equipment necessary to the maintenance of a continuous probe-field. In these places I secreted myself and thought seriously about the likelihood of an encephalic/neural linkage with one of Kommfleet's interstellar frigates.

My body was a trial. Diderits had long ago informed me that it —that *I*—was still "sexually viable," but this was something I hadn't yet put to the test, nor did I wish to. Tyrannized by morbidly vivid images of human viscera, human excreta, human decay, I had been rebuilt of metal, porcelain, and plastic *as if* from the very substances—skin, bone, hair, cartilage—that these inorganic materials derided. I was a contradiction, a quasi-immortal masquerading as one of the ephemera who had saved me from their own short-lived lot. Still another paradox was the fact that my aversion to the organic was itself a human (i.e., an organic) emotion. That was why I so fervently wanted out. For over a year and a half on Diroste I had hoped that Rumer and the others would see their mistake and exile me not only from themselves, but from the body that was a deadly daily reminder of my total estrangement.

But Rumer was adamant in her love, and I had been a prisoner in the Port Iranani Galenshall—with but one chilling respite—ever since the Haft Paykar explosion and cave-in. Now I was being given into the hands of a new wardress, and as I sat amid the enamel-encased engines of *Nizami* I couldn't help wondering what sort of prison the House of Compassionate Sharers must be. . . .

Among the passengers of a monorail car bound outward from Manitou Port, Wardress Kefa in the window seat beside me, I sat tense and stiff. Anthrophobia. Lorca, I told myself repeatedly, you must exercise self-control. Amazingly, I did. From Manitou Port we rode the sleek underslung bullet of our car through rugged, sparsely-populated terrain toward Wolf Run Summit, and I controlled myself.

"You've never been 'home' before?" Wardress Kefa asked me.

"No. Earth isn't home. I was born on GK-world Dai-Han, Wardress. And as a young man I was sent as an administrative colonist to Diroste, where—"

"Where you were born again," Wardress Kefa interrupted. "Nevertheless, this is where we began."

The shadows of the mountains slid across the wraparound glass of our car, and the imposing white pylons of the monorail system flashed past us like the legs of giants. Yes. Like huge, naked cyborgs hiding among the mountains' aspens and pines.

"Where I met Rumer Montieth, I was going to say; where I eventually got married and settled down to the life of a bureaucrat who happens to be married to power. You anticipate me, Wardress." I didn't add that now Earth and Diroste were equally alien to me, that the probeship *Nizami* had bid fair to assume first place among my loyalties.

A 'rail from Wolf Run came sweeping past us toward Manitou Port. The sight pleased me; the vibratory hum of the passing 'rail lingered sympathetically in my hearing, and I refused to talk, even though the Wardress clearly wanted to draw me out about my former life. I was surrounded and beset. Surely this woman had all she needed to know of my past from Diderits and my wife. My annoyance grew.

"You're very silent, Mr. Lorca."

"I have no innate hatred of silences."

"Nor do I, Mr. Lorca—unless they're empty ones."

Hands in lap, humming bioelectrically, inaudibly, I looked at my tiny guardian with disdain. "There are some," I told her, "who are unable to engage in a silence without stripping it of its unspoken cargo of significance."

To my surprise the woman laughed heartily. "That certainly isn't true of you, is it?" Then, a wry expression playing on her lips, she shifted her gaze to the hurtling countryside and said nothing else until it came time to disembark at Wolf Run Summit.

Wolf Run was a resort frequented principally by Kommfleet officers and members of the administrative hierarchy stationed at Port Manitou. Civi Korps personnel had built quaint, gingerbread chateaus among the trees and engineered two of the slopes above the hamlet for year-round skiing. "Many of these people," Wardress Kefa explained, indicating a crowd of men and women beneath the deck of Wolf Run's main lodge, "work inside Shays Mountain, near the light-probe port, in facilities built originally for satellite-tracking and missile-launch detection. Now they monitor the display-boards for Kommfleet orbiters and shuttles; they program the cruising and descent lanes of these vehicles. Others are demographic and wildlife managers, bent on resettling Earth as efficiently as it may be done. Tedious work, Mr. Lorca. They come here to play." We passed below the lodge on a path of unglazed vitrifoam. Two or three of Wolf Run's bundled visitors stared at me, presumably because I was in my tunic sleeves and conspicuously undaunted by the spring cold. Or maybe their stares were for my guardian. . . .

"How many of these people are customers of yours, Wardress?"

"That isn't something I can divulge." But she glanced back over her shoulder as if she had recognized someone.

"What do they find at your establishment they can't find in Manitou Port?"

"I don't know, Mr. Lorca; I'm not a mind reader."

To reach the House of Compassionate Sharers from Wolf Run, we had to go on foot down a narrow path worked reverently into the flank of the mountain. It was very nearly a two-hour hike. I couldn't believe the distance or Wardress Kefa's stamina. Swinging her arms, jolting herself on stiff legs, she went down the mountain with a will. And in all the way we walked we met no other hikers.

At last we reached a clearing giving us an open view of a steep, pine-peopled glen: a grotto that fell away beneath us and led our eyes to an expanse of smooth white sky. But the Wardress pointed directly down into the foliage.

"There," she said. "The House of Compassionate Sharers."

I saw nothing but afternoon sunlight on the aspens, boulders huddled in the mulch cover, and swaying tunnels among the trees. Squinting, I finally made out a geodesic structure built from the very materials of the woods. Like an upland sleight, a wavering mirage, the House slipped in and out of my vision, blending, emerging, melting again. It was a series of irregular domes as hard to hold as water vapor—but after several redwinged blackbirds flew noisily across the plane of its highest turret, the House remained for me in stark relief; it had shed its invisibility.

"It's more noticeable," Wardress Kefa said, "when its external shutters have been cranked aside. Then the House sparkles like a dragon's eye. The windows are stained glass."

"I'd like to see that. Now it appears camouflaged."

"That's deliberate, Mr. Lorca. Come."

When we were all the way down, I could see of what colossal size the House really was: it reared up through the pine needles and displayed its interlocking polygons to the sky. Strange to think that no one in a passing helicraft was ever likely to catch sight of it . . .

Wardress Kefa led me up a series of plank stairs, spoke once at the door, and introduced me into an antechamber so clean and military that I thought "barracks" rather than "bawdyhouse." The ceiling and walls were honeycombed, and the natural flooring was redolent of the outdoors. My guardian disappeared, returned without her coat, and escorted me into a much smaller room shaped like a tapered well. By means of a wooden hand-crank she opened the shutters, and varicolored light filtered in upon us through the room's slant-set windows. On elevated cushions that snapped and rustled each time we moved, we sat facing each other.

"What now?" I asked the Wardress.

"Just listen: The Sharers have come to the House of their own volition, Mr. Lorca; most lived and worked on extrakomm worlds toward Glaktik Center before being approached for duty here.

The ones who are here accepted the invitation. They came to offer their presences to people very like yourself."

"Me? Are they misconceived machines?"

"I'm not going to answer that. Let me just say that the variety of services the Sharers offer is surprisingly wide. As I've told you, for some visitants the Sharers are simply a convenient means of satisfying exotically aberrant tastes. For others they're a way back to the larger community. We take whoever comes to us for help, Mr. Lorca, in order that the Sharers not remain idle nor the House vacant."

"So long as whoever comes is wealthy and influential?"

She paused before speaking. "That's true enough. But the matter's out of my hands, Mr. Lorca. I'm an employee of Glaktik Komm, chosen for my empathetic abilities. I don't make policy. I don't own title to the House."

"But you *are* its madam. Its 'wardress,' rather."

"True. For the last twenty-two years. I'm the first and only wardress to have served here, Mr. Lorca, and I love the Sharers. I love their devotion to the fragile mentalities who visit them. Even so, despite the time I've lived among them, I still don't pretend to understand the source of their transcendent concern. That's what I wanted to tell you."

"You think me a 'fragile mentality'?"

"I'm sorry—but you're here, Mr. Lorca, and you certainly aren't fragile of *limb,* are you?" The Wardress laughed. "I also wanted to ask you to . . . well, to restrain your crueler impulses when the treatment itself begins."

I stood up and moved away from the little woman. How had I borne her presence for as long as I had?

"Please don't take my request amiss. It isn't *specifically* personal, Mr. Lorca. I make it of everyone who comes to the House of Compassionate Sharers. Restraint is an unwritten corollary of the only three rules we have here. Will you hear them?"

I made a noise of compliance.

"First, that you do not leave the session chamber once you've entered it. Second, that you come forth immediately upon my summoning you. . . ."

"And third?"

"That you do not kill the Sharer."

All the myriad disgusts I had been suppressing for seven or eight hours were now perched atop the ladder of my patience, and, rung by painful rung, I had to step them back down. Must a rule be made to prevent a visitant from murdering the partner he had bought? Incredible. The Wardress herself was just perceptibly sweating, and I noticed too how grotesquely distended her earlobes were.

"Is there a room in this establishment for a wealthy and influential patron? A private room?"

"Of course," she said. "I'll show you."

It had a full-length mirror. I undressed and stood in front of it. Only during my first "period of adjustment" on Dirosto had I spent much time looking at what I had become. Later, back in the Port Iranani Galenshall, Diderits had denied me any sort of reflective surface at all—looking glasses, darkened windows, even metal spoons. The waxen perfection of my features ridiculed the ones another Dorian Lorca had possessed before the Haft Paykar Incident. Cosmetic mockery. Faintly corpselike, speciously paradigmatic, I was both more than I was supposed to be and less.

In Wardress Kefa's House the less seemed preeminent. I ran a finger down the inside of my right arm, scrutinizing the track of one of the intubated veins through which circulated a serum that Diderits called hematocybin: an efficient, "low-maintenance" blood substitute, combative of both fatigue and infection, which requires changing only once every six D-months. With a proper supply of hematocybin and a plastic recirculator I can do the job myself, standing up. That night, however, the ridge of my vein, mirrored only an arm's length away, was more horror than miracle. I stepped away from the looking glass and closed my eyes.

Later that evening Wardress Kefa came to me with a candle and a brocaded dressing gown. She made me put on the gown in front of her, and I complied. Then, the robe's rich and symbolic embroidery on my back, I followed her out of my first-floor chamber to a rustic stairwell seemingly connective to all the rooms in the House.

The dome contained countless smaller domes and five or six

primitive staircases, at least. Not a single other person was about. Lit flickeringly by Wardress Kefa's taper as we climbed one of these sets of stairs, the House's mid-interior put me in mind of an Escheresque drawing in which verticals and horizontals become hopelessly confused and a figure who from one perspective seems to be going up a series of steps, from another seems to be coming down them. Presently the Wardress and I stood on a landing above this topsy-turvy well of stairs (though there were still more stairs above us), and, looking down, I experienced an unsettling reversal of perspectives. Vertigo. Why hadn't Diderits, against so human a susceptibility, implanted tiny gyrostabilizers in my head? I clutched a railing and held on.

"You can't fall," Wardress Kefa told me. "It's an illusion. A whim of the architects."

"Is it an illusion behind this door?"

"Oh, the Sharer's real enough, Mr. Lorca. Please. Go on in." She touched my face and left me, taking her candle with her.

After hesitating a moment I went through the door to my assignation, and the door locked of itself. I stood with my hand on the butterfly shape of the knob and felt the night working in me and the room. The only light came from the stove-bed on the opposite wall, for the fitted polygons overhead were still blanked out by their shutters and no candles shone here. Instead, reddish embers glowed behind an isinglass window beneath the stove-bed, strewn with quilts, on which my Sharer awaited me.

Outside, the wind played harp music in the trees.

I was trembling rhythmically, as when Rumer had come to me in the "Black Pavilion." Even though my eyes adjusted rapidly, automatically, to the dark, it was still difficult to see. Temporizing, I surveyed the dome. In its high central vault hung a cage in which, disturbed by my entrance, a bird hopped skittishly about. The cage swayed on its tether.

Go on, I told myself.

I advanced toward the dais and leaned over the unmoving Sharer who lay there. With a hand on either side of the creature's head, I braced myself. The figure beneath me moved, moved weakly, and I drew back. But because the Sharer didn't stir again, I reassumed my previous stance; the posture of either a lover or a man called upon to identify a disfigured corpse. But identification was impossible; the embers under the bed gave too feeble a sheen. In the chamber's darkness even a lover's kiss would have fallen clumsily. . . .

"I'm going to touch you," I said. "Will you let me do that?"

The Sharer lay still.

Then, willing all of my senses into the cushion of synthetic flesh at my forefinger's tip, I touched the Sharer's face.

Hard, and smooth, and cool.

I moved my finger from side to side; and the hardness, smoothness, coolness continued to flow into my pressuring fingertip. It was like touching the pate of a death's-head, the cranial cap of a human being: bone rather than metal. My finger distinguished between these two possibilities, deciding on bone; and, half panicked, I concluded that I had traced an arc on the skull of an intelligent being who wore his every bone on the outside, like an armor of calcium. Could that be? If so, how could this organism—this entity, this *thing*—express compassion?

I lifted my finger away from the Sharer. Its tip hummed with a pressure now relieved and emanated a faint warmth.

A death's-head come to life . . .

Maybe I laughed. In any case, I pulled myself onto the platform and straddled the Sharer. I kept my eyes closed, though not tightly. It didn't seem that I was straddling a skeleton.

"Sharer," I whispered. "Sharer, I don't know you yet."

Gently, I let my thumbs find the creature's eyes, the sockets in the smooth exoskeleton, and both thumbs returned to me a hardness and a coldness that were unquestionably metallic in origin. Moreover, the Sharer didn't flinch—even though I'd anticipated that probing his eyes, no matter how gently, would provoke at least an involuntary pulling away. Instead, the Sharer lay still and tractable under my hands.

And why not? I thought. *Your eyes are nothing but two pieces of sophisticated optical machinery.* . . .

It was true. Two artificial, light-sensing, image-integrating units gazed up at me from the sockets near which my thumbs probed, and I realized that even in this darkness my Sharer, its vision mechanically augmented beyond my own, could *see* my blind face staring down in a futile attempt to create an image out of the information my hands had supplied me. I opened my eyes and held them open. I could see only shadows, but my thumbs could *feel* the cold metal rings that held the Sharer's photosensitive units so firmly in its skull.

"An animatronic construct," I said, rocking back on my heels. "A soulless robot. Move your head if I'm right."

The Sharer continued motionless.

"All right. You're a sentient creature whose eyes have been replaced with an artificial system. What about that? Lord, are we brothers then?"

I had a sudden hunch that the Sharer was very old, a senescent being owing its life to prosthetics, transplants, and imitative organs of laminated silicone. Its life, I was certain, had been *extended* by these contrivances, not saved. I asked the Sharer about my feeling, and very, very slowly it moved the helmetlike skull housing its artificial eyes and its aged, compassionate mind. Uncharitably I then believed myself the victim of a deception, whether the Sharer's or Wardress Kefa's I couldn't say. Here, after all, was a creature who had chosen to prolong its organic condition rather than to escape it, and it had willingly made use of the same materials and methods Diderits had brought into play to save me.

"You might have died," I told it. "Go too far, Sharer—go too far with these contrivances and you may forfeit suicide as an option."

Then, leaning forward again, saying, "I'm still not through, I still don't know you," I let my hands come down the Sharer's bony face to its throat. Here a shield of cartilage graded upward into its jaw and downward into the plastically silken skin covering the remainder of its body, internalizing all but the defiantly naked skull of the Sharer's skeletal structure. A death's-head with the body of a man . . .

That was all I could take. I rose from the stove-bed and, cinching my dressing gown tightly about my waist, crossed to the other side of the chamber. There was no furniture in the room but the stove-bed (if that qualified), and I had to content myself with sitting in a lotus position on the floor. I sat that way all night, staving off dreams.

Diderits had said that I needed to dream. If I didn't dream, he warned, I'd be risking hallucinations and eventual madness; in the Port Iranani Galenshall he'd seen to it that drugs were administered to me every two days and my sleep period monitored by an ARC machine and a team of electroencephalographers. But my dreams were almost always nightmares, descents into klieg-lit charnel houses, and I infinitely preferred the risk of going psychotic. There was always the chance someone would take pity and disassemble me, piece by loving piece. Besides, I had lasted two E-weeks now on nothing but grudging catnaps, and so far I still had gray matter upstairs instead of scrambled eggs. . . .

I crossed my fingers.

A long time after I'd sat down, Wardress Kefa threw open the door. It was morning. I could tell because the newly-canted shutters outside our room admitted a singular roaring of light. The entire chamber was illumined, and I saw crimson wall-hangings, a mosaic of red and purple stones on the section of the floor, and a tumble of scarlet quilts. The bird in the suspended cage was a red-winged blackbird.

"Where is it from?"

"You could use a more appropriate pronoun."

"*He? She?* Which is the more appropriate, Wardress Kefa?"

"Assume the Sharer masculine, Mr. Lorca."

"My sexual proclivities have never run that way, I'm afraid."

"Your sexual proclivities," the Wardress told me stingingly, "enter into this only if you persist in thinking of the House as a brothel rather than a clinic and the Sharers as whores rather than therapists!"

"Last night I heard two or three people clomping up the stairs in their boots, that and a woman's raucous laughter."

"A visitant, Mr. Lorca, *not* a Sharer."

"I didn't think she was a Sharer. But it's difficult to believe I'm in a 'clinic' when that sort of noise disrupts my midnight meditations, Wardress."

"I've explained that. It can't be helped."

"All right, all right. Where is *he* from, this 'therapist' of mine?"

"An interior star. But where he's from is of no consequence in your treatment. I matched him to your needs, as I see them, and soon you'll be going back to him."

"Why? To spend another night sitting on the floor?"

"You won't do that again, Mr. Lorca. And you needn't worry. Your reaction wasn't an uncommon one for a newcomer to the House."

"Revulsion?" I cried. "Revulsion's therapeutic?"

"I don't think you were as put off as you believe."

"Oh? Why not?"

"Because you talked to the Sharer. You addressed him directly, not once but several times. Many visitants never get that far during their first session, Mr. Lorca."

"Talked to him?" I said dubiously. "Maybe. Before I found out what he was."

"Ah. Before you found out what he was." In her heavy green jacket and swishy pantaloons the tiny woman turned about and departed the well of the sitting room.

I stared bemusedly after her for a long time.

Three nights after my first "session," the night of my conversation with Wardress Kefa, I entered the Sharer's chamber again. Everything was as it had been, except that the dome's shutters were open and moonlight coated the mosaic work on the floor. The Sharer awaited me in the same recumbent, unmoving posture, and inside its cage the redwinged blackbird set one of its perches to rocking back and forth.

Perversely, I had decided not to talk to the Sharer this time—but I did approach the stove-bed and lean over him. *Hello,* I thought, and the word very nearly came out. I straddled the Sharer and studied him in the stained moonlight. He looked just as my sense of touch had led me to conclude previously . . . like a skull, oddly flattened and beveled, with the body of a man. But despite the chemical embers glowing beneath his dais the Sharer's body had no warmth, and to know him more fully I resumed tracing a finger over his alien parts.

I discovered that at every conceivable pressure point a tiny scar existed, or the tip of an implanted electrode, and that miniature canals into which wires had been sunk veined his inner arms and legs. Just beneath his sternum a concave disc about eight centimeters across, containing neither instruments nor any other surface features, had been set into the Sharer's chest like a stainless-steel brooch. It seemed to hum under the pressure of my finger as I drew my nail silently around the disc's circumference. What was it for? What did it mean? Again, I almost spoke.

I rolled toward the wall and lay stretched out beside the unmoving Sharer. Maybe he *couldn't* move. On my last visit he had moved his dimly phosphorescent head for me, of course, but that only feebly, and maybe his immobility was the result of some cybergamic dysfunction. I had to find out. My resolve not to speak deserted me, and I propped myself up on my elbow.

"Sharer . . . Sharer, can you move?"

The head turned toward me slightly, signaling . . . well, what?

"Can you get off this platform? Try. Get off this dais under your own power."

To my surprise the Sharer nudged a quilt to the floor and in a moment stood facing me. Moonlight glinted from the photosensitive units serving the creature as eyes and gave his bent, elongated body the appearance of a piece of Inhodlef Era statuary, primitive work from the extrakomm world of Glaparcus.

"Good," I praised the Sharer; "very good. Can you tell me what you're supposed to share with me? I'm not sure we have as much in common as our Wardress seems to think."

The Sharer extended both arms toward me and opened his tightly closed fists. In the cups of his palms he held two items I hadn't discovered during my tactile examination of him. I accepted these from the Sharer. One was a small metal disc, the other a thin metal cylinder. Looking them over, I found that the disc reminded me of the larger, mirrorlike bowl set in the alien's chest, while the cylinder seemed to be a kind of penlight.

Absently, I pulled my thumb over the head of the penlight; a ridged metal sheath followed the motion of my thumb, uncovering a point of ghostly red light stretching away into the cylinder seemingly deeper than the penlight itself. I pointed this instrument at the wall, at our bedding, at the Sharer himself—but it emitted no beam. When I turned the penlight on my wrist, the results were predictably similar; not even a faint red shadow appeared along the edge of my arm. Nothing. The cylinder's light existed internally, a beam continuously transmitted and retransmitted between the penlight's two poles. Pulling back the sheath on the instrument's head had in no way interrupted the operation of its self-regenerating circuit.

I stared wonderingly into the hollow of redness, then looked up. "Sharer what's this thing for?"

The Sharer reached out and took from my other hand the disc I had so far ignored. Then he placed this small circle of metal in the smooth declivity of the larger disc in his chest, where it apparently adhered—for I could no longer see it. That done, the Sharer stood distressingly immobile, even more like a statue than he had seemed a moment before, one arm frozen across his body and his hand stilled at the edge of the sunken plate in which the smaller disc had just adhered. He looked dead and self-commemorating.

"Lord!" I exclaimed. "What've you done, Sharer? Turned yourself off? That's right, isn't it?"

The Sharer neither answered nor moved.

Suddenly I felt sickeningly weary, opiate-weary, and I knew that I wouldn't be able to stay on the dais with this puzzle-piece being from an anonymous sun standing over me like a dark angel from my racial subconscious. I thought briefly of manhandling the Sharer across the room, but didn't have the will to touch this catatonically rigid being, this sculpture of metal and bone, and so dismissed the idea. Nor was it likely that Wardress Kefa would help me, even if I tried to summon her with murderous poundings and cries—a bitterly amusing prospect. Wellaway, another night propped against the chamber's far wall, keeping sleep at bay . . .

Is this what you wanted me to experience, Rumer? The frustration of trying to piece together my own "therapy"? I looked up through one of the dome's unstained polygons in lethargic search of the constellation Auriga. Then I realized that I wouldn't recognize it even if it happened to lie within my line of sight. Ah, Rumer, Rumer . . .

"You're certainly a pretty one," I told the Sharer. Then I pointed the penlight at his chest, drew back the sheath on its head, and spoke a single onomatopoeic word: *"Bang."*

Instantly a beam of light sang between the instrument in my hand and the plate in the Sharer's chest. The beam died at once (I had registered only its shattering brightness, not its color), but the disc continued to glow with a residual illumination.

The Sharer dropped his frozen arm and assumed a posture more limber, more suggestive of life. He looked . . . expectant.

I could only stare. Then I turned the penlight over in my hands, pointed it again at the Sharer, and waited for another coursing of light. To no purpose. The instrument still burned internally, but it wouldn't relume the alien's inset disc, which, in any case, continued to glow dimly. Things were all at once interesting again. I gestured with the penlight.

"You've rejoined the living, haven't you?"

The Sharer acknowledged this with a slight turn of the head.

"Forgive me, Sharer, but I don't want to spend another night sitting on the floor. If you can move again, how about over there?" I pointed at the opposite wall. "I don't want you hovering over me."

Oddly, he obeyed. But he did so oddly, without turning around. He cruised backward as if on invisible coasters—his legs moving a little, yes, but not enough to propel him so smoothly, so quickly, across the chamber. Once against the far wall, the Sharer settled into the motionless but expectant posture he had assumed after his "activation" by the penlight. I could see that he still had some degree of control over his own movements, for his long fingers curled and uncurled and his skull nodded eerily in the halo of moonlight pocketing him. Even so, I realized that he had truly moved only at my voice command and my simultaneous gesturing with the penlight. And what did *that* mean?

. . . Well, that the Sharer had relinquished control of his body to the manmachine Dorian Lorca, retaining for himself just those meaningless reflexes and stirrings that convince the manipulated of their own autonomy. It was an awesome prostitution, even if Wardress Kefa would have frowned to hear me say so. Momentarily I rejoiced in it, for it seemed to free me from the demands of an artificial eroticism, from the need to figure through what was expected of me. The Sharer would obey my simplest wrist-turning,

my briefest word; all I had to do was *use* the control he had literally handed to me.

This virtually unlimited power, I thought then, was a therapy
whose value Rumer would understand only too well. This was a
harsh assessment, but, penlight in hand, I felt that I too was a kind
of marionette . . .

Insofar as I could, I tried to come to grips with the physics of
the Sharer's operation. First, the disc-within-a-disc on his chest apparently broke the connections ordinarily allowing him to exercise
the senile powers that were still his. And, second, the penlight's
beam restored and amplified these powers but delivered them into
the hands of the speaker of imperatives who wielded the penlight.
I recalled that in Earth's lunar probeship yards were crews of
animatronic laborers programmed for fitting and welding. A single
trained supervisor could direct from fifteen to twenty receiver-
equipped laborers with one penlight and a microphone—

"Sharer," I commanded, blanking out this reverie, pointing the
penlight, "go there. . . . No, no, not like that. Lift your feet.
March for me. . . . That's right, a *goosestep*."

While Wardress Kefa's third rule rattled in the back of my mind
like a challenge, for the next several hours I toyed with the Sharer.
After the marching I set him to calisthenics and interpretative
dance, and he obeyed, moving more gracefully than I would have
imagined possible. Here—then there—then back again. All he
lacked was Beethoven's piano sonatas for an accompaniment.

At intervals I rested, but always the fascination of the penlight
drew me back, almost against my will, and I once again played
puppetmaster.

"Enough, Sharer, enough." The sky had a curdled quality suggestive of dawn. Catching sight of the cage overhead, I was taken
by an irresistible impulse. I pointed the penlight at the cage and
commanded, "Up, Sharer. Up, up, up."

The Sharer floated up from the floor and glided effortlessly toward the vault of the dome: a beautiful, aerial walk. Without
benefit of hawsers or scaffolds or wings the Sharer levitated. Hovering over the stove-bed he had been made to surrender, hovering
over everything in the room, he reached the cage and swung before it with his hands touching the scrolled ironwork on its little

door. I dropped my own hands and watched him. So tightly was I gripping the penlight, however, that my knuckles must have resembled the caps of four tiny bleached skulls.

A great deal of time went by, the Sharer poised in the gelid air awaiting some word from me.

Morning began coming in the room's polygonal windows.

"Take the bird out," I ordered the Sharer, moving my penlight. "Take the bird out of the cage and kill it." This command, sadistically heartfelt, seemed to me a foolproof, indirect way of striking back at Rumer, Diderits, the Wardress, and the Third Rule of the House of Compassionate Sharers. More than anything, against all reason, I wanted the redwinged blackbird dead. And I wanted the Sharer to kill it.

Dawn made clear the cancerous encroachment of age in the Sharer's legs and hands, as well as the full horror of his cybergamically rigged death's-head. He looked like he had been unjustly hanged. And when his hands went up to the cage, instead of opening its door the Sharer lifted the entire contraption off the hook fastening it to its tether and then accidentally lost his grip on the cage.

I watched the cage fall—land on its side—bounce—bounce again. The Sharer stared down with his bulging, silver-ringed eyes, his hands still spread wide to accommodate the fallen cage.

"Mr. Lorca." Wardress Kefa was knocking at the door. "Mr. Lorca, what's going on, please?"

I arose from the stove-bed, tossed my quilt aside, straightened my heavy robes. The Wardress knocked again. I looked at the Sharer swaying in the half-light like a sword or a pendulum, an instrument of severance. The night had gone faster than I liked.

Again, the purposeful knocking.

"Coming," I barked.

In the dented cage there was a flutter of crimson, a stillness, and then another bit of melancholy flapping. I hurled my penlight across the room. When it struck the wall, the Sharer rocked back and forth for a moment without descending so much as a centimeter. The knocking continued.

"You have the key, Wardress. Open the door."

She did, and stood on its threshold taking stock of the games we had played. Her eyes were bright but devoid of censure, and I swept past her wordlessly, burning with shame and bravado.

I slept that day—all that day—for the first time since leaving my own world. And I dreamed. I dreamed that I was connected to a mechanism pistoning away on the edge of the Haft Paykar diggings, siphoning deadly gases out of the shafts and perversely recirculating them through the pump with which I shared a symbiomechanic linkage. Amid a series of surreal turquoise sunsets and intermittent gusts of sand, this pistoning went on, and on, and on. When I awoke I lifted my hands to my face, intending to scar it with my nails. But a moment later, as I had known it would, the mirror in my chamber returned me a perfect, unperturbed Dorian Lorca. . . .

"May I come in?"

"I'm the guest here, Wardress. So I suppose you may."

She entered and, quickly intuiting my mood, walked to the other side of the chamber. "You slept, didn't you? And you dreamed?"

I said nothing.

"You dreamed, didn't you?"

"A nightmare, Wardress. A long and repetitious nightmare, notable only for being different from the ones I had on Diroste."

"A start, though. You weren't monitored during your sleep, after all, and even if your dream *was* a nightmare, Mr. Lorca, I believe you've managed to survive it. Good. All to the good."

I went to the only window in the room, a hexagonal pane of dark blue through which it was impossible to see anything. "Did you get him down?"

"Yes. And restored the birdcage to its place." Her tiny feet made pacing sounds on the hardwood. "The bird was unharmed."

"Wardress, what's all this about? Why have you paired me with . . . with this particular Sharer?" I turned around. "What's the point?"

"You're not estranged from your wife only, Mr. Lorca. You're—"

"I know that. I've *known* that."

"And I know that you know it. Give me a degree of credit.

. . . You also know," she resumed, "that you're estranged from yourself, body and soul at variance—"

"Of course, damn it! And the argument between them's been stamped into every pseudo-organ and circuit I can lay claim to!"

"Please, Mr. Lorca, I'm trying to explain. This interior 'argument' you're so aware of . . . it's really a metaphor for an attitude you involuntarily adopted after Diderits performed his operations. And a metaphor can be taken apart and explained."

"Like a machine."

"If you like." She began pacing again. "To take inventory you have to surmount that which is to be inventoried. You go outside, Mr. Lorca, in order to come back in." She halted and fixed me with a colorless, lopsided smile.

"All of that," I began cautiously, "is clear to me. 'Know thyself,' saith Diderits and the ancient Greeks. . . . Well, if anything, my knowledge has *increased* my uneasiness about not only myself, but others—and not only others, but the very phenomena permitting us to spawn." I had an image of crimson-gilted fish firing upcurrent in a roiling, untidy barrage. "What I know hasn't cured anything, Wardress."

"No. That's why we've had you come here. To extend the limits of your knowledge and to involve you in relationships demanding a recognition of others as well as self."

"As with the Sharer I left hanging up in the air?"

"Yes. Distance is advisable at first, perhaps inevitable. You needn't feel guilty. In a night or two you'll be going back to him, and then we'll just have to see."

"Is this the only Sharer I'm going to be . . . working with?"

"I don't know. It depends on the sort of progress you make."

But for the Wardress Kefa, the Sharer in the crimson dome, and the noisy, midnight visitants I had never seen, there were times when I believed myself the only occupant of the House. The thought of such isolation, although not unwelcome, was an anchoritic fantasy: I knew that breathing in the chambers next to mine, going about the arcane business of the lives they had bartered away, were humanoid creatures difficult to imagine; harder still, once lodged in the mind, to put out of it. To what num-

ber and variety of beings had Wardress Kefa indentured her
love . . . ?

I had no chance to ask this question. We heard an insistent
clomping on the steps outside the House and then muffled voices
in the antechamber.

"Who's that?"

The Wardress put her hand to silence me and opened the door
to my room. "A moment," she called. "I'll be with you in a moment." But her husky voice didn't carry very well, and whoever
had entered the House set about methodically knocking on doors
and clomping from apartment to apartment, all the while bellow-
ing the Wardress's name. "I'd better go talk with them," she told
me apologetically.

"But who is it?"

"Someone voice-coded for entrance, Mr. Lorca. Nothing to
worry about." And she went into the corridor, giving me a scent of
spruce needles and a vision of solidly hewn rafters before the door
swung to.

But I got up and followed the Wardress. Outside I found her
face to face with two imposing persons who looked exactly alike in
spite of their being one a man and the other a woman. Their faces
had the same lantern-jawed mournfulness, their eyes a hooded
look under prominent brows. They wore filigreed pea jackets, ski
leggings, and fur-lined caps bearing the interpenetrating-galaxies
insignia of Glaktik Komm. I judged them to be in their late thirties, E-standard, but they both had the domineering, glad-handing
air of high-ranking veterans in the bureaucratic establishment, people who appreciate their positions just to the extent that their positions can be exploited. I knew. I had once been an official of the
same stamp.

The man, having been caught in midbellow, was now trying to
laugh. "Ah, Wardress, Wardress."

"I didn't expect you this evening," she told the two of them.

"We were granted a proficiency leave for completing the Salous
blueprint in advance of schedule," the woman explained, "and so
caught a late 'rail from Manitou Port to take advantage of the
leave. We hiked down in the dark." Along with her eyebrows she
lifted a hand lantern for our inspection.

"We *took* a proficiency leave," the man said, "even if we *were* here last week. And we deserved it too." He went on to tell us that "Salous" dealt with reclaiming the remnants of aboriginal populations and pooling them for something called integrative therapy. "The Great Plains will soon be our bordello, Wardress. There, you see: you and the Orhas are in the same business . . . at least until we're assigned to stage-manage something more prosaic." He clapped his gloved hands together and looked at me. "You're new, aren't you? Who are you going to?"

"Pardon me," the Wardress interjected wearily. "Who do *you* want tonight?"

The man looked at his partner with a mixture of curiosity and concern. "Cleva?"

"The mouthless one," Cleva responded at once. "Drugged, preferably."

"Come with me, Orhas," the Wardress directed. She led them first to her own apartment and then into the House's midinterior, where the three of them disappeared from my sight. I could hear them climbing one of the sets of stairs.

Shortly thereafter the Wardress returned to my room.

"They're twins?"

"In a manner of speaking, Mr. Lorca. Actually they're clonemates: Cleva and Cleirach Orha, specialists in Holosyncretic Management. They do abstract computer planning involving indigenous and alien populations, which is why they know of the House at all and have an authorization to come here."

"Do they always appear here together? Go upstairs together?"

The Wardress's silence clearly meant yes.

"That's a bit kinky, isn't it?"

She gave me an angry look whose implications immediately silenced me. I started to apologize, but she said: "The Orhas are the only visitants to the House who arrive together, Mr. Lorca. Since they share a common upbringing, the same genetic material, and identical biochemistries, it isn't surprising that their sexual preferences should coincide. In Manitou Port, I'm told, is a third clonemate who was permitted to marry, and her I've never seen either here or in Wolf Run Summit. It seems there's a *degree* of variety even among clonal siblings."

"Do these two come often?"

"You heard them in the House several days ago."

"They have frequent leaves then?"

"Last time was an overnighter. They returned to Manitou Port in the morning, Mr. Lorca. Just now they were trying to tell me that they intend to be here for a few days."

"For treatment," I said.

"You know better. You're baiting me, Mr. Lorca." She had taken her graying scalplock into her fingers, and was holding its fan of hair against her right cheek. In this posture, despite her pre-occupation with the arrival of the Orhas, she looked very old and very innocent.

"Who is the 'mouthless one,' Wardress?"

"Goodnight, Mr. Lorca. I only returned to tell you goodnight." And with no other word she left.

It was the longest I had permitted myself to talk with her since our first afternoon in the House, the longest I had been in her presence since our claustrophobic 'rail ride from Manitou Port. Even the Orhas, bundled to the gills, as vulgar as sleek bullfrogs, hadn't struck me as altogether insufferable.

Wearing neither coat nor cap, I took a walk through the glens below the House, touching each wind-shaken tree as I came to it and trying to conjure out of the darkness a viable memory of Rumer's smile. . . .

"Sex as weapon," I told my Sharer, who sat propped on the stove-bed amid ten or twelve quilts of scarlet and off-scarlet. "As prince consort to the Governor of Diroste, that was the only weapon I had access to. . . . Rumer employed me as an emissary, Sharer, an espionage agent, a protocol officer, whatever state business required. I received visiting representatives of Glaktik Komm, mediated disputes in the Port Iranani business community, and went on biannual inspection tours of the Fetneh and Furak District mines. I did a little of everything, Sharer."

As I paced, the Sharer observed me with a macabre, but somehow not unsettling, penetration. The hollow of his chest was exposed, and, as I passed him, an occasional metallic wink caught the corner of my eye.

I told him the story of my involvement with a minor official in Port Iranani's department of immigration, a young woman whom I had never called by anything but her maternal surname, Humay. There had been others besides this woman, but Humay's story was the one I chose to tell. Why? Because alone among my ostensible "lovers," Humay I had never lain with. I had never chosen to.

Instead, to her intense bewilderment, I gave Humay ceremonial pendants, bracelets, ear-pieces, brooches, necklaces, and die-cut cameos of gold on silver, all from the collection of Rumer Montieth, Governor of Diroste—anything, in short, distinctive enough to be recognizable to my wife at a glance. Then, at those state functions requiring Rumer's attendance upon a visiting dignitary, I arranged for Humay to be present; sometimes I accompanied her myself, sometimes I found her an escort among the unbonded young men assigned to me as aides. Always I insured that Rumer should see Humay, if not in a reception line then in the promenade of the formal recessional. Afterwards I asked Humay, who never seemed to have even a naïve insight into the purposes of my game, to hand back whatever piece of jewelry I had given her for ornament, and she did so. Then I returned the jewelry to Rumer's sandalwood box before my wife could verify what her eyes had earlier that evening tried to tell her. Everything I did was designed to create a false impression of my relationship with Humay, and I wanted my dishonesty in the matter to be conspicuous.

Finally, dismissing Humay for good, I gave her a cameo of Rumer's that had been crafted in the Furak District. I learned later that she had flung this cameo at an aide of mine who entered the offices of her department on a matter having nothing to do with her. She created a disturbance, several times raising my name. Ultimately (in two days' time), she was disciplined by a transfer to the frontier outpost of Yagme, the administrative center of the Furak District, and I never saw her again.

"Later, Sharer, when I dreamed of Humay, I saw her as a woman with mother-of-pearl flesh and ruby eyes. In my dreams she *became* the pieces of jewelry with which I'd tried to incite my wife's sexual jealousy—blunting it even as I incited it."

The Sharer regarded me with hard but sympathetic eyes.

Why? I asked him. Why had I dreamed of Humay as if she were

an expensive clockwork mechanism, gilded, beset with gemstones, invulnerably enameled? And why had I so fiercely desired Rumer's jealousy?

The Sharer's silence invited confession.

After the Haft Paykar Incident (I went on, pacing), after Diderits had fitted me with a total prosthesis, my nightmares often centered on the young woman who'd been exiled to Yagme. Although in Port Iranani I hadn't once touched Humay in an erotic way, in my monitored nightmares I regularly descended into either a charnel catacomb or a half-fallen quarry—it was impossible to know which—and there forced myself, without success, on the bejeweled automaton she had become. In every instance Humay waited for me underground; in every instance she turned me back with coruscating laughter. Its echoes always drove me upward to the light, and in the midst of nightmare I realized that I wanted Humay far less than I did residency in the secret, subterranean places she had made her own. The klieg lights that invariably directed my descent always followed me back out, too, so that Humay was always left kilometers below exulting in the dark. . . .

My Sharer got up and took a turn around the room, a single quilt draped over his shoulders and clutched loosely together at his chest. This was the first time since I had been coming to him that he had moved so far of his own volition, and I sat down to watch. Did he understand me at all? I had spoken to him as if his understanding were presupposed, a certainty—but beyond a hopeful *feeling* that my words meant something to him I'd had no evidence at all, not even a testimonial from Wardress Kefa. All of the Sharer's "reactions" were really nothing but projections of my own ambiguous hopes.

When he at last returned to me, he extended both hideously canaled arms and opened his fists. In them, the disc and the penlight. It was an offering, a compassionate, selfless offering, and for a moment I stared at his open hands in perplexity. What did they want of me, this Sharer, Wardress Kefa, the people who had sent me here? How was I supposed to buy either their forbearance or my freedom? By choosing power over impotency? By manipulation? . . . But these were altogether different questions, and I hesitated.

The Sharer then placed the small disc in the larger one beneath his sternum. Then, as before, a thousand esoteric connections severed, he froze. In the hand still extended toward me, the penlight glittered faintly and threatened to slip from his insensible grasp. I took it carefully from the Sharer's fingers, pulled back the sheath on its head, and gazed into its red-lit hollow. I released the sheath and pointed the penlight at the disc in his chest.

If I pulled the sheath back again, he would become little more than a fully integrated, *external* prosthesis—as much at my disposal as the hands holding the penlight.

"No," I said. "Not this time." And I flipped the penlight across the chamber, out of the way of temptation. Then, using my fingernails, I pried the small disc out of its electromagnetic moorings above the Sharer's heart.

He was restored to himself.

As was I to myself. As was I.

A day later, early in the afternoon, I ran into the Orhas in the House's midinterior. They were coming unaccompanied out of a lofty, seemingly sideways-canted door as I stood peering upward from the access corridor. Man and woman together, mirror images ratcheting down a Moebius strip of stairs, the Orhas held my attention until it was too late for me to slip away unseen.

"The new visitant," Cleirach Orha informed his sister when he reached the bottom step. "We've seen you before."

"Briefly," I agreed. "The night you arrived from Manitou Port for your proficiency leave."

"What a good memory you have," Cleva Orha said. "We also saw you the day *you* arrived from Manitou Port. You and the Wardress were just setting out from Wolf Run Summit together. Cleirach and I were beneath the ski lodge, watching."

"You wore no coat," her clonemate said in explanation of their interest.

They both stared at me curiously. Neither was I wearing a coat in the well of the House of Compassionate Sharers—even though the temperature inside hovered only a few degrees above freezing and we could see our breaths before us like the ghosts of ghosts. . . . I was a queer one, wasn't I? My silence made them nervous and brazen.

"No coat," Cleva Orha repeated, "and the day cold enough to fur your spittle. 'Look at that one,' Cleirach told me; 'thinks he's a polar bear.' We laughed about that, studling. We laughed heartily."

I nodded, nothing more. A coppery taste of bile, such as I hadn't experienced for several days, flooded my mouth, and I wanted to escape the Orhas' warty good humor. They were intelligent people, otherwise they would never have been cloned, but face to face with their flawed skins and their loud, insinuative sexuality I began to feel my newfound stores of tolerance overbalancing like a tower of blocks. It was a bitter test, this meeting below the stairs, and one I was on the edge of failing.

"We seem to be the only ones in the House this month," the woman volunteered. "Last month the Wardress was gone, the Sharers had a holiday, and Cleirach and I had to content ourselves with incestuous buggery in Manitou Port."

"Cleva!" the man protested, laughing.

"It's true." She turned to me. "It's true, studling. And that little she-goat—Kefa, I mean—won't even tell us why the Closed sign was out for so long. Delights in mystery, that one."

"That's right," Cleirach went on. "She's an exasperating woman. She begrudges you your privileges. You have to tread lightly on her patience. Sometimes you'd like to take *her* into a chamber and find out what makes her tick. A bit of exploratory surgery, heyla!" Saying this, he showed me his trilling tongue.

"She's a maso-ascetic, Brother."

"I don't know. There are many mansions in this House, Cleva, several of which she's refused to let us enter. Why?" He raised his eyebrows suggestively, as Cleva had done the night she lifted her hand-lantern for our notice. The expressions were the same.

Cleva Orha appealed to me as a disinterested third party: "What do you think, studling? Is Wardress Scalplock at bed and at bone with one of her Sharers? Or does she lie by herself, maso-ascetically, under a hide of untanned elk hair? What do you think?"

"I haven't really thought about it." Containing my anger, I tried to leave. "Excuse me, Orha-clones."

"Wait, wait, wait," the woman said mincingly, half-humorously. "You know our names and a telling bit of our background. That puts you up, studling. We won't have that. You can't go without giving us a name."

Resenting the necessity, I told them my name.

"From where?" Cleirach Orha asked.

"Colony World GK-11. We call it Diroste."

Brother and sister exchanged a glance of sudden enlightenment, after which Cleva raised her thin eyebrows and spoke in a mocking rhythm: "Ah ha, the mystery solved. Out and back our Wardress went and therefore closed her House."

"Welcome, Mr. Lorca. Welcome."

"We're going up to Wolf Run for an after-bout of toddies and P-nol. What about you? Would you like to go? The climb wouldn't be anything to a warmblooded studling like you. Look, Cleirach. Biceps unbundled and his sinuses still clear."

In spite of the compliment I declined.

"Who have *you* been with?" Cleirach Orha wanted to know. He bent forward conspiratorially. "We've been with a native of an extrakomm world called Trope. That's the local name. Anyhow, there's not another such being inside of a hundred light-years, Mr. Lorca."

"It's the face that intrigues us," Cleva Orha explained, saving me from an immediate reply to her brother's question. And then she reached out, touched my arm, and ran a finger down my arm to my hand. "Look. Not even a goose bump. Cleirach, you and I are suffering the shems and trivs, and our earnest Mr. Lorca's standing here bare-boned."

Brother was annoyed by this analysis. There was something he wanted to know, and Cleva's non sequiturs weren't advancing his case. Seeing that he was going to ask me again, I rummaged about for an answer that was neither informative nor tactless.

Cleva Orha, meanwhile, was peering intently at her fingertips. Then she looked at my arm, again at her fingers, and a second time at my arm. Finally she locked eyes with me and studied my face as if for some clue to the source of my reticence.

Ah, I thought numbly, she's recognized me for what I am. . . .

"Mr. Lorca can't tell you who he's been with, Cleirach," Cleva Orha told her clonemate, "because he's not a visitant to the House at all and he doesn't choose to violate the confidences of those who are."

Dumbfounded, I said nothing.

Cleva put her hand on her brother's back and guided him past me into the House's antechamber. Over her shoulder she bid me good afternoon in a toneless voice. Then the Orha-clones very deliberately let themselves out the front door and began the long climb to Wolf Run Summit.

What had happened? It took me a moment to figure it out. Cleva Orha had recognized me as a human-machine and from this recognition drawn a logical but mistaken inference: she believed me, like the "mouthless one" from Trope, a slave of the House. . . .

During my next tryst with my Sharer I spoke for an hour, two hours, maybe more, of Rumer's infuriating patience, her dignity, her serene ardor. I had moved her—maneuvered her—to the expression of these qualities by my own hollow commitment to Humay and the others before Humay who had engaged me only physically. Under my wife's attentions, however, I preened sullenly, demanding more than Rumer—than any woman in Rumer's position—had it in her power to give. My needs, I wanted her to know, my needs were as urgent and as real as Diroste's.

And at the end of one of these vague encounters Rumer seemed both to concede the legitimacy of my demands and to decry their intemperance by removing a warm pendant from her throat and placing it like an accusation in my palm.

"A week later," I told the Sharer, "was the inspection tour of the diggings at Haft Paykar."

These things spoken, I did something I had never done before in the Wardress's House: I went to sleep under the hand of my Sharer. My dreams were dreams rather than nightmares, and clarified ones at that, shot through with light and accompanied from afar by a peaceful funneling of sand. The images that came to me were haloed arms and legs orchestrated within a series of shifting yellow, yellow-orange, and subtly-red discs. The purr of running sand behind these movements conferred upon them the benediction of mortality, and that, I felt, was good.

I awoke in a blast of icy air and found myself alone. The door to the Sharer's apartment was standing open on the shaft of the stairwell, and I heard faint, angry voices coming across the emptiness between. Disoriented, I lay on my stove-bed staring toward the door, a square of shadow feeding its chill into the room.

"*Dorian!*" a husky voice called. "*Dorian!*"

Wardress Kefa's voice, diluted by distance and fear. A door opened, and her voice hailed me again, this time with more clarity. Then the door slammed shut, and every sound in the House took on a smothered quality, as if mumbled through cold, semiporous wood.

I got up, dragging my bedding with me, and reached the narrow porch on the stairwell with a clear head. Thin starlight filtered through the unshuttered windows in the ceiling. Nevertheless, looking from stairway to stairway to stairway inside the House, I had no idea behind which door the Wardress now must be.

Because there existed no connecting stairs among the staggered landings of the House, my only option was to go down. I took the steps two at a time, very nearly plunging.

At the bottom I found my Sharer with both hands clenched about the outer stair rail. He was trembling. In fact, his chest and arms were quivering so violently that he seemed about to shake himself apart. I put my hands on his shoulders and tightened my grip until the tremors wracking him threatened to wrack my systems, too. Who would come apart first?

"Go upstairs," I told the Sharer. "Get the hell upstairs."

I heard the Wardress call my name again. Although by now she had squeezed some of the fear out of her voice, her summons was still distance-muffled and impossible to pinpoint.

The Sharer either couldn't or wouldn't obey me. I coaxed him, cursed him, goaded him, tried to turn him around so that he was heading back up the steps. Nothing availed. The Wardress, summoning me, had inadvertently called the Sharer out as my proxy, and he now had no intention of giving back to me the role he'd just usurped. The beautifully paired planes of his skull turned to-ward me, bringing with them the stainless-steel rings of his eyes. These were the only parts of his body that didn't tremble, but they were helpless to countermand the agues shaking him. As inhuman and unmoving as they were, the Sharer's features still managed to convey stark, unpitiable entreaty. . . .

I sank to my knees, felt about the insides of the Sharer's legs, and took the penlight and the disc from the two pocket-like inci-sions tailored to these instruments. Then I stood and used them.

"Find Wardress Kefa for me, Sharer," I commanded, gesturing with the penlight at the windows overhead. "Find her."

And the Sharer floated up from the steps through the midin-terior of the House. In the crepuscular starlight, rocking a bit, he seemed to pass through a knot of curving stairs into an open space where he was all at once brightly visible.

"Point to the door," I said, jabbing the penlight uncertainly at several different landings around the well. "Show me the one."

My words echoed, and the Sharer, legs dangling, inscribed a slow half-circle in the air. Then he pointed toward one of the nearly hidden doorways.

I stalked across the well, found a likely-seeming set of stairs, and climbed them with no notion at all of what was expected of me.

Wardress Kefa didn't call out again, but I heard the same faint, somewhat slurred voices that I'd heard upon waking and knew that they belonged to the Orhas. A burst of muted female laughter, twice repeated, convinced me of this, and I hesitated on the landing.

"All right," I told my Sharer quietly, turning him around with a turn of the wrist, "go on home."

Dropping through the torus of a lower set of stairs, he found the porch in front of our chamber and settled upon it like a clumsily-handled puppet. And why not? I was a clumsy puppetmaster. Be-cause there seemed to be nothing else I could do, I slid the pen-light into a pocket of my dressing gown and knocked on the Orhas' door.

"Come in," Cleva Orha said. "By all means, Sharer Lorca, come in."

I entered and found myself in a room whose surfaces were all burnished as if with beeswax. The timbers shone. Whereas in the other chambers I had seen nearly all the joists and rafters were rough-hewn, here they were smooth and splinterless. The scent of sandalwood pervaded the air, and opposite the door was a carven screen blocking my view of the chamber's stove-bed. A tall wooden lamp illuminated the furnishings and the three people arrayed around the lamp's border of light like iconic statues.

"Welcome," Cleirach Orha said. "Your invitation was from the Wardress, however, not us." He wore only a pair of silk pantaloons drawn together at the waist with a cord, and his right forearm was under Wardress Kefa's chin, restraining her movement without quite cutting off her wind.

His disheveled clonemate, in a dressing gown very much like mine, sat crosslegged on a cushion and toyed with a wooden stiletto waxed as the beams of the chamber were waxed. Her eyes were too wide, too lustrous, as were her brother's, and I knew this was the result of too much placenol in combination with too much Wolf Run small-malt in combination with the Orhas' innate meanness. The woman was drugged, and drunk, and, in consequence of these things, malicious to a turn. Cleirach didn't appear quite so far gone as his sister, but all he had to do to strangle the Wardress, I understood, was raise the edge of his forearm into her trachea. I felt again the familiar sensation of being out of my element, gill-less in a sluice of stinging salt water. . . .

"Wardress Kefa—" I began.

"She's all right," Cleva Orha assured me. "Perfectly all right." She tilted her head so that she was gazing at me out of her right eye alone, and then barked a hoarse, deranged-sounding laugh.

"Let the Wardress go," I told her clonemate.

Amazingly, Cleirach Orha looked intimidated. "Mr. Lorca's an anproz," he reminded Cleva. "That little letter opener you're cleaning your nails with, it's not going to mean anything to him."

"Then let her go, Cleirach. Let her go."

Cleirach released the Wardress, who, massaging her throat with both hands, ran to the stove-bed. She halted beside the carven screen and beckoned me with a doll-like hand. "Mr. Lorca . . . Mr. Lorca, please . . . will you see to him first? I beg you."

"I'm going back to Wolf Run Summit," Cleirach informed his sister, and he slipped on a night jacket, gathered up his clothes, and left the room. Cleva Orha remained seated on her cushion, her head titled back as if she were tasting a bitter potion from a heavy metal goblet.

Glancing doubtfully at her, I went to the Wardress. Then I stepped around the wooden divider to see her Sharer.

The Tropeman lying there was a slender creature, almost slight. There was a ridge of flesh where his mouth ought to be, and his eyes were an organic variety of crystal, uncanny and depthful stones. One of these brandy-colored stones had been dislodged in its socket by Cleva's "letter opener"; and although the Orhas had failed to pry the eye completely loose, the Tropeman's face was streaked with blood from their efforts. The streaks ran down into the bedding under his narrow, fragile head and gave him the look of an aborigine in war paint. Lacking external genitalia, his sexless body was spread-eagled atop the quilts so that the burn marks on his legs and lower abdomen cried out for notice as plangently as did his face.

"Sweet light, sweet light," the Wardress chanted softly, over and over again, and I found her locked in my arms, hugging me tightly above her beloved, butchered ward, this Sharer from another star.

"He's not dead," Cleva Orha said from her cushion. "The rules . . . the rules say not to kill 'em and we go by the rules, brother and I."

"What can I do, Wardress Kefa?" I whispered, holding her. "What do you want me to do?"

Slumped against me, the Wardress repeated her consoling chant and held me about the waist. So, fearful that this being with eyes like precious gems would bleed to death as we delayed, each of us undoubtedly ashamed of our delay, we delayed—and I held the Wardress, pressed her head to my chest, gave her a warmth I hadn't before believed in me. And she returned this warmth in undiluted measure.

Wardress Kefa, I realized, was herself a Compassionate Sharer; she was as much a Sharer as the bleeding Tropeman on the stove-bed or that obedient creature whose electrode-studded body and luminous death's-head had seemed to mock the efficient, mechanical deadness in myself—a deadness that, in turning away from Rumer, I had made a god of. In the face of this realization my disgust with the Orhas was transfigured into something very unlike disgust; a mode of perception, maybe; a means of adapting. An answer had been revealed to me, and, without its being either easy or uncomplicated, it was still, somehow, very simple: I, too, was a Compassionate Sharer, Monster, machine, anproz, the designation didn't matter any longer. Wherever I might go, I was forevermore a ward of this tiny woman's House—my fate, inescapable and sure.

The Wardress broke free of my embrace and knelt beside the Tropeman. She tore a piece of cloth from the bottom of her tunic. Wiping the blood from the Sharer's face, she said, "I heard him calling me while I was downstairs, Mr. Lorca. Encephalogoi. 'Brain words,' you know. And I came up here as quickly as I could. Cleirach took me aside. All I could do was shout for you. Then, not even that."

Her hands touched the Sharer's burns, hovered over the wounded eye, moved about with a knowledge the Wardress herself seemed unaware of.

"We couldn't get it all the way out," Cleva Orha laughed. "Wouldn't come. Cleirach tried and tried."

I found the cloned woman's pea jacket, leggings and tunic. Then I took her by the elbow and led her down the stairs to her brother. She reviled me tenderly as we descended, but otherwise didn't protest.

"You," she predicted once we were down, ". . . you we'll never get."

She was right. It was a long time before I returned to the House of Compassionate Sharers, and, in any case, upon learning of their sadistic abuse of one of the wards of the House, the authorities in Manitou Port denied the Orhas any future access to it. A Sharer, after all, was an expensive commodity.

But I did return. After going back to Diroste and living with Rumer the remaining forty-two years of her life, I applied to the House as a novitiate. I am here now. In fact as well as in metaphor, I am today one of the Sharers.

My brain cells die, of course, and there's nothing anyone can do to stop utterly the depredations of time—but my body seems to be that of a middle-aged man and I still move inside it with ease. Visitants seek comfort from me, as once, against my will, I sought comfort here: and I try to give it to them . . . even to the ones who have only a muddled understanding of what a Sharer really is. My battles aren't really with these unhappy people; they're with the advance columns of my senility (I don't like to admit this) and the shock troops of my memory, which is still excessively good. . . .

Wardress Kefa has been dead seventeen years, Diderits twenty-three, and Rumer two. That's how I keep score now. Death has also carried off the gem-eyed Tropeman and the Sharer who drew the essential Dorian Lorca out of the prosthetic rind he had mistaken for himself.

I intend to be here a while longer yet. I have recently been given a chamber into which the light sifts with a painful white brilliance reminiscent of the sands of Diroste or the snows of Wolf Run Summit. This is all to the good. Either way, you see, I die at home. . . .

PARTICLE THEORY

by Edward Bryant

*This is the sort of story that with perfect justice
could go into any good mainstream collection as an
example of one of the year's best. It does happen
to be science fiction, a subtle and able kind, but it
shows what can be done entirely outside Uncle
Hugo's pulp tradition.*

I see my shadow flung like black iron against the wall. My sundeck blazes with untimely summer. Eliot was wrong; Frost, right.
Nanoseconds . . .

Death is as relativistic as any other apparent constant. I wonder: *am I dying?*

I thought it was a cliché with no underlying truth.

"Lives *do* flash in a compressed instant before dying eyes," said
Amanda. She poured me another glass of burgundy the color
of her hair. The fire highlighted both. "A psychologist named
Noyes—" She broke off and smiled at me. "You really want to hear
this?"

"Sure." The fireplace light softened the taut planes of her face. I
saw a flicker of the gentler beauty she had possessed thirty years
before.

"Noyes catalogued testimonial evidence for death's-door phenomena in the early seventies. He termed it 'life review,' the second of three clearly definable steps in the process of dying; like a movie, and not necessarily linear."

I drink. I have a low threshold of intoxication. I ramble. "Why does it happen? How?" I didn't like the desperation in my voice. We were suddenly much further apart than the geography of the table separating us; I looked in Amanda's eyes for some memory of Lisa. "Life goes shooting off—or we recede from it—like Earth and an interstellar probe irrevocably severed. Mutual recession at light-speed, and the dark fills in the gap." I held my glass by the stem, rotated it, peered through the distorting bowl.

Pine logs crackled. Amanda turned her head and her eyes' image shattered in the flames.

The glare, the glare—

When I was thirty I made aggrieved noises because I'd screwed around for the past ten years and not accomplished nearly as much as I should. Lisa only laughed, which sent me into a transient rage and a longer-lasting sulk before I realized hers was the only appropriate response.

"Silly, silly," she said. "A watered-down Byronic character, full of self-pity and sloppy self-adulation." She blocked my exit from the kitchen and said millimeters from my face, "It's not as though you're waking up at thirty to discover that only fifty-six people have heard of you."

I stuttered over a weak retort.

"Fifty-seven?" She laughed; I laughed.

Then I was forty and went through the same pseudo-menopausal trauma. Admittedly, I hadn't done any work at all for nearly a year, and any *good* work for two. Lisa didn't laugh this time; she did what she could, which was mainly to stay out of my way while I alternately moped and raged around the coast house southwest of Portland. Royalties from the book I'd done on the fusion break-through kept us in groceries and mortgage payments.

"Listen, maybe if I'd go away for a while—" she said. "Maybe it would help for you to be alone." Temporary separations weren't alien to our marriage; we'd once figured that our relationship got measurably rockier if we spent more than about sixty percent of our time together. It had been a long winter and we were overdue; but then Lisa looked intently at my face and decided not to leave. Two months later I worked through the problems in my skull, and asked her for solitude. She knew me well—well enough to laugh again because she knew I was waking out of another mental hibernation.

She got onto a jetliner on a gray winter day and headed east for my parents' old place in southern Colorado. The jetway for the flight was out of commission that afternoon, so the airline people had to roll out one of the old wheeled stairways. Just before she stepped into the cabin, Lisa paused and waved back from the head of the stairs; her dark hair curled about her face in the wind.

Two months later I'd roughed out most of the first draft for my initial book about the reproductive revolution. At least once a week I would call Lisa and she'd tell me about the photos she was taking river-running on an icy Colorado or Platte. Then I'd use her as a sounding board for speculations about ectogenesis, heterogynes, or the imminent emergence of an exploited human hostmother class.

"So what'll we do when you finish the first draft, Nick?"

"Maybe we'll take a leisurely month on the Trans-Canadian Railroad."

"Spring in the provinces . . ."

Then the initial draft was completed and so was Lisa's Colorado adventure. "Do you know how badly I want to see you?" she said.

"Almost as badly as I want to see you."

"Oh, no," she said. "Let me tell you—"

What she told me no doubt violated state and federal laws and probably telephone company tariffs as well. The frustration of only hearing her voice through the wire made me twine my legs like a contortionist.

"Nick, I'll book a flight out of Denver. I'll let you know."

I think she wanted to surprise me. Lisa didn't tell me when she booked the flight. The airline let me know.

And now I'm fifty-one. The pendulum has swung and I again bitterly resent not having achieved more. There is so much work left undone; should I live for centuries, I still could not complete it all. That, however, will not be a problem.

I am told that the goddamned level of acid phosphatase in my goddamned blood is elevated. How banal that single fact sounds, how sterile; and how self-pitying, the phraseology. Can't I afford a luxurious tear, Lisa?

Lisa?

Death: I wish to determine my own time.

"Charming," I said much later. "End of the world."

My friend Denton, the young radio astronomer, said, "Christ almighty! Your damned jokes. How can you make a pun about this?"

"It keeps me from crying," I said quietly. "Wailing and breast-beating won't make a difference."

"Calm, so calm." She looked at me peculiarly.

"I've seen the enemy," I said. "I've had time to consider it."

Her face was thoughtful, eyes focused somewhere beyond this cluttered office. "*If* you're right," she said, "it could be the most fantastic event a scientist could observe and record." Her eyes refocused and met mine. "Or it might be the most frightening; a final horror."

"Choose one," I said.

"If I believed you at all."

"I'm dealing in speculations."

"Fantasies," she said.

"However you want to term it." I got up and moved to the door. "I don't think there's much time. You've never seen where I live. Come—" I hesitated, "—visit me if you care to. I'd like that to have you there."

"Maybe," she said.

I should not have left the situation ambiguous.

I didn't know that in another hour, after I had left her office; pulled my car out of the Gamow Peak parking lot and driven down to the valley, Denton would settle herself behind the wheel of her sports car and gun it onto the Peak road. Tourists saw her go off the switchback. A Highway Department crew pried her loose from the embrace of Lotus and lodgepole.

When I got the news I grieved for her, wondering if this were the price of belief. I drove to the hospital and, because no next of kin had been found and Amanda intervened, the doctors let me stand beside the bed.

I had never seen such still features, never such stasis short of actual death. I waited an hour, seconds sweeping silently from the wall clock, until the urge to return home was overpowering.

I could wait no longer because daylight was coming and I would tell no one.

Toward the beginning:

I've tolerated doctors as individuals; as a class they terrify me. It's a dread like shark attacks or dying by fire. But eventually I made the appointment for an examination, drove to the sparkling white clinic on the appointed day and spent a surly half hour reading a year-old issue of *Popular Science* in the waiting room.

"Mr. Richmond?" the smiling nurse finally said. I followed her back to the examination room. "Doctor will be here in just a minute." She left. I sat apprehensively on the edge of the examination table. After two minutes I heard the rustling of my file being removed from the outside rack. Then the door opened.

"How's it going?" said my doctor. "I haven't seen you in a while."

"Can't complain," I said, reverting to accustomed medical ritual. "No flu so far this winter. The shot must have been soon enough."

Amanda watched me patiently. "You're not a hypochondriac. You don't need continual reassurance—or sleeping pills, any more. You're not a medical groupie, God knows. So what is it?"

"Uh," I said. I spread my hands helplessly.

"Nicholas." Get-on-with-it-I'm-busy-today sharpness edged her voice.

"Don't imitate my maiden aunt."

"All right, *Nick*," she said. "What's wrong?"

"I'm having trouble urinating."

She jotted something down. Without looking up. "What kind of trouble?"

"Straining."

"For how long?"

"Six, maybe seven months. It's been a gradual thing."

"Anything else you've noticed?"

"Increased frequency."

"That's all?"

"Well," I said, "afterwards, I, uh, dribble."

She listed, as though by rote: "Pain, burning, urgency, hesitancy, change in stream of urine? Incontinence, change in size of stream, change in appearance of urine?"

"What?"

"Darker, lighter, cloudy, blood discharge from penis, VD exposure, fever, night sweats?"

I answered with a variety of nods or monosyllables.

"Mmm." She continued to write on the pad, then snapped it shut. "Okay, Nick, would you get your clothes off?" And when I had stripped, "Please lie on the table. On your stomach."

"The greased finder?" I said. "Oh shit."

Amanda tore a disposable glove off the roll. It crackled as she put it on. "You think I get a thrill out of this?" She's been my GP for a long time.

When it was over and I sat gingerly and uncomfortably on the edge of the examining table, I said, "Well?"

Amanda again scribbled on a sheet. "I'm sending you to a urologist. He's just a couple of blocks away. I'll phone over. Try to get an appointment in—oh, inside of a week."

"Give me something better," I said, "or I'll go to the library and check out a handbook of symptoms."

She met my eyes with a candid blue gaze. "I want a specialist to check out the obstruction."

"You found something when you stuck your finger in?"

"Crude, Nicholas." She half smiled. "Your prostate is hard—stony. There could be a number of reasons."

"What John Wayne used to call the Big C?"

"Prostatic cancer," she said, "is relatively infrequent in a man of your age." She glanced down at my records. "Fifty."

"Fifty-one," I said, wanting to shift the tone, trying, failing. "You didn't send me a card on my birthday."

"But it's not impossible," Amanda said. She stood. "Come on

up to the front desk. I want an appointment with you after the urology results come back." As always, she patted me on the shoulder as she followed me out of the examination room. But this time there was slightly too much tension in her fingers.

I was seeing grassy hummocks and marble slabs in my mind and didn't pay attention to my surroundings as I exited the waiting room.

"Nick?" A soft Oklahoma accent.

I turned back from the outer door, looked down, saw tousled hair. Jackie Denton, one of the bright young minds out at the Gamow Peak Observatory, held the well-thumbed copy of *Popular Science* loosely in her lap. She honked and snuffled into a deteriorating Kleenex. "Don't get too close. Probably doesn't matter at this point. Flu. You?" Her green irises were red-rimmed.

I fluttered my hands vaguely. "I had my shots."

"Yeah." She snuffed again. "I was going to call you later on from work. See the show last night?"

I must have looked blank.

"Some science writer," she said. "Rigel went supernova."

"Supernova," I repeated stupidly.

"Blam, you know? *Blooie*." She illustrated with her hands and the magazine flipped onto the carpet. "Not that you missed anything. It'll be around for a few weeks—biggest show in the skies."

A sudden ugly image of red-and-white aircraft warning lights merging in an actinic flare sprayed my retinas. I shook my head. After a moment I said, "First one in our galaxy in—how long? Three hundred and fifty years? I wish you'd called me."

"A little longer. Kepler's star was in 1604. Sorry about not calling—we were all a little busy, you know?"

"I can imagine. When did it happen?"

She bent to retrieve the magazine. "Just about midnight. Spooky. I was just coming off shift." She smiled. "Nothing like a little cosmic cataclysm to take my mind off jammed sinuses. Just as well; no sick leave tonight. That's why I'm here at the clinic. Kris says no excuses."

Krishnamurthi was the Gamov director. "You'll be going back

up to the peak soon?" She nodded. "Tell Kris I'll be in to visit. I want to pick up a lot of material."

"For sure."

The nurse walked up to us. "Ms. Denton?"

"Mmph." She nodded and wiped her nose a final time. Struggling up from the soft chair, she said, "How come you didn't read about Rigel in the papers? It made every morning edition."

"I let my subscriptions lapse."

"But the TV news? The radio?"

"I didn't watch, and I don't have a radio in the car."

Before disappearing into the corridor to the examination rooms, she said, "That country house of yours must really be isolated."

The ice drips from the eaves as I drive up and park beside the garage. Unless the sky deceives me there is no new weather front moving in yet; no need to protect the car from another ten centimeters of fresh snow.

Sunset comes sooner at my house among the mountains; shadows stalk across the barren yard and suck heat from my skin. The peaks are, of course, deliberate barriers blocking off light and warmth from the coastal cities. Once I personified them as friendly giants, amiable *lummoxen* guarding us. No more. Now they are only mountains again, the Cascade Range.

For an instant I think I see a light flash on, but it is just a quick sunset reflection on a window. The house remains dark and silent. The poet from Seattle's been gone for three months. My coldness—her heat. I thought that transference would warm me. Instead she chilled. The note she left me in the vacant house was a sonnet about psychic frostbite.

My last eleven years have not been celibate, but sometimes they feel like it. Entropy ultimately overcomes all kinetic force.

Then I looked toward the twilight east and saw Rigel rising. Luna wouldn't be visible for a while, so the brightest object in the sky was the exploded star. It fixed me to this spot by my car with the intensity of an aircraft landing light. The white light that shone down on me had left the supernova five hundred years before (a detail to include in the inevitable article—a graphic illustration of interstellar distances never fails to awe readers).

Tonight, watching the 100 billion-degree baleful eye that was

Rigel convulsed, I know *I* was awed. The cataclysm glared, brighter than any planet. I wondered whether Rigel—unlikely, I knew—had had a planetary system; whether guttering mountain ranges and boiling seas had preceded worlds frying. I wondered whether, five centuries before, intelligent beings had watched stunned as the stellar fire engulfed their skies. Had they time to rail at the injustice? There are 100 billion stars in our galaxy; only an estimated three stars go supernova per thousand years. Good odds: Rigel lost.

Almost hypnotized, I watched until I was abruptly rocked by the wind rising in the darkness. My fingers were stiff with cold. But as I started to enter the house I looked at the sky a final time. Terrifying Rigel, yes—but my eyes were captured by another phenomenon in the north. A spark of light burned brighter than the surrounding stars. At first I thought it was a passing aircraft, but its position remained stationary. Gradually; knowing the odds and unwilling to believe, I recognized the new supernova for what it was.

In five decades I've seen many things. Yet watching the sky I felt like I was a primitive, shivering in uncured furs. My teeth chattered from more than the cold. I wanted to hide from the universe. The door to my house was unlocked, which was lucky—I couldn't have fitted a key into the latch. Finally I stepped over the threshold. I turned on all the lights, denying the two stellar pyres burning in the sky.

My urologist turned out to be a dour black man named Sharpe who treated me, I suspected, like any of the other specimens that turned up in his laboratory. In his early thirties, he'd read several of my books. I appreciated his having absolutely no respect for his elders or for celebrities.

"You'll give me straight answers?" I said.

"Count on it."

He also gave me another of those damned urological fingers. When I was finally in a position to look back at him questioningly, he nodded slowly and said, "There's a nodule."

Then I got a series of blood tests for an enzyme called acid phosphatase. "Elevated," Sharpe said.

Finally, at the lab, I was to get the cystoscope; a shiny metal tube which would be run up my urethra. The biopsy forceps would be inserted through it. "Jesus, you're kidding." Sharpe shook his head. I said, "If the biopsy shows a malignancy . . ."

"I can't answer a silence."

"Come on," I said. "You've been straight until now. What are the chances of curing a malignancy?"

Sharpe had looked unhappy ever since I'd walked into his office. Now he looked unhappier. "Ain't my department," he said. "Depends on many factors."

"Just give me a simple figure."

"Maybe thirty percent. All bets are off if there's a metastasis." He met my eyes while he said that, then busied himself with the cystoscope. Local anesthetic or not, my penis burned like hell.

I had finally gotten through to Jackie Denton on a private line the night of the second supernova. "I thought last night was a madhouse," she said. "You should see us now. I've only got a minute."

"I just wanted to confirm what I was looking at," I said, "I saw the damn thing actually blow."

"You're ahead of everybody at Gamow. We were busily focusing on Rigel—" Electronic *wheeps* garbled the connection. "Nick, are you still there?"

"I think somebody wants the line. Just tell me a final thing: is it a full-fledged supernova?"

"Absolutely. As far as we can determine now, it's a genuine. Type II."

"Sorry it couldn't be the biggest and best of all."

"Big enough," she said. "It's good enough. This time it's only about nine light-years away. Sirius A."

"Eight point seven light-years," I said automatically. "What's that going to mean?"

"Direct effects? Don't know. We're thinking about it." It sounded like her hand cupped the mouthpiece; then she came back on the line. "Listen, I've got to go. Kris is screaming for my head. Talk to you later."

"All right," I said. The connection broke. On the dead line I thought I heard the 21-centimeter basic hydrogen hiss of the universe. Then the dial tone cut in and I hung up the receiver.

Amanda did not look at all happy. She riffled twice through what I guessed were my laboratory test results. "All right," I said from the patient's side of the wide walnut desk. "Tell me."

"*Mr. Richmond? Nicholas Richmond?*"

"*Speaking.*"

"*This is Mrs. Kurnick, with Trans-West Airways. I'm calling from Denver.*"

"*Yes?*"

"*We obtained this number from a charge slip. A ticket was issued to Lisa Richmond—*"

"*My wife. I've been expecting her sometime this weekend. Did she ask you to phone ahead?*"

"*Mr. Richmond, that's not it. Our manifest shows your wife boarded our Flight 903, Denver to Portland, tonight.*"

"*So? What is it? What's wrong? Is she sick?*"

"*I'm afraid there's been an accident.*"

Silence choked me. "*How bad?*" *The freezing began.*

"*Our craft went down about ten miles northwest of Glenwood Springs, Colorado. The ground parties at the site say there are no survivors. I'm sorry, Mr. Richmond.*"

"*No one?*" I said, "I mean—"

"*I'm truly sorry,*" said Mrs. Kurnick. "*If there's any change in the situation, we will be in touch immediately.*"

Automatically I said, "*Thank you.*"

I had the impression that Mrs. Kurnick wanted to say something else; but after a pause, she only said, "*Good night.*"

On a snowy Colorado mountainside I died.

"The biopsy was malignant," Amanda said.

"Well," I said. "That's pretty bad." She nodded. "Tell me about my alternatives." *Ragged bits of metal slammed into the mountainside like teeth.*

My case was unusual only in a relative sense. Amanda told me that prostatic cancer is the penalty men pay for otherwise good health. If they avoid every other health hazard, twentieth-century men eventually get zapped by their prostates. In my case, the problem was about twenty years early; my bad luck. *Cooling metal snapped and sizzled in the snow, was silent.*

Assuming that the cancer hadn't already metastasized, there were several possibilities; but Amanda had, at this stage, little hope for either radiology or chemotherapy. She suggested a radical prostatectomy.

"I wouldn't suggest it if you didn't have a hell of a lot of valuable years left," she said. "It's not usually advised for older patients. But you're in generally good condition; you could handle it."

Nothing moved on the mountainside. "What all would come out?" I said.

"You already know the ramifications of 'radical'."

I didn't mind so much the ligation of the spermatic tubes—I should have done that a long time before. At fifty-one I could handle sterilization with equanimity, but—

"Sexually dysfunctional?" I said. "Oh my God." I was aware of my voice starting to tighten. "I can't do that."

"You sure as hell can," said Amanda firmly. "How long have I known you?" She answered her own question. "A long time. I know you well enough to know that what counts isn't all tied up in your penis."

I shook my head silently.

"Listen, damn it, cancer death is worse."

"No," I said stubbornly. "Maybe. Is that the whole bill?"

It wasn't. Amanda reached my bladder's entry on the list. It would be excised as well.

"Tubes protruding from me?" I said. "*If* I live, I'll have to spend the rest of my life toting a plastic bag as a drain for my urine?"

Quietly she said, "You're making it too melodramatic."

"But am I right?"

After a pause, "Essentially, yes."

And all that was the essence of it; the *good* news, all assuming that the carcinoma cells wouldn't jar loose during surgery and migrate off to the other organs. "No," I said. The goddamned lousy, loathsome unfairness of it all slammed home. "Goddamn it, no. It's my choice; I won't live that way. If I just die, I'll be done with it."

"Nicholas! Cut the self-pity."

"Don't you think I'm entitled to some?"

"Be reasonable."

"You're supposed to comfort me," I said. "Not argue. You've taken all those death-and-dying courses. *You* be reasonable."

The muscles tightened around her mouth. "I'm giving you suggestions," said Amanda. "You can do with them as you damned well please." It had been years since I'd seen her angry.

We glared at each other for close to a minute. "Okay," I said. "I'm sorry."

She was not mollified. "Stay upset, even if it's whining. Get angry, be furious. I've watched you in a deep-freeze for a decade."

I recoiled internally. "I've survived. That's enough."

"No way. You've been sitting around for eleven years in suspended animation, waiting for someone to chip you free of the glacier. You've let people carom past, occasionally bouncing off you with no effect. Well, now it's not some*one* that's shoving you to the wall—it's some*thing*. Are you going to lie down for it? Lisa wouldn't have wanted that."

"Leave her out," I said.

"I can't. You're even more important to me because of her. She was my closest friend, remember?"

"Pay attention to her," Lisa had once said. "She's more sensible than either of us." Lisa had known about the affair; after all, Amanda had introduced us.

"I know." I felt disoriented; denial, resentment, numbness—the roller coaster clattered toward a final plunge.

"Nick, you've got a possibility for a healthy chunk of life left. I want you to have it, and if it takes using Lisa as a wedge, I will."

"I don't want to survive if it means crawling around as a piss-dripping cyborg eunuch." The roller coaster teetered on the brink.

Amanda regarded me for a long moment, then said earnestly, "There's an outside chance, a longshot. I heard from a friend there that the New Mexico Meson Physics Facility is scouting for a subject."

I scoured my memory. "Particle beam therapy?"

"Pions."

"It's chancy," I said.

"Are you arguing?" She smiled.

I smiled too. "No."

"Want to give it a try?"

My smile died. "I don't know. I'll think about it."

"That's encouragement enough," said Amanda. "I'll make some calls and see if the facility's as interested in you as I expect you'll be in them. Stick around home? I'll let you know."

"I haven't said 'yes'. We'll let each other know." I didn't tell Amanda, but I left her office thinking only of death.

Melodramatic as it may sound, I went downtown to visit the hardware stores and look at their displays of pistols. After two hours, I tired of handling weapons. The steel seemed uniformly cold and distant.

When I returned home late that afternoon, there was a single message on my phone-answering machine:

"Nick, this is Jackie Denton. Sorry I haven't called for a while, but you know how it's been. I thought you'd like to know that Kris is going to have a press conference early in the week—probably Monday afternoon. I think he's worried because he hasn't come up with a good theory to cover the three Type II supernovas and the half-dozen standard novas that have occurred in the last few weeks. But then nobody I know has. We're all spending so much time awake nights, we're turning into vampires. I'll get back to you when I know the exact time of the conference. I think it must be about thirty seconds now, so I—" The tape ended.

I mused with winter bonfires in my mind as the machine rewound and reset. Three Type II supernovas? One is merely nature, I paraphrased. Two mean only coincidence. Three make a conspiracy.

Impulsively I slowly dialed Denton's home number; there was no answer. Then the lines to Gamow Peak were all busy. It seemed logical to me that I needed Jackie Denton for more than being my sounding board, or for merely news about the press conference. I needed an extension of her friendship. I thought I'd like to borrow the magnum pistol I knew she kept in a locked desk drawer at her observatory office. I knew I could ask her a favor. She ordinarily used the pistol to blast targets on the peak's rocky flanks after work.

The irritating regularity of the busy signal brought me back to sanity. Just a second, I told myself. Richmond, what the hell are you proposing?

Nothing was the answer. Not yet. Not . . . quite.

Later in the night, I opened the sliding glass door and disturbed the skiff of snow on the second-story deck. I shamelessly allowed myself the luxury of leaving the door partially open so that warm air would spill out around me while I watched the sky. The stars were intermittently visible between the towering banks of strato-cumulus scudding over the Cascades. Even so, the three super-novas dominated the night. I drew imaginary lines with my eyes; connect the dots and solve the puzzle. How many enigmas can you find in this picture?

I reluctantly took my eyes away from the headline phenomena and searched for old standbys. I picked out the red dot of Mars.

Several years ago I'd had a cockamamic scheme that sent me to a Mesmerist—that's how she'd billed herself—down in Eugene. I'd been driving up the coast after covering an aerospace medical conference in Oakland. Somewhere around Crescent City, I capped a sea-bass dinner by getting blasted on prescribed pills and pro-scribed Scotch. Sometime during the evening, I remembered the computer-enhancement process JPL had used to sharpen the clarity of telemetered photos from such projects as the Mariner fly-bys and Viking Mars lander. It seemed logical to me at the time that memories from the human computer could somehow be enhanced, brought into clarity through hypnosis. Truly stoned fantasies. But they somehow sufficed as rationale and incentive to wind up at Madame Guzmann's "Advice/Mesmerism/Health" establishment across the border in Oregon. Madame Guzmann had skin the color of her stained hardwood door; she made a point of looking and dressing the part of a stereotype we *gajos* would think of as Gypsy. The scarf and crystal ball strained the image. I think she was Vietnamese. At any rate she convinced me she could hypno-tize, and then she nudged me back through time.

Just before she ducked into the cabin, Lisa paused and waved back from the head of the stairs; her dark hair curled about her face in the wind.

I should have taken to heart the lesson of stasis: entropy is not so easily overcome.

What Madame Guzmann achieved was to freeze-frame that last image of Lisa. Then she zoomed me in so close it was like standing beside Lisa. I sometimes still see it in my nightmares: Her eyes focus distantly. Her skin has the graininess of a newspaper photo. I look but cannot touch. I can speak but she will not answer. I shiver with the cold—

—and slid the glass door further open.

There! An eye opened in space. A glare burned as cold as a refrigerator light in a night kitchen. Mars seemed to disappear, swallowed in the glow from the nova distantly behind it. Another one, I thought. The new eye held me fascinated, pinned as securely as a child might fasten a new moth in the collection.

Nick?

Who is it?

Nick . . .

You're an auditory hallucination.

There on the deck the sound of laughter spiraled around me. I thought it would shake loose the snow from the trees. The mountain stillness vibrated.

The secret, Nick.

What secret?

You're old enough at fifty-one to decipher it.

Don't play with me.

Who's playing? Whatever time is left—

Yes?

You've spent eleven years now dreaming, drifting, letting others act on you.

I know.

Do you? Then act on that. Choose your actions. No lover can tell you more. Whatever time is left—

Shivering uncontrollably, I gripped the rail of the deck. A fleeting pointillist portrait in black and white dissolved into the trees. From branch to branch, top bough to bottom, crusted snow broke and fell, gathering momentum. The trees shed their mantle. Powder swirled up to the deck and touched my face with stinging diamonds.

Eleven years was more than half what Rip van Winkle slept. "Damn it." I said. "Damn you." We prize our sleep. The grave rested peacefully among the trees. "Damn you." I said again, looking up at the sky.

On a snowy Oregon mountainside I was no longer dead.

And yes, Amanda. Yes.

After changing planes at Albuquerque, we flew into Los Alamos on a small feeder called Ross Airlines. I'd never flown before on so ancient a DeHavilland Twin Otter, and I hoped never to again; I'd take a Greyhound out of Los Alamos first. The flight attendant and half the other sixteen passengers were throwing up in the turbulence as we approached the mountains. I hadn't expected the mountains. I'd assumed Los Alamos would lie in the same sort of southwestern scrub desert surrounding Albuquerque. Instead I found a small city nestled a couple of kilometers up a wooded mountainside.

The pilot's unruffled voice came on the cabin intercom to announce our imminent landing, the airport temperature, and the fact that Los Alamos has more Ph.D.'s per capita than any other American city. "Second only to Akademgorodok," I said, turning away from the window toward Amanda. The skin wrinkled around her closed eyes. She hadn't had to use her airsick bag. I had a feeling that despite old friendships, a colleague and husband who was willing to oversee the clinic, the urgency of helping a patient, and the desire to observe the exotic experiment, Amanda might be regretting accompanying me to what she'd termed "the meson factory."

The Twin Otter made a landing approach like a strafing run and then we were down. As we taxied across the apron I had a sudden sensation of déjà-vu: the time a year ago when a friend had flown me north in a Cessna. The airport in Los Alamos looked much like the civil air terminal at Sea-Tac where I'd met the Seattle poet. It happened that we were both in line at the snack counter.

I'd commented on her elaborate Haida-styled medallion. We took the same table and talked; it turned out she'd heard of me.

"I really admire your stuff," she said.

So much for my ideal poet using only precise images. Wry thought. She was—is—a first-rate poet. I rarely think of her as anything but "the poet from Seattle." Is that kind of depersonalization a symptom?

Amanda opened her eyes, smiled wanly, said, "I could use a doctor." The flight attendant cracked the door and thin New Mexican mountain air revived us both.

Most of the New Mexico Meson Physics Facility was buried beneath a mountain ridge. Being guest journalist as well as experimental subject, I think we were given a more exhaustive tour than would be offered most patients and their doctors. Everything I saw made me think of expensive sets for vintage science fiction movies: the interior of the main accelerator ring, glowing eggshell white and curving away like the space-station corridors in *2001;* the linac and booster areas; the straight-away tunnel to the meson medical channel; the five-meter bubble chamber looking like some sort of time machine.

I'd visited both FermiLab in Illinois and CERN in Geneva, so I had a general idea of what the facilities were all about. Still I had a difficult time trying to explain to Amanda the *Alice in Wonderland* mazes that constituted high energy particle physics. But then so did Delaney, the young woman who was the liaison biophysicist for my treatment. It became difficult sorting out the mesons, pions, hadrons, leptons, baryons, J's, fermions and quarks, and such quantum qualities as strangeness, color, baryonness and charm. Especially charm, that ephemeral quality accounting for why certain types of radioactive decay should happen, but don't. I finally bogged down in the midst of quarks, antiquarks, charmed quarks, neoquarks and quarklets.

Some wag had set a sign on the visitors' reception desk in the administration center reading: "Charmed to meet you." "It's a joke, right?" said Amanda tentatively.

"It probably won't get any funnier," I said.

Delaney, who seemed to load every word with deadly earnestness, didn't laugh at all. "Some of the technicians think it's funny. I don't."

We rehashed the coming treatment endlessly. Optimistically I took notes for the book: *The primary problem with a radiological approach to the treatment of cancer is that hard radiation not only kills the cancerous cells, it also irradiates the surrounding healthy tissue. But in the mid-nineteen seventies, cancer researchers found a more promising tool: shaped beams of subatomic particles which can be selectively focused on the tissue of tumors.*

Delaney had perhaps two decades on Amanda; being younger seemed to give her a perverse satisfaction in playing the pedagogue. "Split atomic nuclei on a small scale—"

"Small?" said Amanda innocently.

"—smaller than a fission bomb. Much of the binding force of the nucleus is miraculously transmuted to matter."

"Miraculously?" said Amanda. I looked up at her from the easy cushion shot I was trying to line up on the green velvet. The three of us were playing rotation in the billiards annex of the NMMPF recreation lounge.

"Uh," said Delaney, the rhythm of her lecture broken. "Physics shorthand."

"Reality shorthand," I said, not looking up from the cue now. "Miracles are as exact a quality as charm."

Amanda chuckled. "That's all I wanted to know."

The miracle pertinent to my case was atomic glue, mesons, one of the fission-formed particles. More specifically, my miracle was the negatively charged pion, a subclass of meson. Electromagnetic fields could focus pions into a controllable beam and fire it into a particular target—me.

"There are no miracles in physics," said Delaney seriously. "I used the wrong term."

I missed my shot. A gentle stroke, and gently the cue ball rolled into the corner pocket, missing the eleven. I'd set things up nicely, if accidentally, for Amanda.

She assayed the table and smiled. "Don't come unglued."

"That's very good," I said. Atomic glue does become unstuck, thanks to pions' unique quality. When they collide and are captured by the nucleus of another atom, they reconvert to pure energy; a tiny nuclear explosion.

Amanda missed her shot too. The corners of Delaney's mouth curled in a small gesture of satisfaction. She leaned across the table, hands utterly steady. "Multiply pions, multiply target nuclei, and you have a controlled aggregate explosion releasing considerably more energy than the entering pion beam. *Hah!*"

She sank the eleven and twelve: then ran the table. Amanda and I exchanged glances. "Rack 'em up," said Delaney.

"Your turn," Amanda said to me.

In my case the NMMPF medical channel would fire a directed pion beam into my recalcitrant prostate. If all went as planned, the pions intercepting the atomic nuclei of my cancer cells would convert back into energy in a series of atomic flares. The cancer cells being more sensitive, tissue damage should be restricted, localized in my carcinogenic nodule.

Thinking of myself as a nuclear battlefield in miniature was wondrous. Thinking of myself as a new Stage Field or an Oak Ridge was ridiculous.

Delaney turned out to be a pool shark *par excellence*. Winning was all-important and she won every time. I decided to interpret that as a positive omen.

"It's time," Amanda said.

"You needn't sound as though you're leading a condemned man to the electric chair." I tied the white medical smock securely about me, pulled on the slippers.

"I'm sorry. Are you worried?"

"Not so long as Delaney counts me as part of the effort toward a Nobel Prize."

"She's good." Her voice rang too hollow in the sterile tiled room. We walked together into the corridor.

"Me. I'm bucking for a Kalinga Prize," I said.

Amanda shook her head. Cloudy hair played about her face. "I'll just settle for a positive prognosis for my patient." Beyond the door, Delaney and two technicians with a gurney waited for me.

There is a state beyond indignity that defines being draped naked on my belly over a bench arrangement, with my rear spread and facing the medical channel. Rigidly clamped, a ceramic target tube opened a separate channel through my anus to the prostate. Monitoring equipment and shielding shut me in. I felt hot and vastly uncomfortable. Amanda had shot me full of chemicals, not all of whose names I'd recognized. Now dazed, I couldn't decide which of many discomforts was the most irritating.

"Good luck," Amanda had said. "It'll be over before you know it." I'd felt a gentle pat on my flank.

I thought I heard the phasing-up whine of electrical equipment. I could tell my mind was closing down for the duration: I couldn't even remember how many billion electron-volts were about to route a pion beam up my backside. I heard sounds I couldn't iden-tify; perhaps an enormous metal door grinding shut.

My brain swam free in a chemical river; I waited for something to happen.

I thought I heard machined ball bearings rattling down a chute; no, particles screaming past the giant bending magnets into the medical channel at 300,000 kilometers per second; flashing toward me through the series of adjustable filters; slowing, slowing, losing energy as they approach; then through the final tube and into my body. Inside . . .

The pion sails the inner atomic seas for a relativistically finite time. Then the perspective inhabited by one is inhabited by two. The pion drives toward the target nucleus. At a certain point the pion is no longer a pion; what was temporarily matter transmutes back to energy. The energy flares, expands, expends and fades. Other explosions detonate in the spaces within the patterns un-derlying larger patterns.

Darkness and light interchange.

The light coalesces into a ball; massive, hot, burning against the darkness. Pierced, somehow stricken, the ball begins to collapse in upon itself. Its internal temperature climbs to a critical level. At 600 million degrees, carbon muclei fuse. Heavier elements form. When the fuel is exhausted, the ball collapses further; again the temperature is driven upward; again heavier elements form and are in turn consumed. The cycle repeats until the nuclear furnace

*manufactures iron. No further nuclear reaction can be triggered;
the heart's fire is extinguished. Without the outward balance of fusion reaction, the ball initiates the ultimate collapse. Heat reaches
100 billion degrees. Every conceivable nuclear reaction is consum-
mated.*

*The ball explodes in a final convulsive cataclysm. Its energy
flares, fades, is eaten by entropy. The time it took is no more than
the time it takes Sollight to reach and illuminate the Earth.*

"How do you feel?" Amanda leaned into my field of vision,
eclipsing the fluorescent rings overhead.

"Feel?" I seemed to be talking through a mouthful of cotton
candy.

"Feel."

"Compared to what?" I said.

She smiled. "You're doing fine."

"I had one foot on the accelerator," I said.

She looked puzzled, then started to laugh. "It'll wear off soon."
She completes her transit and the lights shone back in my face.

"No hand on the brake," I mumbled. I began to giggle. Something pricked my arm.

I think Delaney wanted to keep me under observation in New
Mexico until the anticipated ceremonies in Stockholm. I didn't
have time for that. I suspected none of us did. Amanda began to
worry about my moody silences; she ascribed them at first to my
medication and then to the two weeks' tests Delaney and her col-
leagues were inflicting on me.

"To hell with this," I said. "We've got to get out of here."
Amanda and I were alone in my room.

"What?"

"Give me a prognosis."

She smiled. "I think you may as well shoot for the Kalinga."

"Maybe." I quickly added, "I'm not a patient any more; I'm an
experimental subject."

"So? What do we do about it?"

We exited NMMPF under cover of darkness and struggled a
half kilometer through brush to the highway. There we hitched a
ride into town.

"This is crazy," said Amanda, picking thistle out of her sweater.

"It avoids a strong argument," I said as we neared the lights of Los Alamos.

The last bus of the day had left. I wanted to wait until morning. Over my protests, we flew out on Ross Airlines. "Doctor's orders," said Amanda, teeth tightly together, as the Twin Otter bumped onto the runway.

I dream of pions. I dream of colored balloons filled with hydrogen, igniting and flaming up in the night. I dream of Lisa's newsprint face. Her smile is both proud and sorrowful.

Amanda had her backlog of patients and enough to worry about, so I took my nightmares to Jackie Denton at the observatory. I told her of my hallucinations in the accelerator chamber. We stared at each other across the small office.

"I'm glad you're better, Nick, but—"

"That's not it," I said. "Remember how you hated my article about poetry glorifying the new technology? Too fanciful?" I launched into speculation, mixing with abandon pion beams, doctors, supernovas, irrational statistics, carcinogenic nodes, fire balloons and gods.

"Gods?" she said. "*Gods? Are* you going to put that in your next column?"

I nodded.

She looked as though she were inspecting a newly foundout psychopath. "No one needs that in the press now, Nick. The whole planet's upset already. The possibility of nova radiation damaging the ozone layer, the potential for genetic damage, all that's got people spooked."

"It's only speculation."

She said, "You don't yell 'fire' in a crowded theater."

"Or in a crowded world?"

Her voice was unamused. "Not now."

"And if I'm right?" I felt weary. "What about it?"

"A supernova? No way. Sol simply doesn't have the mass."

"But a nova?" I said.

"Possibly," she said tightly. "But it shouldn't happen for a few billion years. Stellar evolution—"

"—is theory," I said. *"Shouldn't* isn't *won't.* Tonight look again at that awesome sky."

Denton said nothing.

"Could you accept a solar flare? A big one?"

I read the revulsion in her face and knew I should stop talking; but I didn't. "Do you believe in God? Any god?" She shook her head. I had to get it all out. "How about concentric universes, one within the next like Chinese carved ivory spheres?" Her face went white. "Pick a card," I said, "any card. A wild card."

"God damn you, shut up." On the edge of the desk, her knuckles were as white as her lips.

"Charming," I said, ignoring the incantatory power of words, forgetting what belief could cost. I do not think she deliberately drove her Lotus off the Peak road. I don't want to believe that. Surely she was coming to join me.

Maybe, she'd said.

Nightmares should be kept home. So here I stand on my sundeck at high noon for the Earth. No need to worry about destruction of the ozone layer and the consequent skin cancer. There will be no problem with mutational effects and genetic damage. I need not worry about deadlines or contractual commitments. I regret that no one will ever read my book about pion therapy.

All that—maybe.

The sun shines bright—The tune plays dirgelike in my head.

Perhaps I am wrong. The flare may subside. Maybe I am not dying. No matter.

I wish Amanda were with me now, or that I were at Jackie Denton's bedside, or even that I had time to walk to Lisa's grave among the pines. Now there is no time.

At least I've lived as long as I have now by choice.

That's the secret, Nick . . .

The glare illuminates the universe.

THE TASTE OF
THE DISH
AND THE SAVOR
OF THE DAY

by John Brunner

*A science fiction story about a gourmet cook?
And with the ring of the authentic connoisseur of
the palate about it? Who else but John Brunner
could bring it off . . . one of the very few sf au-
thors with the proper qualifications for it. He wrote
that he had a lot of fun writing it, and the élan of
the telling enhances the flavor very well!*

The Baron's circumstances had altered since our only previous
encounter a year ago. This I was prepared for. His conversation at
that time had made it abundantly clear that he had, as the charm-
ingly archaic phrase goes, "expectations."

I was by no means sure they would materialize. . . . Still, even
though I half suspected him of being a confidence trickster, that
hadn't stopped me from taking a considerable liking to him. After

all, being a novelist makes me a professional liar myself, in a certain sense.

So, finding myself obliged to visit my publishers in Paris, I dropped a note to what turned out to be an address the Baron had left. He answered anyway, in somewhat flowery fashion, saying how extremely pleased he would be were I to dine with him *tête-à-tête* at home—home being an apartment in an expensive block only a few minutes from what Parisians still impenitently call *l'Etoile*. I was as much delighted as surprised; for him to have moved to such a location implied that there had indeed been substance in his former claims.

Yet from the moment of my arrival I was haunted by a sense of incongruity.

I was admitted by a manservant who ushered me into a *salon*, cleanly but plainly decorated, and furnished in a style neither fashionable nor *démodé*, but nonetheless entirely out of keeping, consisting mainly of the sort of chairs you see at a pavement cafe, with a couple of tables to match and a pair of cane-and-wicker armchairs. The impression was of a collection put together in the thirties by a newly married couple down on their luck, who had hoped to replace everything by stages and found they couldn't afford to after having children.

I was still surveying the room when the Baron himself entered, and his appearance added to my feeling of unease. He greeted me with a restrained version of his old effusiveness; he settled me solicitously in one of the armchairs—it creaked abominably!—and turned to pour me an *aperitif*. I took the chance of observing him in detail. And noticed. . . .

For example, that although it was clean and crisply pressed and was of excellent quality, the suit he had on this evening was one I remembered from a year ago—then trespassing on, now drifting over, the verge of shabbiness. His shoes were to match: brilliantly polished, yet discernibly wrinkled. In general, indeed, so far as his appearance was concerned, whatever he could attend to for himself—as his manicure, his shave, the set of his tie knot—was without a flaw. But his haircut, it immediately struck me, was scarcely the masterpiece of France's finest barber.

Nor was his manner of a piece with what I would have predicted. I recalled him as voluble, concerned to create a memorable impact; in place of that warmth which, affected or not, had made him an agreeable companion, there was a stiltedness, a sense of going through formally prescribed routines.

He gave the impression of being . . . how shall I define it? Out of focus!

Furthermore, the *aperitif* he handed me was unworthy of his old aspirations: nothing but a commonplace vermouth with a chip of a tired lemon dropped into it as by afterthought. For himself he took only a little Vichy water.

Astonished that someone who, whatever his other attributes, was indisputably a *gourmet,* should thus deny himself, I was about to inquire why he was so abstemious. Then it occurred to me that he must have had bad news from his doctor. Or, on reflection (which took half a second), might wish me to believe so. I was much more prepared now than I had been a year ago to accept that he was a genuine hereditary baron. However, even if one is a scion of a family that lost its worldly goods apart from a miserly pittance in the Events of 1789, one can still be a con man. There is no incompatibility between those roles any more than there is between being an author and being a sucker. So I forbore to comment and was unable to decide whether or not a shadow of disappointment crossed his face.

By the time when I declined a second helping of that indifferent vermouth, I might well have been in the mood to regret my decision to recontact the Baron and have decided to limit my visit to the minimum consistent with politeness, but for an aroma which had gradually begun to permeate the air a few minutes after I sat down. It was inexpressibly delectable and savory, setting my taste buds to tingle *a l'avance.* Perhaps everything was going to be for the best after all. A dinner which broadcast such olfactory harbingers was bound to be worthwhile!

Except that when we actually went to table, it wasn't.

At my own place I found a sort of symbolic gesture in the direction of an *hors d'oeuvre:* a limp leaf of lettuce, a lump of cucumber, a soft tomato, and some grated carrot that had seen better days before it met the *mandoline,* over which a bit of salt and oil had been sprinkled. To accompany this mini-feast I was given a dose of dry white *ordinaire* from a bottle without a label. Before the Baron, though, the servant set no food, only pouring for him more Vichy water which he sipped at in a distracted manner while his eyes followed my glass on its way to my lips and the discovery that such a wine would have shamed a *restaurant des routiers sans panneau*. His face was pitiable. He looked envious!

Of rabbit food and immature vinegar?

I was so confused, I could not comment. I made what inroads I could on the plate before me, trying to preserve at least a polite expression on my own face. And thinking about the servant. Had I not seen the fellow elsewhere?

As he answered the door to me, I'd scarcely glanced at him. Now, when he came to check whether I'd finished with my first course—I yielded it with relief—I was able to take a longer, though still covert, look. And concluded: yes, I had seen him.

Moreover I recalled when and where. During my last trip to France, in Guex-sur-Saône where they had held that year's French National Science Fiction Congress—and incidentally where I had met the Baron—and, what is more, he had been in the same car as the Baron.

But a year ago he could not possibly have afforded a manservant! He had not even been able to afford his bill at the Restaurant du Tertre to which he had recommended, and accompanied, me and my wife and the friends we were with; he still owed me an embarrassing trifle of seven francs eighty which I was not proposing to mention again if he did not, because the meal had been an incredibly good value.

The incongruities here began at last to form a pattern in my mind. Had he received the benefit of his "expectations" and then let silly pride tempt him into an extravagance he now regretted? Was it because, thinking a servant appropriate to his new station in life, he had hired one, that he still wore the same suit and couldn't afford to have his hair properly barbered? Was it economy rather than health that drove him to refrain from even such poor refreshment as a guest was offered in this apartment which, though in a smart *quartier,* either was furnished out of a flea market or hadn't been refurnished since what one buys at flea markets was last in style?

Hmm . . . !

The interior of the head of a professional writer is a little like a mirror-maze and a little like a haunted house. From the most trivial impetus, the mind inside can find countless unpredictable directions in which to jump. While I was waiting for the main course to be brought in, mine took off towards the past and reviewed key details of our meeting in Guex.

Of all the science fiction events I have attended—and in the course of twenty-five years there have been not a few—that one was the most chaotic it has been my misfortune to participate in. The organizers chose a date already preempted by a reunion of *anciens combattants de la Resistance,* so that all the hotels in the center of town were full and we had been farmed out to somewhere miles away. It was, I suppose, entirely in keeping with the rest of the arrangements that on the last evening of the congress we should find ourselves, and the only other English people present—the guest of honor, his wife, and their baby—abandoned in front of the cinema where the congress was being held because the committee and anyone else who was *au fait* had piled into cars and gone into the country for dinner. So many people had turned up for the reunion of the Resistance, there wasn't a restaurant in walking distance with a vacant table.

Hungry and stranded, we made the acquaintance of the Baron: a youngish man—I'd have said thirty-two and prematurely world-weary—lean, with a certain old-fashioned elegance, and out of place. I'd exchanged a word or two with him earlier in the day, when he'd chanced on me standing about, as usual, waiting for one of the organizers to put in an appearance so I could find out what was happening, and asked me whether a member of the public might attend the movie then showing, since he had a few hours to kill. Seemingly he had enjoyed the picture, for he had stayed over or come back for another.

Emerging now, drawing on unseasonable gloves with an air of distraction as though he were vaguely put out by the absence of a coachman to convey him to his next destination, he spotted and remembered me and approached with a flourish of his hat to thank me for the trivial service I'd performed.

My answer was doubtless a curt one. Sensing something amiss, he inquired whether he might in turn be of assistance. We exclaimed . . . choosing, of course, terms less than libelous, though we were inclined to use strong language.

Ah! Well, if we would accept a suggestion from someone who was almost as much a stranger as ourselves . . . ? (We would.) And did we have transportation? (We did, although my car was at the hotel twenty minutes' walk away.) In that case, we might be interested to know that he had been informed of a certain restaurant, not widely advertised, in a village a few kilometers distant, and had wondered whether during his brief stay in Guex he might sample its cuisine. He had precise directions for finding it. It was reputed to offer outstanding value. Were we . . . ?

We were. And somehow managed to cram into my car and not die of suffocation on the way; it's theoretically designed for four, but no more than three can be comfortable. Still, we got there.

The evening proved to be an education—on two distinct levels.

I found myself instantly compelled to admire the deftness with which our chance acquaintance inserted data about himself into a discussion about an entirely different subject. Even before I came back with the car, the others had learned about his aristocratic background; I noticed he was already being addressed as *Monsieur le Baron*. His technique was superb! Always on the *qui vive* for new tricks that might enable me to condense the detail a reader needs to know into a form which doesn't slow down the story, I paid fascinated attention. Almost without our noticing that he was monopolizing the conversation, we were told about his lineage, his ancestors' sufferings at the rude hands of the mob, the death of the elderly aunt for whose funeral he had come to Guex, a lady of remarkable age whose existence he had been ignorant of until a lawyer wrote and advised him he might benefit under her will. . . . (The French are far less coy about discussing bequests than are we Anglophones.)

But on the other and much more impressive hand, within—I swear? five minutes of our being seated in the restaurant, the word had got around behind the scenes that someone of *grand standing* was present tonight. In turn the waiter—it was too small a restaurant to boast a headwaiter—and the *sommelier* and the *chef* and finally the proprietor put in their successive appearances at our table as *M. le Baron* proceeded with the composition of our meal. He laid down that there should not be an excess of fennel with the trout, and that the Vouvray should be cellar-cool and served in chilled glasses but on no account iced, which would incarcerate its "nose" and prevent it from competing with the fennel (he was right); that with the subsequent *escalope de veau Marengo* one should not drink the Sancerre, of which the *patron* was so proud, but a Sain-Pourcain only two years old (he was right about that too), just so long as the *saucier* did not add more than a splash—what he actually said was *une goutte goutteuse,* a phrase that stuck in my mind because it literally means "a drop with the gout"—of wine-vinegar to the salad dressing. And so on.

I was not the only one to be impressed. When we had finished our dessert, the owner sent us a complimentary glass apiece of a local liqueur scented with violets, wild strawberries, and something called *reine de bois,* which I later discovered to be woodruff. It was so delicious, we asked where else it could be got, and were told regretfully that it was not generally available, being compounded to a secret recipe dating back two centuries or more. Well, one meets that kind of thing quite frequently in France. . . .

Let me draw a veil over the arrival of the bill, except to mention that after my eyes and the Baron's had met and I'd summed up the situation, I let an extra fifty-franc note rest for a moment on the table. The dexterity with which it became forty-two francs twenty reminded me of the skill of a cardsharp. I don't think even the waiter noticed.

Well, he was after all in Guex on the sort of business that doesn't conduce to commonsensical precautions; attending a funeral, I wouldn't think to line my billfold with a wad of spare cash against the chance of going out to dinner with a group of foreign strangers. I let the matter ride. The meal had been superb and worth far more than we were being charged.

Whether for that reason, though, or because he had found out he was in the company of two writers, or simply because the wines and the liqueur had made him garrulous, he appended to the information he had earlier imparted a few more precise details. His elderly aunt had possessed a *chateau* nearby (not a castle—the word corresponds quite exactly to the English term "manor house" and needs not necessarily have turrets and a moat), and although the lawyers were still wrangling, it did seem he must be the closest of her surviving relatives. So he might just, with luck, look forward to inheriting a country seat in keeping with his patent—patent of nobility, that is, a term I'd previously run across only in history books.

By then we were all very mellow, and so we toasted his chances in another round of the exquisite liqueur. After which we drove back to Guex.

Carefully.

Arriving at his hotel, we said good-by in a flurry of alcoholic *bonhomie,* exchanging names and addresses though I don't think we honestly imagined we would meet again, for tomorrow was the last day of the congress, and the Baron had said that directly after the funeral—scheduled for the morning—he was obliged to return to Paris.

But we did in fact cross paths next day. As we were emerging from the cinema after the closing ceremony of the congress, a large black limousine passed, which unmistakably belonged to a firm of undertakers. It stopped and backed up, and from its window the Baron called a greeting. With him were three other passengers, all men.

And although I'd only seen him for as long as it took me and my wife to shake hands with the Baron and confirm our intention of getting in touch again one day, I was certain that one of them was the same who now was bringing in a cart from the kitchen, on which reposed a dish whose lid when lifted freed into the air the concentrated version of the odor I had already detected in diluted form.

I was instantly detached from the here and now. I had to close my eyes. Never have my nostrils been assailed by so delectable a scent! My mouth watered until I might have drowned in saliva but that all my glands—the very cells of my body!—wanted to experience the aroma and declined to be insulated against it.

When I recovered, more at a loss than ever, I found that something brown and nondescript-looking had been dumped on my plate, which was chipped; that a half-full glass of red wine as sour as the white had been set alongside, while the Baron's water glass had been topped up: and that he was eating busily.

Busily?

This was not the person I had met last year. That version of the Baron not only cared about but loved his food—paid deliberate and sensitive attention to every mouthful of any dish that warranted it. Now he was shoveling the stuff up, apparently determined to clear his plate in record time. And that was absurd. For, as I discovered when I sampled my unprepossessing dollop of what's-it, its flavor matched its aroma. I had taken only a small forkful; nonetheless, as I rolled it across my tongue, choirs sang and flowers burst into bloom and new stars shone in the heavens. I simply did not believe what I was eating.

In the upshot I was reluctant even to swallow that first morsel. I had never dreamed it was possible to create in the modern world a counterpart of ambrosia, the food of the gods. I was afraid to let it slide down my throat for fear the second taste might fall short of the first.

When I did finally get it down in a sort of belated convulsion, I found that the Baron had cleared his plate and was regarding me with a strange expression.

"Ah, you must be enjoying it," he said.

Even as I sought words to express my delight, I could feel a tingling warmth moving down me—down not so much in the gravitational as the evolutionary sense, to lower and lower levels of being, so that instead of just registering on palate and tastebuds and olfactory nerves this stuff, this stew, seemed to be transfusing energy directly into my entire system.

But I did not say so. For I could suddenly read on my host's face what I could also hear unmistakably in his tone of voice: such hopelessness as Mephistopheles might know, something which would be to despair as starvation is to appetite. He spoke as a man who, after long and bitter experience, now knew he would never again enjoy anything.

The tissues of my body were crying out for that miraculous incredible food. I fought and thought for half eternity except that in retrospect I judge it to have been seconds.

And pushed away my plate.

I doubt I shall match that act of will until my dying day. But it was my turn to rise to the occasion, as he had done for stranded foreigners at Guex, and trust to being helped over the consequences.

He stared at me. "Is it possible," he inquired, "that in fact you do not like it?"

"*Mais si!*" I cried. "I do! But. . . ." It came to me without warning what I ought to say. "But it's the only food I've tasted in my life which is so delicious that it frightens me."

In one of his books William Burroughs hypothesizes a drug to which a person would become addicted after a single dose. I had perhaps had that remark vaguely at the back of my mind. Without having read it, possibly I might not have—Ah, but I had, and I did.

There was a frozen pause. Then a smile spread over the Baron's face so revolutionizing in its effect that it was like the spring thaw overtaking an arctic landscape.

"I knew I was right," he said. "I knew! If anyone could understand, it must be an artist of some kind—an author, a poet. . . . We shall withdraw so that you may smoke a cigar, and I shall instruct Gregoire to bring something to make good the deficiencies of this repast."

He clapped his hands. The servant entered promptly, and stopped dead on seeing my plate practically as full as when he had handed it to me.

"Your dish does not meet with the approval of my guest," the Baron said. "Remove it. Bring fruit and nuts to the *salon*."

Pushing back my chair, anxious to leave the room, I found the fellow glaring at me. And took stock of him properly for the first time. I cannot say he was ill-favored; he was of a type one might pass by the thousand on the streets of any city in France. But, as though he had been insulted to his very marrow by my unwillingness to eat what he had prepared, he was regarding me with indescribable malevolence. For a heartbeat or two I could have believed in the Evil Eye.

How had the Baron, a person of taste, hit on this clown for his "gentleman's gentleman"? Was this some hanger-on of his aunt's, tied to him as a condition of her will?

Well, doubtless I should be enlightened soon enough. The time for speculation was over.

As soon as he had recalled Gregoire to his duties, which were sullenly undertaken, the Baron escorted me into the *salon* and from a corner cupboard produced a bottle I thought I recognized. Noticing that I was staring at it, he turned it so that I could read the label. Yes, indeed; it did say *Le Digestif du Tertre*. When he drew the cork and poured me some, I acknowledged the aroma of violets and strawberries and woodruff like an old friend.

The bottle was full; in fact I doubt it had been previously opened. Yet the Baron poured none for himself. Now I could brace myself to ask why.

He answered with the greatest possible obliquity.

"Because," he said, "Gregoire is more than two hundred years old."

I must have looked like a figure in a cartoon film. I had a cigar in one hand and a burning match in the other, and my mouth fell ajar in disbelief and stayed that way until the flame scorched me back to life. Cursing, I disposed of the charred stick and licked my finger.

And was at long last able to say, *"What?"*

"To be precise," the Baron amplified, "he was born in the year the American Revolution broke out, and by the time the French Revolution was launched in imitation of it he was already a turnspit and apprentice *saucier* in the kitchens of my late aunt's *chateau* near Guex . . . which did turn out to devolve on me as her closest surviving relative, but which unfortunately was not accompanied by funds which would have permitted the repair of its neglected fabric. A shame! I found it necessary to realize its value in ready money, and the sum was dismayingly small after the *sacre* lawyer took his share. I said, by the way, my aunt. This is something of a misnomer. According to inconvertible proofs shown to me by Gregoire, she was my great-aunt at least eleven times over."

I had just had time to visualize a sort of slantwise genealogical tree in which aunts and uncles turned out to be much younger than any of their nephews and nieces, when he corrected himself.

"By that I mean she was my eleven-times-great aunt. Sister of an ancestor on my father's mother's side who was abridged by the guillotine during the Terror, for no fouler crime than having managed his estates better than most of his neighbors and occasionally saved a bit of cash in consequence."

Having made those dogmatic statements, he fixed me with an unwavering gaze and awaited my response.

Was I in two minds? No, I was in half a dozen. Out of all the assumptions facing me, the simplest was that the Baron—whom I'd suspected of setting me up for a confidence trick—had himself been brilliantly conned.

Only. . . .

By whom? By Gregoire? But in that case he would have carried on with the act when I refused to finish my meal, not scowled as though he wished me to drop dead.

And in addition there was the matter of the food itself. I was having to struggle, even after one brief taste, against the urge to run back and take more, especially since its seductive aroma still permeated the air.

My uncertainty showed on my face. The Baron said, "I can tell that you are not convinced. But I will not weary you by detailing the evidence which had persuaded me. I will not even ask you to credit the argument I put forward—I shall be content if you treat it as one of your fantastic fictions and merely judge whether the plot can be resolved on a happy ending . . . for I swear *I* can't see such an outcome. But already you have proof, do you not? Consult the cells of your body. Are they not reproaching you for eating so little of what was offered?"

Gregoire entered, favoring me with another savage glare, deposited a bowl containing a couple of oranges and some walnuts more or less within reach of me, and went out again. This gave me a chance to bring my chaotic mind under control.

As the door shut, I managed to say, "Who—who invented it?"

The Baron almost crowed with relief, but the sweat pearling on his face indicated how afraid he had been that I would mock him.

"Gregoire's father did," he answered. "A failed alchemist who was driven to accept a post in the kitchens of my family home and there continued his experiments while becoming a renowned *chef*.

From Gregoire, though he is a person exceedingly difficult to talk to, I have the impression that his employers believed him to be compounding the Philosophers' Stone and hoped, I imagine, that one day they might find themselves eating off plates of gold that yesterday were pewter . . . But he was in fact obsessed with the Elixir of Life, which, I confess, has always struck me as being by far the most possible of the alchemical goals. Doubtless the succession of delectable dishes which issued from his kitchen and were in part answerable for the decline in my ancestors' fortunes, for such was their fame that the king himself, and many of his relatives and courtiers, used to invite themselves for long stays at our *chateau,* despite the cramped accommodation it had to offer. . . . I digress; forgive me.

"As I was about to say, those marvelous dishes were each a step along the path towards his supreme achievement. Ironically, for himself it was too late. Earlier he had been misled into believing that mercury was a sovereign cure for old age, and his frame was so ravaged by ill-judged experiments with it that when he did finally hit on the ideal combination he could only witness its effects on his son, not benefit in person.

"He left his collection of recipes to his son, having previously taught the boy to cook the perfected version by means of such repeated beatings that the child could, and I suspect sometimes did, mix the stuff while half asleep.

"But, possibly because of the mercury poisoning which had made him 'mad as a hatter,' to cite that very apt English phrase, Gregoire *père* overlooked a key point. He omitted to teach the boy how to read and write.

"Finding that his sole bequest from his father was a satchel full of papers, he consulted the only member of the family who had been kind to him: a spinster lady, sister of the then Baron. She did know how to read."

"This is supposed to be the lady you buried just under a year ago?" I demanded.

He gave me a cool look of reproach. "Permit me to lay all before you and reserve your comments . . . ?"

I sighed and nodded and leaned back in my uncomfortable, noisy chair.

"But you are, as it happens, correct," he admitted when he had retrieved the thread of his narrative.

"I cannot show you the satchel I alluded to. Gregoire is keenly aware of its value, though I often suspect he is aware of little else outside his daily cycle from one meal to another. Only because it must have dawned on his loutish brain that he would have to make some adjustments following the death of my—my *aunt,* did he force himself to part with it long enough for me and her lawyer to examine the contents.

"We found inside nearly eighty sheets of paper and five of parchment, all in the same crabbed hand, with what I later established to be a great use of alchemical jargon and an improbably archaic turn of phrase—seventeenth rather than eighteenth century, say the experts I've consulted. How did I get the documents into the hands of experts?

"Well, the lawyer—who is a fool—showed little or no interest in them. He disliked my aunt as you would expect a bigoted peasant to do, inasmuch as since time immemorial it had been known in the district that she lived alone except for a male companion and never put in an appearance at church. Moreover he was furious at having found that in the estate there was only a fraction of the profit he had looked forward to.

"However, he does possess a photocopier and before Gregoire's terror overcame him to the point of insisting on being given back all his precious papers, I had contrived to feed six or seven of them through the machine. If you're equipped to judge them, I can show them to you. I warn you, though: the language is impenetrably ancient and technical. Have you wondered why my inheritance has not improved my *facon de vivre?* It is upon the attempt to resolve the dilemma posed by Gregoire's patrimony that I've expended what meager income my portion yields. New clothes, new furniture—such trivia can wait, for if what I believe to be true is true I shall later on have all the time imaginable to make good these transient deficiencies!"

He spoke in the unmistakable tone of someone trying to reassure himself. As much to provide a distraction which would help me not to think about that strange food as for my less selfish reason, I said, "How did Gregoire get his claws into you?"

He laid his finger across his lips with reflex speed. "Do not say such things! Gregoire is the sole repository of a secret which, had it been noised abroad, would have been the downfall of empires!"

Which told me one thing I wanted to know: among the half-dozen papers the Baron had contrived to copy there was *not* the recipe of the dish served to us tonight.

"But your aunt is dead," I countered.

"After more than two hundred years! And I'm convinced she expired thanks to industrial pollution—poisonous organic compounds, heavy metals, disgusting effluents ruining what would otherwise be wholesome foodstuffs. . . ."

But his voice tailed away. While he was speaking I had reached for the nuts, cracked one against another in my palm, and was sampling the flesh. There was nothing memorable about this particular nut, but it was perfectly good, and I found I could savor it. Moreover I could enjoy the rich smoke of my cigar. I made it obvious I was doing so—cruelly, perhaps, from the Baron's point of view, for his eyes hung on my every movement and he kept biting his lower lip. Something, though, made me feel that my behavior was therapeutic for him. I rubbed salt on the wound by topping up my glass of liqueur without asking permission.

"And in what manner," I inquired, "did your aunt spend her two centuries of existence? Waiting out a daily cycle from one meal to the next, always of the same food, as you've said Gregoire docs?"

The Baron slumped.

"I suppose so," he admitted. "At first, with that delirious sensation on one's palate, one thinks, 'Ah, this is the supreme food, which will never cloy!' After the hundredth day, after the two hundredth . . . Well, you have seen.

"You asked me how Gregoire snared me. It was simple—simple enough for his dull wits to work out a method! How could I decline to share a conveyance, *en route* to and from the funeral, with my late aunt's sole loyal retainer? How could I decline to agree when, in the hearing of her lawyer and his *hussier,* he offered to cook me her favorite meal if I would provide him with the cost of the ingredients? The sum was—well, let me say substantial. Luckily the lawyer, upon whom may there be defecation, was willing to part with a few *sous* as an advance against my inheritance.

"And what he gave me was the dish you sampled tonight. With neither garnishing nor salad nor. . . . Nothing! He has never learned to cook anything else, for his father's orders were explicit: eat this alone, and drink spring water. But he caught me at my most vulnerable moment. Overwhelmed by the subtlety of the dish, its richness, its fragrance, its ability to arouse appetite even in a person who, like myself at that time, is given over to the most melancholy reflections, I was netted like a pigeon."

In horrified disbelief I said, "For almost a year you have eaten this same dish over and over, without even a choice of wines to set it off? Without dessert? Without *anything?*"

"But it does work!" he cried. "The longevity of my aunt is evidence! Even though during the Nazi occupation it was hard to find certain important spices, she—Wait! Perhaps it wasn't modern pollution that hastened her end. Perhaps it was lack of those special ingredients while the *sales Boches* were overrunning our beloved country. Perhaps Gregoire kept them back for himself, cheated the helpless old lady who had been the only one to help him when he was orphaned!"

"And kept her elixir to herself, content to watch her brother die, and his wife, and their children and the rest of the family, in the hope of inheriting the lot, which she eventually did. And she then spent her fortune on the food because only Gregoire would tell her how much it was going to cost to buy the necessary ingredients."

The Baron gaped at me. "You talk as if this is all common knowledge," he whispered. I made a dismissive gesture.

"If the recipe works, what other reason can there be for the fact that the rest of her generation aren't still among us?"

"Under the Directory—" he parried.

"If they'd known they had a chance of immortality, it would have made sense for them to realize their assets and bribe their way to safety. You said just now that you will have unimaginable time before you if what you think is actually true. Why didn't the same thought occur to your forebears? Because this old bitch kept the news from them—correct?"

The corners of his mouth turned down. "Truly, life can do no more than imitate art. I invited you to treat this like a plot for a story, and thus far I cannot fault your logic."

"Despite which you plan to imitate someone who shamed not only your family name but indeed her nation and her species?" I crushed my cigar into the nearest ashtray and gulped the rest of my liqueur. "I am appalled! I am revolted! The gastronomic masters of the ages have performed something approaching a miracle. They've transformed what to savages is mere refueling into a series of splendid compositions akin to works of art, akin to symphonies, to landscapes, to statues! To leaf through a book like *Larousse Gastronomique* is to find the civilized counterpart of Homer and Vergil—a paean to the heroes who instead of curtailing life amplified it!"

"I think the same—" he began. I cut him short.

"You used to think so, of which I'm well aware. Now you cannot! Now, by your own decision, you've been reduced to the plight of a prisoner who has to coax and wheedle his jailer before he gets even his daily ration of slop. If a single year has done this to you, what will ten years do, or fifty, or a hundred? What use are you going to make of your oversize life-span? Do you have plans to reform the world? How appropriate will they be when for decades your mind has been clouded by one solitary obsession?"

I saw he was wavering, and I rammed home my advantage.

"And think what you'll be giving up—what you have given up already, on the say-so of a half-moronic turnspit so dullwitted his father couldn't teach him to read! This liqueur, for a start!" I helped myself to more again and in exaggerated pantomime relished another swig. "Oh, how it brings back that delectable *truite flambée au fenouil* which preceded it, and the marvelous veal, and that salad which on your instructions was dressed as lightly as dewfall. . . ."

I am not what they call in French *croyant*. But if there are such things as souls and hells, I think maybe that night I saved one of the former from the latter.

Given my lead, lent reassurance by the way I could see envy gathering in the Baron's face, I waxed lyrical about—making a random choice—oysters *Bercy* and *moules en brochette* and lobster *a*

l'armoricaine, invoking some proper wines to correspond. I en-
thused over quail and partridge and grouse, and from the air I con-
jured vegetables to serve with them, artichokes and cardoons and
salsify and other wonders that the soil affords. These I dressed
with sauces so delightfully seasoned I could have sworn their perfume was in the room. I did not, of course, forget that supreme
miracle, the truffle, nor did I neglect the crepe or the *faux mous-
seron* or the beefsteak mushroom, which is nothing like a steak but
gave me *entrée,* as it were, to the main course.

Whereupon I became ecstatic. Roasts and grills, and pies and
casseroles and pasties were succeeded by a roll call of those
cheeses which make walking through a French street market like
entering Aladdin's cave. Then I reviewed fruits of all sizes, shapes,
colors, flavors: plums and pomegranates, quinces and medlars,
pineapples and nectarines. Then I briefly touched on a few des-
serts, like *profiteroles* and *crêpes* and *tarte alsacienne.* . . .

I was poised to start all over again at the beginning if I must; I
had scarcely scraped the surface of even French *cuisine,* and beyond Europe lay China and the Indies and a whole wide world of
fabulous fare. But I forbore. I saw suddenly that one shiny drop
on the Baron's cheek was not perspiration after all. It was a tear.

Falling silent, I waited.

At length the Baron rose with the air of a man going to face the
firing squad. Stiffly, he selected a glass for himself from the tray
beside the liqueur bottle, poured himself a slug, and turned to face
me, making a half bow.

"Mon ami," he said with great formality. "I am forever in your
debt. Or at any rate, for the duration of my—my *natural* life."

I was afraid he was going to take the drink like medicine, or
poison. But instead he checked as he raised it to his lips, inhaled,
gave an approving nod, closed his eyes and let a little of it roll
around his tongue, smiling.

It was more like it!

He took a second and more generous swig and resumed his
chair.

"That is," he murmured, "a considerable relief. I can after all
now appreciate this. I had wondered whether my sense of taste
might prove to be negated—whether the food I have subsisted on

might entail addiction. . . . The latter possibility no doubt remains; however, when all else fails there is always the treatment called *le dindon froid."*

Or, as they say in English, cold turkey. . . . Whatever his other faults, I realized, one could not call the Baron a coward.

"Ach!" he went on. "In principle I knew all you have told me months ago. You are right in so many ways, I'm embarrassed by your perspicuity. Am I the person to reform the world? I, whom they have encouraged since childhood to believe that the world's primary function is to provide me with a living regardless of whether or not I have worked to earn it? Sometimes I've been amused to the point of laughing aloud by the silliness of my ambition. And yet—and yet. . . .

"Figurez-vous, mon vieux what it is like always to have a voice saying in your head, 'Suppose this time the dish that sustained your aunt two hundred years can be developed into the vehicle of true immortality?' There's no denying that it's a wonderful hybrid between *cuisine* and medicine."

That I was obliged to grant.

"So, you see, I'm stuck with an appalling moral dilemma," the Baron said. He emptied his glass and set it aside. "It occurs to me," he interpolated, "that I may just have incurred a second one —perhaps infringing Gregoire's father's injunction about eating nothing except his food constitutes a form of suicide? But luckily I feel better for it, so the riddle can be postponed. . . . Where was I? Oh, yes, my dilemma. If I break my compact with Gregoire, what's to become of him? If there is no employer to provide him with the funds he needs to buy his ingredients and the kitchen and the pans and stove to cook them, will he die? Or will he be driven like a junkie to robbery and possibly murder? *Mon brave, mon ami,* what the hell am I to do about Gregoire?"

It was as though my panegyric on gastronomy had drained my resources of both speech and enthusiasm. Perhaps more of the liqueur would restore them; I took some.

"By the way," the Baron said, copying me, "an amusing coincidence! While I was still in Guex-sur-Saône, I recalled. . . . Are you all right?"

"I—I think so. Yes," I said.

For a moment I'd been overcome by an irresolvable though fortunately transient problem. I was thinking over the discourse I'd improvised about cookery when it suddenly dawned on me that I'd praised to the skies things I'd never run across. I hadn't tasted half of what I'd talked about with such excitement, and as for the wines, why, only a millonaire could aspire to keep that lot in his cellar!

This *digestif du Tertre* must be powerful stuff on an empty belly!

Recovering, I said, "Please go on."

"I was about to say that after poring over the papers of Gregoire's that I'd managed to copy, I recalled what the *patron* of the Restaurant du Tertre had said about basing his *digestif* on an eighteenth-century recipe. Thinking that if he had such a recipe he might help me decipher some of those by Gregoire's father, I went back to the restaurant, ostensibly of course to buy a bottle of their speciality—I did in fact buy that very bottle yonder.

"And when, after chatting with the *patron* for a while, I produced the most apposite-seeming of the half-dozen recipes I'd acquired, he was appalled. After scarcely more than a glance, he declared that this was identical with the recipe used for his liqueur and was on the verge of trying to bribe me and prevent it coming to the notice of a commercial manufacturer!"

Chuckling, he helped himself to half a glassful.

"I mention that not so much as an example of how small-minded people in commerce tend to be—though is it not better that something outstanding should be shared if there is a means of creating enough of it, rather than kept for the private profit of a few? —No! I cite it as evidence that had he not been obsessed with his alchemical aspirations, Gregoire's father could have become a culinary pioneer to stand beside Carême and Brillat-Savarin, indeed take precedence of them! What a tragedy that his genius was diverted into other channels and that his son—Well!"

"And yet . . ." I said.

"And yet . . ." he echoed, with a heavy sigh.

And that was when I had the only brilliant inspiration of my life.

Or possibly, as I wondered later, credit ought to go to the *digestif*.

At all events, we dined the following night at the Tour d'Argent. And, apart from drinking rather too much so that he wished a hangover on himself, the Baron made an excellent recovery—which removed his last objection to my scheme.

I have one faint regret about the whole affair, and that is that nowadays I have rather less time for my writing. On the other hand, I no longer feel the intense financial pressure which so often compelled me to cobble together an unessential bit of made-work simply so that I could meet the bills that month. My routine outgoings are automatically taken care of by the admirable performance of my holdings in Eurobrita Health Food SA, a concern whose product we often patronize and can recommend.

What did we do about Gregoire?

Oh, that was inspiration. What the Baron had overlooked, you see, was the fact that, despite my having slandered him for effect, Gregoire was not absolutely stupid. He couldn't be. I confirmed that the moment I put my head around the door of the kitchen he was working in and found it fitted with an electric stove and separate glass fronted high-level oven, a far cry from the kitchens at the family *chateau* with their open fires of wood. A few minutes of questioning, and he opened up like a mussel in a hot pan, as though he had never before been asked about the one thing he really understood: cooking equipment. Which, given the character I'd deduced for his longest term employer, was not I suppose very surprising.

It emerged that he had advanced by way of coal-fired cast-iron ranges, and then gas, and had even had experience of bottled gas and kerosene stoves, and had gone back to wood during hard times.

Well, with his enormous experience of different sorts of kitchens, did he not think it time he was put in charge of a really large one, with staff under him? And what is more, I pressed, we can give you a title!

His sullenness evaporated on the instant. *That* was the ambition he had cherished all his two centuries of life: to be addressed with an honorific. Truly he was a child of the years before the Revolution! It is not quite the sort of title one used to have in those days, of course, but his experience with so many various means of cooking had borne it in on him that there had been certain changes in the world.

And now, in a room larger than the great hall of the *chateau*, full of vast stainless steel vats and boilers, to which the necessary ingredients are delivered by the truckload—being much cheaper bought in bulk—Gregoire rejoices in the status of *Controleur du Service de Surveillance Qualitative,* and everybody, even the Baron, calls him *Maître*.

He learned almost before he could grow a beard that he must never discuss his longevity with anybody except his employer; so there has been no trouble on the score; his uncertainty in a big city was put down to the fact that he had been isolated near Guex in a small backward village. Inevitably, someone is sooner or later going to notice that on his unvarying diet he doesn't visibly age.

But that will be extremely good for sales.

JEFFTY IS FIVE

by Harlan Ellison

This was the kick-off story of a special issue of
Fantasy and Science Fiction *dedicated to Harlan
Ellison, that phenomenon of one. It is an example
of Harlan at his nostalgic best with a charm and
mood that seems quite apart from the hard-ar-
mored warrior of Hollywood that he actually is.
But it is that contradiction that makes Ellison so
human that even those who hate his guts admire
his ability.*

When I was five years old, there was a little kid I played with:
Jeffty. His real name was Jeff Kinzer, and everyone who played
with him called him Jeffty. We were five years old together, and
we had good times playing together.

When I was five, a Clark Bar was as fat around as the gripping
end of a Louisville Slugger, and pretty nearly six inches long, and
they used real chocolate to coat it, and it crunched very nicely
when you bit into the center, and the paper it came wrapped in
smelled fresh and good when you peeled off one end to hold the
bar so it wouldn't melt onto your fingers. Today, a Clark Bar is as
thin as a credit card, they use something artificial and awful-tast-

ing instead of pure chocolate, the thing is soft and soggy, it costs
fifteen or twenty cents instead of a decent, correct nickel, and they
wrap it so you think it's the same size it was twenty years ago, only
it isn't; it's slim and ugly and nasty tasting and not worth a penny,
much less fifteen or twenty cents.

When I was that age, five years old, I was sent away to my Aunt
Patricia's home in Buffalo, New York for two years. My father
was going through "bad times," and Aunt Patricia was very beautiful and had married a stockbroker. They took care of me for two
years. When I was seven, I came back home and went to find
Jeffty, so we could play together.

I was seven. Jeffty was still five. I didn't notice any difference. I
didn't know: I was only seven.

When I was seven years old I used to lie on my stomach in front
of our Atwater Kent radio and listen to swell stuff. I had tied the
ground wire to the radiator, and I would lie there with my coloring
books and my Crayolas (when there were only sixteen colors in
the big box), and listen to the NBC red network: Jack Benny on
the Jell-O Program, Amos 'n' Andy, Edgar Bergen and Charlie
McCarthy on the Chase and Sanborn Program. One Man's Family, First Nighter; the NBC blue network: Easy Aces, the Jergens
Program with Walter Winchell, Information Please, Death Valley
Days; and best of all, the Mutual Network with The Green Hor-
net, The Lone Ranger, The Shadow and Quiet Please. Today, I
turn on my car radio and go from one end of the dial to the other
and all I get is 100 string orchestras, banal housewives and in-
sipid truckers discussing their kinky sex lives with arrogant talk
show hosts, country and western drivel and rock music so loud it
hurts my ears.

When I was ten, my grandfather died of old age and I was "a
troublesome kid," and they sent me off to military school, so I
could be "taken in hand."

I came back when I was fourteen. Jeffty was still five.

When I was fourteen years old, I used to go to the movies on
Saturday afternoons and a matinee was ten cents and they used
real butter on the popcorn and I could always be sure of seeing a
western like Lash LaRue, or Wild Bill Elliott as Red Ryder with
Bobby Blake as Little Beaver, or Roy Rogers, or Johnny Mack

Brown; a scary picture like *House of Horrors* with Rondo Hatton as the Strangler, or *The Cat People,* or *The Mummy,* or *I Married a Witch* with Fredric March and Veronica Lake; plus an episode of a great serial like The Shadow with Victor Jory, or Dick Tracy or Flash Gordon; and three cartoons; a James Fitzpatrick Travel Talk; Movietone News; a singalong and, if I stayed on till evening, Bingo or Keno; and free dishes. Today, I go to movies and see Clint Eastwood blowing people's heads apart like ripe cantaloupes.

At eighteen, I went to college. Jeffty was still five. I came back during the summers, to work at my Uncle Joe's jewelry store. Jeffty hadn't changed. Now I knew there was something different about him, something wrong, something weird. Jeffty was still five years old, not a day older.

At twenty-two I came home for keeps. To open a Sony television franchise in town, the first one. I saw Jeffty from time to time. He was five.

Things are better in a lot of ways. People don't die from some of the old diseases any more. Cars go faster and get you there more quickly on better roads. Shirts are softer and silkier. We have paperback books even though they cost as much as a good hardcover used to. When I'm running short in the bank I can live off credit cards till things even out. But I still think we've lost a lot of good stuff. Did you know you can't buy linoleum any more, only vinyl floor covering? There's no such thing as oilcloth any more; you'll never again smell that special, sweet smell from your grandmother's kitchen. Furniture isn't made to last thirty years or longer because they took a survey and found that young homemakers like to throw their furniture out and bring in all new color-coded borax every seven years. Records don't feel right; they're not thick and solid like the old ones, they're thin and you can bend them . . . that doesn't seem right to me. Restaurants don't serve cream in pitchers any more, just that artificial glop in little plastic tubs, and one is never enough to get coffee the right color. Everywhere you go, all the towns look the same with Burger Kings and MacDonald's and 7-Elevens and motels and shopping centers. Things may be better, but why do I keep thinking about the past?

What I mean by five years old is not that Jeffty was retarded. I don't think that's what it was. Smart as a whip for five years old; very bright, quick, cute, a funny kid.

But he was three feet tall, small for his age, and perfectly formed, no big head, no strange jaw, none of that. A nice, normal-looking five-year-old kid. Except that he was the same age as I was: twenty-two.

When he spoke, it was with the squeaking, soprano voice of a five year old; when he walked it was with the little hops and shuffles of a five year old; when he talked to you, it was about the concerns of a five year old . . . comic books, playing soldier, using a clothes pin to attach a stiff piece of cardboard to the front fork of his bike so the sound it made when the spokes hit was like a motorboat, asking questions like *why does that thing do that like that,* how high is up, how old is old, why is grass green, what's an elephant look like? At twenty-two, he was five.

Jeffty's parents were a sad pair. Because I was still a friend of Jeffty's, still let him hang around with me in the store, sometimes took him to the county fair or to the miniature golf or the movies, I wound up spending time with *them.* Not that I much cared for them, because they were so awfully depressing. But then, I suppose one couldn't expect much more from the poor devils. They had an alien thing in their home, a child who had grown no older than five in twenty-two years, who provided the treasure of that special childlike state indefinitely, but who also denied them the joys of watching the child grow into a normal adult.

Five is a wonderful time of life for a little kid . . . or it *can* be, if the child is relatively free of the monstrous beastliness other children indulge in. It is a time when the eyes are wide open and the patterns are not yet set; a time when one has not yet been hammered into accepting everything as immutable and hopeless; a time when the hands cannot do enough, the mind cannot learn enough, the world is infinite and colorful and filled with mysteries. Five is a special time before they take the questing, unquenchable, quixotic soul of the young dreamer and thrust it into dreary schoolroom boxes. A time before they take the trembling hands that want to hold everything, touch everything, figure everything out, and make them lie still on desktops. A time before people begin saying "act your age" and "grow up" or "you're behaving like a baby." It is a time when a child who acts adolescent is still cute and responsive and everyone's pet. A time of delight, of wonder, of innocence.

Jeffty had been stuck in that time, just five, just so.

But for his parents it was an ongoing nightmare from which no one—not social workers, not priests, not child psychologists, not teachers, not friends, not medical wizards, not psychiatrists, no one—could slap or shake them awake. For seventeen years their sorrow had grown through stages of parental dotage to concern, from concern to worry, from worry to fear, from fear to confusion, from confusion to anger, from anger to dislike, from dislike to naked hatred, and finally, from deepest loathing and revulsion to a stolid, depressive acceptance.

John Kinzer was a shift foreman at the Balder Tool & Die plant. He was a thirty year man. To everyone but the man living it, his was a spectacularly uneventful life. In no way was he remarkable . . . save that he had fathered a twenty-two-year-old five year old.

John Kinzer was a small man, soft, with no sharp angles, with pale eyes that never seemed to hold mine for longer than a few seconds. He continually shifted in his chair during conversations, and seemed to see things in the upper corners of the room, things no one else could see . . . or wanted to see. I suppose the word that best suited him was *haunted*. What his life had become . . . well, *haunted* suited him.

Leona Kinzer tried valiantly to compensate. No matter what hour of the day I visited, she always tried to foist food on me. And when Jeffty was in the house she was always at *him* about eating: "Honey, would you like an orange? A nice orange? Or a tangerine? I have tangerines. I could peel a tangerine for you." But there was clearly such fear in her, fear of her own child, that the offers of sustenance always had a faintly ominous tone.

Leona Kinzer had been a tall woman, but the years had bent her. She seemed always to be seeking some area of wall-papered wall or storage niche into which she could fade, adopt some chintz or rose-patterned protective coloration and hide forever in plain sight of the child's big brown eyes, pass her a hundred times a day and never realize she was there, holding her breath, invisible. She always had an apron tied around her waist. And her hands were red from cleaning. As if by maintaining the environment immaculately she could pay off her imagined sin: having given birth to this strange creature.

Neither of them watched television very much. The house was usually dead silent, not even the sibilant whispering of water in the pipes, the creaking of timbers settling, the humming of the refrigerator. Awfully silent, as if time itself had taken a detour around that house.

As for Jeffty, he was inoffensive. He lived in that atmosphere of gentle dread and dulled loathing, and if he understood it, he never remarked in any way. He played, as a child plays, and seemed happy. But he must have sensed, in the way of a five year old, just how alien he was in their presence.

Alien. No, that wasn't right. He was *too* human, if anything. But out of phase, out of synch with the world around him and resonating to a different vibration than his parents, God knows. Nor would other children play with him. As they grew past him, they found him at first childish, then uninteresting, then simply frightening as their perceptions of aging became clear and they could see he was not affected by time as they were. Even the little ones, his own age, who might wander into the neighborhood, quickly came to shy away from him like a dog in the street when a car backfires.

Thus, I remained his only friend. A friend of many years. Five years. Twenty-two years. I liked him; more than I can say. And never knew exactly why. But I did, without reserve.

But because we spent time together, I found I was also—polite society—spending time with John and Leona Kinzer. Dinner, Saturday afternoons sometimes, an hour or so when I'd bring Jeffty back from a movie. They were grateful: slavishly so. It relieved them of the embarrassing chore of going out with him, of having to pretend before the world that they were loving parents with a perfectly normal, happy, attractive child. And their gratitude extended to hosting me. Hideous, every moment of their depression, hideous.

I felt sorry for the poor devils, but I despised them for their inability to love Jeffty, who was eminently lovable.

I never let on, even during the evenings in their company that were awkward beyond belief.

We would sit there in the darkening living room—*always* dark or darkening, as if kept in shadow to hold back what the light might reveal to the world outside through the bright eyes of the house—we would sit and silently stare at one another. They never knew what to say to me.

"So how are things down at the plant," I'd say to John Kinzer.

He would shrug. Neither conversation nor life suited him with any ease or grace. "Fine, just fine," he would say, finally.

And we would sit in silence again.

"Would you like a nice piece of coffee cake?" Leona would say. "I made it fresh just this morning." Or deep dish green apple pie. Or milk and toll house cookies. Or a brown betty pudding.

"No, no, thank you, Mrs. Kinzer; Jeffty and I grabbed a couple of cheeseburgers on the way home." And again, silence.

Then, when the stillness and the awkwardness became too much even for them (and who knew how long that total silence reigned when they were alone, with that thing they never talked about any more, hanging between them), Leona Kinzer would say, "I think he's asleep."

John Kinzer would say, "I don't hear the radio playing."

Just so, it would go on like that, until I could politely find excuse to bolt away on some flimsy pretext. Yes, that was the way it would go on, every time, just the same . . . except once.

"I don't know what to do any more," Leona said. She began crying. "There's no change, not one day of peace."

Her husband managed to drag himself out of the old easy chair and went to her. He bent and tried to soothe her, but it was clear from the graceless way in which he touched her graying hair that the ability to be compassionate had been stunned in him. "Shhh, Leona, it's all right. Shhh." But she continued crying. Her hands scraped gently at the antimacassars on the arms of the chair.

Then she said, "Sometimes I wish he had been stillborn."

John looked up into the corners of the room. For the nameless shadows that were always watching him? Was it God he was seeking in those spaces? "You don't mean that," he said to her, softly, pathetically, urging her with body tension and trembling in his voice to recant before God took notice of the terrible thought. But she meant it; she meant it very much.

I managed to get away quickly that evening. They didn't want witnesses to their shame. I was glad to go.

And for a week I stayed away. From them, from Jeffty, from their street, even from that end of town.

I had my own life. The store, accounts, suppliers' conferences, poker with friends, pretty women I took to well-lit restaurants, my own parents, putting anti-freeze in the car, complaining to the laundry about too much starch in the collars and cuffs, working out at the gym, taxes, catching Jan or David (whichever one it was) stealing from the cash register. I had my own life.

But not even *that* evening could keep me from Jeffty. He called me at the store and asked me to take him to the rodeo. We chummed it up as best a twenty-two year old with other interests *could* . . . with a five year old. I never dwelled on what bound us together; I always thought it was simply the years. That, and affection for a kid who could have been the little brother I never had. (Except I *remembered* when we had played together, when we had both been the same age; I *remembered* that period, and Jeffty was still the same.)

And then, one Saturday afternoon, I came to take him to a double feature, and things I should have noticed so many times before, I first began to notice only that afternoon.

I came walking up to the Kinzer house, expecting Jeffty to be sitting on the front porch steps, or in the porch glider, waiting for me. But he was nowhere in sight.

Going inside, into that darkness and silence, in the midst of May sunshine, was unthinkable. I stood on the front walk for a few moments, then cupped my hands around my mouth and yelled, "Jeffty? Hey, Jeffty, come on out, let's go. We'll be late."

His voice came faintly, as if from under the ground.

"Here I am, Donny."

I could hear him, but I couldn't see him. It was Jeffty, no question about it: as Donald H. Horton, President and Sole Owner of

The Horton TV & Sound Center, no one but Jeffty called me Donny. He had never called me anything else.

(Actually, it isn't a lie. I *am*, as far as the public is concerned, Sole Owner of the Center. The partnership with my Aunt Patricia is only to repay the loan she made me, to supplement the money I came into when I was twenty-one, left to me when I was ten by my grandfather. It wasn't a very big loan, only eighteen thousand, but I asked her to be a silent partner, because of when she had taken care of me as a child.)

"Where are you, Jeffty?"

"Under the porch in my secret place."

I walked around the side of the porch, and stooped down and pulled away the wicker grating. Back in there, on the pressed dirt, Jeffty had built himself a secret place. He had comics in orange crates, he had a little table and some pillows, it was lit by big fat candles, and we used to hide there when we were both . . . five.

"What'cha up to?" I asked, crawling in and pulling the grate closed behind me. It was cool under the porch, and the dirt smelled comfortable, the candles smelled clubby and familiar. Any kid would feel at home in such a secret place: there's never been a kid who didn't spend the happiest, most productive, most deliciously mysterious times of his life in such a secret place.

"Playin'," he said. He was holding something golden and round. It filled the palm of his little hand.

"You forget we were going to the movies?"

"Nope. I was just waitin' for you here."

"Your mom and dad home?"

"Momma."

I understood why he was waiting under the porch. I didn't push it any further. "What've you got there?"

"Captain Midnight Secret Decoder Badge," he said, showing it to me on his flattened palm.

I realized I was looking at it without comprehending what it was for a long time. Then it dawned on me what a miracle Jeffty had in his hand. A miracle that simply could *not* exist.

"Jeffty," I said softly, with wonder in my voice, "where'd you get that?"

"Came in the mail today. I sent away for it."

"It must have cost a lot of money."

"Not so much. Ten cents an' two inner wax seals from two jars of Ovaltine."

"May I see it?" My voice was trembling, and so was the hand I extended. He gave it to me and I held the miracle in the palm of my hand. It was *wonderful*.

You remember. *Captain Midnight* went on the radio nationwide in 1940. It was sponsored by Ovaltine. And every year they issued a Secret Squadron Decoder Badge. And every day at the end of the program, they would give you a clue to the next day's installment in a code that only kids with the official badge could decipher. They stopped making those wonderful Decoder Badges in 1949. I remember the one I had in 1945; it was beautiful. It had a magnifying glass in the center of the code dial. *Captain Midnight* went off the air in 1950, and though it was a short-lived television series in the mid-Fifties, and though they issued Decoder Badges in 1955 and 1956, as far as the *real* badges were concerned, they never made one after 1949.

The Captain Midnight Code-O-Graph I held in my hand, the one Jeffty said he had gotten in the mail for ten cents (*ten cents!!!*) and two Ovaltine labels, was brand new, shiny gold metal, not a dent or a spot of rust on it like the old ones you can find at exorbitant prices in collectible shoppes from time to time . . . it was a *new* Decoder. And the date on it was *this* year.

But *Captain Midnight* no longer existed. Nothing like it existed on the radio. I'd listened to the one or two weak imitations of old-time radio the networks were currently airing, and the stories were dull, the sound effects bland, the whole feel of it wrong, out of date, cornball. Yet I held a *new* Code-O-Graph.

"Jeffty, tell me about this," I said.

"Tell you what, Donny? It's my new Capt'n Midnight Secret Decoder Badge. I use it to figger out what's gonna happen tomorrow."

"Tomorrow how?"

"On the program."

"*What* program?!"

He stared at me as if I was being purposely stupid. "On Capt'n *Mid*night! Boy!" I was being dumb.

I still couldn't get it straight. It was right there, right out in the open, and I still didn't know what was happening. "You mean one of those records they made of the old-time radio programs? Is that what you mean, Jeffty?"

"What records?" he asked. He didn't know what *I* meant.

We stared at each other, there under the porch. And then I said, very slowly, almost afraid of the answer, "Jeffty, how do you hear *Captain Midnight?*"

"Every day. On the radio. On my radio. Every day at five-thirty."

News. Music, dumb music, and news. That's what was on the radio every day at five-thirty. Not *Captain Midnight*. The Secret Squadron hadn't been on the air in twenty years.

"Can we hear it tonight?" I asked.

"Boy!" he said. I was being dumb. I knew it from the way he said it; but I didn't know *why*. Then it dawned on me: this was Saturday. *Captain Midnight* was on Monday through Friday. Not on Saturday or Sunday.

"We goin' to the movies?"

He had to repeat himself twice. My mind was somewhere else. Nothing definite. No conclusions. No wild assumptions leapt to. Just off somewhere trying to figure it out, and concluding—as *you* would have concluded, as *any*one would have concluded rather than accepting the truth, the impossible and wonderful truth—just finally concluding there was a simple explanation I didn't yet perceive. Something mundane and dull, like the passage of time that steals all good, old things from us, packratting trinkets and plastic in exchange. And all in the name of Progress.

"We goin' to the movies, Donny?"

"You bet your boots we are, kiddo," I said. And I smiled. And I handed him the Code-O-Graph. And he put it in his side pants pocket. And we crawled out from under the porch. And we went to the movies. And neither of us said anything about *Captain Midnight* all the rest of that day. And there wasn't a ten-minute stretch, all the rest of that day, that I didn't think about it.

It was inventory all that next week. I didn't see Jeffty till late Thursday. I confess I left the store in the hands of Jan and David,

told them I had some errands to run, and left early. At 4:00. I got
to the Kinzers' right around 4:45. Leona answered the door, looking exhausted and distant. "Is Jeffty around?" She said he was upstairs in his room . . .

. . . listening to the radio.

I climbed the stairs two at a time.

All right, I had finally made that impossible, illogical leap. Had
the stretch of belief involved anyone but Jeffty, adult or child, I
would have reasoned out more explicable answers. But it *was*
Jeffty, clearly another kind of vessel of life, and what he might experience should not be expected to fit into the ordered scheme.

I admit it: I *wanted* to hear what I heard.

Even with the door closed, I recognized the program:
"There he goes, Tennessee! Get him!"

There was the heavy report of a rifle shot and the keening whine
of the slug ricocheting, and then the same voice yelled trium-
phantly, *"Got him! D-e-a-a-a-a-d center!"*

He was listening to the American Broadcasting Company, 790
kilocycles, and he was hearing *Tennessee Jed,* one of my most favorite programs from the Forties, a western adventure I had not
heard in twenty years, because it had not existed for twenty years.

I sat down on the top step of the stairs, there in the upstairs hall
of the Kinzer home, and I listened to the show. It wasn't a rerun
of an old program, because there were occasional references in the
body of the drama to current cultural and technological developments, and phrases that had not existed in common usage in the
Forties: aerosol spray cans, laseracing of tattoos, Tanzania, the
word "uptight."

I could not ignore the fact. Jeffty was listening to a *new* segment
of *Tennessee Jed.*

I ran downstairs and out the front door to my car. Leona must
have been in the kitchen. I turned the key and punched on the
radio and spun the dial to 790 kilocycles. The ABC station. Rock
music.

I sat there for a few moments, then ran the dial slowly from one
end to the other. Music, news, talk shows. No *Tennessee Jed.* And
it was a Blaupunkt, the best radio I could get. I wasn't missing
some perimeter station. It simply was not there!

After a few moments I turned off the radio and the ignition and went back upstairs quietly. I sat down on the top step and listened to the entire program. It was *wonderful*.

Exciting, imaginative, filled with everything I remembered as being most innovative about radio drama. But it was modern. It wasn't an antique, re-broadcast to assuage the need of that dwindling listenership who longed for the old days. It was a new show, with all the old voices, but still young and bright. Even the commercials were for currently available products, but they weren't as loud or as insulting as the screamer ads one heard on the radio these days.

And when *Tennessee Jed* went off at 5:00, I heard Jeffty spin the dial on his radio till I heard the familiar voice of the announcer Glenn Riggs proclaim, *"Presenting Hop Harrigan! America's ace of the airwaves!"* There was the sound of an airplane in flight. It was a prop plane, *not* a jet! Not the sound kids today have grown up with, but the sound *I* grew up with, the *real* sound of an airplane, the growling, revving, throaty sound of the kind of airplanes G-8 and His Battle Aces flew, the kind Captain Midnight flew, the kind Hop Harrigan flew. And then I heard Hop say, *"CX-4 calling control tower. CX-4 calling control tower. Standing by!"* A pause, then, *"Okay, this is Hop Harrigan . . . coming in!"*

And Jeffty, who had the same problem all of us kids had in the Forties with programming that pitted equal favorites against one another on different stations, having paid his respects to Hop Harrigan and Tank Tinker, spun the dial and went back to ABC where I heard the stroke of a gong, the wild cacophony of nonsense Chinese chatter, and the announcer yelled, *"T-e-e-e-rry and the Pirates!"*

I sat there on the top step and listened to Terry and Connie and Flip Corkin and, so help me God, Agnes Moorehead as The Dragon Lady, all of them in a new adventure that took place in a Red China that had not existed in the days of Milton Caniff's 1937 version of the Orient, with river pirates and Chiang Kai-shek and warlords and the naive Imperialism of American gunboat diplomacy.

Sat, and listened to the whole show, and sat even longer to hear *Superman* and part of *Jack Armstrong, the All-American boy,* and

part of *Captain Midnight,* and John Kinzer came home and neither he nor Leona came upstairs to find out what had happened to
me, or where Jeffty was, and sat longer, and found I had started
crying, and could not stop, just sat there with tears running down
my face, into the corners of my mouth, sitting and crying until
Jeffty heard me and opened his door and saw me and came out
and looked at me in childish confusion as I heard the station break
for the Mutual Network and they began the theme music of *Tom
Mix,* "When it's Round-up Time in Texas and the Bloom is on the
Sage," and Jeffty touched my shoulder and smiled at me and said,
"Hi, Donny. Wanna come in an' listen to the radio with me?"

Hume denied the existence of an absolute space, in which each
thing has its place; Borges denies the existence of one single time,
in which all events are linked.

Jeffty received radio programs from a place that could not, in
logic, in the natural scheme of the space-time universe as conceived by Einstein, exist. But that wasn't all he received. He got
mail order premiums that no one was manufacturing. He read
comic books that had been defunct for three decades. He saw
movies with actors who had been dead for twenty years. He was
the receiving terminal for endless joys and pleasures of the past
that the world had dropped along the way. On its headlong suicidal flight toward New Tomorrows, the world had razed its treas-
urehouse of simple happiness, had poured concrete over its play-
grounds, had abandoned its elfin stragglers, and all of it was being
impossibly, miraculously shunted back into the present through
Jeffty. Revivified, updated, the traditions maintained but contem-
poraneous. Jeffty was the unbidding Aladdin whose very nature
formed the magic lampness of his reality.

And he took me into his world.

Because he trusted me.

We had breakfast of Quaker Puffed Wheat Sparkies and warm
Ovaltine we drank out of *this* year's little Orphan Annie Shake-Up
Mugs. We went to the movies and while everyone else was seeing a
comedy starring Goldie Hawn and Ryan O'Neal, Jeffty and I were
enjoying Humphrey Bogart as the professional thief Parker in

John Huston's brilliant adaptation of the Donald Westlake novel, *Slayground*. The second feature was Spencer Tracy, Carole Lombard and Laird Cregar in the Val Lewton-produced film of *Leinengen Versus the Ants*.

Twice a month we went down to the newsstand and bought the current pulp issues of *The Shadow, Doc Savage* and *Startling Stories*. Jeffty and I sat together and I read to him from the magazines. He particularly liked the new short novels by Henry Kuttner, "The Dreams of Achilles," and the new Stanley G. Weinbaum series of short stories set in the subatomic particle universe of Redurna. In September we enjoyed the first installment of the new Robert E. Howard Conan novel, *Isle of the Black Ones,* in *Weird Tales;* and in August were only mildly disappointed by Edgar Rice Burroughs' fourth novella in the Jupiter series featuring John Carter of Barsoom—"Corsairs of Jupiter." But the editor of *Argosy All-Story Weekly* promised there would be two more stories in the series, and it was such an unexpected revelation for Jeffty and me that it dimmed our disappointment at the lessened quality of the current story.

We read comics together, and Jeffty and I both decided—separately, before we came together to discuss it—that our favorite characters were Doll Man, Airboy and The Heap. We also adored the George Carlson strips in *Jingle Jangle Comics,* particularly the Pie-Face Prince of Old Pretzleburg stories, which we read together and laughed over, even though I had to explain some of the subtler puns to Jeffty, who was too young to have that kind of subtle wit.

How to explain it? I can't. I had enough physics in college to make some offhand guesses, but I'm more likely wrong than right. The laws of the conservation of energy occasionally break. These are laws that physicists call "weakly violated." Perhaps Jeffty was a catalyst for the weak violation of conservation laws we're only now beginning to realize exist. I tried doing some reading in the area—muon decay of the "forbidden" kind: gamma decay that doesn't include the muon neutrino among its products—but nothing I encountered, not even the latest readings from the Swiss Institute for Nuclear Research near Zurich gave me an insight. I was thrown back on a vague acceptance of the philosophy that the real name for "science" is *magic*.

No explanations, but enormous good times.

The happiest time of my life.

I had the "real" world, the world of my store and my friends and my family, the world of profit & loss, of taxes and evenings with young women who talked about going shopping or the United Nations, of the rising cost of coffee and microwave ovens. And I had Jeffty's world, in which I existed only when I was with him. The things of the past he knew as fresh and new, I could experience only when in his company. And the membrane between the two worlds grew ever thinner, more luminous and transparent. I had the best of both worlds. And knew, somehow, that I could carry nothing from one to the other.

Forgetting that, for just a moment, betraying Jeffty by forgetting, brought an end to it all.

Enjoying myself so much, I grew careless and failed to consider how fragile the relationship between Jeffty's world and my world really was. There is a reason why the present begrudges the existence of the past. I never really understood. Nowhere in the beast books, where survival is shown in battles between claw and fang, tentacle and poison sac, is there recognition of the ferocity the present always brings to bear on the past. Nowhere is there a detailed statement of how the present lies in wait for What-Was, waiting for it to become Now-This-Moment so it can shred it with its merciless jaws.

Who could know such a thing . . . at any age . . . and certainly not at my age . . . who could understand such a thing?

I'm trying to exculpate myself. I can't. It was my fault.

It was another Saturday afternoon.

"What's playing today?" I asked him, in the car, on the way downtown.

He looked up at me from the other side of the front seat and smiled one of his best smiles. "Ken Maynard in *Bullwhip Justice* an' *The Demolished Man.*" He kept smiling, as if he'd really put one over on me. I looked at him with disbelief.

"You're *kid*ding!" I said, delighted. "Bester's *The Demolished Man?*" He nodded his head, delighted at my being delighted. He knew it was one of my favorite books. "Oh, that's super!"

"Super *duper*," he said.

"Who's in it?"

"Franchot Tone, Evelyn Keyes, Lionel Barrymore and Elisha Cook, Jr." He was much more knowledgeable about movie actors than I'd ever been. He could name the character actors in any movie he'd ever seen. Even the crowd scenes.

"And cartoons?" I asked.

"Three of 'em, a *Little Lulu,* a *Donald Duck* and a *Bugs Bunny.* An' a *Pete Smith Specialty* an' a *Lew Lehr Monkeys is da C-r-r-r-aziest Peoples.*"

"Oh boy!" I said. I was grinning from ear to ear. And then I looked down and saw the pad of purchase order forms on the seat. I'd forgotten to drop it off at the store.

"Gotta stop by the Center," I said. "Gotta drop off something. It'll only take a minute."

"Okay," Jeffty said, "but we won't be late, will we?"

"Not on your tintype, kiddo," I said.

When I pulled into the parking lot behind the Center, he decided to come in with me and we'd walk over to the theater, it's not a large town. There are only two movie houses, the Utopia and the Lyric. We were going to the Utopia, only three blocks from the Center.

I walked into the store with the pad of forms, and it was bedlam. David and Jan were handling two customers each, and there were people standing around waiting to be helped. Jan turned a look on me and her face was a horror-mask of pleading. David was running from the stockroom to the showroom and all he could murmur as he whipped past was, "Help!" and then he was gone.

"Jeffty," I said, crouching down, "listen, give me a few minutes. Jan and David are in trouble with all these people. We won't be late, I promise. Just let me get rid of a couple of these customers." He looked nervous, but nodded okay.

I motioned to a chair and said, "Just sit down for a while and I'll be right with you."

He went to the chair, good as you please, though he knew what was happening, and he sat down.

I started taking care of people who wanted color television sets. This was the first really substantial batch of units we'd gotten in— color television was only now becoming reasonably priced and this was Sony's first promotion—and it was bonanza time for me. I could see paying off the loan and being out in front for the first time with the Center. It was business.

In my world, good business comes first.

Jeffty sat there and stared at the wall. Let me tell you about the wall.

Stanchion and bracket designs had been rigged from floor to within two feet of the ceiling. Television sets had been stacked artfully on the wall. Thirty-three television sets. All playing at the same time. Black and white, color, little ones, big ones, all going at the same time.

Jeffty sat and watched thirty-three television sets, on a Saturday afternoon. We can pick up a total of thirteen channels including the UHF educational stations. Golf was on one channel; baseball was on a second; celebrity bowling was on a third; the fourth channel was a religious seminar; a teen-age dance show was on the fifth; the sixth was a rerun of a situation comedy; the seventh was a rerun of a police show; eighth was a nature program showing a man flycasting endlessly; ninth was news and conversation; tenth was a stock car race; eleventh was a man doing logarithms on a blackboard; twelfth was a woman in a leotard doing sitting-up exercises; and on the thirteenth channel was a badly-animated cartoon show in Spanish. All but six of the shows were repeated on three sets. Jeffty sat and watched that wall of television on a Saturday afternoon while I sold as fast and as hard as I could, to pay back my Aunt Patricia and stay in touch with my world. It was business.

I should have known better. I should have understood about the present and the way it kills the past. But I was selling with both hands. And when I finally glanced over at Jeffty, half an hour later, he looked like another child.

He was sweating. That terrible fever sweat when you have stomach flu. He was pale, as pasty and pale as a worm, and his little hands were gripping the arms of the chair so tightly I could see his knuckles in bold relief. I dashed over to him, excusing myself from the middle-aged couple looking at the new 21″ Mediterranean model.

"Jeffty!"

He looked at me, but his eyes didn't track. He was in absolute terror. I pulled him out of the chair and started toward the front door with him, but the customers I'd deserted yelled at me, "Hey!" The middle-aged man said, "You wanna sell me this thing or don't you?"

I looked from him to Jeffty and back again. Jeffty was like a zombie. He had come where I'd pulled him. His legs were rubbery and his feet dragged. The past, being eaten by the present, the sound of something in pain.

I clawed some money out of my pants pocket and jammed it into Jeffty's hand. "Kiddo . . . listen to me . . . get out of here right now!" He still couldn't focus properly. "*Jeffty,*" I said as tightly as I could, "*listen* to me!" The middle-aged customer and his wife were walking toward us. "Listen, kiddo, get out of here right this minute. Walk over to the Utopia and buy the tickets. I'll be right behind you." The middle-aged man and his wife were almost on us. I shoved Jeffty through the door and watched him stumble away in the wrong direction, then stop as if gathering his wits, turn and go back past the front of the Center and in the direction of the Utopia. "Yes sir," I said, straightening up and facing them, "yes, ma'am, that is one terrific set with some sen*s*ational features! If you'll just step back here with me . . ."

There was a terrible sound of something hurting, but I couldn't tell from which channel, or from which set, it was coming.

Most of it I learned later, from the girl in the ticket booth, and from some people I knew who came to me to tell me what had happened. By the time I got to the Utopia, nearly twenty minutes later, Jeffty was already beaten to a pulp and had been taken to the Manager's office.

"Did you see a very little boy, about five years old, with big brown eyes and straight brown hair . . . he was waiting for me?"

"Oh, I think that's the little boy those kids beat up?"

"What!?! *Where is he?*"

"They took him to the Manager's office. No one knew who he was or where to find his parents—"

A young girl wearing an usher's uniform was placing a wet paper towel on his face.

I took the towel away from her and ordered her out of the office. She looked insulted and snorted something rude, but she left. I sat on the edge of the couch and tried to swab away the blood from the lacerations without opening the wounds where the blood had caked. Both his eyes were swollen shut. His mouth was ripped badly. His hair was matted with dried blood.

He had been standing in line behind two kids in their teens. They started selling tickets at 12:30 and the show started at 1:00. The doors weren't opened till 12:45. He had been waiting, and the kids in front of him had had a portable radio. They were listening to the ballgame. Jeffty had wanted to hear some program, God knows what it might have been, *Grand Central Station, Land of the Lost,* God only knows which one it might have been.

He had asked if he could borrow their radio to hear the program for a minute, and it had been a commercial break or something, and the kids had given him the radio, probably out of some malicious kind of courtesy that would permit them to take offense and rag the little boy. He had changed the station . . . and they'd been unable to get it to go back to the ballgame. It was locked into the past, on a station that was broadcasting a program that didn't exist for anyone but Jeffty.

They had beaten him badly . . . as everyone watched.

And then they had run away.

I had left him alone, left him to fight off the present without sufficient weaponry. I had betrayed him for the sale of a 21″ Mediterranean console television, and now his face was pulped meat. He moaned something inaudible and sobbed softly.

"Shhh, it's okay, kiddo, it's Donny. I'm here. I'll get you home, it'll be okay."

I should have taken him straight to the hospital. I don't know why I didn't. I should have. I should have done that.

When I carried him through the door, John and Leona Kinzer just stared at me. They didn't move to take him from my arms. One of his hands was hanging down. He was conscious, but just barely. They stared, there in the semi-darkness of a Saturday afternoon in the present. I looked at them. "A couple of kids beat him up at the theater." I raised him a few inches in my arms and extended him. They stared at me, at both of us, with nothing in their eyes, without movement. "Jesus Christ," I shouted, "he's been beaten! He's your son! Don't you even want to touch him? What the hell kind of people are you?!"

Then Leona moved toward me very slowly. She stood in front of us for a few seconds, and there was a leaden stoicism in her face that was terrible to see. It said, *I have been in this place before, many times, and I cannot bear to be in it again; but I am here now.*

So I gave him to her. God help me, I gave him over to her.

And she took him upstairs to bathe away his blood and his pain.

John Kinzer and I stood in our separate places in the dim livingroom of their home, and we stared at each other. He had nothing to say to me.

I shoved past him and fell into a chair. I was shaking.

I heard the bath water running upstairs.

After what seemed a very long time Leona came downstairs, wiping her hands on her apron. She sat down on the sofa and after a moment John sat down beside her. I heard the sound of rock music from upstairs.

"Would you like a piece of nice pound cake?" Leona said.

I didn't answer. I was listening to the sound of the music. Rock music. On the radio. There was a table lamp on the end table beside the sofa. It cast a dim and futile light in the shadowed living room. Rock music from the present, on a radio upstairs? I started to say something, and then *knew* . . .

I jumped up just as the sound of hideous crackling blotted out the music, and the table lamp dimmed and dimmed and flickered.

I screamed something, I don't know what it was, and ran for the stairs.

Jeffty's parents did not move. They sat there with their hands folded, in that place they had been for so many years.

I fell twice rushing up the stairs.

There isn't much on television that can hold my interest. I bought an old cathedral-shaped Philco radio in a second-hand store, and I replaced all the burnt-out parts with the original tubes from old radios I could cannibalize that still worked. I don't use transistors or printed circuits. They wouldn't work. I've sat in front of that set for hours sometimes, running the dial back and forth as slowly as you can imagine, so slowly it doesn't look as if it's moving at all sometimes.

But I can't find *Captain Midnight* or *The Land of the Lost* or *The Shadow* or *Quiet Please*.

So she did love him, still, a little bit, even after all those years. I can't hate them: they only wanted to live in the present world again. That isn't such a terrible thing.

It's a good world, all things considered. It's much better than it used to be, in a lot of ways. People don't die from the old diseases any more. They die from new ones, but that's Progress, isn't it?

Isn't it?

Tell me.

Somebody please tell me.

THE SCREWFLY
SOLUTION

by Raccoona Sheldon

Based upon a very effective and romantically scientific discovery that has enhanced agriculture in many places, this is the event as seen from the recipient's point of view. It's the sort of thing that readers expect from the mysterious James Tiptree, Jr. And we mention that because Tiptree is no longer a mystery. "He" is the person signing this story. Just add Alice.

The young man sitting at 2° N, 75° W sent a casually venomous glance up at the nonfunctional shoofly *ventilador* and went on reading his letter. He was sweating heavily, stripped to his shorts in the hotbox of what passed for a hotel room in Cuyapán.

How do other wives *do* it? I stay busy-busy with the Ann Arbor grant review programs and the seminar, saying brightly, "Oh yes, Alan is in Colombia setting up a biological pest control program, isn't it wonderful?" But inside I imagine you being surrounded by nineteen-year-old raven-haired cooing beauties, every one panting with social dedication and filthy rich. And forty inches of bosom busting out of her delicate lingerie. I even figured it in centimeters, that's 101.6 centimeters of busting. Oh, darling, darling, do what you want only *come home safe*.

Alan grinned fondly, briefly imagining the only body he longed for. His girl, his magic Anne. Then he got up to open the window another cautious notch. A long pale mournful face looked in—a goat. The room opened on the goatpen, the stench was vile. Air, anyway. He picked up the letter.

Everything is just about as you left it, except that the Peedsville horror seems to be getting worse. They're calling it the Sons of Adam cult now. Why can't they *do* something, even if it is a religion? The Red Cross has set up a refugee camp in Ashton, Georgia. Imagine, refugees in the U.S.A. I heard two little girls were carried out all slashed up. Oh, Alan.

Which reminds me, Barney came over with a wad of clippings he wants me to send you. I'm putting them in a separate envelope; I know what happens to very fat letters in foreign POs. He says, in case you don't get them, what do the following have in common? Peedsville, Sao Paulo, Phoenix, San Diego, Shanghai, New Delhi, Tripoli, Brisbane, Johannesburg and Lubbock, Texas. He says the hint is, remember where the Intertropical Convergence Zone is now. That makes no sense to me, maybe it will to your superior ecological brain. All I could see about the clippings was that they were fairly horrible accounts of murders or massacres of women. The worst was the New Delhi one, about "rafts of female corpses" in the river. The funniest (!) was the Texas Army officer who shot his wife, three daughters and his aunt, because God told him to clean the place up.

Barney's such an old dear, he's coming over Sunday to help me take off the downspout and see what's blocking it. He's dancing on air right now, since you left his spruce budworm-moth antipheromone program finally paid off. You know he tested over 2,000 compounds? Well, it seems that good old 2,097 *really* works. When I asked him what it does he just giggles, you know how shy he is with women. Anyway, it seems that a one-shot spray program will save the forests, without harming a single other thing. Birds and people can eat it all day, he says.

Well sweetheart, that's all the news except Amy goes back to

Chicago to school Sunday. The place will be a tomb, I'll miss her frightfully in spite of her being at the stage where I'm her worst enemy. The sullen sexy subteens, Angie says. Amy sends love to her Daddy. I send you my whole heart, all that words can't say.

Your Anne

Alan put the letter safely in his notefile and glanced over the rest of the thin packet of mail, refusing to let himself dream of home and Anne. Barney's "fat envelope" wasn't there. He threw himself on the rumpled bed, yanking off the lightcord a minute before the town generator went off for the night. In the darkness the last of places Barney had mentioned spread themselves around a misty globe that turned, troublingly, briefly in his mind. Something . . .

But then the memory of the hideously parasitized children he had worked with at the clinic that day took possession of his thoughts. He set himself to considering the data he must collect. *Look for the vulnerable link in the behavioral chain*—how often Barney—Dr. Barnhard Braithwaite—had pounded it into his skull. Where was it, where? In the morning he would start work on bigger canefly cages . . .

At that moment, five thousand miles North, Anne was writing:

Oh, darling, darling, your first three letters are here, they all came together. I *knew* you were writing. Forget what I said about swarthy heiresses, that was all a joke. My darling I know, I know . . . us. Those dreadful canefly larvae, those poor little kids. If you weren't my husband I'd think you were a saint or something. (I do anyway.)

I have your letters pinned up all over the house, makes it a lot less lonely. No real news here except things feel kind of quiet and spooky. Barney and I got the downspout out, it was full of a big rotted hoard of squirrel-nuts. They must have been dropping them down the top, I'll put a wire over it. (Don't worry, I'll use a ladder this time.)

Barney's in an odd, grim mood. He's taking this Sons of Adam thing very seriously, it seems he's going to be on the investigation committee if that ever gets off the ground. The weird part is that nobody seems to be doing anything, as if it's just too big. Selina Peters has been printing some acid comments, like When one man kills his wife you call it murder, but when enough do it we call it a lifestyle. I think it's spreading, but nobody knows because the media have been asked to down-play it. Barney says it's being viewed as a form of contagious hysteria. He insisted I send you this ghastly interview, printed on thin paper. It's *not* going to be published, of course. The Quietness is worse, though, it's like something terrible was going on just out of sight. After reading Barney's thing I called up Pauline in San Diego to make sure she was all right. She sounded funny, as if she wasn't saying everything . . . my own sister. Just after she said things were great she suddenly asked if she could come and stay here awhile next month, I said come right away, but she wants to sell her house first. I wish she'd hurry.

Oh, the diesel car is okay now, it just needed its filter changed. I had to go out to Springfield to get one but Eddie installed it for only $2.50. He's going to bankrupt his garage.

In case you didn't guess, those places of Barney's are all about latitude 30° N or S—the horse latitudes. When I said not exactly, he said remember the equatorial convergence zone shifts in winter, and to add in Libya, Osaka, and a place I forget—wait, Alice Springs, Australia. What has this to do with anything, I asked. He said, "Nothing—I hope." I leave it to you, great brains like Barney can be weird.

Oh my dearest, here's all of me to all of you. Your letters make life possible. But don't feel you *have* to, I can tell how tired you must be. Just know we're together, always everywhere.

                                                                Your Anne

Oh PS I had to open this to put Barney's thing in, it wasn't the secret police. Here it is. All love again. A.

In the goat-infested room where Alan read this, rain was drumming on the roof. He put the letter to his nose to catch the faint perfume once more, and folded it away. Then he pulled out the yellow flimsy Barney had sent and began to read, frowning.

PEEDSVILLE CULT/SONS OF ADAM SPECIAL. Statement by driver Sgt. Willard Mews, Globe Fork, Ark. We hit the road-block about 80 miles west of Jacksonville. Major John

Heinz of Ashton was expecting us, he gave us an escort of two riot vehicles headed by Capt. T. Parr. Major Heinz appeared shocked to see that the NIH medical team included two women doctors. He warned us in the strongest terms of the danger. So Dr. Patsy Putnam (Urbana, Ill.), the psychologist, decided to stay behind at the Army cordon. But Dr. Elaine Fay (Clinton, N.J.) insisted on going with us, saying she was the epi-something (epidemiologist).

We drove behind one of the riot cars at 30 mph for about an hour without seeing anything unusual. There were two big signs saying "SONS OF ADAM—LIBERATED ZONE." We passed some small pecan packing plants and a citrus processing plant. The men there looked at us but did not do anything unusual. I didn't see any children or women of course. Just outside Peedsville we stopped at a big barrier made of oil drums in front of a large citrus warehouse. This area is old, sort of a shantytown and trailer park. The new part of town with the shopping center and developments is about a mile further on. A warehouse worker with a shotgun came out and told us to wait for the Mayor. I don't think he saw Dr. Elaine Fay then, she was sitting sort of bent down in back.

Mayor Blount drove up in a police cruiser and our chief, Dr. Premack, explained our mission from the Surgeon General. Dr. Premack was very careful not to make any remarks insulting to the Mayor's religion. Mayor Blount agreed to let the party go on into Peedsville to take samples of the soil and water and so on and talk to the doctor who lives there. The mayor was about 6' 2", weight maybe 230 or 240, tanned, with grayish hair. He was smiling and chuckling in a friendly manner.

Then he looked inside the car and saw Dr. Elaine Fay and he blew up. He started yelling we had to all get the hell back. But Dr. Premack managed to talk to him and cool him down and finally the Mayor said Dr. Fay should go into the warehouse office and stay there with the door closed. I had to stay there too and see she didn't come out, and one of the Mayor's men would drive the party.

So the medical people and the Mayor and one of the riot

vehicles went on into Peedsville and I took Dr. Fay back into the warehouse office and sat down. It was real hot and stuffy. Dr. Fay opened a window, but when I heard her trying to talk to an old man outside I told her she couldn't do that and closed the window. The old man went away. Then she wanted to talk to me but I told her I did not feel like conversing. I felt it was real wrong, her being there.

So then she started looking through the office files and reading papers there. I told her that was a bad idea, she shouldn't do that. She said the government expected her to investigate. She showed me a booklet or magazine they had there, it was called *Man Listens To God* by Reverend McIllhenny. They had a carton full in the office. I started reading it and Dr. Fay said she wanted to wash her hands. So I took her back along a kind of enclosed hallway beside the conveyor to where the toilet was. There were no doors or windows so I went back. After awhile she called out that there was a cot back there, she was going to lie down. I figured that was all right because of the no windows, also I was glad to be rid of her company.

When I got to reading the book it was very intriguing. It was very deep thinking about how man is now on trial with God and if we fulfill our duty God will bless us with a real new life on Earth. The signs and portents show it. It wasn't like, you know, Sunday school stuff. It was deep.

After awhile I heard some music and saw the soldiers from the other riot car were across the street by the gas tanks, sitting in the shade of some trees and kidding with the workers from the plant. One of them was playing a guitar, not electric, just plain. It looked so peaceful.

Then Mayor Blount drove up alone in the cruiser and came in. When he saw I was reading the book he smiled at me sort of fatherly, but he looked tense. He asked me where Dr. Fay was and I told him she was lying down in back. He said that was okay. Then he kind of sighed and went back down the hall, closing the door behind him. I sat and listened to the guitar man, trying to hear what he was singing. I felt really hungry, my lunch was in Dr. Premack's car.

After awhile the door opened and Mayor Blount came back in. He looked terrible, his clothes were messed up and he had bloody scrape marks on his face. He didn't say anything, he just looked at me hard and fierce, like he might have been disoriented. I saw his zipper was open and there was blood on his clothing and also on his (private parts). I didn't feel frightened, I felt something important had happened. I tried to get him to sit down. But he motioned me to follow him back down the hall, to where Dr. Fay was. "You must see," he said. He went into the toilet and I went into a kind of little room there, where the cot was. The light was fairly good, reflected off the tin roof from where the walls stopped. I saw Dr. Fay lying on the cot in a peaceful appearance. She was lying straight, her clothing was to some extent different but her legs were together. I was glad to see that. Her blouse was pulled up and I saw there was a cut or incision on her abdomen. The blood was coming out there, or it had been coming out there, like a mouth. It wasn't moving at this time. Also her throat was cut open.

I returned to the office. Mayor Blount was sitting down, looking very tired. He had cleaned himself off. He said, "I did it for you. Do you understand?"

He seemed like my father, I can't say it better than that. I realized he was under a terrible strain, he had taken a lot on himself for me. He went on to explain how Dr. Fay was very dangerous, she was what they call a cripto-female (crypto?), the most dangerous kind. He had exposed her and purified the situation. He was very straightforward, I didn't feel confused at all, I knew he had done what was right.

We discussed the book, how man must purify himself and show God a clean world. He said some people raise the question of how can man reproduce without women but such people miss the point. The point is that as long as man depends on the old filthy animal way God won't help him. When man gets rid of his animal part which is woman, this is the signal God is awaiting. Then God will reveal the new true clean way, maybe angels will come bringing new souls, or maybe we will live forever, but it is not our place to speculate, only to obey. He said some men here had seen an Angel of the Lord. This was very deep, it seemed like it echoed inside me, I felt it was inspiration.

Then the medical party drove up and I told Dr. Premack that Dr. Fay had been taken care of and sent away, and I got in the car to drive them out of the Liberated Zone. However four of the six soldiers from the roadblock refused to leave. Capt. Parr tried to argue them out of it but finally agreed they could stay to guard the oil-drum barrier.

I would have liked to stay too the place was so peaceful but they needed me to drive the car. If I had known there would be all this hassle I never would have done them the favor. I am not crazy and I have not done anything wrong and my lawyer will get me out. That is all I have to say.

In Cuyapán the hot afternoon rain had temporarily ceased. As Alan's fingers let go of Sgt. Willard Mews's wretched document he caught sight of pencil-scrawled words in the margin. Barney's spider hand. He squinted.

Man's religion and metaphysics are the voices of his glands. Schönweiser, 1878.

Who the devil Schönweiser was Alan didn't know, but he knew what Barney was conveying. This murderous crackpot religion of McWhosis was a symptom, not a cause. Barney believed something was physically affecting the Peedsville men, generating psychosis, and a local religious demagog had sprung up to "explain" it.

Well, maybe. But cause or effect, Alan thought only of one thing: eight hundred miles from Peedsville to Ann Arbor. Anne should be safe. She *had* to be.

He threw himself on the lumpy cot, his mind going back exultantly to his work. At the cost of a million bites and cane-cuts he was pretty sure he'd found the weak link in the canefly cycle. The male mass-mating behavior, the comparative scarcity of ovulant females. It would be the screwfly solution all over again with the sexes reversed. Concentrate the pheromone, release sterilized females. Luckily the breeding populations were comparatively isolated. In a couple of seasons they ought to have it. Have to let them go on spraying poison meanwhile, of course; damn pity, it was slaughtering everything and getting in the water, and the caneflies had evolved to immunity anyway. But in a couple of seasons, maybe three, they could drop the canefly populations below reproductive viability. No more tormented human bodies with those stinking larvae in the nasal passages and brain. . . . He drifted off for a nap, grinning.

Up north, Anne was biting her lip in shame and pain.

Sweetheart, I shouldn't admit it but your wife is a bit jittery. Just female nerves or something, nothing to worry about. Everything is normal up here. It's so eerily normal, nothing in the papers, nothing anywhere except what I hear through Barney and Lillian. But Pauline's phone won't answer out in San Diego; the fifth day some strange man yelled at me and banged the phone down. Maybe she's sold her house—but why wouldn't she call?

Lillian's on some kind of Save-the-Women committee, like we were an endangered species, ha-ha—you know Lillian. It seems the Red Cross has started setting up camps. But she says, after the first rush, only a trickle are coming out of what they call "the affected areas". Not many children, either, even little boys. And they have some air-photos around Lubbock showing what look like mass graves. Oh, Alan . . . so far it seems to be mostly spreading west, but something's happening to St. Louis, they're cut off. So many places seem to have just vanished from the news, I had a nightmare that there isn't a woman left alive down there. And nobody's *doing* anything. They talked about spraying with tranquillizers for awhile and then that died out. What could it do? Somebody at the U.N. had proposed a convention on—you won't believe this—*femicide*. It sounds like a deodorant spray.

Excuse me honey, I seem to be a little hysterical. George Searles came back from Georgia talking about God's Will—Searles the life-long atheist. Alan, something crazy is happening.

But there are no facts. Nothing. The Surgeon General issued a report on the bodies of the Rahway Rip-Breast Team—I guess I didn't tell you about that. Anyway, they could find no pathology. Milton Baines wrote a letter saying in the present state of the art we can't distinguish the brain of a saint from the psychopathic killer, so how could they expect to find what they don't know how to look for?

Well, enough of these jitters. It'll be all over by the time you get back, just history. Everything's fine here, I fixed the car's muffler again. And Amy's coming home for the vacations, *that'll* get my mind off faraway problems.

Oh, something amusing to end with—Angie told me what Barney's enzyme does to the spruce budworm. It seems it blocks the male from turning around after he connects with the female, so he mates with her *head* instead. Like clockwork with a cog missing. There're going to be some pretty puzzled female spruceworms. Now why couldn't Barney tell me that? He really is such a sweet shy old dear. He's given me some stuff to put in, as usual. I didn't read it.

Now don't worry my darling everything's fine.

I love you, I love you so.

Always, all ways your Anne

Two weeks later in Cuyapán when Barney's enclosures slid out of the envelope, Alan didn't read them either. He stuffed them into the pocket of his bush-jacket with a shaking hand and started bundling his notes together on the rickety table, with a scrawled note to Sister Dominique on top. *Anne, Anne my darling.* The hell with the canefly, the hell with everything except that tremor in his fearless girl's handwriting. The hell with being five thousand miles away from his woman, his child, while some deadly madness raged. He crammed his meager belongings into his duffel. If he hurried he could catch the bus through to Bogotá and maybe make the Miami flight.

In Miami he found the planes north jammed. He failed a quick standby; six hours to wait. Time to call Anne. When the call got through some difficulty he was unprepared for the rush of joy and relief that burst along the wires.

"Thank God—I can't believe it—Oh, Alan, my darling, are you really—I can't believe—"

He found he was repeating too, and all mixed up with the canefly data. They were both laughing hysterically when he finally hung up.

Six hours. He settled in a frayed plastic chair opposite *Aerolineas Argentinas,* his mind half back at the clinic, half on the throngs moving by him. Something was oddly different here, he perceived presently. Where was the decorative fauna he usually enjoyed in Miami, the parade of young girls in crotch-tight pastel jeans? The flounces, boots, wild hats and hairdos and startling expanses of newly-tanned skin, the brilliant fabrics barely confining the bob of breasts and buttocks? Not here—but wait; looking closely, he glimpsed two young faces hidden under unbecoming parkas, their bodies draped in bulky nondescript skirts. In fact, all down the long vista he could see the same thing: hooded ponchos, heaped on clothes and baggy pants, dull colors. A new style? No, he thought not. It seemed to him their movements suggested furtiveness, timidity. And they moved in groups. He watched a lone girl struggle to catch up with others ahead of her, apparently strangers. They accepted her wordlessly.

They're frightened, he thought. Afraid of attracting notice. Even that gray-haired matron in a pantsuit resolutely leading a flock of kids was glancing around nervously.

And at the Argentine desk opposite he saw another odd thing: two lines had a big sign over them, *Mujeres.* Women. They were crowded with the shapeless forms and very quiet.

The men seemed to be behaving normally; hurrying, lounging, griping and joking in the lines as they kicked their luggage along. But Alan felt an undercurrent of tension, like an irritant in the air. Outside the line of storefronts behind him a few isolated men seemed to be handing out tracts. An airport attendant spoke to the nearest man; he merely shrugged and moved a few doors down.

To distract himself Alan picked up a *Miami Herald* from the next seat. It was surprisingly thin. The international news occupied him for awhile; he had seen none for weeks. It too had a strange empty quality, even the bad news seemed to have dried up. The African war which had been going on seemed to be over, or went unreported. A trade summit-meeting was haggling over grain and steel prices. He found himself at the obituary pages, columns of close-set type dominated by the photo of an unknown defunct ex-senator. Then his eye fell on two announcements at the bottom of the page. One was too flowery for quick comprehension, but the other stated in bold plain type:

THE FORSETTE FUNERAL HOME
REGRETFULLY ANNOUNCES
IT WILL NO LONGER ACCEPT
FEMALE CADAVERS

Slowly he folded the paper, staring at it numbly. On the back was an item headed *Navigational Hazard Warning,* in the shipping news. Without really taking it in, he read:

AP/Nassau: The excursion liner *Carib Swallow* reached port under tow today after striking an obstruction in the Gulf Stream off Cape Hatteras. The obstruction was identified as part of a commercial trawler's seine floated by female corpses. This confirms reports from Florida and the Gulf of the use of such seines, some of them over a mile in length. Similar reports coming from the Pacific coast and as far away as Japan indicate a growing hazard to coastwide shipping.

Alan flung the thing into a trash receptacle and sat rubbing his forehead and eyes. Thank God he had followed his impulse to come home. He felt totally disoriented, as though he had landed by error on another planet. Four and a half hours more to wait. . . . At length he recalled the stuff from Barney he had thrust in his pocket, and pulled it out and smoothed it.

The top item, however, seemed to be from Anne, or at least the Ann Arbor News. Dr. Lillian Dash, together with several hundred other members of her organization, had been arrested for demonstrating without a permit in front of the White House. They seemed to have started a fire in an oil drum, which was considered particularly heinous. A number of women's groups had participated, the total struck Alan as more like thousands than hundreds. Extraordinary security precautions were being taken, despite the fact that the President was out of town at the time.

The next item had to be Barney's, if Alan could recognize the old man's acerbic humor.

UP/Vatican City 19 June. Pope John IV today intimated that he does not plan to comment officially on the so-called Pauline Purification cults advocating the elimination of women as a means of justifying man to God. A spokesman emphasized that the Church takes no position on these cults but repudiates any doctrine involving a "challenge" to or from God to reveal His further plans for man.

Cardinal Fazzoli, spokesman for the European Pauline movement, reaffirmed his view that the Scriptures define woman as merely a temporary companion and instrument of Man. Women, he states, are nowhere defined as human, but merely as a transitional expedient or state. "The time of transition to full humanity is at hand," he concluded.

The next item appeared to be a thin-paper Xerox from a recent issue of *Science:*

SUMMARY REPORT OF THE AD HOC EMERGENCY COMMITTEE OF FEMICIDE

The recent world-wide though localized outbreaks of femicide appear to represent a recurrence of similar outbreaks by some group or sect which are not uncommon in world history in times of psychic stress. In this case the root cause is undoubtedly the speed of social and technological change, augmented by population pressure, and the spread and scope are aggravated by instantaneous world communications, thus exposing more susceptible persons. It is not viewed as a medical or epidemiological problem; no physical pathology has been found. Rather it is more akin to the various manias which swept Europe in the 17th century, e.g., the Dancing Manias, and like them, should run its course and disappear. The chiliastic cults which have sprung up around the affected areas appear to be unrelated, having in common only the idea that a new means of human reproduction will be revealed as a result of the "purifying" elimination of women.

We recommend that (1) inflammatory and sensational reporting be suspended; (2) refugee centers be set up and maintained for women escapees from the focal areas; (3) containment of affected areas by military cordon be continued and enforced; and (4) after a cooling-down period and the subsidence of the mania, qualified mental health teams and appropriate professional personnel go in to undertake rehabilitation.

SUMMARY OF THE MINORITY
REPORT OF THE AD HOC COMMITTEE

The nine members signing this report agree that there is no evidence for epidemiological contagion of femicide in the strict sense. *However,* the geographical relation of the focal areas of outbreak strongly suggest that they cannot be dismissed as purely psychosocial phenomena. The initial outbreaks have occurred around the globe near the 30th parallel, the area of principal atmospheric downflow of upper winds coming from the Intertropical Convergence Zone. An agent or condition in the upper equatorial atmosphere would thus be expected to reach ground level along the 30th parallel, with certain seasonal variations. One principal variation is that the downflow moves north over the East Asian continent during the late winter months, and these areas south of it (Arabia, Western India, parts of North Africa) have in fact been free of outbreaks until recently, when the downflow zone has moved south. A similar downflow occurs in the Southern Hemisphere, and outbreaks have been reported along the 30th parallel running through Pretoria and Alice Springs, Australia. (Information from Argentina is currently unavailable.)

This geographical correlation cannot be dismissed, and it is therefore urged that an intensified search for a physical cause be instituted. It is also urgently recommended that the rate of spread from known focal points be correlated with wind condition. A watch for similar outbreaks along the secondary down-welling zones at 60° north and south should be kept.

(signed for the minority)
Barnhard Braithwaite

Alan grinned reminiscently at his old friend's name, which seemed to restore normalcy and stability to the world. It looked as if Barney was onto something, too, despite the prevalence of horses' asses. He frowned, puzzling it out.

Then his face slowly changed as he thought how it would be, going home to Anne. In a few short hours his arms would be around her, the tall, secretly beautiful body that had come to obsess him. Theirs had been a late-blooming love. They'd married, he supposed now, out of friendship, even out of friends' pressure. Everyone said they were made for each other, he big and chunky and blond, she willowy brunette; both shy, highly controlled, cerebral types. For the first few years the friendship had held, but sex hadn't been all that much. Conventional necessity. Politely reassuring each other, privately—he could say it now—disappointing.

But then, when Amy was a toddler, something had happened. A miraculous inner portal of sensuality had slowly opened to them, a liberation into their own secret unsuspected heaven of fully physical bliss . . . Jesus, but it had been a wrench when the Colombia thing had come up. Only their absolute sureness of each other had made him take it. And now, to be about to have her again, trebly desirable from the spice of separation—feeling-seeing-hearing-smelling-grasping. He shifted in his seat to conceal his body's excitement, half mesmerized by fantasy.

And Amy would be there, too; he grinned at the memory of that prepubescent little body plastered against him. She was going to be a handful, all right. His manhood understood Amy a lot better than her mother did; no cerebral phase for Amy . . . But Anne, his exquisite shy one, with whom he'd found the way into the almost unendurable transports of the flesh . . . First the conventional greeting, he thought; the news, the unspoken, savored, mounting excitement behind their eyes; the light touches; then the seeking of their own room, the falling clothes, the caresses, gentle at first—the flesh, the *nakedness*—the delicate teasing, the grasp, the first thrust—

—A terrible alarm-bell went off in his head. Exploded from his dream, he stared around, then finally down at his hands. *What was he doing with his open clasp-knife in his fist?*

Stunned, he felt for the last shreds of his fantasy, and realized that the tactile images had not been of caresses, but of a frail neck strangling in his fist, the thrust had been the Plunge of a blade seeking vitals. In his arms, legs, phantasms of striking and trampling bones cracking. And Amy—

Oh God, Oh God—

Not sex, bloodlust.

That was what he had been dreaming. The sex was there, but it was driving some engine of death.

Numbly he put the knife away, thinking only over and over, it's got me. It's got me. Whatever it is, it's got me. *I can't go home*.

After an unknown time he got up and made his way to the United counter to turn in his ticket. The line was long. As he waited, his mind cleared a little. What could he do, here in Miami? Wouldn't it be better to get back to Ann Arbor and turn himself in to Barney? Barney could help him, if anyone could. Yes, that was best. But first he had to warn Anne.

The connection took even longer this time. When Anne finally answered he found himself blurting unintelligibly, it took awhile to make her understand he wasn't talking about a plane delay.

"I tell you, I've caught it. Listen, Anne, for God's sake. If I should come to the house don't let me come near you. I mean it. I'm going to the lab, but I might lose control and try to get to you. Is Barney there?"

"Yes, but darling—"

"Listen. Maybe he can fix me, maybe this'll wear off. But I'm not safe, Anne, Anne, I'd kill you, can you understand? Get a —get a weapon. I'll try not to come to the house. But if I do, don't let me get near you. Or Amy. It's a sickness, it's real. Treat me—treat me like a fucking wild animal. Anne, say you understand, say you'll do it."

They were both crying when he hung up.

He went shaking back to sit and wait. After a time his head seemed to clear a little more. *Doctor, try to think*. The first thing he thought of was to take the loathsome knife and throw it down a trash-slot. As he did so he realized there was one more piece of Barney's material in his pocket. He uncrumpled it; it seemed to be a clipping from *Nature*.

At the top was Barney's scrawl: "Only guy making sense. U.K. infected now, Oslo, Copenhagen out of communication. Damfools still won't listen. Stay put."

Communication from Professor Ian
MacIntyre, Glasgow Univ.

A potential difficulty for our species has always been implicit in the close linkage between the behavioural expression of aggression /predation and sexual reproduction in the male. This close linkage involves (a) many of the same neuromuscular pathways which are utilized both in predatory and sexual pursuit, grasping, mounting, etc., and (b) similar states of adrenergic arousal which are activated in both. The same linkage is seen in the males of many other species; in some, the expression of aggression and copulation alternate or even coexist, an all-too-familiar example being the common house cat. Males of many species bite, claw, bruise, tread or otherwise assault receptive females during the act of intercourse; indeed, in some species the male attack is necessary for female ovulation to occur.

In many if not all species it is the aggressive behaviour which appears first, and then changes to copulatory behaviour when the appropriate signal is presented (*e.g.,* the three-tined sickleback and the European robin). Lacking the inhibiting signal, the male's fighting response continues and the female is attacked or driven off.

It seems therefore appropriate to speculate that the present crisis might be caused by some substance, perhaps at the viral or enzymatic level, which effects a failure of the switching or triggering function in the higher primates. (Note: Zoo gorillas and chimpanzees have recently been observed to attack or destroy their mates; rhesus not.) Such a dysfunction could be expressed by the failure of mating behaviour to modify or supervene over the aggressive/predatory response; *i.e.,* sexual stimulation would produce attack only, the stimulation discharging itself through the destruction of the stimulating object.

In this connection it might be noted that exactly this condition is a commonplace of male functional pathology, in those cases where murder occurs as a response to and apparent completion of, sexual desire.

It should be emphasized that the aggression/copulation linkage discussed here is specific to the male; the female response (*e.g.,* lordotic reflex) being of a different nature.

Alan sat holding the crumpled sheet a long time; the dry, stilted Scottish phrases seemed to help clear his head, despite the sense of brooding tension all around him. Well, if pollution or whatever had produced some substance, it could presumably be countered, filtered, neutralized. Very very carefully, he let himself consider his life with Anne, his sexuality. Yes; much of their loveplay could be viewed as genitalized, sexually-gentled savagery. Play-preda-tion . . . He turned his mind quickly away. Some writer's phrase occurred to him: "The panic element is all sex." Who? Fritz Leiber? The violation of social distance, maybe; another threaten-ing element. Whatever, it's our weak link, he thought. Our vulner-ability . . . The dreadful feeling of *rightness* he had experienced when he found himself knife in hand, fantasizing violence, came back to him. As though it was the right, the only way. Was that what Barney's budworms felt when they mated with their females wrong-end-to?

At length, he became aware of body need and sought a toilet. The place was empty, except for what he took to be a heap of clothes blocking the door of the far stall. Then he saw the red-brown pool in which it lay, and the bluish mounds of bare, thin buttocks. He backed out, not breathing, and fled into the nearest crowd, knowing he was not the first to have done so.

Of course. Any sexual drive. Boys, men, too.

At the next washroom he watched to see men enter and leave normally before he ventured in.

Afterward he returned to sit, waiting, repeating over and over to himself: *Go to the lab. Don't go home. Go straight to the lab.* Three more hours; he sat numbly at 26° N, 81° W, breathing, breathing . . .

Dear Diary. Big scene tonite, Daddy came home!!! Only he acted so funny, he had the taxi wait and just held onto the door-way, he wouldn't touch me or let us come near him. (I mean funny weird, not funny Ha-ha.) He said, I have something to tell you, this is getting worse not better. I'm going to sleep in the lab but I want you to get out, Anne, Anne, I can't trust myself any more. First thing in the morning you both get on the plane for Martha's and stay there. So I thought he had to be joking. I mean with the dance next week and Aunt Martha lives in Whitehorse where there's nothing nothing nothing. So I was yelling and Mother was yelling and Daddy was groaning. Go now! And then he started crying. Crying!!! So I realized, wow, this is serious, and

I started to go over to him but Mother yanked me back and then I saw she had this big KNIFE!!! And she shoved me in back of her and started crying too Oh Alan, Oh Alan, like she was insane. So I said, Daddy, I'll never leave you, it felt like the perfect thing to say. And it was thrilling, he looked at me real sad and deep like I was a grown-up while Mother was treating me like I was a mere infant as usual. But Mother ruined it raving Alan the child is mad, darling go. So he ran out the door yelling Be gone, Take the car, Get out before I come back.

Oh I forgot to say I was wearing what but my gooby green with my curltites still on, wouldn't you know of all the shitty luck, how could I have known such a beautiful scene was ahead we never know life's cruel whimsy. And mother is dragging out suitcases yelling Pack your things hurry! So she's going I guess but I am not repeat not going to spend the fall sitting in Aunt Martha's grain silo and lose the dance and all my summer credits. And Daddy was trying to communicate with us, right? I think their relationship is obsolete. So when she goes upstairs I am splitting, I am going to go over to the lab and see Daddy.

Oh PS Diane tore my yellow jeans she promised me I could use her pink ones Ha-ha that'll be the day.

I ripped that page out of Amy's diary when I heard the squad car coming. I never opened her diary before but when I found she'd gone I looked . . . Oh, my darling little girl. She went to him, my little girl, my poor little fool child. Maybe if I'd taken time to explain, maybe—

Excuse me, Barney. The stuff is wearing off, the shots they gave me. I didn't feel anything. I mean, I knew somebody's daughter went to see her father and he killed her. And cut his throat. But it didn't mean anything.

Alan's note, they gave me that but then they took it away. Why did they have to do that? His last handwriting, the last words he wrote before his hand picked up the, before he—

I remember it. *"Sudden and light as that, the bonds gave And we learned of finalities besides the grave. The bonds of our humanity have given, we are finished. I love—"*

I'm all right, Barney, really. Who wrote that, Robert Frost? *The bonds gave*. . . . Oh, he said, tell Barney: *The terrible rightness*. What does that mean?

You can't answer that, Barney dear. I'm just writing this to stay sane, I'll put it in your hidey-hole. Thank you, thank you Barney dear. Even as blurry as I was, I knew it was you. All the time you were cutting off my hair and rubbing dirt on my face, I knew it was right because it was you. Barney I never thought of you as those horrible words you said. You were always Dear Barney.

By the time the stuff wore off I had done everything you said, the gas, the groceries. Now I'm here in your cabin. With those clothes you made me put on I guess I do look like a boy, the gas man called me "Mister."

I still can't really realize, I have to stop myself from rushing back. But you saved my life, I know that. The first trip in I got a paper, I saw where they bombed the Apostle Islands refuge. And it had about those three women stealing the Air Force plane and bombing Dallas, too. Of course they shot them down, over the Gulf. Isn't it strange how we do nothing? Just get killed by ones and twos. Or more, now they've started on the refuges. . . . Like hypnotized rabbits. We're a toothless race.

Do you know I never said "we" meaning women before? "We" was always me and Alan, and Amy of course. Being killed selectively encourages group identification. . . . You see how sane-headed I am.

But I still can't really realize.

My first trip in was for salt and kerosene. I went to that little Red Deer store and got my stuff from the old man in the back, as you told me—you see, I remembered! He called me "Boy," but I think maybe he suspects. He knows I'm staying in your cabin.

Anyway, some men and boys came in the front. They were all so *normal,* laughing and kidding, I just couldn't believe, Barney. In fact I started to go out past them when I heard one of them say "Heinz saw an angel." An *angel.* So I stopped and listened. They said it was big and sparkly. Coming to see if man is carrying out God's will, one of them said. And he said, Moosenee is now a liberated zone, and all up by Hudson Bay. I turned and got out the back, fast. The old man had heard them too. He said to me quietly, I'll miss the kids.

Hudson Bay, Barney, that means it's coming from the north too, doesn't it? That must be about 60°.

But I have to go back once again, to get some fishhooks. I can't live on bread. Last week I found a deer some poacher had killed, just the head and legs. I made a stew. It was a doe. Her eyes; I wonder if mine look like that now.

I went to get the fishhooks today. It was bad, I can't ever go back. There were some men in front again, but they were different. Mean and tense. No boys. And there was a new sign out in front, I couldn't see it; maybe it says Liberated Zone too.

The old man gave me the hooks quick and whispered to me, "Boy, them woods'll be full of hunters next week." I almost ran out.

About a mile down the road a blue pickup started to chase me. I guess he wasn't from around there, I ran the VW into a logging draw and he roared on by. After a long while I drove out and came on back, but I left the car about a mile from here and hiked in. It's surprising how hard it is to pile enough brush to hide a yellow VW.

Barney, I can't stay here. I'm eating perch raw so nobody will see my smoke, but those hunters will be coming through. I'm going to move my sleeping bag out to the swamp by that big rock, I don't think many people go there.

Since the last lines I moved out. It feels safer. Oh, Barney, how did this *happen?*

Fast, that's how. Six months ago I was Dr. Anne Alstein. Now I'm a widow and bereaved mother, dirty and hungry, squatting in a swamp in mortal fear. Funny if I'm the last woman left alive on Earth. I guess the last one around here, anyway. Maybe some holed out in the Himalayas, or sneaking through the wreck of New York City. How can we last?

We can't.

And I can't survive the winter here, Barney. It gets to 40° below. I'd have to have a fire, they'd see the smoke. Even if I worked my way south, the woods end in a couple hundred miles. I'd be potted like a duck. No. No use. Maybe somebody is trying something somewhere, but it won't reach here in time . . . and what do I have to live for?

No. I'll just make a good end, say up on that rock where I can see the stars. After I go back and leave this for you. I'll wait to see the beautiful color in the trees one last time.

I know what I'll scratch for an epitaph.

HERE LIES THE SECOND MEANEST
PRIMATE ON EARTH.

Good-bye, dearest dearest Barney.

I guess nobody will ever read this, unless I get the nerve and energy to take it to Barney's. Probably I won't. Leave it in a Baggie, I have one here; maybe Barney will come and look. I'm up on the big rock now. The moon is going to rise soon, I'll do it then. Mosquitoes, be patient. You'll have all you want.

The thing I have to write down is that I saw an angel too. This morning. It was big and sparkly, like the man said; like a Christmas tree without the tree. But I knew it was real because the frogs stopped croaking and two bluejays gave alarm calls. That's important; it was *really there*.

I watched it, sitting under my rock. It didn't move much. It sort of bent over and picked up something, leaves or twigs, I couldn't see. Then it did something with them around its middle, like putting them into an invisible sample-pocket.

Let me repeat—it was *there*. Barney, if you're reading this, THERE ARE THINGS HERE. And I think they've done whatever it is to us. Made us kill ourselves off.

Why? Well, it's a nice place, if it wasn't for people. How do you get rid of people? Bombs, death-rays—all very primitive. Leave a big mess. Destroy everything, craters, radioactivity, ruin the place.

This way there's no muss, no fuss. Just like what we did to the screwfly. Pinpoint the weak link, wait a bit while we do it for them. Only a few bones around; make good fertilizer.

Barney dear, good-bye. I saw it. It was there.

But it wasn't an angel.

I think I saw a real-estate agent.

EYES OF AMBER

by Joan D. Vinge

This has an affinity with John Varley's story only insofar as both tales utilize the known techniques of space exploration without having to throw in Buck Rogers' rocket ships and all that. What we have here is an alien civilization on an alien—and for Terrestrials uninhabitable—world . . . and the peculiarities of attempting meaningful conversation between mutually exclusive mentalities.

The beggar woman shuffled up the silent evening street to the rear of Lord Chwiul's townhouse. She hesitated, peering up at the softly glowing towers, then clawed at the watchman's arm. "A word with you master—"

"Don't touch me, hag!" The guard raised his spearbutt in disgust.

A deft foot kicked free of the rags and snagged him off balance. He found himself sprawled on his back in the spring melt, the speartip dropping toward his belly, guided by a new set of hands. He gaped, speechless. The beggar tossed an amulet onto his chest.

"Look at it, fool! I have business with your lord." The beggar woman stepped back, the speartip tapped him impatiently.

The guard squirmed in the filth and wet, holding the amulet up close to his face in the poor light. "You . . . you are the one? You may pass—"

"Indeed!" Muffled laughter. "Indeed I may pass—for many things, in many places. The Wheel of Change carries us all." She lifted the spear. "Get up, fool . . . and no need to escort me, I'm expected."

The guard climbed to his feet, dripping and sullen, and stood back while she freed her wing membranes from the folds of cloth. He watched them glisten and spread as she gathered herself to leap effortlessly to the tower's entrance, twice his height above. He waited until she had vanished inside before he even dared to curse her.

"Lord Chwiul?"

"T'uupieh, I presume." Lord Chwiul leaned forward on the couch of fragrant mosses, peering into the shadows of the hall.

"*Lady* T'uupieh." T'uupieh strode forward into light, letting the ragged hood slide back from her face. She took a fierce pleasure in making no show of obeisance, in coming forward directly as nobility to nobility. The sensuous ripple of a hundred tiny *miih* hides underfoot made her calloused feet tingle. *After so long, it comes back too easily . . .*

She chose the couch across the low, waterstone table from him, stretching languidly in her beggar's rags. She extended a finger claw and picked a juicy *kelet* berry from the bowl in the table's scroll-carven surface; let it slide into her mouth and down her throat, as she had done so often, so long ago. And then, at last, she glanced up, to measure his outrage.

"You dare to come to me in this manner—"

Satisfactory. *Yes, very . . . "I* did not come to you. You came to me . . . you sought my services." Her eyes wandered the room with affected casualness, taking in the elaborate frescoes that surfaced the waterstone walls even in this small, private room . . . particularly in this room? she wondered. How many midnight meetings, for what varied intrigues, were held in this room? Chwiul was not the wealthiest of his family or clan: and appearances of wealth and power counted in this city, in this world—for wealth and power were everything.

"I sought the services of T'uupieh the Assassin. I'm surprised to find that the Lady T'uupieh dared to accompany her here." Chwiul had regained his composure; she watched his breath frost, and her own, as he spoke.

"Where one goes, the other follows. We are inseparable. You should know that better than most, my lord." She watched his long, pale arm extend to spear several berries at once. Even though the nights were chill he wore only a body-wrapping tunic, which let him display the intricate scaling of jewels that danced and spiraled over his wing surfaces.

He smiled; she saw the sharp fangs protrude slightly. "Because my brother made the one into the other, when he seized your lands? I'm surprised you would come at all—how did you know you could trust me?" His movements were ungraceful; she remembered how the jewels dragged down fragile, translucent wing membranes and slender arms, until flight was impossible. Like every noble, Chwiul was normally surrounded by servants who answered his every whim. Incompetence, feigned or real, was one more trapping of power, one more indulgence that only the rich could afford. She was pleased that the jewels were not of high quality.

"I don't trust you," she said, "I trust only myself. But I have friends, who told me you were sincere enough—in this case. And of course, I did not come alone."

"Your outlaws?" Disbelief. "That would be no protection."

Calmly she separated the folds of cloth that held her secret companion at her side.

"It is true," Chwiul trilled softly. "They call you Demon's Consort!"

She turned the amber lens of the demon's precious eye so that it could see the room, as she had seen it, and then settled its gaze on Chwiul. He drew back slightly, fingering moss.

"'A demon has a thousand eyes, and a thousand thousand torments for those who offend it.'" She quoted from the Book of Ngoss, whose rituals she had used to bind the demon to her.

Chwiul stretched nervously, as if he wanted to fly away. But he only said, "Then I think we understand each other. And I think I have made a good choice: I know how well you have served the Overlord, and other court members . . . I want you to kill someone for me."

"Obviously."

"I want you to kill Klovhiri."

T'uupieh started, very slightly. "You surprise me in return, Lord Chwiul. Your own brother?" *And the usurper of my lands. How I have ached to kill him, slowly, so slowly, with my own hands. . . . But always he is too well guarded.*

"And your sister too—my lady." Faint overtones of mockery. "I want his whole family eliminated; his mate, his children . . ."

Klovhiri . . . and Ahtseet. Ahtseet, her own younger sister, who had been her closest companion since childhood, her only family since their parents had died. Ahtseet, whom she had cherished and protected; dear, conniving, traitorous little Ahtseet—who could forsake pride and decency and family honor to mate willingly with the man who had robbed them of everything . . . Anything to keep the family lands, Ahtseet had shrilled; anything to keep her position. But that was not the way! Not by surrendering; but by striking back—T'uupieh became aware that Chwiul was watching her reaction with unpleasant interest. She fingered the dagger at her belt.

"Why?" She laughed, wanting to ask, *"How?"*

"That should be obvious. I'm tired of coming second. I want what he has—your lands, and all the rest. I want him out of my way, and I don't want anyone else left with a better claim to his inheritance than I have."

"Why not do it yourself? Poison them, perhaps . . . it's been done before."

"No. Klovhiri has too many friends, too many loyal clansmen, too much influence with the Overlord. It has to be an 'accidental' murder. And no one would be better suited than you, my lady, to do it for me."

T'uupieh nodded vaguely, assessing. No one could be better chosen for a desire to succeed than she . . . and also, for a position from which to strike. All she had lacked until now was the opportunity. From the time she had been dispossessed, through the fading days of autumn and the endless winter—for nearly a third of her life, now—she had haunted the wild swamp and fenland of her estate. She had gathered a few faithful servants, a few malcontents, a few cutthroats, to harry and murder Klovhiri's retainers, ruin his phib nets, steal from his snares and poach her own game. And for survival, she had taken to robbing whatever travelers took the roads that passed through her lands.

Because she was still nobility, the Overlord had at first toler-ated, and then secretly encouraged her banditry: Many wealthy foreigners traveled the routes that crossed her estate, and for a certain commission, he allowed her to attack them with impunity. It was a sop, she knew, thrown to her because he had let his favor-ite, Klovhiri, have her lands. But she used it to curry what favor she could, and after a time the Overlord had begun to bring her more discreet and profitable business—the elimination of certain enemies. And so she had become an assassin as well—and found that the calling was not so very different from that of noble: both required nerve, and cunning, and an utter lack of compunction. And because she was T'uupieh, she had succeeded admirably. But because of her vendetta, the rewards had been small . . . until now.

"You do not answer," Chwiul was saying. "Does that mean your nerve fails you, in kith-murder, where mine does not?"

She laughed sharply. "That you say it proves twice that your judgment is poorer than mine. . . . No, my nerve does not fail me. Indeed, my blood burns with desire! But I hadn't thought to lay Klovhiri under the ice, just to give my lands to his brother. Why should I do that favor for you?"

"Because obviously you cannot do it alone. Klovhiri hasn't managed to have you killed, in all the time you've plagued him; which is a testament to your skill. But you've made him too wary—you can't get near him, when he keeps himself so well protected. You need the cooperation of someone who has his trust—someone like myself. I can make him yours."

"And what will be my reward, if I accept? Revenge is sweet; but revenge is not enough."

"I will pay what you ask."

"My estate." She smiled.

"Even you are not so naive—"

"No." She stretched a wing toward nothing in the air. "I am not so naive. I know its value . . ." The memory of a golden-clouded summer's day caught her—of soaring, soaring, on the warm up-drafts above the streaming lake . . . seeing the fragile rose-red of the manor towers spearing light far off above the windswept tide of the trees . . . the saffron and crimson and aquamarine of ammo-nia pools bright with dissolved metals, that lay in the gleaming melt-surface of her family's land, the land that stretched forever, like the summer . . . "I know its value." Her voice hardened. "And that Klovhiri is still the Overlord's pet. As you say, Klovhiri has many powerful friends, and they will become your friends when he dies. I need more strength, more wealth, before I can buy enough influence to hold what is mine again. The odds are not in my favor—now."

"You are carved from ice, T'uupieh. I like that." Chwiul leaned forward. His amorphous red eyes moved along her outstretched body; trying to guess what lay concealed beneath the rags in the shadowy foxfire-light of the room. His eyes came back to her face.

She showed him neither annoyance nor amusement. "I like no man who likes that in me."

"Not even if it meant regaining your estate?"

"As a mate of yours?" Her voice snapped like a frozen branch. "My lord—I have just about decided to kill my sister for doing as much. I would sooner kill myself."

He shrugged, lying back on the couch. "As you wish . . ." He waved a hand in dismissal. "Then what will it take to be rid of my brother—and of you as well?"

"Ah." She nodded, understanding more. "You wish to buy my services, and to buy me off, too. That may not be so easy to do. But—," *But I will make the pretense, for now.* She speared berries from the bowl in the tabletop, watched the silky sheet of emerald-tinted ammonia water that curtained one wall. It dropped from heights within the tower into a tiny plunge basin, with a music that would blur conversation for anyone who tried to listen outside. Discretion, and beauty. . . . The musky fragrance of the mossy couch brought back her childhood suddenly, disconcertingly: the memory of lying in a soft bed, on a soft spring night. . . . "But as the seasons change, change moves me in new directions. Back into the city, perhaps. I like your tower, Lord Chwiul. It combines discretion and beauty."

"Thank you."

"Give it to me, and I'll do what you ask."

Chwiul sat up, frowning. "My townhouse!" Recovering, "Is that all you want?"

She spread her fingers, studied the vestigial webbing between them. "I realize it is rather modest." She closed her hand. "But considering what satisfaction will come from earning it, it will suffice. And you will not need it, once I succeed."

"No . . ." he relaxed somewhat. "I suppose not. I will scarcely miss it, after I have your lands."

She let it pass. "Well then, we are agreed. Now, tell me, where is the key to Klovhiri's lock? What is your plan for delivering him —and his family—into my hands?"

"You are aware that your sister and the children are visiting here, in my house, tonight? And that Klovhiri will return before the new day?"

"I am aware." She nodded, with more casualness than she felt; seeing that Chwiul was properly, if silently, impressed at her nerve in coming here. She drew her dagger from its sheath beside the demon's amber eye and stroked the serrated blade of water stone-impregnated wood. "You wish me to slit their throats, while they sleep under your very roof?" She managed the right blend of incredulity.

"No!" Chwiul frowned again. "What sort of fool do you—" he broke off. "With the new day, they will be returning to the estate by the usual route. I have promised to escort them, to ensure their safety along the way. There will also be a guide, to lead us through the bogs. But the guide will make a mistake . . ."

"And I will be waiting." T'uupieh's eyes brightened. During the winter the wealthy used sledges for travel on long journeys— preferring to be borne over the frozen melt by membranous sails, or dragged by slaves where the surface of the ground was rough and crumpled. But as spring came and the surface of the ground began to dissolve, treacherous sinks and pools opened like blossoms to swallow the unwary. Only an experienced guide could read the surfaces, tell sound waterstone from changeable ammonia-water melt. "Good," she said softly. "Yes, very good. . . . Your guide will see them safely foundered in some slushhole, and then I will snare them like changeling phibs."

"Exactly. But I want to be there when you do; I want to watch. I'll make some excuse to leave the group, and meet you in the swamp. The guide will mislead them only if he hears my signal."

"As you wish. You've paid well for the privilege. But come alone. My followers need no help, and no interference." She sat up, let her long, webbed feet down to rest again on the sensuous hides of the rug.

"And if you think that I'm a fool, and playing into your hands myself, consider this. You will be the obvious suspect when Klovhiri is murdered. I'll be the only witness who can swear to the Overlord that your outlaws weren't the attackers. Keep that in mind."

She nodded. "I will."

"How will I find you, then?"

"You will not. My thousand eyes will find you." She rewrapped the demon's-eye in its pouch of rags.

Chwiul looked vaguely disconcerted. "Will—*it* take part in the attack?"

"It may, or it may not; as it chooses. Demons are not bound to the Wheel of Change like you and I. But you will surely meet it face to face—although it has no face—if you come." She brushed the pouch at her side. "Yes—do keep in mind that I have my safeguards too, in this agreement. A demon never forgets."

She stood up at last, gazing once more around the room. "I shall be comfortable here." She glanced back at Chwiul. "I will look for you, come the new day."

"Come the new day." He rose, his jeweled wings catching light.

"No need to escort me. I shall be discreet." She bowed, as an equal, and started toward the shadowed hall. "I shall definitely get rid of your watchman. He doesn't know a lady from a beggar."

"The Wheel turns once more for me, my demon. My life in the swamps will end with Klovhiri's life. I shall move into town . . . and I shall be lady of my manor again, when the fishes sit in the trees!"

T'uupieh's alien face glowed with malevolent joy as she turned away, on the display screen above the computer terminal. Shannon Wyler leaned back in his seat, finished typing his translation, and pulled off the wire headset. He smoothed his long, blond, slicked-back hair, the habitual gesture helping him reorient to his surroundings. When T'uupieh spoke he could never maintain the objectivity he needed to help him remember he was still on Earth, and not really on Titan, orbiting Saturn, some fifteen hundred million kilometers away. *T'uupieh, whenever I think I love you, you decide to cut somebody's throat. . . .*

He nodded vaguely at the congratulatory murmurs of the staff and technicians, who literally hung on his every word waiting for new information. They began to thin out behind him, as the computer reproduced copies of the transcript. Hard to believe he'd been doing this for over a year now. He looked up at his concert posters on the wall, with nostalgia but no regret.

Someone was phoning Marcus Reed: he sighed, resigned.

" 'Vhen the fishes sit in the trees'? Are you being sarcastic?"

He looked over his shoulder at Dr. Garda Bach's massive form. "Hi, Garda. Didn't hear you come in."

She glanced up from a copy of the translation, tapped him lightly on the shoulder with her forked walking stick. "I know, dear boy. You never hear anything when T'uupieh speaks. But what do you mean by this?"

"On Titan that's summer—when the triphibians metamorphose for the third time. So she means maybe five years from now, our time."

"Ah! Of course. The old brain is not what it was . . ." She shook her gray-white head; her black cloak swirled out melodramatically.

He grinned, knowing she didn't mean a word of it. "Maybe learning Titanese on top of fifty other languages is the straw that breaks the camel's back."

"*Ja . . . ja . . .* maybe it is . . ." She sank heavily into the next seat over, already lost in the transcript. He had never, he thought, expected to like the old broad so well. He had become aware of her Presence while he studied linguistics at Berkeley—she was the *grande dame* of linguistic studies, dating back to the days when there had still been unrecorded languages here on Earth. But her skill at getting her name in print and her face on television, as an expert on what everybody "really meant", had convinced him that her true talent lay in merchandising. Meeting her at last, in person, hadn't changed his mind about that; but it had convinced him forever that she knew her stuff about cultural linguistics. And that, in turn, had convinced him her accent was a total fraud. But despite the flamboyance, or maybe even because of it, he found that her now-archaic views on linguistics were much closer to his own feelings about communication than the views of either one of his parents.

Garda sighed. "Remarkable, Shannon! You are simply remarkable—your feel for a wholly alien language amazes me. Whatever vould ve have done if you had not come to us?"

"Done without, I expect." He savored the special pleasure that came of being admired by someone he respected. He looked down again at the computer console, at the two shining green-lit plates of plastic thirty centimeters on a side, that together gave him the versatility of a virtuoso violinist and a typist with a hundred thousand keys: His link to T'uupieh, his voice—the new IBM synthesizer, whose touch-sensitive control plates could be manipulated to re-create the impossible complexities of her language. God's gift to the world of linguistics . . . except that it required the sensitivity and inspiration of a musician to fully use its range.

He glanced up again and out the window, at the now familiar fog-shrouded skyline of Coos Bay. Since very few linguists were musicians, their resistance to the synthesizer had been like a brick wall. The old guard of the aging New Wave—which included His Father the Professor and His Mother the Communications Engineer—still clung to a fruitless belief in mathematical computer translation. They still struggled with ungainly programs weighed down by endless morpheme lists, that supposedly would someday generate any message in a given language. But even after years of refinement, computer-generated translations were still uselessly crude and sloppy.

At graduate school there had been no new languages to seek out, and no permission for him to use the synthesizer to explore the old ones. And so—after a final, bitter family argument—he had quit graduate school. He had taken his belief in the synthesizer into the world of his second love, music; into a field where, he hoped, real communication still had some value. Now, at twenty-four, he was Shann the Music Man, the musician's musician, a hero to an immense generation of aging fans and a fresh new generation that had inherited their love for the ever-changing music called "rock". And neither of his parents had willingly spoken to him in years.

"No false modesty," Garda was chiding. "What could we have done, without you? You yourself have complained enough about your mother's methods. You know we would not have a tenth of the information about Titan we've gained from T'uupieh, if she had gone on using that damned computer translation."

Shannon frowned faintly, at the sting of secret guilt. "Look, I know I've made some cracks—and I meant most of them—but I'd never have gotten off the ground if she hadn't done all the preliminary analysis before I even came." His mother had already been on the mission staff, having worked for years at NASA on the esoterics of computer communication with satellites and space probes; and because of her linguistic background, she had been made head of the newly pulled-together staff of communications specialists by Marcus Reed, the Titan project director. She had been in charge of the initial phonic analysis, using the computer to compress the alien voice range into one audible to humans, then breaking up the complex sounds into more, and simpler, human phones . . . she had identified phonemes, separated morphemes, fitted them into a grammatical framework, and assigned English sound equivalents to it all. Shannon had watched her on the early TB interviews, looking unhappy and ill at ease while Reed held court for the spellbound press. But what Dr. Wyler the Communications Engineer had had to say, at last, had held them on the edge of his seat; and unable to resist, he had taken the next plane to Coos Bay.

"Vell, I meant no offense," Garda said. "Your mother is obviously a skilled engineer. But she needs a little more—flexibility."

"You're telling me." He nodded ruefully. "She'd still love to see the synthesizer drop through the floor. She's been out of joint ever since I got here. At least Reed appreciates my 'value'." Reed had welcomed him like a long-lost son when he first arrived at the institute. . . . Wasn't he a skilled linguist as well as an inspired musician, didn't he have some time between gigs, wouldn't he like to extend his visit, and get an insider's view of his mother's work? He had agreed, modestly, to all three—and then the television cameras and reporters had sprung up as if on cue, and he understood clearly enough that they were not there to record the visit of Dr. Wyler's kid, but Shann the Music Man.

But he had gotten his first session with a voice from another world. And with one hearing, he had become an addict . . . because their speech was music. Every phoneme was formed of two or three superposed sounds, and every morpheme was a blend of phonemes, flowing together like water. They spoke in chords, and the result was a choir, crystal bells ringing, the shattering of glass chandeliers . . .

And so he had stayed on and on, at first only able to watch his mother and her assistants with agonized frustration: His mother's computer-analysis methods had worked well in the initial transphonemicizing of T'uupieh's speech, and they had learned enough very quickly to send back clumsy responses using the probe's echo-locating device, to keep T'uupieh's interest from wandering. But typing input at a keyboard, and expecting even the most sophisticated programming to transform it into another language, still would not work even for known human languages. And he knew, with an almost religious fervor, that the synthesizer had been designed for just this miracle of communication; and that he alone could use it to capture directly the nuances and subtleties machine translation could never supply. He had tried to approach his mother about letting him use it, but she had turned him down flat, "This is a research center, not a recording studio."

And so he had gone over her head to Reed, who had been delighted. And when at last he felt his hands moving across the warm, faintly tingling plates of light, tentatively recreating the speech of another world, he had known that he had been right all along. He had let his music commitments go to hell, without a regret, almost with relief, as he slid back into the field that had always come first.

Shannon watched the display, where T'uupieh had settled back with comfortable familiarity against the probe's curving side, half obscuring his view of the camp. Fortunately both she and her followers treated the probe with obsessive care, even when they dragged it from place to place as they constantly moved to camp. He wondered what would have happened if they had inadvertently set off its automatic defense system—which had been designed to protect it from aggressive animals; which delivered an electric shock that varied from merely painful to fatal. And he wondered what would have happened if the probe and its "eyes" hadn't fit so neatly into T'uupieh's beliefs about demons. The idea that he might never have known her, or heard her voice. . . .

More than a year had passed already since he, and the rest of the world, had heard the remarkable news that intelligent life existed on Saturn's major moon. He had no memory at all of the first two flybys to Titan, back in '79 and '81—although he could clearly remember the 1990 orbiter that had caught fleeting glimpses of the surface through Titan's swaddling of opaque, golden clouds. But the handful of miniprobes it had dropped had proved that Titan profited from the same "greenhouse effect" that made Venus a boiling hell. And even though the seasonal temperatures never rose above two hundred degrees Kelvin, the few photographs had shown, unquestionably, that life existed there. The discovery of life, after so many disappointments throughout the rest of the solar system, had been enough to initiate another probe mission, one designed to actually send back data from Titan's surface.

That probe had discovered a life form with human intelligence . . . or rather, the life form had discovered the probe. And T'uupieh's discovery had turned a potentially ruined mission into a success: The probe had been designed with a main, immobile data processing unit, and ten "eyes," or subsidiary units, that were to be scattered over Titan's surface to relay information. The release of the subsidiary probes during landing had failed, however, and all of the "eyes" had come down within a few square kilometers of its own landing in the uninhabited marsh. But T'uupieh's self-interested fascination and willingness to appease her "demon" had made up for everything.

Shannon looked up at the flat wall-screen again, at T'uupieh's incredible, unhuman face—a face that was as familiar now as his own in the mirror. She sat waiting with her incredible patience for a reply from her "demon": She would have been waiting for over an hour by the time her transmission reached him across the gap between their worlds; and she would have to wait as long again, while they discussed a response and he created the new translation. She spent more time now with the probe than she did with her own people. *The loneliness of command* . . . he smiled. The almost flat profile of her moon-white face turned slightly toward him—toward the camera lens; her own fragile mouth smiled gently, not quite revealing her long, sharp teeth. He could see one red pupilless eye, and the crescent nose-slit that half ringed it; her frosty cyanide breath shone blue-white, illuminated by the ghostly haloes of St. Elmo's fire that wreathed the probe all through Titan's interminable eight-day nights. He could see balls of light hanging like Japanese lanterns on the drooping snarl of ice-bound branches in a distant thicket.

It was unbelievable . . . or perfectly logical; depending on which biological expert was talking . . . that the nitrogen- and ammonia-based life on Titan should have so many analogs with oxygen- and water-based life on Earth. But T'uupieh was not human, and the music of her words time and again brought him messages that made a mockery of any ideals he tried to harbor about her, and their relationship. So far in the past year she had assassinated eleven people, and with her outlaws had murdered God knew how many more, in the process of robbing them. The only reason she cooperated with the probe, she had as much as said, was because only a demon had a more bloody reputation; only a demon could command her respect. And yet, from what little she had been able to show them and tell them about the world she lived in, she was no better or no worse than anyone else—only more competent. Was she a prisoner of an age, a culture, where blood was something to be spilled instead of shared? Or was it something biologically innate that let her philosophize brutality, and brutalize philosophy—

Beyond T'uupieh, around the nitrogen campfire, some of her outlaws had begun to sing—the alien folk melodies that in translation were no more than simple, repetitious verse. But heard in their pure, untranslated form, they layered harmonic complexity on complexity: musical speech in a greater pattern of song. Shannon reached out and picked up the headset again, forgetting everything else. He had had a dream, once, where he had been able to sing in chords—

Using the long periods of waiting between their communications, he had managed, some months back, to record a series of the alien songs himself, using the synthesizer. They had been spare and uncomplicated versions compared to the originals, because even now his skill with the language couldn't help wanting to make them his own. Singing was a part of religious ritual, T'uupieh had told him, "But they don't sing because they're religious; they sing because they like to sing." Once, privately, he had played one of his own human compositions for her on the synthesizer, and transmitted it. She had stared at him (or into the probe's golden eye) with stony, if tolerant, silence. She never sang herself, although he had sometimes heard her softly harmonizing. He wondered what she would say if he told her that her outlaws' songs had already earned him his first Platinum Record. Nothing, probably . . . but knowing her, if he could make the concepts clear, she would probably be heartily in favor of the exploitation.

He had agreed to donate the profits of the record to NASA (and although he had intended that all along, it had annoyed him to be asked by Reed), with the understanding that the gesture would be kept quiet. But somehow, at the next press conference, some reporter had known just what question to ask, and Reed had spilled it all. And his mother, when asked about her son's sacrifice, had murmured, "Saturn is becoming a three-ring circus," and left him wondering whether to laugh or swear.

Shannon pulled a crumpled pack of cigarettes out of the pocket of his caftan and lit one. Garda glanced up, sniffing, and shook her head. She didn't smoke, or anything else (although he suspected she ran around with men), and she had given him a long, wasted lecture about it, ending with, "Vell, at least they're not tobacco." He shook his head back at her.

"What do you think about T'uupieh's latest victims, then?"

Garda flourished the transcript, pulling his thoughts back. "Vill she kill her own sister?"

He exhaled slowly around the words, "Tune in tomorrow, for our next exciting episode! I think Reed will love it; that's what I think." He pointed at the newspaper lying on the floor beside his chair. "Did you notice we've slipped to page three?" T'uupieh had fed the probe's hopper some artifacts made of metal—a thing she had said was only known to the "Old Ones"; and the scientific speculation about the existence of a former technological culture had boosted interest in the probe to front page status again. But even news of that discovery couldn't last forever . . . "Gotta keep those ratings up, folks. Keep those grants and donations rolling in."

Garda clucked. "Are you angry at Reed, or at T'uupieh?"

He shrugged dispiritedly. "Both of 'em. I don't see why she won't kill her own sister—" He broke off, as the subdued noise of the room's numerous project workers suddenly intensified, and concentrated: Marcus Reed was making an entrance, simultaneously solving everyone else's problems, as always. Shannon marveled at Reed's energy, even while he felt something like disgust at the way he spent it. Reed exploited everyone, and everything, with charming cynicism, in the ultimate hype for Science—and watching him at work had gradually drained away whatever respect and goodwill Shannon had brought with him to the project. He knew that his mother's reaction to Reed was close to his own, even though she had never said anything to him about it; it surprised him that there was something they could still agree on.

"Dr. Reed—"

"Excuse me, Dr. Reed, but—"

His mother was with Reed now as they all came down the room; looking tight-lipped and resigned, her lab coat buttoned up as if she was trying to avoid contamination. Reed was straight out of *Manstyle* magazine, as usual. Shannon glanced down at his own loose gray caftan and jeans, which had led Garda to remark, "Are you planning to enter a monastery?"

". . . we'd really like to—"

"Senator Foyle wants you to call him back—"

". . . yes, all right; and tell Dinocci he can go ahead and have the probe run another sample. Yes, Max, I'll get to that . . ." Reed gestured for quiet as Shannon and Garda turned in their seats to face him. "Well, I've just heard the news about our 'Robin Hood's' latest hard contract."

Shannon grimaced quietly. He had been the one who had first, facetiously, called T'uupieh "Robin Hood". Reed had snapped it up, and dubbed her ammonia swamps "Sherwood Forest" for the press: After the facts of her bloodthirsty body counts began to come out, and it even began to look like she was collaborating with "the Sheriff of Nottingham," some reporter had pointed out that T'uupieh bore no more resemblance to Robin Hood than she did to Rima the Bird-Girl. Reed had said, laughing, "Well, after all, the only reason Robin Hood stole from the rich was because the poor didn't have any money!" That, Shannon thought, had been the real beginning of the end of his tolerance.

". . . this could be used as an opportunity to show the world graphically the harsh realities of life on Titan—"

"*Ein Moment,*" Garda said. "You're telling us you want to let the public watch this atrocity, Marcus?" Up until now they had never released to the media the graphic tapes of actual murders; even Reed had not been able to argue that that would have served any real scientific purpose.

"No, he's not, Garda." Shannon glanced up as his mother began to speak. "Because we all agreed that we would *not* release any tapes, just for purposes of sensationalism."

"Carly, you know that the press has been after me to release those other tapes, and that I haven't, because we all voted against it. But I feel this situation is different—a demonstration of a unique, alien sociocultural condition. What do you think, Shann?"

Shannon shrugged, irritated and not covering it up. "I don't know what's so damn unique about it: a snuff flick is a snuff flick, wherever you film it. I think the idea stinks." Once, at a party while he was still in college, he had watched a film of an unsuspecting victim being hacked to death. The film, and what all films like it said about the human race, had made him sick to his stomach.

"*Ach*—there's more truth than poetry in that!" Garda said.

Reed frowned, and Shannon saw his mother raise her eyebrows.

"I have a better idea." He stubbed out his cigarette in the ashtray under the panel. "Why don't you let me try to talk her out of it?" As he said it, he realized how much he wanted to try; and how much success could mean, to his belief in communication—to his image of T'uupieh's people and maybe his own.

They both showed surprise, this time. "How?" Reed said.

"Well . . . I don't know yet. Just let me talk to her, try to really communicate with her, find out how she thinks and what she feels; without all the technical garbage getting in the way for a while."

His mother's mouth thinned, he saw the familiar worry-crease form between her brows. "Our job here is to collect that 'garbage.' Not to begin imposing moral values on the universe. We have too much to do as it is."

"What's 'imposing' about trying to stop a murder?" A certain light came into Garda's faded blue eyes. "Now that has real . . . social implications. Think about it, Marcus—"

Reed nodded, glancing at the patiently attentive faces that still ringed him. "Yes—it does. A great deal of human interest . . ." Answering nods and murmurs. "All right, Shann. There are about three days left before morning comes again in 'Sherwood Forest.' You can have them to yourself, to work with T'uupieh. The press will want reports on your progress . . ." He glanced at his watch, and nodded toward the door, already turning away. Shannon looked away from his mother's face as she moved past him.

"Good luck, Shann." Reed threw it back at him absently. "I wouldn't count on reforming Robin Hood; but you can still give it a good try."

Shannon hunched down in his chair, frowning, and turned back to the panel. "In your next incarnation may you come back as a toilet."

T'uupieh was confused. She sat on the hummock of clammy waterstone beside the captive demon, waiting for it to make a reply. In the time that had passed since she'd found it in the swamp, she had been surprised again and again by how little its behavior resembled all the demon-lore she knew. And tonight. . . .

She jerked, startled, as its grotesque, clawed arm came to life suddenly and groped among the icy-silver spring shoots pushing up through the melt at the hummock's foot. The demon did many incomprehensible things (which was fitting) and it demanded offerings of meat and vegetation and even stone—even, sometimes, some part of the loot she had taken from passers-by. She had given it those things gladly, hoping to win its favor and its aid . . . she had even, somewhat grudgingly, given it precious metal ornaments of Old Ones which she had stripped from a whining foreign lord. The demon had praised her effusively for that; all demons hoarded metal, and she supposed that it must need metals to sustain its strength: its domed carapace—gleaming now with the witch-fire that always shrouded it at night—was an immense metal jewel the color of blood. And yet she had always heard that demons preferred the flesh of men and women. But when she had tried to stuff the wing of the foreign lord into its maw it had spit him out with a few dripping scratches, and told her to let him go. Astonished, she had obeyed, and let the fool run off screaming to be lost in the swamp.

And then, tonight— "You are going to kill your sister, T'uupieh," it had said to her tonight, "and two innocent children. How do you feel about that?" She had spoken what had come first, and truthfully, into her mind: "That the new day cannot come soon enough for me! I have waited so long—too long—to take my revenge on Klovhiri! My sister and her brats are a part of his foulness, better slain before they multiply." She had drawn her dagger and driven it into the mushy melt, as she would drive it into their rotten hearts.

The demon had been silent again, for a long time; as it always was. (The lore said that demons were immortal, and so she had always supposed that it had no reason to make a quick response, she had wished, sometimes, it would show more consideration for her own mortality.) Then at last it had said, in its deep voice filled with alien shadows, "But the children have harmed no one. And Ahtseet is your only sister, she and the children are your only blood kin. She has shared your life. You say that once you—" the demon paused, searching its limited store of words, "—cherished her, for that. Doesn't what she once meant to you mean anything now? Isn't there any love left, to slow your hand as you raise it against her?"

"Love!" she had said, incredulous. "What speech is that, oh Soulless One? You mock me—," sudden anger had bared her teeth. "Love is a toy, my demon and I have put my toys behind me. And so has Ahtseet . . . she is no kin of mine. Betrayer, betrayer!" The word hissed like the dying embers of the campfire; she had left the demon in disgust, to rake in the firepit's insulating layer of sulphury ash, and lay on a few more soggy branches. Y'lirr, her second-in-command, had smiled at her from where he lay in his cloak on the ground, telling her that she should sleep. But she had ignored him, and gone back to her vigil on the hill.

Even though this night was chill enough to recrystallize the slowly-thawing limbs of the *safilil* trees, the equinox was long past, and now the fine mist of golden polymer rain presaged the golden days of the approaching summer. T'uupieh had wrapped herself more closely in her own cloak and pulled up the hood, to keep the clinging, sticky mist from fouling her wings and ear membranes; and she had remembered last, her first summer, which she would always remember . . . Ahtseet had been a clumsy, flapping infant as that first summer began, and T'uupieh the child had thought her new sister was silly and useless. But summer slowly transformed the land, and filled her wondering eyes with miracles; and her sister was transformed too, into a playful, easily-led companion who could follow her into adventure. Together they learned to use their wings, and to use the warm updrafts to explore the boundaries and the freedoms of their heritage.

And now, as spring moved into summer once again, T'uupieh clung fiercely to the vision, not wanting to lose it, or to remember that childhood's sweet, unreasoning summer would never come again, even though the seasons returned; for the Wheel of Change swept on, and there was never a turning back. No turning back . . . she had become an adult by the summer's end, and she would never soar with a child's light-winged freedom again. And Ahtseet would never do anything again. Little Ahtseet, always just behind her, like her own fair shadow . . . *No! She would not regret it! She would be glad—*

"Did you ever think, T'uupieh," the demon had said suddenly, "that it is wrong to kill anyone? You don't want to die—no one wants to die too soon. Why should they have to? Have you ever wondered what it would be like if you could change the world into one where you—where you treated everyone else as you wanted them to treat you, and they treated you the same? If everyone could—live and let live . . ." Its voice slipped into blurred overtones that she couldn't hear.

She had waited, but it said no more, as if it were waiting for her to consider what she'd already heard. But there was no need to think about what was obvious: "Only the dead 'live and let live.' I treat everyone as I expect them to treat me; or I would quickly join the peaceful dead! Death is a part of life. We die when fate wills it, and when fate wills it, we kill.

"You are immortal, you have the power to twist the Wheel, to turn destiny as you want. You may toy with idle fantasies, even make them real, and never suffer the consequences. We have no place for such things in our small lives. No matter how much I might try to be like you, in the end I die like all the rest. We can change nothing, our lives are preordained. That is the way, among mortals." And she had fallen silent again, filled with unease at this strange wandering of the demon's mind. But she must not let it prey on her nerves. Day would come very soon, she must not be nervous; she must be totally in control when she led this attack on Klovhiri. No emotion must interfere . . . no matter how much she yearned to feel Klovhiri's blood spill bluely over her hands, and her sister's, and the children's . . . Ahtseet's brats would never feel the warm wind lift them into the sky; or plunge, as she had, into the depths of her rainbow-petaled pools; or see her towers spearing light far off among the trees. *Never! Never!*

She had caught her breath sharply then, as a fiery pinwheel burst through the wall of tangled brush behind her, tumbling past her head into the clearing of the camp. She had watched it circle the fire—spitting sparks, hissing furiously in the quiet air—three and a half times before it spun on into the darkness. No sleeper wakened, and only two stirred. She clutched one of the demon's hard, angular legs, shaken; knowing that the circling of the fire had been a portent . . . but not knowing what it meant. The burning silence it left behind oppressed her; she stirred restlessly, stretching her wings.

And utterly unmoved, the demon had begun to drone its strange, dark thoughts once more, "Not all you have heard about demons is true. We can suffer . . ." it groped for words again, "the—consequences of our acts; among ourselves we fight and die. We *are* vicious, and brutal, and pitiless: But we don't like to be that way. We want to change into something better, more merciful, more forgiving. We fail more than we win . . . but we believe we *can* change. And you are more like us than you realize. You can draw a line between—trust and betrayal, right and wrong, good and evil; you can choose never to cross that line—"

"How, then?" She had twisted to face the amber eye as large as her own head, daring to interrupt the demon's speech. "How can one droplet change the tide of the sea? It's impossible! The world melts and flows, it rises into mist, it returns again to ice, only to melt and flow once more. A wheel has no beginning, and no end; no starting place. There is no 'good', no 'evil' . . . no line between them. Only acceptance. If you were a mortal, I would think you were mad!"

She had turned away again, her claws digging shallow runnels in the polymer-coated stone as she struggled for self-control. *Madness*. . . . Was it possible? she wondered suddenly. Could her demon have gone mad? How else could she explain the thoughts it had put into her mind? Insane thoughts, bizarre, suicidal . . . but thoughts that would haunt her.

Or, could there be a method in its madness? She knew that treachery lay at the heart of every demon. It could simply be lying to her, when it spoke of trust and forgiveness—knowing she must be ready for tomorrow, hoping to make her doubt herself, make her fail. Yes, that was much more reasonable. But then, why was it so hard to believe that this demon would try to ruin her most cherished goals? After all, she held it prisoner; and though her spells kept it from tearing her apart, perhaps it still sought to tear apart her mind, to drive her mad instead. Why shouldn't it hate her, and delight in her torment, and hope for her destruction?

How could it be so ungrateful! She had almost laughed aloud at her own resentment, even as it formed the thought. As if a demon ever knew gratitude! But ever since the day she had netted it in spells in the swamp, she had given it nothing but the best treatment. She had fetched and carried, and made her fearful followers do the same. She had given it the best of everything—anything it desired. At its command she had sent out searchers to look for its scattered eyes, and it had allowed—even encouraged—her to use the eyes as her own, as watchers and protectors. She had even taught it to understand her speech (for it was as ignorant as a baby about the world of mortals), when she realized that it wanted to communicate with her. She had done all those things to win his favor—because she knew that it had come into her hands for a reason; and if she could gain its cooperation, there would be no one who would dare to cross her.

She had spent every spare hour in keeping it company, feeding its curiosity—and her own—as she fed its jeweled maw . . . until gradually, those conversations with the demon had become an end in themselves, a treasure worth the sacrifice of even precious metals. Even the constant waiting for its alien mind to ponder her questions and answers had never tired her, she had come to enjoy sharing even the simple pleasure of its silences, and resting in the warm amber light of its gaze.

T'uupieh looked down at the finely-woven fiber belt which passed through the narrow slits between her side and wing and held her tunic to her. She fingered the heavy, richly-amber beads that decorated it—metal-dyed melt trapped in polished waterstone by the jewelsmith's secret arts—that reminded her always of her demon's thousand eyes. *Her* demon—

She looked away again, toward the fire, toward the cloak-wrapped forms of her outlaws. Since the demon had come to her she had felt both the physical and emotional space that she had always kept between herself as leader and her band of followers gradually widening. She was still completely their leader, perhaps more firmly so because she had tamed the demon; and their bond of shared danger and mutual respect had never weakened. But there were other needs which her people might fill for each other, but never for her.

She watched them sleeping like the dead, as she should be sleeping now; preparing themselves for tomorrow. They took their sleep sporadically, when they could, as all commoners did—as she did now, too, instead of hibernating the night through like proper nobility. Many of them slept in pairs, man and woman; even though they mated with a commoner's chaotic lack of discrimination, whenever a woman felt the season come upon her. T'uupieh wondered what they must imagine when they saw her sitting here with the demon far into the night. She knew what they believed—what she encouraged all to believe—that she had chosen it for a consort, or that it had chosen her. Y'lirr, she saw, still slept alone. She trusted and liked him as well as she did anyone; he was quick and ruthless, and she knew that he worshipped her. But he was a commoner . . . and more importantly, he did not challenge her. Nowhere, even among the nobility, had she found anyone who offered the sort of companionship she craved . . . until now, until the demon had come to her. No, she would not believe that all its words had been lies—

"T'uupieh," the demon called her name buzzingly in the misty darkness. "Maybe you can't change the pattern of fate . . . but you can change your mind. You've already defied fate, by turning outlaw, and defying Klovhiri. Your sister was the one who accepted . . ." unintelligible words, ". . . only let the Wheel take her. Can you really kill her for that? You must understand why she did it, how she *could* do it. You don't have to kill her for that . . . you don't have to kill any of them. You have the strength, the courage, to put vengeance aside, and find another way to your goals. You can choose to be merciful—you can choose your own path through life, even if the ultimate destination of all life is the same."

She stood up resentfully, matching the demon's height, and drew her cloak tightly around her. "Even if I wished to change my mind, it is too late. The Wheel is already in motion . . . and I must get my sleep, if I am to be ready for it." She started away toward the fire; stopped, looking back. "There is nothing I can do now, my demon. I cannot change tomorrow. Only you can do that. Only you."

She heard it, later, calling her name softly as she lay sleepless on the cold ground. But she turned her back toward the sound and lay still, and at last sleep came.

Shannon slumped back into the embrace of the padded chair, rubbing his aching head. His eyelids were sandpaper, his body was a weight. He stared at the display screen, at T'uppieh's back turned stubbornly toward him as she slept beside the nitrogen campfire. "Okay, that's it. I give up. She won't even listen. Call Reed and tell him I quit."

"That you've quit trying to convince T'uupieh," Garda said. "Are you sure? She may yet come back. Use a little more emphasis on—spiritual matters. We must be certain we have done all we can to . . . change her mind."

To save her soul, he thought sourly. Garda had gotten her early training at an institute dedicated to translating the Bible; he had discovered in the past few hours that she still had a hidden desire to proselytize. *What soul?* "We're wasting our time. It's been six hours since she walked out on me. She's not coming back. . . . And I mean quit everything. I don't want to be around for the main event, I've had it."

"You don't mean that," Garda said. "You're tired, you need the rest too. When T'uppich wakes, you can talk to her again."

He shook his head, pushing back his hair. "Forget it. Just call Reed." He looked out the window, at dawn separating the mist-wrapped silhouette of seaside condominiums from the sky.

Garda shrugged, disappointed, and turned to the phone.

He studied the synthesizer's touch boards again, still bright and waiting, still calling his leaden, weary hands to try one more time. At least when he made this final announcement, it wouldn't have to be direct to the eyes and ears of a waiting world: He doubted that any reporter was dedicated enough to still be up in the glass-walled observation room at this hour. Their questions had been endless earlier tonight, probing his feelings and his purpose and his motives and his plans, asking about 'Robin Hood's' morality, or lack of it, and his own; about a hundred and one other things that were nobody's business but his own.

The music world had tried to do the same thing to him once, but then there had been buffers—agents, publicity staffs—to protect him. Now, when he'd had so much at stake, there had been no protection, only Reed at the microphone eloquently turning the room into a sideshow, with Shann the Man as chief freak; until Shannon had begun to feel like a man staked out on an anthill and smeared with honey. The reporters gazed down from on high critiquing T'uppieh's responses and criticizing his own, and filled the time gaps when he needed quiet to think with infuriating interruptions. Reed's success had been total in wringing every drop of pathos and human interest out of his struggle to prevent T'uupieh's vengeance against the innocents . . . and by that, had managed to make him fail.

No. He sat up straighter, trying to ease his back. No, he couldn't lay it on Reed. By the time what he'd had to say had really counted, the reporters had given up on him. The failure belonged to him, only him: his skill hadn't been great enough, his message hadn't been convincing enough—he was the one who hadn't been able to see through T'uppieh's eyes clearly enough to make her see through his own. He had had his chance to really communicate, for once in his life—to communicate something important. And he'd sunk it.

A hand reached past him to set a cup of steaming coffee on the shelf below the terminal. "One thing about this computer—," a voice said quietly, "—it's programmed for a good cup of coffee."

Startled, he laughed without expecting to; he glanced up. His mother's face looked drawn and tired, she held another cup of coffee in her hand. "Thanks." He picked up the cup and took a sip, felt the hot liquid slide down his throat into his empty stomach. Not looking up again, he said, "Well, you got what you wanted. And so did Reed. He got his pathos, and he gets his murders too."

She shook her head. "This isn't what I wanted. I don't want to see you give up everything you've done here, just because you don't like what Reed is doing with part of it. It isn't worth that. Your work means too much to this project . . . and it means too much to you."

He looked up.

"*Ja,* she is right, Shannon. You can't quit now—we need you too much. And T'uupieh needs you."

He laughed again, not meaning it. "Like a cement yo-yo. What are you trying to do, Garda, use my own moralizing against me?"

"She's telling you what any blind man could see tonight; if he hadn't seen it months ago . . ." His mother's voice was strangely distant. "That this project would never have had this degree of success without you. That you were right about the synthesizer. And that losing you now might—"

She broke off, turning away to watch as Reed came through the doors at the end of the long room. He was alone, this time, for once, and looking rumpled. Shannon guessed that he had been sleeping when the phone call came and was irrationally pleased at waking him up.

Reed was not so pleased. Shannon watched the frown that might be worry, or displeasure, or both, forming on his face as he came down the echoing hall toward them. "What did she mean, you want to quit? Just because you can't change an alien mind?" He entered the cubicle, and glanced down at the terminal—to be sure that the remote microphones were all switched off, Shannon guessed. "You knew it was a long shot, probably hopeless . . . you have to accept that she doesn't want to reform, accept that the values of an alien culture are going to be different from your own—"

Shannon leaned back, feeling a muscle begin to twitch with fatigue along the inside of his elbow. "I can accept that. What I can't accept is that you want to make us into a bunch of damn panderers. Christ, you don't even have a good reason! I didn't come here to play sound track for a snuff flick. If you go ahead and feed the world those murders, I'm laying it down. I don't want to give all this up, but I'm not staying for a kill-porn carnival."

Reed's frown deepened, he glanced away. "Well? What about the rest of you? Are you still privately branding me an accessory to murder, too? Carly?"

"No, Marcus—not really." She shook her head. "But we all feel that we shouldn't cheapen and weaken our research by making a public spectacle of it. After all, the people of Titan have as much right to privacy and respect as any culture on Earth."

"*Ja*, Marcus—I think we all agree about that."

"And just how much privacy does anybody on Earth have today? Good God—remember the Tasaday? And that was thirty years ago. There isn't a single mountain top or desert island left that the all-seeing eye of the camera hasn't broadcast all over the world. And what do you call the public crime surveillance laws—our own lives are one big peep show."

Shannon shook his head. "That doesn't mean we have to—"

Reed turned cold eyes on him. "And I've had a little too much of your smartass piety, Wyler. Just what do you owe your success as a musician to, if not publicity?" He gestured at the posters on the walls. "There's more hard sell in your kind of music than any other field I can name."

"I have to put up with some publicity push, or I couldn't reach the people, I couldn't do the thing that's really important to me—communicate. That doesn't mean I like it."

"You think I enjoy this?"

"Don't you?"

Reed hesitated. "I happen to be good at it, which is all that really matters. Because you may not believe it, but I'm still a scientist, and what I care about most of all is seeing that research gets its fair slice of the pie. You say I don't have a good reason for pushing our findings: Do you realize that NASA lost all the data from our Neptune probe just because somebody in effect got tired of waiting for it to get to Neptune, and cut off our funds? The real problem on these long outer-planet missions isn't instrumental reliability, it's financial reliability. The public will pay out millions for one of your concerts, but not one cent for something they don't understand—"

"I don't make—"

"People want to forget their troubles, be entertained . . . and who can blame them? So in order to compete with movies, and sports, and people like you—not to mention ten thousand other worthy government and private causes—we have to give the public what it wants. It's my responsibility to deliver that, so that the 'real scientists' can sit in their neat, bright institutes with half a billion dollars' worth of equipment around them, and talk about 're-spect for research.'"

He paused; Shannon kept his gaze stubbornly. "Think it over. And when you can tell me how what you did as a musician is morally superior to, or more valuable than what you're doing now, you can come to my office and tell me who the real hypocrite is. But think it over, first—all of you." Reed turned and left the cubicle.

They watched in silence, until the double doors at the end of the room hung still. "Vell . . ." Garda glanced at her walking stick, and down at her cloak. "He does have a point."

Shannon leaned forward, tracing the complex beauty of the synthesizer terminal, feeling the combination of chagrin and caffeine pushing down his fatigue: "I know he does. But that isn't the point I was trying to get at! I didn't want to change T'uupieh's mind, or quit either, just because I objected to selling this project. It's the *way* it's being sold, like some kind of kill-porn show perversion, that I can't take—" When he was a child, he remembered, rock concerts had had a kind of notoriety; but they were as respectable as a symphony orchestra now, compared to the "thrill-shows" that had eclipsed them as he was growing up: where "experts" gambled their lives against a million dollar pot, in front of a crowd who came to see them lose; where masochists made a living by self-mutilation; where they ran *cinema verité* films of butchery and death.

"I mean, is that what everybody really wants? Does it really make everybody feel good to watch somebody else bleed? Or are they going to get some kind of moral superiority thing out of watching it happen on Titan instead of here?" He looked up at the display, at T'uupieh, who still lay sleeping, unmoving and unmoved. "If I could have changed T'uupieh's mind, or changed what happens here, then maybe I could have felt good about something. At least about myself. But who am I kidding . . ." T'uupieh had been right all along; and now he had to admit it to himself: that there had never been any way he could change either one. "T'uupieh's just like the rest of them, she'd rather cut off your hand than shake it . . . and doing it vicariously means we're no better. And none of us ever will be." The words to a song older than he was slipped into his mind, with sudden irony. " 'One man's hands can't build,' " he began to switch off the terminal, "anything."

"You need to sleep . . . ve all need to sleep." Garda rose stiffly from her chair.

"'. . . but if one and one and fifty make a million,'" his mother matched his quote softly.

Shannon turned back to look at her, saw her shake her head; she felt him looking at her, glanced up. "After all, if T'uupieh could have accepted that everything she did was morally evil, what would have become of her? She knew: It would have destroyed her—we would have destroyed her. She would have been swept away and drowned in the tide of violence." His mother looked away at Garda, back at him. "T'uupieh is a realist, whatever else she is."

He felt his mouth tighten against the resentment that sublimated a deeper, more painful emotion; he heard Garda's grunt of indignation.

"But that doesn't mean that you were wrong—or that you failed."

"That's big of you." He stood up, nodding at Garda, and toward the exit, "Come on."

"Shannon."

He stopped, still facing away.

"I don't think you failed. I think you did reach T'uupieh. The last thing she said was 'only you can change tomorrow' . . . I think she was challenging the demon to go ahead; to do what she didn't have the power to do herself. I think she was asking you to help her."

He turned, slowly. "You really believe that?"

"Yes, I do." She bent her head, freed her hair from the collar of her sweater.

He moved back to his seat, his hands brushed the dark, unresponsive touchplates on the panel. "But it wouldn't do any good to talk to her again. Somehow the demon has to stop the attack itself. If I could use the 'voice' to warn them. . . . Damn the time lag!" By the time his voice reached them, the attack would have been over for hours. How could he change anything tomorrow, if he was always two hours behind?

"I know how to get around the time-lag problem."

"How?" Garda sat down again, mixed emotions showing on her broad, seamed face. "He can't send a varning ahead of time; no one knows when Klovhiri will pass. It would come too soon, or too late."

Shannon straightened up. "Better to ask, 'why?' Why are you changing your mind?"

"I never changed my mind," his mother said mildly. "I never liked this either. When I was a girl, we used to believe that our actions *could* change the world; maybe I've never stopped wanting to believe that."

"But Marcus is not going to like us meddling behind his back, anyway." Garda waved her staff. "And what about the point that perhaps we do need this publicity?"

Shannon glanced back irritably. "I thought you were on the side of the angels, not the devil's advocate."

"I am!" Garda's mouth puckered. "But—"

"Then what's such bad news about the probe making a last minute rescue? It'll be a sensation."

He saw his mother smile, for the first time in months. "Sensational . . . if T'uupieh doesn't leave us stranded in the swamp for our betrayal."

He sobered: "Not if you really think she wants our help. And I know she wants it . . . I *feel* it. But how do we beat the time lag?"

"I'm the engineer, remember? I'll need a recorded message from you, and some time to play with that." His mother pointed at the computer terminal.

He switched on the terminal and moved aside. She sat down, and started a program documentation on the display; he read, REMOTE OPERATIONS MANUAL. "Let's see . . . I'll need feedback on the approach of Klovhiri's party."

He cleared his throat. "Did you really mean what you said, before Reed came in?"

She glanced up, he watched one response form on her face, and then fade into another smile, "Garda—have you met My Son, the Linguist?"

"And when did you ever pick up on that Pete Seeger song?"

"And My Son, the Musician . . ." the smile came back to him. "I've listened to a few records, in my day." The smile turned inward, toward a memory. "I don't suppose I ever told you that I fell in love with your father because he reminded me of Elton John."

T'uupieh stood silently, gazing into the demon's unwavering eye. A new day was turning the clouds from bronze to gold; the brightness seeped down through the glistening, snarled hair of the treetops, glanced from the green translucent cliff-faces and sweating slopes to burnish the demon's carapace with light. She gnawed the last shreds of flesh from a bone, forcing herself to eat, scarcely aware that she did. She had already sent out watchers in the direction of the town, to keep watch for Chwiul . . . and Klovhiri's party. Behind her the rest of her band made ready now, testing weapons and reflexes or feeding their bellies.

And still the demon had not spoken to her. There had been many times when it had chosen not to speak for hours on end; but after its mad ravings of last night, the thought obsessed her that it might never speak again. Her concern grew, lighting the fuse of her anger, which this morning was already short enough; until at last she strode recklessly forward and struck it with her open hand. "Speak to me, *mala 'ingga!*"

But as her blow landed a pain like the touch of fire shot up the muscles of her arm. She leaped back with a curse of surprise, shaking her hand. The demon had never lashed out at her before, never hurt her in any way: But she had never dared to strike it before, she had always treated it with calculated respect. *Fool!* She looked down at her hand, half afraid to see it covered with burns that would make her a cripple in the attack today. But the skin was still smooth and unblistered, only bright with the smarting shock.

"T'uupieh! Are you all right?"

She turned to see Y'lirr, who had come up behind her looking half-frightened, half-grim. "Yes," she nodded, controlling a sharper reply at the sight of his concern. "It was nothing." He carried her double-arched bow and quiver, she put out her smarting hand and took them from him casually, slung them at her back. "Come, Y'lirr, we must—"

"T'uupieh." This time it was the demon's eerie voice that called her name. "T'uupieh, if you believe in my power to twist fate as I like, then you must come back and listen to me again."

She turned back, felt Y'lirr hesitate behind her. "I believe truly in all your powers, my demon!" She rubbed her hand.

The amber depths of its eye absorbed her expression, and read her sincerity; or so she hoped. "T'uupieh, I know I did not make you believe what I said. But I want you to—," its words blurred unintelligibly, "—in me. I want you to know my name. T'uupieh, my name is—"

She heard a horrified yowl from Y'lirr behind her. She glanced around—seeing him cover his ears—and back, paralyzed by disbelief.

"—Shang'ang."

The word struck her like the demon's fiery lash, but the blow this time struck only in her mind. She cried out, in desperate protest; but the name had already passed into her knowledge, *too late!*

A long moment passed; she drew a breath, and shook her head. Disbelief still held her motionless as she let her eyes sweep the brightening camp, as she listened to the sounds of the wakening forest, and breathed in the spicy acridness of the spring growth. And then she began to laugh. She had heard a demon speak its name, and she still lived—and was not blind, not deaf, not mad. The demon had chosen her, joined with her, surrendered to her at last!

Dazed with exultation, she almost did not realize that the demon had gone on speaking to her. She broke off the song of triumph that rose in her, listening:

". . . then I command you to take me with you when you go today. I must see what happens, and watch Klovhiri pass."

"Yes! Yes, my—Shang'ang. It will be done as you wish. Your whim is my desire." She turned away down the slope, stopped again as she found Y'lirr still prone where he had thrown himself down when the demon spoke its name. "Y'lirr?" She nudged him with her foot. Relieved, she saw him lift his head; watched her own disbelief echoing in his face as he looked up at her.

"My lady . . . it did not—?"

"No, Y'lirr," she said softly; then more roughly, "Of course it did not! I am truly the Demon's Consort now; nothing shall stand in my way." She pushed him again with her foot, harder. "Get up. What do I have, a pack of sniveling cowards to ruin the morning of my success?"

Y'lirr scrambled to his feet, brushing himself off. "Never that,

T'uupieh! We're ready for any command . . . ready to deliver
your revenge." His hand tightened on his knife hilt.

"And my demon will join us in seeking it out!" The pride she
felt rang in her voice. "Get help to fetch a sledge here, and prepare it. And tell them to move it *gently*."

He nodded, and for a moment as he glanced at the demon she
saw both fear and envy in his eyes. "Good news." He moved off
then with his usual brusqueness, without glancing back at her.

She heard a small clamor in the camp, and looked past him,
thinking that word of the demon had spread already. But then she
saw Lord Chwiul, come as he had promised, being led into the
clearing by her escorts. She lifted her head slightly, in surprise—he
had indeed come alone, but he was riding a *bliell*. They were rare
and expensive mounts, being the only beast she knew of large
enough to carry so much weight, and being vicious and difficult to
train, as well. She watched this one snapping at the air, its fangs
protruding past slack, dribbling lips, and grimaced faintly. She saw
that the escort kept well clear of its stumplike webbed feet, and
kept their spears ready to prod. It was an amphibian, being too
heavy ever to make use of wings, but buoyant and agile when it
swam. T'uupieh glanced fleetingly at her own webbed fingers and
toes, at the wings that could only lift her body now for bare seconds at a time; she wondered, as she had so many times, what
strange turns of fate had formed, or transformed, them all.

She saw Y'lirr speak to Chwiul, pointing her out, saw his in-
solent grin and the trace of apprehension that Chwiul showed
looking up at her; she thought that Y'lirr had said, "She knows its
name."

Chwiul rode forward to meet her, with his face under control as
he endured the demon's scrutiny. T'uupieh put out a hand to
casually—gently—stroke its sensuous jewel-faceted side. Her eyes
left Chwiul briefly, drawn by some instinct to the sky directly
above him—and for half a moment she saw the clouds break
open . . .

She blinked, to see more clearly, and when she looked again it
was gone. No one else, not even Chwiul, had seen the gibbous disc
of greenish gold, cut across by a line of silver and a band of
shadow-black: The Wheel of Change. She kept her face expres-

sionless, but her heart raced. The Wheel appeared only when someone's life was about to be changed profoundly—and usually the change meant death.

Chwiul's mount lunged at her suddenly as he stopped before her. She held her place at the demon's side; but some of the *bliell's* bluish spittle landed on her cloak as Chwiul jerked at its heavy head. "Chwiul!" She let her emotion out as anger. "Keep that slobbering filth under control, or I will have it struck dead!" Her hand fisted on the demon's slick hide.

Chwiul's near-smile faded abruptly, and he pulled his mount back, staring uncomfortably at the demon's glaring eye.

T'uupieh took a deep breath, and produced a smile of her own. "So you did not quite dare to come to my camp alone, my lord."

He bowed slightly, from the saddle. "I was merely hesitant to wander in the swamp on foot, alone, until your people found me."

"I see." She kept the smile. "Well then—I assumed that things went as you planned this morning. Are Klovhiri and his party all on their way into our trap?"

"They are. And their guide is waiting for my sign, to lead them off safe ground into whatever mire you choose."

"Good. I have a spot in mind that is well ringed by heights." She admired Chwiul's self-control in the demon's presence, although she sensed that he was not as easy as he wanted her to believe. She saw some of her people coming toward them, with a sledge to carry the demon on their trek. "My demon will accompany us, by its own desire. A sure sign of our success today, don't you agree?"

Chwiul frowned, as if he wanted to question that, but didn't quite dare. "If it serves you loyally, then yes, my lady. A great honor and a good omen."

"It serves me with true devotion." She smiled again, insinuatingly. She stood back as the sledge came up onto the hummock, watched as the demon was settled onto it, to be sure her people used the proper care. The fresh reverence with which her outlaws treated it—and their leader—was not lost on either Chwiul or herself.

She called her people together, then, and they set out for their destination, picking their way over the steaming surface of the marsh and through the slimy slate-blue tentacles of the fragile, thawing underbrush. She was glad that they covered this ground often, because the pungent spring growth and the ground's mushy unpredictability changed the pattern of their passage from day to day. She wished that she could have separated Chwiul from his ugly mount, but she doubted that he would cooperate, and she was afraid that he might not be able to keep up on foot. The demon was lashed securely onto its sledge, and its sweating bearers pulled it with no hint of complaint.

At last they reached the heights overlooking the main road— though it could hardly be called one now—that led past her family's manor. She had the demon positioned where it could look back along the overgrown trail in the direction of Klovhiri's approach, and sent some of her followers to secret its eyes further down the track. She stood then gazing down at the spot below where the path seemed to fork, but did not. The false fork followed the rippling yellow bands of the cliff-face below her—directly into a sink caused by ammonia-water melt seeping down and through the porous sulphide compounds of the rock. There they would all wallow, while she and her band picked them off like swatting *ngips* . . . she thoughtfully swatted a *ngip* that had settled on her hand. Unless her demon—unless her demon chose to create some other outcome . . .

"Any sign?" Chwiul rode up beside her.

She moved back slightly from the cliff's crumbly edge, watching him with more than casual interest. "Not yet. But soon. She had outlaws posted on the lower slope across the track as well; but not even her demon's eyes could pierce too deeply into the foliage along the road. It had not spoken since Chwiul's arrival, and she did not expect it to reveal its secrets now. "What livery does your escort wear, and how many of them do you want killed for effect?" She unslung her bow, and began to test its pull.

Chwiul shrugged. "The dead carry no tales; kill them all. I shall have Klovhiri's men soon. Kill the guide too—a man who can be bought once, can be bought twice."

"Ah—" She nodded, grinning. "A man with your foresight and discretion will go far in the world, my lord." She nocked an arrow in the bowstring before she turned away to search the road again.

Still empty. She looked away restlessly, at the spiny silver-blue-green of the distant, fog-clad mountains; at the hollow fingers of upthrust ice, once taller than she was, stubby and diminishing now along the edge of the nearer lake. The lake where last summer she had soared . . .

A flicker of movement, a small unnatural noise, pulled her eyes back to the road. Tension tightened the fluid ease of her movement as she made the trilling call that would send her band to their places along the cliff's edge. *At last—* She leaned forward eagerly for the first glimpse of Klovhiri; spotting the guide, and then the sledge that bore her sister and the children. She counted the numbers of the escort, saw them all emerge into her unbroken view on the track. But Klovhiri . . . where was Klovhiri? She turned back to Chwiul, her whisper struck out at him, "Where is he! Where is Klovhiri?"

Chwiul's expression lay somewhere between guilt and guile. "Delayed. He stayed behind, he said there were still matters at court—"

"Why didn't you tell me that?"

He jerked sharply on the *bliell's* rein. "It changes nothing! We can still eradicate his family. That will leave me first in line to the inheritance . . . and Klovhiri can always be brought down later."

"But it's Klovhiri I want, for myself." T'uupieh raised her bow, the arrow tracked toward his heart.

"They'll know who to blame if I die!" He spread a wing defensively. "The Overlord will turn against you for good; Klovhiri will see to that. Avenge yourself on your sister, T'uupieh—and I will still reward you well if you keep the bargain!"

"This is not the bargain we agreed to!" The sounds of the approaching party reached her clearly now from down below; she heard a child's high notes of laughter. Her outlaws crouched, waiting for her signal; and she saw Chwiul prepare for his own signal call to his guide. She looked back at the demon, its amber eye fixed on the travelers below. She started toward it. It could still twist fate for her. . . . *Or had it, already?*

"Go back, go back!" The demon's voice burst over her, down across the silent forest, like an avalanche. "Ambush . . . trap . . . you have been betrayed!"

"—betrayal!"

She barely heard Chwiul's voice below the roaring; she looked back, in time to see the *bliell* leap forward, to intersect her own course toward the demon. Chwiul drew his sword, she saw the look of white fury on his face, not knowing whether it was for her, or the demon itself. She ran toward the demon's sledge, trying to draw her bow; but the *bliell* covered the space between them in two great bounds. Its head swung toward her, jaws gaping. Her foot skidded on the slippery melt, and she went down; the dripping jaws snapped futilely shut above her face. But one flailing leg struck her heavily and knocked her sliding through the melt to the demon's foot—

The demon. She gasped for the air that would not fill her lungs, trying to call its name, saw with incredible clarity the beauty of its form, and the ululating horror of the *bliell* bearing down on them to destroy them both. She saw it rear above her, above the demon —saw Chwiul, either leaping or thrown, sail out into the air—and at last her voice came back to her and she screamed the name, a warning and a plea, "Shang'ang!"

And as the *bliell* came down, lightning lashed out from the demon's carapace and wrapped the *bliell* in fire. The beast's ululations rose off the scale; T'uupieh covered her ears against the piercing pain of its cry. But not her eyes: the demon's lash ceased with the suddenness of lightning, and the *bliell* toppled back and away, rebounding lightly as it crashed to the ground, stone dead. T'uupieh sank back against the demon's foot, supported gratefully as she filled her aching lungs, and looked away—

To see Chwiul, trapped in the updrafts at the cliff's edge, gliding, gliding . . . and she saw the three arrows that protruded from his back, before the currents let his body go, and it disappeared below the rim. She smiled, and closed her eyes.

"T'uupieh! T'uupieh!"

She blinked them open again, resignedly, as she felt her people cluster around her. Y'lirr's hand drew back from the motion of touching her face as she opened her eyes. She smiled again, at him, at them all; but not with the smile she had had for Chwiul. "Y'lirr—" she gave him her own hand, and let him help her up. Aches and bruises prodded her with every small movement, but

she was certain, reassured, that the only real damage was an ooz-
ing tear in her wing. She kept her arm close to her side.

"T'uupieh—"

"My lady—"

"What happened? The demon—"

"The demon saved my life." She waved them silent. "And . . .
for its own reasons, it foiled Chwiul's plot." The realization, and
the implications, were only now becoming real in her mind. She
turned, and for a long moment gazed into the demon's unreadable
eye. Then she moved away, going stiffly to the edge of the cliff to
look down.

"But the contract—," Y'lirr said.

"Chwiul broke the contract! He did not give me Klovhiri." No
one made a protest. She peered through the brush, guessing
without much difficulty the places where Ahtseet and her party
had gone to earth below. She could hear a child's whimpered crying, now. Chwiul's body lay sprawled on the flat, in plain view of
them all, and she thought she saw more arrows bristling from his
corpse. Had Ahtseet's guard riddled him too, taking him for an at-
tacker? The thought pleased her. And a small voice inside her
dared to whisper that Ahtseet's escape pleased her much
more. . . . She frowned suddenly at the thought.

But Ahtseet had escaped, and so had Klovhiri—and so she
might as well make use of that fact, to salvage what she could. She
paused, collecting her still-shaken thoughts. "Ahtseet!" Her voice
was not the voice of the demon, but it echoed satisfactorily. "It's
T'uupieh! See the traitor's corpse that lies before you—your own
mate's brother, Chwiul! He hired murderers to kill you in the
swamp—seize your guide, make him tell you all. It is only by my
demon's warning that you still live."

"Why?" Ahtseet's voice wavered faintly on the wind.

T'uupieh laughed bitterly. "Why, to keep the roads clear of
ruffians. To make the Overlord love his loyal servant more, and
reward her better, dear sister! And to make Klovhiri hate me. May
it eat his guts out that he owes your lives to me! Pass freely
through my lands, Ahtseet; I give you leave—this once."

She drew back from the ledge and moved wearily away, not car-ing whether Ahtseet would believe her. Her people stood waiting, gathered silently around the corpse of the *bliell*.

"What now?" Y'lirr asked, looking at the demon, asking for them all.

And she answered, but made her answer directly to the demon's silent amber eye. "It seems I spoke the truth to Chwiul after all, my demon: I told him he would not be needing his townhouse after today . . . Perhaps the Overlord will call it a fair trade. Perhaps it can be arranged. The Wheel of Change carries us all; but not with equal ease. Is that not so, my beautiful Shang'ang?"

She stroked its day-warmed carapace tenderly, and settled down on the softening ground to wait for its reply.

CHILD OF THE SUN

by James E. Gunn

Interfering with the past—or is it the future—to save society is an old and honorable theme in science fiction. Here we have such a problem spelled out in very human details, with a hero whose very existence and reason for being is never fully disclosed. Which is as it would be if such a thing were to take place. Or maybe it has. Many times.

Ten thousand suns burned in the valley as Ellen McCleary climbed from the desert past the staff village to the cottage on the hills above the project.

Ten thousand giants bestrode the mountains holding lightning in either hand as she opened the cottage door and moved into the cool darkness calling, "Shelly? Shelly? I'm home. Where are you? Michelle? Mrs. Ross?"

Ten thousand trumpets shouted in her ears as she read the message scribbled redly across her bathroom mirror—and moments later found the housekeeper, tied and gagged with her own stockings, behind her bed.

He never knew whether he was troubled by memory or nightmare.

Every few weeks he dreamed about a pendulum. It swung back and forth like the regulator on a clock. He sensed the movement and he heard a sound, not a tick but a swoosh, as if something were moving rapidly through the air. At first he had only a vague impression of things, but gradually details forced themselves into his awareness. The pendulum arm, for instance, was more like a silvery chain with wires running through it down to the weight at the end.

Then scale became apparent. The entire apparatus was big. It swung in a cavern whose sides were so distant they could not be seen, and the wires were thick, like busbars. The weight was a kind of cage, and it was large enough to hold a person standing upright. Somewhere, far beyond the cavern, unpleasantness waited. Here there was only hushed expectancy.

In his dream he could see only the glittering chain and the cage; it swung back and forth, and at the end of each swing, where the pendulum should have slowed before it started its return, the cage blurred as if it were swinging too fast to be seen.

At this point he always realized that the cage was occupied. He was in the cage. And he understood that the pendulum marked not the passage of time but a passage through time.

The dream always ended the same way: the cage arrived with a barely perceptible jar, with a cessation of motion, and he woke up. Even awake he had the sense that somewhere the pendulum still was swinging, he still was in the cage, and eyes were watching him —or perhaps a single eye, like a camera, that occasionally revealed to him a scene of what might be. . . .

He opened his eyes. He was lying on a bed. The sheets and blankets were tangled as if he had been thrashing around in his sleep.

He looked up at the ceiling. Cracks ran across the old plaster like a map of a country he did not recognize. On his left a window let a thin, wintry light through layers of dust. On the right was the rest of the room: shabby, dingy, ordinary. In the center of the room was a black-and-white breakfast table made of metal and plastic; pulled up to it were two matching metal chairs. Beyond the table, toward what appeared to be the door to the room, was a black plastic sofa; a rickety wooden coffee table stood in front of it, and a floor lamp, at one end. Against the left wall was a wooden dresser whose walnut veneer was peeling and, beside it, an imitation walnut wardrobe. Against the right wall was another door which led, no doubt, to a bathroom. Next to the door four-foot partitions separated from the rest of the room a stove, a sink, a refrigerator, and cabinets.

Newspapers advertised it as a studio apartment; once it was called a kitchenette.

The man swung his legs out of bed and sat up, rubbing the sleep out of his face with open hands. He appeared to be a young man, a good-looking man with brown, curly hair and dark eyes and a complexion that looked as if he had been out in the sun. He had a youthful innocence about him, a kind of newly born awareness and childlike interest in everything that made people want to talk to him, to tell him personal problems, secrets they might have shared with no one else.

But after meeting him what people remembered most was his eyes. They seemed older than the rest of him. They looked at people and at things steadily, as if they were trying to understand, as if they were trying to make sense out of what they saw, as if they saw things other people could not see, as if they had seen too much. Or perhaps they were only the eyes of a man who often forgot and was trying to remember. They looked like that now as they surveyed the room and finally returned to the table and the hand-sized tape recorder that rested on it.

He stood up and walked to the table and looked down at the recorder. A cassette was in place. He pushed the lever marked "Play." The cassette hissed for a moment and then a man spoke in a clear, musical voice but with a slight accent, like someone who learned English after adolescence and speaks it better than the natives.

"Your name is Bill Johnson," the voice said. "You have just saved the world from World War III, and you don't remember. You will find stories in the newspapers about the crisis through which the world has passed. But you will find no mention of the part you played.

"For this there are several possible explanations, including the likelihood that I may be lying or deceived or insane. But the explanation on which you must act is that I have told you the truth: you are a man who was born in a future which has almost used up all hope: you were sent to this time and place to alter the events that created that future.

"Am I telling the truth? The only evidence you have is your apparently unique ability to foresee consequences—it comes like a vision, not of the future because the future can be changed, but of what will happen if events take their natural course, if someone does not act, if you do not intervene.

"But each time you intervene, no matter how subtly, you change the future from which you came. You exist in this time and outside of time and in the future, and so each change makes you forget.

"I recorded this message last night to tell you what I know, just as I learned about myself a few weeks ago by listening to a recording like this one, for I am you and we are one, and we have done this many times before. . . ."

After the voice stopped, the man called Bill Johnson picked up a billfold lying beside the recorder; near it were a few coins, a couple of keys on a ring, and a black pocket comb. In the billfold he found thirty-six dollars, a BankAmericard and a plastic-encased Social Security card both made out to Bill Johnson, and a receipt for an insured package dated three days before.

He tossed the billfold back to the table, walked to the stove, ran a little water from the hot water tap into a teakettle, and put it on the stove. He turned on the gas under it and tried to light it several times before he gave up and turned the knob off. He went into the bathroom, came out a few minutes later, and opened the front door. A newspaper lay on the dusty carpet outside. He picked it up, shut the door, and turned on the overhead light. The bulb burned dimly, as if the current was weak. He made himself a cup of instant coffee with tap water and took it to the table.

The newspaper was thin, only eight pages. The man leafed through it quickly before he stopped at one item, stared at it for a long moment as if he were not so much reading it as looking through it, tore it out, folded it, and put it into the billfold. He stood up, went to the dresser, put on his clothes, removed a scratched plastic suitcase from the top of the wardrobe, and put into it two extra pairs of pants, three shirts and a jacket, and a handful of socks and underwear; he put his dirty clothes into a paper sack and packed it, remembered the tape recorder, closed the suitcase, picked up the assorted objects on the table and slipped them into his pockets, and walked to the door.

He looked back. The room had been ordinary before. Now it was anonymous. A series of nonentities had lived here, leaving no impression of themselves upon their surroundings. Time itself in its passage had left a cigarette burn on the table, torn a hole in the cushion of a chair, ripped the sofa, scratched the coffee tables and the walls and the doors a thousand times, deposited loesses of dirt and lint in the corners and under the bed.

Johnson smiled briefly and shut the door behind him.

Downstairs he stooped to drop the keys on the ring into the mail slot in the door marked with a plaque on which was spelled out the word: Manager. Just after the keys hit the floor, the door opened. Johnson found himself looking into the face of a middle-aged woman. Her gray hair was braided and wound around her head; her face was creased into a frown of concern.

"Mr. Johnson," she said. "You're leaving? So sudden?"

"I told you I might." His voice was the voice he had heard from the tape recorder.

"I know. But—" She hesitated. "I thought—maybe—you were so good to my daughter when she had—her trouble—"

"Anyone would have wanted to help," he said.

"I know but—she thought—we thought—"

Johnson spread his hands helplessly, as if he saw time passing and was unable to stop it. "I'm sorry. I have to leave."

"You've been a good tenant," the woman said. "No complaining about the brownouts, which nobody can help God knows, or the gas shortages. You're quiet. You don't take girls to your room. And you're easy to talk to. Mr. Johnson, I hate to see you go. Who will I talk to?"

"There are always people to talk to if you give them a chance. Goodbye," he said. "May the future be kind."

Only when Bill Johnson was alone did he feel like a person. When he was with people he felt that he was being watched. Those occasions had a peculiar quality of unreality, as if he were an actor mouthing lines that someone else had written for him and he was forced to stand off and watch himself perform.

Seeing himself at the corner of the block, wind-swept paper and dust swirling around his legs, waiting without impatience for a city bus to come steaming around the corner. Sitting uneasily over torn plastic, protecting the seat of the pants from the sneaky probe of a broken spring, arriving at last at the interstate bus terminal surrounded by buildings with plyboarded windows scribbled with obscene comments and directions. Purchasing, with the aid of his credit card, a ticket automatically imprinted with a Las Vegas destination; waiting in a television-equipped chair—the viewer long broken and useless—until a faulty public address system announced the departure of his bus in words blurred almost beyond understanding.

Hearing the unending whine of tires on interstate concrete, broken only by chuckhole thumps and the stepdown of gears as the bus pulled off the highway for one of its frequent stops to expel or ingest passengers, to refuel with liquefied coal and resupply with boiler water, to allow passengers to consume lukewarm food at dirty bus stations or anonymous diners. Enduring the procession of drowsy days and sleepless nights. Watching people enter and depart, getting on, getting off, individual worlds of perceptions and relationships curiously intersecting in this other world on wheels careening down the naked edges of the world.

Feeling bodies deposited in the seat beside him, bodies that sometimes remained silent, unanimated lumps of flesh, but sometimes, by a miracle as marvelous as the changing of Pinocchio into a real boy or the mermaid into a woman, transforming themselves into feeling, suffering, rejoicing, talking people.

Listening to the talk, this imperfect mechanism of communication, supplemented in the light by gesture and expression and body position, anonymous in the night but perhaps thereby as honest as the confessional.

Listening to an old man, hair bleached and thinned by the years, face carved by life into uniqueness, recalling the past as the present rolled past the window carrying him to the future, a retirement home where he never again would trouble his children or his grandchildren.

Listening to a girl, with blonde hair and blue eyes and a smooth, unformed face ready for the hand of time to write upon, anticipating rosily her first job, her first apartment, her first big city, her life to come with its romances, pleasures, possessions, and faceless lovers.

Listening to a man of middle years, dark-haired, dark-eyed, already shaped by a knowledge of what life was about and how a man went about facing up to it, touched now by failure and uncertainty, heading toward a new position, determined to make good but disturbed by the possibility of failing again.

Listening to a woman of thirty, her life solidified by marriage and family but somehow incomplete and unsatisfying, achieving neither the heights of bliss nor the bedrock of fulfillment, unconsciously missing the excitements of youth, the uncertainty of what the day would bring, the possibilities of flight and pursuit, looking, although she did not know it, for adventure.

The young man inspected the unrolling fabric of their lives and past it to that part which was yet concealed from them, and he was kind, as everyone must be kind who knows that the future holds bereavement, disappointment, disillusion, and death.

Besides, the times were hard: like the curse of the witch who had not been invited to the christening, the Depression had laid like death across the land for five years, the unemployment rate was nearly eighteen per cent, and the energy shortage was pressing continually harder on the arteries of civilization. A little kindness came cheap enough, but it was scarce all the same.

Between conversations on his rolling world, the man named Bill Johnson occasionally removed a newspaper clipping from his billfold and read it again.

CALIFORNIA GIRL ABDUCTED

Death Valley, CA (AP)—The four-year-old daughter of Ellen McCleary, managing engineer of the Death Valley Solar Power Project, was reported missing today.

McCleary returned from her afternoon duties at the Project to discover her housekeeper, Mrs. Fred Ross, bound and gagged behind her own bed and the McCleary girl, Michelle, gone from the home.

Authorities at the Project and the local sheriff's office have refused to release any information about the possible abductor, but sources close to the Project suggest that oil interests have reason to desire the failure of the Project.

McCleary was recently divorced from her husband of ten years, Stephen Webster. Webster's location is unknown.

Authorities will neither confirm nor deny that the abductor left a message behind.

Below the hill the valley was a lake of flame as Bill Johnson climbed toward the cottage some two hundred yards from the little group of preformed buildings he had left behind. Then, as the path rose, the angle of vision changed and the flame vanished, as if snuffed by a giant finger. Now the valley was lined with thousands of mirrors reflecting the orange-red rays of the dying sun toward a black cylinder towering in their center.

The air coming up the hill off the desert was hot, like a dragon's breath, and brought with it the scent of alkali dust and the feeling of fluids being sucked through the skin until, if the process continued long enough, only the desiccated husk would be left behind for the study of future archeologists. Johnson knocked on the door of the cottage. When there was no answer he knocked again, and turned to look at the valley, arid and lifeless below him like a vision of the future.

A small noise and an outpouring of cool air made him turn. In front of him, in the doorway, stood a middle-aged woman with a face as dry as an alkali flat.

"Mrs. Ross?" Johnson said. "I'm Bill Johnson. I talked on the telephone to Ms. McCleary from Las Vegas, but the connection was bad."

"Ms. McCleary gets lotsa calls," the woman said in a voice like dust. "She don't see nobody."

"I know that," Johnson said. He smiled understandingly. "But she will want to see me. I've come to help in the disappearance of her daughter."

Mrs. Ross was unmoved. "Lotsa nuts bother Ms. McCleary about stuff like that. She don't see nobody."

"I'm sorry to be persistent," Johnson said, and his smile illustrated his regret, "but it is important." His body position was relaxed and reassuring.

The housekeeper looked at him for the first time and hesitated about closing the door. As she hesitated, a woman's voice came from within the darkened house, "Who is it, Mrs. Ross?"

"Just another crank, Ms. McCleary," the housekeeper said, looking behind her, but grasping the door firmly as if in fear that Johnson would burst past her into the sanctity of the cool interior.

Another woman appeared in the doorway. She was tall, slender, dark, good-looking but a bit haggard with concern and sleeplessness. She stared at Johnson angrily as if she blamed him for the events of the past few days. "What do you want?"

"My name is Bill Johnson," he said patiently. "I called you from Las Vegas."

"And I said I didn't want to see you," McCleary said and started to turn away. "Shut the door, Mrs. Ross—" she began.

"I may be the only person who can get your daughter back for you," Johnson said. It was as if he had leaned a hand against the door to keep it from closing.

The tall woman turned toward him again, her body rigid with the effort to control the anxiety within. Johnson smiled confidently but without arrogance, looking not at all like a nut or a crank or a criminal.

"What do you know about my daughter?" McCleary demanded. Then she took a deep breath and turned to Mrs. Ross. "Oh, let him in. He seems harmless enough."

"The sheriff said not to talk to anybody," the housekeeper said. "The sheriff said you was to—"

"I know what the sheriff said, Mrs. Ross," McCleary interrupted. "But I guess it won't matter if I talk to this person. Sometimes," she continued, her voice detached and distant, "I have to talk to somebody." She brought herself back to this place and time. "Let him in and go stand by the telephone in case I find it necessary to call the sheriff." She looked at Johnson as if warning him against making that step necessary.

"I wouldn't want you to do that," he said submissively, and moved forward into darkness. More by sound than sight he followed her footsteps down a hallway into a living room where returning vision and the light filtering through closed drapes over a picture window let him make his way to an upholstered chair. McCleary sat stiffly on the edge of a matching sofa; it was covered with velvet with variable-width stripes of orange and brown and cream. She lit a cigarette. The lingering odors of stale smoke and a littered ashtray on the glass-covered coffee table in front of her suggested that she had been smoking one cigarette after another.

"What do you know about my daughter?" she asked. She was under control now.

"First of all," he said, "she is an important person." He held up a hand to forestall her questions. "Not just to you, overriding as that may be at the moment. Not just because she is a person in a society that values every individual. But because of her potential."

"What do you know about that?" she demanded. A note of doubt had crept into her voice.

"It's hard to explain without making me seem like a crackpot or a fool," Johnson said, leaning toward her to emphasize his sincerity. "I have—special knowledge—which comes to me in the form of —visions."

"I see." Doubt had crystallized into certainty. "You're a psychic."

"No," Johnson said. "I told you it was difficult. But if that's the way you want to think of it—"

"I've had dozens of letters and telephone calls from psychics since my daughter was abducted, Mr. Johnson, and they've all been phonies," she said coldly. "All psychics are phonies. I think you'd better go." She stood up.

He stood up along with her, not submitting to, but resisting his dismissal. He looked into her eyes as if his eyes had the power to compel her belief. "I think I can find your daughter. I think I know how to get her back. If I thought you could do it without my help, I wouldn't be here. I want you to know that I could find myself in great difficulties and my mission in jeopardy."

"Where is my daughter?" It was not the tone of belief but of a final examination.

"With your husband."

"You guessed."

"No."

"You know about the message."

"Was there a message?"

"You're from Steve. He sent you."

"No. But I sense danger to your daughter and perhaps to your husband as well."

She slumped back to the sofa. "What are you then?" she asked. "Are you just a confidence man?" Her tone was pleading, as if it would comfort her if he admitted her guess was right. "What do you want from me? Why don't you leave me alone?" If she had been a more dependent person she might have turned her face from his and cried.

"All I want is to help you," he said, sitting down again, reaching toward her with one hand but not touching her, "and to help you find your daughter."

"I don't have any money," she said. "I can't pay you. If you're preying on my helplessness, it won't gain you anything. If you're seeking notoriety, you will be exposed eventually."

"None of these things matter besides your daughter's safety and her future. Besides, you may not be able to control the events of your life as you have been accustomed to doing, but you are not helpless. I don't want any money. I don't want any word of my part in this to get out to anyone, and certainly not to the press. It would be dangerous to me."

"Then what do you want?"

"I want to get to know you," he said, and as she stiffened he hastened on, "so that I can find your daughter." His glance moved around the room as if he were looking at it for the first and the last time. At the picture window that looked out over the desert valley and the solar power project when the drapes were drawn. Michelle had stood there and watched for her mother's return. At the electronic organ in the corner that neither McCleary nor her daughter could play. At the doors that led to bedrooms where a woman and a man had slept and made love and lain awake in the night. At other doors that led to baths, to the hall, to the kitchen and dining room on the other side of the hall. "I want information about your work, your daughter, your husband, the circumstances of your daughter's abduction—"

She sighed. "Where do you want to start?"

"The message. What did it say?"

"The sheriff told me not to describe it to anyone. He said that knowledge of it would either be guilty knowledge or proof of the abductor's identity."

"You've got to trust somebody some time," Johnson said.

"And the police are not to be trusted, Mr. Johnson?" Through her concern flashed the perceptiveness that had made her director of a major research project.

"From the police you get police-type answers," he said. "Investigation, surveillance, evidence, apprehension. I think you want something else—your daughter back safely and preferably without your husband—"

"My former husband," she corrected.

"Your former husband's injury or punishment."

"Ms. McCleary," said the voice of Mrs. Ross from the hall doorway, "the sheriff is here to see you."

"Thank you, Mrs. Ross," McCleary said.

"Come in, sir," Johnson said. "I've been expecting you."

The room was not much of a jail cell. It was a small room without windows. The walls were paneled in plywood faced with mahogany and decorated with framed prints of famous race horses. In the center of the room was a long table lined with chairs on either side.

It had never been intended for a cell. It was a small dining room off the main cafeteria, where groups could get together for luncheon conversations. Now a young man sat across the table from Johnson, silent and nervous, uncertain about his duties and privileges as a jailer.

He was a junior engineer on the Solar Power Project, and he had been asked to guard the prisoner while the sheriff made arrangements to transport the prisoner to the county jail some forty miles away. The young man fidgeted in his chair, clasped and unclasped his hands, and smiled uncertainly at Johnson.

Johnson smiled back reassuringly. "How is the project going?" he asked.

"What do you mean?" The engineer was a pleasant-looking young man with sandy hair bleached almost white by the sun, a face peeling perpetually from sunburn, and large hairy hands that he didn't know what to do with.

"The Solar Power Project," Johnson said. "How's it going?"

"What do you know about the project?" the engineer demanded, as if he suspected that Johnson, after all, was the hireling of the oil interests.

"Everybody knows about the Solar Power Project," Johnson said. "It's no secret."

"I guess not," the engineer admitted. He looked at the metal table with its printed wood grain as if he wished it were a drawing board. "This is an experimental project, and we've demonstrated that we can get significant amounts of power out of solar energy."

"How much is that?"

"Enough for our own needs and enough more to justify the overhead towers that cross the hills toward Los Angeles," the engineer said with a mixture of pride and defensiveness.

"That is a significant amount."

"During daylight hours, of course."

"Then why is the project still experimental?" Johnson asked.

The young man at last found something to do with one hand. "Well," he said, rubbing his chin and making the day's stubble rasp under his fingers, "there's one problem we haven't solved."

"The daylight problem?"

"No. Energy can always be stored by pumping water, electrolyzing it into hydrogen and oxygen, with batteries or flywheels. The problem is economics: it's cheaper to burn coal, even if you toss in the cost of environmental controls and damage. Almost one-fourth as cheap. And nuclear power costs less than that. Other forms of solar power, including power cells for direct conversion of sunlight into electricity, are either less efficient or more expensive."

"If the project has accomplished its purpose," Johnson asked, "why is it still going on?"

Both the engineer's hands were in motion now as he defended his project and his profession. "We still hope for a breakthrough. Producing cheaper solar cells through integrated factories. Maybe cheaper computer-driven mirrors. Maybe putting solar power plants in space where the sun shines twenty-four hours a day, if we could solve the problem of getting the energy back. Maybe some new method of converting sunlight into useful energy like chlorophyll or the purple dyes found in some primitive sea creatures."

"Nature's method of converting sunlight into energy may still be the most efficient," Johnson said. He looked up at one of the racehorses. It was a shiny red, and it was happily cropping blue grass inside a white rail fence.

"We're trying that, too," the engineer said. "Energy farms for growing trees or grasses. But put it all together and it doesn't add up to a third of the energy needs of the world that once were satisfied by cheap oil."

"What about nuclear energy?" Johnson asked.

"Inherently dangerous—particularly the breeder reactor. Not basically any more dangerous in its total impact than coal or oil, but the risks are concentrated and more visible. So the moratorium on the building of new nuclear power plants has effectively ended the effort to make nuclear energy safe."

"Well," Johnson said, "there's a lot of coal."

The engineer nodded. By now he was treating Johnson like an equal instead of a prisoner. "That's true," he said, "but unlike oil, coal is dirty. It has to be dug and that damages the miners, or the land if it's strip-mined. Sulfur has to be removed, in one way or another, to avoid sulfur dioxide pollution. And the coal will run out, too, in a century or so."

Johnson looked sad. "Then the energy depression is going to get worse until the coal runs out, and after that civilization goes back to the dark ages."

The engineer clasped his hands in front of him, almost in an attitude of prayer. "Unless we can come up with a workable technology for nuclear fusion."

"Fusing atoms of hydrogen together?"

"Making helium atoms and turning into energy the little bit of matter that's left over." The engineer's index fingers had formed a steeple. "The true sunpower—the solar process itself, clean, no radioactivity, inexhaustible, unlimited power without byproducts except heat, and maybe that could be harnessed to perform useful work if we're clever enough. Why, with hydrogen fusion man would have enough power to do anything he ever wanted to do—clean up the environment, raise enough food for everybody, improve living standards all around the world until everybody lives as well as we used to, return to space travel in a big way, reshape the other planets or move them into better orbits, go to the stars—" His voice stopped on a rising note like a preacher describing the pleasures of the life to come.

"But we haven't got it yet," Johnson said.

The engineer's eyes lowered to look at Johnson, and his hands folded themselves across each other. "We just haven't got the hang of it," he said. "There's a trick to it we haven't discovered, and we haven't got much time as civilizations go. For the past decade we've been through an energy depression that shows no signs of letting up. How much longer can we go on? Maybe thirty or forty years, if we're lucky and don't have a revolution or a major war; and if we don't discover the secret to thermonuclear fusion by then the level of civilization will be too low to apply the technology necessary to bring it into general use, and after that there'll be no one capable of thinking about anything except personal survival."

"Pretty grim," Johnson said.

"Ain't it?" the engineer said, and then he smiled. "That's why we keep working. Maybe we can buy a little time, ease the pressures a bit. Maybe somewhere a breakthrough will occur. If we don't find it, maybe our children will."

The engineer was a dreamer. Bill Johnson was a visionary. He knew what was coming, but the engineer jumped when the knock came at the door like the future announcing itself.

"George?" said the voice of Ellen McCleary. "Open up. I want to talk to the prisoner."

Outside the day turned to night. The stars had come out, bright and many-colored, and the Milky Way streamed across the sky like a jeweled veil. The reflected heat from the desert below seemed friendly now against the cool evening breeze pouring down from the hills.

Death Valley, deep and arid basin (Badwater, 280 feet below sea level, is the lowest point in the Western Hemisphere), had al-

*kali and salt flats, briny pools, grotesque rocks, and an annual
average rainfall of 1.4 inches.*

Ellen McCleary stopped a few yards from the cafeteria building
and turned to face Johnson. "I guess you think I'm a silly woman,
not able to know her own mind, first having you arrested and then
setting you free."

"I may think many things about you but not that you're a silly
woman," Johnson said. "That battle has been won; you don't have
to keep fighting it. Your presence here as director of this project is
proof of that."

"I thought about it," she said, shrugging off his interruption but
not looking at him, "and I decided that I couldn't throw away the
chance that you might be able to help. If I can get Shelly back—"
She didn't finish the sentence. Instead she held out an oblong of
stiff white paper. It was a Polaroid snapshot.

He took a few steps back into the light that streamed through
the front window of the cafeteria building. The picture showed
writing—red, broad, smeared—against a shiny black background.

"He wrote it on the bathroom mirror with my lipstick," she
said.

Johnson read the message:

> *Ellen—The Court gave Shelly to you, but I'm going to give
> her what you never could—the full-time love of a full-time
> parent.*

"Is that your former husband's handwriting?" Johnson asked.
He seemed to be looking through the picture rather than at it.

"Yes. His language, too. He's a madman, Mr. Johnson."

"In what way?"

"He—" She paused as if to gather together all the fugitive im-
pressions of a life with another person. She took a deep breath and
began again. "He thinks that the way he feels at the moment is the
only thing that matters. That he may feel differently tomorrow or
even the next moment doesn't count. He'd be willing to kill himself—or Shelly—if he felt like it at the moment." She let her breath
sigh out. "That's what I'm afraid of, I guess."

"Are you sure he's homicidal?"

"I'm making him sound crazier than he is, I know, but what I'm trying to say is that he's an impulsive person who believes that people should only do what feels right to them. He doesn't believe in the past or the future. Now is the only thing that exists for him. He thinks I'm cold and unfeeling, and I see him as childish, and— but I'm talking as if you're a marriage counselor. We tried that, too."

They talked together now in the darkness, two voices without faces, sound without body. "That's all right," Johnson said. "It helps me get the feel of things. Did he have a profession, a talent, a job?"

Her voice held the hint of a shrug. "He was a bit of a lot of things—a bit of a painter, a bit of a writer, a bit of an actor, but a romantic all the time. What really broke things up, though, was when this project got started and I was selected as director. I was in charge, and he was just—around. He had nothing to do, and conditions were pretty primitive for a while. That's when Shelly was conceived—as sort of a sop to his manhood. But it didn't last. He left for a few months when Shelly was about a year old, came back, we quarreled, he left again, and finally I divorced him, got custody of Shelly, and that's about it."

"Not much for what—ten years of marriage?"

"Yes." She sighed. "Shelly is all, and he's taken her."

"Where did you meet?"

"In Los Angeles. At a party at a friend's house. I was a graduate student at Cal Tech; he was an actor. He seemed romantic and strong. I was—flattered, I guess—that he was interested in me. We got married in a whirlwind of emotion, and it was great for a few months. Then things began going bad. I irritated him by worrying about my career, by wanting to talk about where we were going to be next year, ten years from now. He annoyed me by his lack of concern for those things, by his unrelenting demands upon my time, my attention, my emotions. Part of my emotions were invested in other things—in my work, for one—and he could never understand that, or forgive it."

"I understand," Johnson said. "The times your husband left— did he return to Los Angeles?"

"I think he did the first time, although we weren't communicating too well then. But that's where he said he'd been when he came back."

"The second time?"

"I don't know. We didn't communicate at all until the divorce, and then it was through lawyers. Until that." She indicated the photograph in Johnson's hand, a shadowy finger almost touching the white rectangle.

He held it in his fingertips, almost as if he were weighing it. "I suppose the police checked all his friends in Los Angeles."

"And his relatives. That's where he was born and grew up. But they didn't find anything. Nobody has seen him recently. Nobody knows where he might have gone with Shelly."

"Did he have any hobbies?"

"Tennis. He liked tennis. And parties. And girls." The last word had an edge of bitterness.

"Hunting? Mountain climbing?" Johnson's words were tentative, as if he were testing a hypothesis.

She seemed to be shaking her head. "He didn't like the outdoors. Not raw. If he'd liked to hike or hunt, he still might be here," she said ruefully. The blur of a hand gestured at the mountains that rose to the east and the north and the west of them.

"He sounds restless," Johnson said. "Could he stay in one place for long at a time? If he starts moving around, the police will find him."

"He never has been able to stay still before, but if he thought that was the only way to hurt me he might be able to do it."

"Is Mrs. Ross sure he's the one who tied her up?"

"She never knew Steve. I hired her after he left. But she identified his picture."

"There was nobody else with him? Nobody who might be making him do what he did?"

"Not that she could tell. She said he seemed cheerful. Whistled while he tied her up. Said not to worry, I would be back at six o'clock—that I was like a quartz watch, always right on the second. He hated that." She paused and waited in the darkness. When he didn't say anything, she asked, "Is there anything else?"

"Do you have any of his personal belongings?"

"I threw them out. I didn't want anything to remind me of him.

Or to remind Shelly either, I guess. Except this." She handed Johnson another white oblong.

He took it into the light. It was the picture of a blond young man in tennis clothing, looking up into the sun with the net and court behind him, squinting a little, laughing, strikingly handsome and vital and alive, as if time had been captured and made to stand still for him and he would never grow old.

"Can I keep the pictures?" Johnson asked.

"Yes," she said. Her disembodied voice held a nod. "Can you find Shelly for me?"

"Yes," he said. It was not boastful nor a promise but a statement of fact. "Don't worry. I'll see that she gets back to you." That was a promise. "May the future be kind," he said. Then he walked out of the light into the darkness. His footsteps sounded more distant on the path until the night was still.

Los Angeles was a carnival of life, a sprawling, vivid city of contrasts between the rich and the poor, between the extravagant and the impecunious, between mansions and slums.

Los Angeles, founded 1781, cattle ranching center under Spanish and Mexicans, expanded with railroads, oil, motion pictures, and aircraft manufacturing, obtains water from Colorado and Owens Rivers and Mono Basin, and power from Hoover Dam.

The smog was gone, removed not so much by the elimination of automobile exhaust fumes but by the elimination of the automobile. Except for the occasional antique gasoline-powered machines that rolled imperiously along the nearly deserted freeways, the principal method of transportation was the coal-fueled steam-powered bus. The smokestacks, too, had been stopped, either by smoke and fume scrubbers or by the Depression.

Watts was sullen. Unlike an earlier period when minorities felt that they were being cheated of an affluence available to everyone else, the citizens shared what was clearly a widespread and apparently growing distress and general decline in civilization. The riots of discrimination were clearly past, and the riots of desperation had not yet begun.

Through this strange city went a man who did not know his name, troubled by a past he could not remember and visions of a

future he could not forget, trying to put together a portrait of a
man who had as many images as there were people who knew him,
seeking the vision that would reveal a place where a man and a
child might be unnoticed, asking questions and getting always the
same replies.

At a Spanish bungalow with peeling pink stucco, "No, we don't
know him."

At a walled studio with sagging gates, echoing sound stages, and
decaying location sets that looked like a premonition of the society
outside its walls, "No, we haven't used him in years."

At a comfortable ranch house in the valley, surrounded by orange trees, "The police have been here twice already. We've answered all their questions."

At a tennis club still maintaining standards and the muted
sprong-sprong of court activity, "He hasn't been around for
months."

At a high school where hopeless teachers tried to impart knowledge whose value they no longer found credible to listless students
who were there only because society had no other place for them,
"We can show you only the yearbooks," and in them pictures of a
face without character and listings of activities without meaning.

And then, unexpectedly, at a bar along the Strip, half facade
and half-corrupt, like a painted whore, "Yeah, I seen him a couple
of months ago, him and a fellow with a cap on—you know one of
those things with a whatchmacallit on the front—yeah, a visor—like
a sea captain, you know—yeah, Gregory Peck as Captain Ahab.
Reason I remember—it wasn't his style, you know. It was always
girls with him. You could see him turn up the charm like one of
those things that dim and brighten lights—a rheostat?—yeah, I
guess. With guys he was cool, you know?—like he didn't care what
they thought of him. But with this guy it was different. Like he
wanted something from the guy. No. I didn't hear what they was
talking about. I had sixty-seventy customers in here that night.
The noise you wouldn't believe sometimes. You're lucky I remembered seeing him."

A search of the dock area, all up and down the coast, until
finally at the small boat marina near Alamitos Beach State Park, a
marina with many empty docks, "Steve? Sure, he borrowed my

cruiser for a couple of hours about two weeks ago. No, he didn't tell me where he was going, but I trusted him and he brought it back. Of course I didn't think he was running dope past the border. There's no point in that now, is there? What with the new laws and everything? Anyway, he was gone only a couple of hours. Well, I gave him the keys about one o'clock in the afternoon, and he was back with them before four. Sure I'm certain about the time. I remember—I told him I was having a party on board that evening, and I had to get her cleaned up and provisioned. Matter of fact, I asked if he wanted to join the party—a guy like Steve gives a party real class, and the girls come back—but he couldn't. You can push her up to thirty knots, but she's a real fuel eater at that speed. No, I didn't see anybody with him. May have been, but I didn't see anybody. Want to look at the boat? Why not? I bought it from a fellow in Long Beach five years ago when fuel got so expensive. Now I hardly ever go out in it. Use it sort of like a floating bar and bedroom . . ."

Brass rails, gleaming teak decks, white paint shining in the sun, the spoked wheel, touch it, feel its response, sense the directions it has gone, the hands that have held it and steered the boat. The cabin below, all compact and efficient, bunks and tables, kitchen and head, immaculate, haunted by ghosts, crowded together here laughing, crying, drunken, reckless, desperate . . .

And back to the dock, certain now, seeing a vision of a place available by water within an hour's range of the cruiser, at most thirty nautical miles from the small boat marina . . .

And at the head of the dock, waiting for him, a tall, slender woman, dark-haired, dark-eyed, good-looking but a bit more haggard now. "So," she said, "he took her away by water. I would never have suspected him of having that much imagination."

Johnson looked at her and saw the past. "You didn't give him credit for much."

"You don't seem surprised at seeing me," she said.

"No."

She hesitated, looking down at her feet in their red canvas shoes that matched her red slacks. "I guess I owe you an apology," she said finally.

"No."

"I suspected you," she went on, looking up at him, letting him see her guilt. "The police suspected you too—of having had some contact with Steve, of being his emissary, at least of knowing him, perhaps where he was living, perhaps being willing to sell him out."

"You have reason to suspect people," Johnson said. The odor of fish and oily salt water surrounded them.

"So we had you followed. And you did the police work to find him. You don't know how difficult this is for me, do you?"

"Yes," he said.

"You did it better than the police. You found him. Maybe you really are what you say you are."

"That's a reasonable assumption."

"The world isn't reasonable," she complained. "People aren't reasonable. You did find him, didn't you? Tell me that you found him."

"I found him," Johnson said simply, "but I haven't gone to him yet. I haven't got Shelly back for you yet."

"I'm not asking you to tell me where he is," Ellen McCleary said, a bit unsteadily, looking at Johnson's face hopefully, "but I'm asking you to take me with you."

"I can get Shelly back without damage to her or your former husband if I go alone," Johnson said. "With you along the chances get much slimmer."

She got angry at that. "Who are you to say? What do you know about him or me or Shelly? What right have you to meddle in our lives?"

"Only the outcome can justify any of us," he said. "Good intentions, emotional involvements, rights—all these are only the absolution we give ourselves for lack of foresight. Look out there." He motioned toward the smooth blue swells of the Pacific gleaming with highlights in the sunshine. "Quite a difference from your wasteland. That's fertility. That's promise. We came from the sea, and in the sea lies our future."

"My desert is not as lifeless as it looks," she said. "We get energy from it, energy we need, energy we must have."

"The lowest kind of energy—heat. You waste a lot when you have to pump it up into electricity."

"Like all energy it comes from the sun."

"Not all," he said. The wind was coming in off the ocean and blowing away the old smells of rot and waste. "I won't take you with me. You can have me followed, of course, but I ask you not to do that. What will it be? Your desert of old memories or my sea of hope?"

She shook her head slowly, helplessly. "I can't promise."

"Then neither can I," he said, and left her standing at the edge of the water as he walked quickly to the street and the nearest public transportation.

The ferry ride was a pleasant interlude, a break in the feeling of urgency that drove Johnson. He could not hurry the ship, and he existed for the moment, like the smiling young man in the tennis clothes, outside of time. From San Pedro Bay to Santa Catalina, he watched the blue water curl under the bow, white and playful, and the smooth blue surface of the Pacific extending undisturbed to the end of the world.

Johnson studied it as if he had never before seen the protean sea or the creatures that lived in it—small darting fish like dark shapes changing instantly into silver when pursued by large solitary predators, and distantly, across the horizon, the gray unbelievable backs of whales. The breeze, laden with salt, blew across his face and tugged at his hair and clothing, and he smiled.

He left the ferry at Avalon as soon as the ship had tied up in its slip.

Santa Catalina, discovered in 1542 by Cabrillo, bought in 1919 by William Wrigley and developed as a pleasure resort, has museums, aquarium, bird haven, and casino.

Few people got off the ferry—the pleasure business was an early casualty of the Depression—and Johnson paid no attention to them. He rented a bicycle from a stand at the end of the pier and peddled up the main road among the wooded hills, got off and walked the bicycle where the hills were too steep to ride, stopped for a moment when he had reached the high point, with Black Jack Peak to his right and the Pacific spread out in front of him again like hope regained, then coasted rapidly down the hills, past

Middle Ranch and along the west coast where the ocean flashed blue between the trees.

Just short of Catalina Harbor, he stopped, pulled the bicycle off the road and behind some trees, and walked up through the woods along a barely discernible path until the trees began to thin and he found himself close to a small clearing. A small cabin stood in the middle of the clearing. As Johnson stood without moving, the sound of a child's happy voice came to him and then a man's deeper voice followed, surprisingly, by a third voice and a fourth, the child's squeal of laughter, and a man's chuckle.

Johnson moved through the last of the trees into the dust of the clearing. Now he could see the front porch of the cabin. On the edge of the porch sat a child with short dark hair and lively blue eyes. She was dressed in a red knitted shirt and dirty jeans. Her feet were bare, her hands were squeezed ecstatically between her knees, and she stared enraptured at finger puppets on the hands of a light-haired young man.

In a hoarse voice the young man chanted:

"Today I'll brew, tomorrow bake;
Merrily I'll dance and sing.
Tomorrow will a baby bring:
The lady cannot stop my game . . ."

The little girl shouted with delight, "Rumpelstiltskin is my name!"

The young man was laughing with her until he saw Johnson. He stopped laughing. The puppets fell off his fingers as he reached behind him. The little girl stopped laughing, too, and looked at Johnson. In repose her face looked a great deal like the face of Ellen McCleary with the young man's blue eyes and spontaneity.

"Hello," Johnson said. He moved forward slowly, like a man moving among wild animals, so as not to frighten them into flight or attack.

"Don't tell me you've come to read the meter," said the young man sitting on the porch, "or that you just wandered here by mistake."

Johnson eased himself down in the center of the clearing with his back to the ocean that gleamed through the trees a deeper blue than the sky. He sat cross-legged and helpless in the dust and said, "No, I came here to talk to you, Steve Webster."

Webster brought his right hand out from behind him. It had a revolver in it. He supported the butt on his knee and pointed it in Johnson's general direction. "If you're from my wife, tell her to leave me alone—me and Shelly—or she'll regret it." Webster's voice was harsh, and the little girl stirred nervously beside him, looking at her father's face, down at the gun, and then at Johnson.

"I've talked to your former wife," Johnson said, "but I'm not here in her behalf alone. I'm here as much for your sake as hers, but mostly for Shelly's sake."

"That's a lot of crap," Webster said, straightening the gun a little.

"You're frightening your daughter," Johnson said to him.

"She wasn't frightened before you came," Webster said.

"I realize that you and your daughter have been happy together," Johnson said. He spread his hands as if he were weighing sunbeams on his palms. "But how long can it last? How long before the authorities locate you?"

Webster waved the ugly gun in the air as if he had forgotten he held it. "That doesn't matter. Maybe they'll find us tomorrow, maybe never. Now we're happy. We're together. Whatever happens can never change that."

"Suppose," Johnson said, "it could last forever. You can't always be a little girl and her father playing games in a cabin in the woods. Shelly will grow up without schooling, without friends. Is that the thing to do for your daughter?"

"A man has got to do what he thinks is right," Webster said stubbornly. "Now is all any of us have got. Next month, next year, maybe something else will happen. Something good, something bad—you can't live for that. Nobody knows what's going to happen."

Johnson's lips tightened but Webster didn't seem to notice.

"Nobody's found me yet," Webster said, and then his eyes focused on Johnson again. "Except you." He noticed the gun in his hand and pointed it more purposefully at Johnson. "Except you," he repeated.

The little girl began to cry.

"Wouldn't that spoil it?" Johnson said. "Having Shelly see me shot by her father?"

"Yeah," Webster said. "Run inside the cabin, Shelly," he said, looking only at Johnson. The little girl didn't move. "Go on, now. Get in the cabin." The little girl cried harder. "See what you're making me do?" he complained to Johnson.

Johnson put his hands out in the dust in a gesture of helplessness. "I'm not a threat to you, and you can't save anything by getting rid of me. If I can find you, others can. In any case, you couldn't stay here long. You'll need food, clothing, books. Word about a man and a little girl living here is bound to get out. You'll have to move. The moment you move the police will spot you. It's hopeless, Steve."

Webster waved the gun in the air. "I can always choose another ending."

"For yourself? Ellen said you might do that."

"Yeah?" Webster looked interested. "Maybe for once Ellen was right."

"But that's not the way it ought to be," Johnson said. "You're old enough to make your own decisions, but you ought to leave Shelly out of this. She's got a right to live, a right to decide what she wants to do with her life."

"That's true," Webster admitted. He started to lower the gun to his knee again, and then lifted it to point at Johnson again. "But what does a little girl know about life?"

"She'll get bigger and able to make her own decisions if you give her a chance," Johnson said.

"A chance," Webster repeated. He raised the gun until it pointed directly at Johnson, aiming it, tightening his finger on the trigger. "That's what the world never gave me. That's what Ellen never gave me."

Johnson sat in the dust, not moving, looking at the deadly black hole in the muzzle of the gun.

Gradually Webster's finger relaxed. He lowered the revolver to the porch beside him as if he had forgotten it. "But you're not to blame," he said.

"I suppose I'm to blame," a woman's voice said from the edge of the clearing. Ellen McCleary stepped out from among the trees.

Webster seemed surprised and delighted to see her. "Ellen," he said, "it was good of you to come to see me."

"Mommy," Shelly said. She tried to get up and run to her mother, but Webster held her wrist firmly in his hand and would not let her go.

"That's all right, Shelly," Ellen said, moving easily toward the porch where her former husband and her daughter sat. She no longer seemed tired, now that she had reached the end of her search. "Let Shelly go," she said to Webster.

"Not bloody likely," he said.

"Not to me," Ellen said. "Let her go with this man."

Webster glanced at Johnson. Neither of them said anything.

"Let's leave Shelly out of this," Ellen said. "It's between us, isn't it?"

"Maybe it is," Webster said. His fingers loosened on Shelly's wrist.

The little girl had stopped crying when her mother appeared. Now she looked back and forth between her parents, on the edge of tears but holding them back.

"We did it to each other," Ellen said, "let's not do it to Shelly. She's not guilty of anything."

"That's true," Webster said. "You and I—we're guilty, all right."

"Go to Mr. Johnson, Shelly," Ellen said. Her voice was quiet but it held a quality of command.

Webster's hand fell away, and he pushed the little girl affectionately toward Johnson. "Go on, Shelly," he said with rough tenderness. "That man's going to take you for a walk."

Johnson held out his arms to the little girl. She looked at her father and then at her mother, and turned to run to Johnson.

"That's a kind thing to do," Ellen said.

"Oh, I can be kind," Webster said. He grinned, and his face was warm and likeable.

Johnson got slowly to his knees in the dust of the clearing and then to his feet.

"It's a matter of knowing what kindness is," Webster said.

"If you're fixed in the present," Ellen said, "I suppose that would be a problem."

Johnson took Shelly's hand and began moving out of the clearing.

"Now, now," Webster cautioned, "let's not be unkind. We are put here on this earth to be kind to one another. And we have come together now to be kind to one another as we were not kind before."

Johnson and Shelly had reached the protection of the trees and moved among them. The odor of green growing things rose around them.

"The problem," Ellen said, "is that we don't know what the other one means by kindness. What is kindness to you may be unkindness to me, and the other way around."

As Johnson and Shelly moved down the path, the voices gradually faded behind them.

"Don't start with me again," Webster said.

"I'm not," she said. "Believe me, I'm not. But it's all over, Steve. I didn't come here alone, you know."

"You mean you brought police," he said. His voice was rising.

"I couldn't find you by myself," she said. "But I didn't bring them. You brought them. By what you did. Don't make it worse, Steve. Give yourself up." The rest was indistinguishable. But the sound of voices, louder, shouting, came to them until hands reached out of bushes beside the path to grab them both.

A man's voice said, "You're not Webster."

Another man's voice, on the other side of the path, said, "That's all right, little girl, we're police officers."

A shot came from the clearing some two hundred yards away. For a moment the world seemed frozen—the leaves were still, the birds stopped singing, even the distant sea ceased its restless motion. And then everything burst into sound and activity again, bodies pounded past Johnson toward the clearing, dust hung in the air, and Shelly was crying.

"Where's my Mommy?" she said. "Where's my Daddy?"

Johnson held her tightly in his arms and tried to comfort her, but there was nothing he could say that would not leave her poorer than she had been a few moments ago.

Then he heard footsteps approaching on the path.

"Hello, Shelly," Ellen said heavily.

"Mommy!" the little girl said, and Johnson let her go to her mother.

After a moment, Ellen said over the child's head, "You knew what was going to happen, didn't you?"

"Only if certain things happened."

"If I had not come here Steve might still be alive," she said, "and if you hadn't been here both Shelly and I might be dead."

"People do what they must—like active chemicals, participating in every reaction. Some persons serve their life purposes by striding purposefully toward their destinations; others, by flailing out wildly in all directions."

"What about you?"

"Others slide through life without being noticed and affect events through their presence rather than their actions," Johnson said. "I am—a catalyst. A substance that assists a reaction without participating in it."

"I don't know what you are," Ellen said. "But I've got a lot to thank you for."

"What are you going to do now?"

"I'm going to sit down and think for a long time. Maybe Steve was right. Maybe I was neglecting Shelly."

"Children can be smothered as well as neglected," Johnson said. "They must be loved enough to be let go by people who love themselves enough to do what they must do to be people."

"You think I should go back to my project."

"For Shelly's sake."

"And yours?"

"And everyone's. But that's just a guess."

"You're a strange man, Bill Johnson, and I should ask you questions, but I have the feeling that whatever answers you gave or didn't give, it wouldn't matter. So—let me ask you just one." She hesitated. "Will you come to see me again when all this is over. I—I'd like you to see me as something other than a suspicious, harried mother."

An expression like pain passed across Johnson's face and was gone. "I can't," he said.

"I understand."

"No, you don't," he said. "Just understand—I would like to know you better. But I can't."

And he stood on the hillside, dappled by the light that came through the leaves and was reflected up from the ocean, and he watched them walk down the path toward the road that would take them back to the boat, back to the mainland.

In the distance a frigate bird sailed alone in the sky, circling a spot in the ocean, turning and circling and finding nothing.

The rented room was lit only by the flickering of an old neon sign outside the window. Johnson sat at a wooden table, pressed down a key on the cassette recorder in front of him, and after a moment began to speak.

"Your name is Bill Johnson," he said. "You have just returned to her mother the little girl who will grow up to perfect the thermonuclear power generator, and you don't remember. You may find a small item in the newspaper about it, but you will find no mention of the part you played in recovering the girl.

"For this there are several possible explanations. . . ."

After he had finished, he sat silently for several minutes while the cassette continued to hiss, until he remembered to reach forward and press the lever marked "Stop."

BROTHER

by Clifford D. Simak

Surely the Grand Master that the Science Fiction Writers of America declared him to be, Simak is beloved for his combination of the farthest futures and the weirdest events with a homey and warm passion for the gentle virtues of the simple rural life. This is the kind of note we like to end an anthology with and we hope you all agree.

He was sitting in his rocking chair on the stone-flagged patio when the car pulled off the road and stopped outside his gate. A stranger got out of it, unlatched the gate and came up the walk. The man coming up the walk was old—not as old, judged the man in the rocking chair, as he was, but old. White hair blowing in the wind and a slow, almost imperceptible, shuffle in his gait.

The man stopped before him. "You are Edward Lambert?" he asked. Lambert nodded. "I am Theodore Anderson," said the man. "From Madison. From the university."

Lambert indicated the other rocker on the patio. "Please sit down," he said. "You are far from home."

Anderson chuckled. "Not too far. A hundred miles or so."

"To me, that's far," said Lambert. "In all my life I've never been more than twenty miles away. The spaceport across the river is as far as I've ever been."

"You visit the port quite often?"

"At one time, I did. In my younger days. Not recently. From here, where I sit, I can see the ships come in and leave."

"You sit and watch for them?"

"Once I did. Not now. I still see them now and then. I no longer watch for them."

"You have a brother, I understand, who is out in space."

"Yes, Phil. Phil is the wanderer of the family. There were just the two of us. Identical twins."

"You see him now and then? I mean, he comes back to visit."

"Occasionally. Three or four times, that is all. But not in recent years. The last time he was home was twenty years ago. He was always in a hurry. He could only stay a day or two. He had great tales to tell."

"But you, yourself, stayed home. Twenty miles, you said, the farthest you've ever been away."

"There was a time," said Lambert, "when I wanted to go with him. But I couldn't. We were born late in our parents' life. They were old when we were still young. Someone had to stay here with them. And after they were gone, I found I couldn't leave. These hills, these woods, the streams had become too much a part of me."

Anderson nodded. "I can understand that. It is reflected in your writing. You became the pastoral spokesman of the century. I am quoting others, but certainly you know that."

Lambert grunted. "Nature writing. At one time, it was in the great American tradition. When I first started writing it, fifty years ago, it had gone out of style. No one understood it, no one wanted it. No one saw the need for it. But now it's back again. Every damn fool who can manage to put three words together is writing it again."

"But none as well as you."

"I've been at it longer. I have more practice doing it."

"Now," said Anderson, "there is greater need of it. A reminder of a heritage that we almost lost."

"Perhaps," said Lambert.

"To get back to your brother. . . ."

"A moment, please," said Lambert. "You have been asking me a lot of questions. No preliminaries. No easy build up. None of the usual conversational amenities. You simply came barging in and began asking questions. You tell me your name and that you are from the university, but that is all. For the record, Mr. Anderson, please tell me what you are."

"I am sorry," said Anderson. "I'll admit to little tact, despite the fact that is one of the basics of my profession. I should know its value. I'm with the psychology department and. . . ."

"Psychology?"

"Yes, psychology."

"I would have thought," said Lambert, "that you were in English or, perhaps, ecology or some subject dealing with the environment. How come a psychologist would drop by to talk with a nature writer?"

"Please bear with me," Anderson pleaded. "I went at this all wrong. Let us start again. I came, really, to talk about your brother."

"What about my brother? How could you know about him? Folks hereabouts know, but no one else. In my writings, I have never mentioned him."

"I spent a week last summer at a fishing camp only a few miles from here. I heard about him then."

"And some of those you talked with told you I never had a brother."

"That is it, exactly. You see, I have this study I have been working on for the last five years. . . ."

"I don't know how the story ever got started," said Lambert, "that I never had a brother. I have paid no attention to it, and I don't see why you. . . ."

"Mr. Lambert," said Anderson, "please pardon me. I've checked the birth records at the county seat and the census. . . ."

"I can remember it," said Lambert, "as if it were only yesterday, the day my brother left. We were working in the barn, there across the road. The barn is no longer used now and, as you can see, has fallen in upon itself. But then it was used. My father farmed the meadow over there that runs along the creek. That land grew, still would grow if someone used it, the most beautiful corn that you ever saw. Better corn than the Iowa prairie land. Better than any place on earth. I farmed it for years after my father died, but I no longer farm it. I went out of the farming business a good ten years ago. Sold off all the stock and machinery. Now I keep a little kitchen garden. Not too large. It needn't be too large. There is only. . . ."

"You were saying about your brother?"

"Yes, I guess I was. Phil and I were working in the barn one day. It was a rainy day—no, not really a rainy day, just drizzling. We were repairing harness. Yes, harness. My father was a strange man in many ways. Strange in reasonable sorts of ways. He didn't believe in using machinery any more than necessary. There was never a tractor on the place. He thought horses were better. On a small place like this, they were. I used them myself until I finally had to sell them. It was an emotional wrench to sell them. The horses and I were friends. But, anyhow, the two of us were working at the harness when Phil said to me, out of the thin air, that he was going to the port and try to get a job on one of the ships. We had talked about it, off and on, before, and both of us had a hankering to go, but it was a surprise to me when Phil spoke up and said that he was going. I had no idea that he had made up his mind. There is something about this that you have to understand—the time, the circumstance, the newness and excitement of travel to the stars in that day of more than fifty years ago. There were days, far back in our history, when New England boys ran off to sea. In that time of fifty years ago, they were running off to space. . . ."

Telling it, he remembered it, as he had told Anderson, as if it were only yesterday. It all came clear and real again, even to the musty scent of last year's hay in the loft above them. Pigeons were cooing in the upper reaches of the barn, and, up in the hillside pasture, a lonesome cow was bawling. The horses stamped in their stalls and made small sounds, munching at the hay remaining in their mangers.

"I made up my mind last night," said Phil, "but I didn't tell you because I wanted to be sure. I could wait, of course, but if I wait, there's the chance I'll never go. I don't want to live out my life here wishing I had gone. You'll tell pa, won't you? After I am gone. Sometime this afternoon, giving me a chance to get away."

"He wouldn't follow you," said Edward Lambert. "It would be best for you to tell him. He might reason with you, but he wouldn't stop your going."

"If I tell him, I will never go," said Phil. "I'll see the look upon his face and I'll never go. You'll have to do this much for me, Ed. You'll have to tell him so I won't see the look upon his face."

"How will you get on a ship? They don't want a green farm boy. They want people who are trained."

"There'll be a ship," said Phil, "that is scheduled to lift off, but with a crew member or two not there. They won't wait for them, they won't waste the time to hunt them down. They'll take anyone who's there. In a day or two, I'll find that kind of ship."

Lambert remembered once again how he had stood in the barn door, watching his brother walking down the road, his boots splashing in the puddles, his figure blurred by the mistlike drizzle. For a long time after he could no longer see him, long after the grayness of the drizzle had blotted out his form, he had still imagined he could see him, an ever smaller figure trudging down the road. He recalled the tightness in his chest, the choke within his throat, the terrible, gut-twisting heaviness of grief at his brother's leaving. As if a part of him were gone, as if he had been torn in two, as if only half of him were left.

"We were twins," he told Anderson. "Identical twins. We were closer than most brothers. We lived in one another's pocket. We did everything together. Each of us felt the same about the other. It took a lot of courage for Phil to walk away like that."

"And a lot of courage and affection on your part," said Anderson, "to let him walk away. But he did come back again?"

"Not for a long time. Not until after both our parents were dead. Then he came walking down the road, just the way he'd left. But he didn't stay. Only for a day or two. He was anxious to be off. As if he were being driven."

Although that was not exactly right, he told himself. Nervous. Jumpy. Looking back across his shoulder. As if he were being followed. Looking back to make sure the Follower was not there.

"He came a few more times," he said. "Years apart. He never stayed too long. He was anxious to get back."

"How can you explain this idea that people have that you never had a brother?" asked Anderson. "How do you explain the silence of the records?"

"I have no explanation," Lambert said. "People get some strange ideas. A thoughtless rumor starts—perhaps no more than a question: 'About this brother of his? Does he really have a brother? Was there ever any brother?' And others pick it up and build it up and it goes on from there. Out in these hills there's not much to talk about. They grab at anything there is. It would be an intriguing thing to talk about—that old fool down in the valley who thinks he has a brother that he never had, bragging about this non-existent brother out among the stars. Although it seems to me that I never really bragged. I never traded on him."

"And the records? Or the absence of the records?"

"I just don't know," said Lambert. "I didn't know about the records. I've never checked. There was never any reason to. You see, I know I have a brother."

"Do you think that you may be getting up to Madison?"

"I know I won't," said Lambert. "I seldom leave this place. I no longer have a car. I catch a ride with a neighbor when I can to go to the store and get the few things that I need. I'm satisfied right here. There's no need to go anywhere."

"You've lived here alone since your parents died?"

"That is right," said Lambert. "And I think this has gone far enough. I'm not sure I like you, Mr. Anderson. Or should that be Dr. Anderson? I suspect it should. I'm not going to the university to answer questions that you want me to or to submit to tests in this study of yours. I'm not sure what your interest is and I'm not even faintly interested. I have other, more important things to do."

Anderson rose from the chair. "I am sorry," he said. "I had not meant. . . ."

"Don't apologize," said Lambert.

"I wish we could part on a happier note," said Anderson.

"Don't let it bother you," said Lambert. "Just forget about it. That's what I plan to do."

He continued sitting in the chair long after the visitor had left.

A few cars went past, not many, for this was a lightly traveled road, one that really went nowhere, just an access for the few families that lived along the valley and back in the hills.

The gall of the man, he thought, the arrogance of him, to come storming in and asking all those questions. That study of his—perhaps a survey of the fantasies engaged in by an aged population. Although it need not be that; it might be any one of a number of other things.

There was, he cautioned himself, no reason to get upset by it. It was not important; bad manners never were important to anyone but those who practiced them.

He rocked gently back and forth, the rockers complaining on the stones, and gazed across the road and valley to the place along the opposite hill where the creek ran, its waters gurgling over stony shallows and swirling in deep pools. The creek held many memories. There, in long, hot summer days, he and Phil had fished for chubs, using crooked willow branches for rods because there was no money to buy regular fishing gear—not that they would have wanted it even if there had been. In the spring great shoals of suckers had come surging up the creek from the Wisconsin River to reach their spawning areas. He and Phil would go out and seine them, with a seine rigged from a gunny sack, its open end held open by a barrel hoop.

The creek held many memories for him and so did all the land, the towering hills, the little hidden valleys, the heavy hardwood forest that covered all except those few level areas that had been cleared for farming. He knew every path and byway of it. He knew what grew on and lived there and where it grew or lived. He knew of the secrets of the few surrounding square miles of countryside, but not all the secrets; no man was born who could know all the secrets.

He had, he told himself, the best of two worlds. Of two worlds, for he had not told Anderson, he had not told anyone, of that secret link that tied him to Phil. It was a link that never had seemed strange because it was something they had known from the time when they were small. Even apart, they had known what the other might be doing. It was no wondrous thing to them; it was something they had taken very much for granted. Years later, he had read in learned journals the studies that had been made of identical twins, with the academic speculation that in some strange manner they seemed to hold telepathic powers which operated only between the two of them—as if they were, in fact, one person in two different bodies.

That was the way of it, most certainly, with him and Phil, although whether it might be telepathy, he had never even wondered until he stumbled on the journals. It did not seem, he thought, rocking in the chair, much like telepathy, for telepathy, as he understood it, was the deliberate sending and receiving of mental messages; it had simply been a knowing, of where the other was and what he might be doing. It had been that way when they were youngsters and that way ever since. Not a continued knowing, not continued contact, if it was contact. Through the years, however, it happened fairly often. He had known through all the years since Phil had gone walking down the road the many planets that Phil had visited, the ships he'd traveled on—had seen it all with Phil's eyes, had understood it with Phil's brain, had known the names of the places Phil had seen and understood, as Phil had understood, what had happened in each place. It had not been a conversation: they had not talked with one another; there had been no need to talk. And although Phil had never told him, he was certain Phil had known what he was doing and where he was and what he might be seeing. Even on the few occasions that Phil had come to visit, they had not talked about it; it was no subject for discussion since both accepted it.

In the middle of the afternoon, a beat-up car pulled up before the gate, the motor coughing to a stuttering halt. Jake Hopkins, one of his neighbors up the creek, climbed out, carrying a small basket. He came up on the patio and, setting the basket down, sat down in the other chair.

"Katie sent along a loaf of bread and a blackberry pie," he said. "This is about the last of the blackberries. Poor crop this year. The summer was too dry."

"Didn't do much blackberrying myself this year," said Lambert. "Just out a time or two. The best ones are on that ridge over yonder, and I swear that hill gets steeper year by year."

"It gets steeper for all of us," said Hopkins. "You and I, we've been here a long time, Ed."

"Tell Katie thanks," said Lambert. "There ain't no one can make a better pie than she. Pies, I never bother with them, although I purely love them. I do some cooking, of course, but pies take too much time and fuss."

"Hear anything about this new critter in the hills?" asked Hopkins.

Lambert chuckled. "Another one of those wild talks, Jake. Every so often, a couple of times a year, someone starts a story. Remember that one about the swamp beast down at Millville? Papers over in Milwaukee got hold of it, and a sportsman down in Texas read about it and came up with a pack of dogs. He spent three days at Millville, floundering around in the swamps, lost one dog to a rattler, and, so I was told, you never saw a madder white man in your life. He felt that he had been took, and I suppose he was, for there was never any beast. We get bear and panther stories, and there hasn't been a bear or panther in these parts for more than forty years. Once, some years ago, some damn fool started a story about a big snake. Big around as a nail keg and thirty feet long. Half the county was out hunting it."

"Yes, I know," said Hopkins. "There's nothing to most of the stories, but Caleb Jones told me one of his boys saw this thing, whatever it may be. Like an ape, or a bear that isn't quite a bear. All over furry, naked. A snowman, Caleb thinks."

"Well, at least," said Lambert, "that is something new. There hasn't been anyone, to my knowledge, claimed to see a snowman here. There have been a lot of reports, however, from the West Coast. It just took a little time to transfer a snowman here."

"One could have wandered east."

"I suppose so. If there are any of them out there, that is. I'm not too sure there are."

"Well, anyhow," said Hopkins, "I thought I'd let you know. You are kind of isolated here. No telephone or nothing. You never even run in electricity."

"I don't need either a telephone or electricity," said Lambert. "The only thing about electricity that would tempt me would be a refrigerator. And I don't need that. I got the springhouse over there. It's as good as any refrigerator. Keeps butter sweet for weeks. And a telephone. I don't need a telephone. I have no one to talk to."

"I'll say this," said Hopkins. "You get along all right. Even without a telephone or the electric. Better than most folks."

"I never wanted much," said Lambert. "That's the secret of it— I never wanted much."

"You working on another book?"

"Jake, I'm always working on another book. Writing down the things I see and hear and the way I feel about them. I'd do it even if no one was interested in them. I'd write it down even if there were no books."

"You read a lot," said Hopkins. "More than most of us."

"Yes, I guess I do," said Lambert. "Reading is a comfort."

And that was true, he thought. Books lined up on a shelf were a group of friends—not books, but men and women who talked with him across the span of continents and centuries of time. His books, he knew, would not live as some of the others had. They would not long outlast him, but at times he liked to think of the possibility that a hundred years from now someone might find one of his books, in a used bookstore, perhaps, and, picking it up, read a few paragraphs of his, maybe liking it well enough to buy it and take it home, where it would rest on the shelves awhile, and might, in time, find itself back in a used bookstore again, waiting for someone else to pick it up and read.

It was strange, he thought, that he had written of things close to home, of those things that most passed by without even seeing, when he could have written of the wonders to be found light-years from earth—the strangenesses that could be found on other planets circling other suns. But of these he had not even thought to write, for they were secret, an inner part of him that was of himself alone, a confidence between himself and Phil that he could not have brought himself to violate.

"We need some rain," said Hopkins. "The pastures are going. The pastures on the Jones place are almost bare. You don't see the grass; you see the ground. Caleb has been feeding his cattle hay for the last two weeks, and if we don't get some rain, I'll be doing the same in another week or two. I've got one patch of corn I'll get some nubbins worth the picking, but the rest of it is only good for fodder. It does beat hell. A man can work his tail off some years and come to nothing in the end."

They talked for another hour or so—the comfortable, easy talk of countrymen who were deeply concerned with the little things that loomed so large for them. Then Hopkins said good-by and, kicking his ramshackle car into reluctant life, drove off down the road.

When the sun was just above the western hills, Lambert went inside and put on a pot of coffee to go with a couple of slices of Katie's bread and a big slice of Katie's pie. Sitting at the table in the kitchen—a table on which he'd eaten so long as memory served —he listened to the ticking of the ancient family clock. The clock, he realized as he listened to it, was symbolic of the house. When the clock talked to him, the house talked to him as well—the house using the clock as a means of communicating with him. Perhaps not talking to him, really, but keeping close in touch, reminding him that it still was there, that they were together, that they did not stand alone. It had been so through the years; it was more so than ever now, a closer relationship, perhaps arising from the greater need on both their parts.

Although stoutly built by his maternal great-grandfather the house stood in a state of disrepair. There were boards that creaked and buckled when he stepped on them, shingles that leaked in the rainy season. Water streaks ran along the walls, and in the back part of the house, protected by the hill that rose abruptly behind it, where the sun's rays seldom reached, there was the smell of damp and mold.

But the house would last him out, he thought, and that was all that mattered. Once he was no longer here, there'd be no one for it to shelter. It would outlast both him and Phil, but perhaps there would be no need for it to outlast Phil. Out among the stars, Phil had no need of the house. Although, he told himself, Phil would be coming home soon. For he was old and so, he supposed, was Phil. They had, between the two of them, not too many years to wait.

Strange, he thought, that they, who were so much alike, should have lived such different lives—Phil, the wanderer, and he, the stay-at-home, and each of them, despite the differences in their lives, finding so much satisfaction in them.

His meal finished, he went out on the patio again. Behind him, back of the house, the wind soughed through the row of mighty evergreens, those alien trees planted so many years ago by that old great-grandfather. What a cross-grained conceit, he thought— to plant pines at the base of a hill that was heavy with an ancient growth of oaks and maples, as if to set off the house from the land on which it was erected.

The last of the fireflies were glimmering in the lilac bushes that flanked the gate, and the first of the whippoorwills were crying mournfully up the hollows. Small, wispy clouds partially obscured the skies, but a few stars could be seen. The moon would not rise for another hour or two.

To the north a brilliant star flared out, but watching it, he knew it was not a star. It was a spaceship coming in to land at the port across the river. The flare died out, then flickered on again, and this time did not die out but kept on flaring until the dark line of the horizon cut it off. A moment later, the muted rumble of the landing came to him, and in time it too died out, and he was left alone with the whippoorwills and fireflies.

Someday, on one of those ships, he told himself, Phil would be coming home. He would come striding down the road as he always had before, unannounced but certain of the welcome that would be waiting for him. Coming with the fresh scent of space upon him, crammed with wondrous tales, carrying in his pocket some alien trinket as a gift that, when he was gone, would be placed on the shelf of the old breakfront in the living room, to stand there with the other gifts he had brought on other visits.

There had been a time when he had wished it had been he rather than Phil who had left. God knows, he had ached to go. But once one had gone, there had been no question that the other must stay on. One thing he was proud of—he had never hated Phil for going. They had been too close for hate. There could never be hate between them.

There was something messing around behind him in the pines. For some time now, he had been hearing the rustling but paying no attention to it. It was a coon, most likely, on its way to raid the cornfield that ran along the creek just east of his land. The little animal would find poor pickings there, although there should be enough to satisfy a coon. There seemed to be more rustling than a coon would make. Perhaps it was a family of coons, a mother and her cubs.

Finally, the moon came up, a splendor swimming over the great dark hill behind the house. It was a waning moon that, nevertheless, lightened up the dark. He sat for a while longer and began to feel the chill that every night, even in the summer, came creeping from the creek and flowing up the hollows.

He rubbed an aching knee, then got up slowly and went into the house. He had left a lamp burning on the kitchen table, and now he picked it up, carrying it into the living room and placing it on the table beside an easy chair. He'd read for an hour or so, he told himself, then be off to bed.

As he picked a book off the shelf behind the chair, a knock came at the kitchen door. He hesitated for a moment and the knock came again. Laying down the book, he started for the kitchen, but before he got there, the door opened, and a man came into the kitchen. Lambert stopped and stared at the indistinct blur of the man who'd come into the house. Only a little light came from the lamp in the living room, and he could not be sure.

"Phil?" he asked, uncertain, afraid that he was wrong.

The man stepped forward a pace or two. "Yes, Ed," he said. "You did not recognize me. After all the years, you don't recognize me."

"It was so dark," said Lambert, "that I could not be sure."

He strode forward with his hand held out, and Phil's hand was there to grasp it. But when their hands met in the handshake, there was nothing there. Lambert's hand closed upon itself.

He stood stricken, unable to move, tried to speak and couldn't, the words bubbling and dying and refusing to come out.

"Easy, Ed," said Phil. "Take it easy now. That's the way it's always been. Think back. That has to be the way it's always been. I am a shadow only. A shadow of yourself."

But that could not be right, Lambert told himself. The man who stood there in the kitchen was a solid man, a man of flesh and bone, not a thing of shadow.

"A ghost," he managed to say. "You can't be a ghost."

"Not a ghost," said Phil. "An extension of yourself. Surely you had known."

"No," said Lambert. "I did not know. You are my brother, Phil."

"Let's go into the living room," said Phil. "Let's sit down and talk. Let's be reasonable about this. I rather dreaded coming, for I knew you had this thing about a brother. You know as well as I do you never had a brother. You are an only child."

"But when you were here before. . . ."

"Ed, I've not been here before. If you are only honest with yourself, you'll know I've never been. I couldn't come back, you see, for then you would have known. And up until now, maybe not even now, there was no need for you to know. Maybe I made a mistake in coming back at all."

"But you talk," protested Lambert, "in such a manner as to refute what you are telling me. You speak of yourself as an actual person."

"And I am, of course," said Phil, "you made me such a person. You had to make me a separate person or you couldn't have believed in me. I've been to all the places you have known I've been, done all the things that you know I've done. Not in detail, maybe, but you know the broad outlines of it. Not at first, but later on, within a short space of time, I became a separate person. I was, in many ways, quite independent of you. Now let's go in and sit down and be comfortable. Let us have this out. Let me make you understand, although in all honesty, you should understand, yourself."

Lambert turned and stumbled back into the living room and let himself down, fumblingly, into the chair beside the lamp. Phil remained standing, and Lambert, staring at him, saw that Phil was his second self, a man similar to himself, almost identical to himself—the same white hair, the same bushy eyebrows, the same crinkles at the corners of his eyes, the same planes to his face.

He fought for calmness and objectivity. "A cup of coffee, Phil?" he asked. "The pot's still on the stove, still warm."

Phil laughed. "I cannot drink," he said, "or eat. Or a lot of other things. I don't even need to breathe. It's been a trial sometimes, although there have been advantages. They have a name out in the stars for me. A legend. Most people don't believe in me. There are too many legends out there. Some people do believe in me. There are people who'll believe in anything at all."

"Phil," said Lambert, "that day in the barn. When you told me you were leaving, I did stand in the door and watch you walk away."

"Of course you did," said Phil. "You watched me walk away, but you knew then what it was you watched. It was only later that you made me into a brother—a twin brother, was it not?"

"There was a man here from the university," said Lambert. "A professor of psychology. He was curious. He had some sort of study going. He'd hunted up the records. He said I never had a brother. I told him he was wrong."

"You believed what you said," Phil told him. "You knew you had a brother. It was a defensive mechanism. You couldn't live with yourself if you had thought otherwise. You couldn't admit the kind of thing you are."

"Phil, tell me. What kind of thing am I?"

"A breakthrough," said Phil. "An evolutionary breakthrough. I've had a lot of time to think about it, and I am sure I'm right. There was no compulsion on my part to hide and obscure the facts, for I was the end result. I hadn't done a thing; you were the one who did it. I had no guilt about it. And I suppose you must have. Otherwise, why all this smokescreen about dear brother Phil."

"An evolutionary breakthrough, you say. Something like an amphibian becoming a dinosaur?"

"Not that drastic," said Phil. "Surely you have heard of people who had several personalities, changing back and forth without warning from one personality to another. But always in the same body. You read the literature on identical twins—one personality in two different bodies. There are stories about people who could mentally travel to distant places, able to report, quite accurately, what they had seen."

"But this is different, Phil."

"You still call me Phil."

"Dammit, you are Phil."

"Well, then, if you insist. And I am glad you do insist. I'd like to go on being Phil. Different, you say. Of course, it's different. A natural evolutionary progression beyond the other abilities I mentioned. The ability to split your personality and send it out on its own, to make another person that is a shadow of yourself. Not mind alone, something more than mind. Not quite another person, but almost another person. It is an ability that made you different, that set you off from the rest of the human race. You couldn't face that. No one could. You couldn't admit, not even to yourself, that you were a freak."

"You've thought a lot about this."

"Certainly I have. Someone had to. You couldn't, so it was up to me."

"But I don't remember any of this ability. I still can see you walking off. I have never felt a freak."

"Certainly not. You built yourself a cover so fast and so secure you even fooled yourself. A man's ability for self-deception is beyond belief."

Something was scratching at the kitchen door, as a dog might scratch to be let in.

"That's the Follower," said Phil. "Go and let him in."

"But a Follower. . . ."

"That's all right," said Phil. "I'll take care of him. The bastard has been following me for years."

"If it is all right. . . ."

"Sure, it is all right. There's something that he wants, but we can't give it to him."

Lambert went across the kitchen and opened the door. The Follower came in. Never looking at Lambert, he brushed past him into the living room and skidded to a halt in front of Phil.

"Finally," shouted the Follower, "I have run you to your den. Now you cannot elude me. The indignities that you have heaped upon me—the learning of your atrocious language so I could converse with you, the always keeping close behind you, but never catching up, the hilarity of my acquaintances who viewed my obsession with you as an utter madness. But always you fled before me, afraid of me when there was no need of fear. Talk with you, that is all I wanted."

"I was not afraid of you," said Phil. "Why should I have been? You couldn't lay a mitt upon me."

"Clinging to the outside of a ship when the way was barred inside to get away from me! Riding in the cold and emptiness of space to get away from me. Surviving the cold and space—what kind of creature are you?"

"I only did that once," said Phil, "and not to get away from you. I wanted to see what it would be like. I wanted to touch interstellar space, to find out what it was. But I never did find out. And I don't mind telling you that once one got over the wonder and the terror of it, there was very little there. Before the ship touched down, I damn near died of boredom."

The Follower was a brute, but something about him said he was more than simple brute. In appearance, he was a cross between a bear and ape, but there was something manlike in him, too. He was a hairy creature, and the clothing that he wore was harness rather than clothing, and the stink of him was enough to make one gag.

"I followed you for years," he bellowed, "to ask you a simple question, prepared well to pay you if you give me a useful answer. But you always slip my grasp. If nothing else, you pale and disappear. Why did you do that? Why not wait for me: Why not speak to me? You force me to subterfuge, you force me to set up ambush. In very sneaky and expensive manner, which I deplore, I learned position of your planet and location where you home, so I could come and wait for you to trap you in your den, thinking that even such as you surely must come home again. I prowl the deep woodlands while I wait, and I frighten inhabitants of here, without wishing to, except they blunder on me, and I watch your den and I wait for you, seeing this other of you and thinking he was you, but realizing, upon due observation, he was not. So now. . . ."

"Now just a minute," said Phil. "Hold up. There is no reason to explain."

"But explain you must, for to apprehend you, I am forced to very scurvy trick in which I hold great shame. No open and above board. No honesty. Although one thing I have deduced from my observations. You are no more, I am convinced, than an extension of this other."

"And now," said Phil, "you want to know how it was done. This is the question that you wish to ask."

"I thank you," said the Follower, "for your keen perception, for not forcing me to ask."

"But first," said Phil, "I have a question for you. If we could tell you how it might be done, if we were able to tell you and if you could turn this information to your use, what kind of use would you make of it?"

"Not myself," said the Follower. "Not for myself alone, but for my people, for my race. You see, I never laughed at you; I did not jest about you as so many others did. I did not term you ghost or spook. I knew more to it than that. I saw ability that if rightly used. . . ."

"Now you're getting around to it," said Phil. "Now tell us the use."

"My race," said the Follower, "is concerned with many different art forms, working with crude tools and varying skills and in stubborn materials that often take unkindly to the shaping. But I tell myself that if each of us could project ourselves and use our second selves as medium for the art, we could shape as we could wish, creating art forms that are highly plastic, that can be worked over and over again until they attain perfection. And, once perfected, would be immune against time and pilferage. . . ."

"With never a thought," said Phil, "as to its use in other ways. In war, in thievery. . . ."

The Follower said, sanctimoniously, "You cast unworthy aspersions upon my noble race."

"I am sorry if I do," said Phil. "Perhaps it was uncouth of me. And now, as to your question, we simply cannot tell you. Or I don't think that we can tell you. How about it, Ed?"

Lambert shook his head. "If what both of you say is true, if Phil really is an extension of myself, then I must tell you I do not have the least idea of how it might be done. If I did it, I just did it, that was all. No particular way of doing it. No ritual to perform. No technique I'm aware of."

"Ridiculous that is," cried the Follower. "Surely you can give me hint or clue."

"All right, then," said Phil, "I'll tell you how to do it. Take a species and give them two million years in which they can evolve, and you might come to it. Might, I say. You can't be certain of it. It would have to be the right species, and it must experience the right kind of social and psychological pressure, and it must have the right kind of brain to respond to these kinds of pressures. And if all of this should happen, then one day one member of the species may be able to do what Ed has done. But that one of them is able to do it does not mean that others will. It may be no more than a wild talent, and it may never occur again. So far as we know, it's not happened before. If it has, it's been hidden, as Ed has hidden his ability, even from himself, forced to hide it from himself because of the human conditioning that would make such an ability unacceptable."

"But all these years," said the Follower, "all these years, he has kept you as you are. That seems. . . ."

"No," said Phil. "Not that at all. No conscious effort on his part. Once he created me, I was self-sustaining."

"I sense," the Follower said, sadly, "that you tell me true. That you hold nothing back."

"You sense it, hell," said Phil. "You read our minds, that is what you did. Why, instead of chasing me across the galaxy, didn't you read my mind long ago and have done with it?"

"You would not stand still," said the Follower, accusingly. "You would not talk with me. You never bring this matter to the forefront of your mind so I have a chance to read it."

"I'm sorry," said Phil, "that it turned out this way for you. But until now, you must realize, I could not talk with you. You make the game too good. There was too much zest in it."

The Follower said, stiffly, "You look upon me and you think me brute. In your eyes I am. You see no man of honor, no creature of ethics. You know nothing of us and you care even less. Arrogant you are. But, please believe me, in all that's happened, I act with honor according to my light."

"You must be weary and hungry," said Lambert. "Can you eat our food? I could cook up some ham and eggs, and the coffee is still hot. There is a bed for you. It would be an honor to have you as our guest."

"I thank you for your confidence, for your acceptance of me," said the Follower. "It warms—how do you say it—the cockle of the heart. But the mission's done and I must be going now. I have wasted too much time. If you, perhaps, could offer me conveyance to the spaceport."

"That's something I can't do," said Lambert. "You see, I have no car. When I need a ride, I bum one from a neighbor, otherwise I walk."

"If you can walk, so can I," said the Follower. "The spaceport is not far. In a day or two, I'll find a ship that is going out."

"I wish you'd stay the night," said Lambert. "Walking in the dark. . . ."

"Dark is best for me," said the Follower. "Less likely to be seen. I gather that few people from other stars wander about this countryside. I have no wish to frighten your good neighbors."

He turned briskly and went into the kitchen, heading for the door, not waiting for Lambert to open it for him.

"Good-by, pal," Phil called after him.

The Follower did not answer. He slammed the door behind him.

When Lambert came back into the living room, Phil was standing in front of the fireplace, his elbow on the mantel.

"You know, of course," he said, "that we have a problem."

"Not that I can see," said Lambert. "You will stay, won't you. You will not leave again. We are both getting old."

"If that is what you want. I could disappear, snuff myself out. As if I'd never been. That might be for the best, more comfortable for you. It could be disturbing to have me about. I do not eat or sleep. I can attain a satisfying solidity but only with an effort and only momentarily. I command enough energy to do certain tasks, but not over the long haul."

"I have had a brother for a long, long time," said Lambert. "That's the way I want it. After all this time, I would not want to lose you."

He glanced at the breakfront and saw that the trinkets Phil had brought on his other trips still stood solidly in place.

Thinking back, he could remember, as if it were only yesterday, I watching from the barn door as Phil went trudging down the road through the gray veil of the drizzle.

"Why don't you sit down and tell me," he said, "about that incident out in the Coonskin system. I knew about it at the time, of course, but I never caught quite all of it."